Out of the Blue
Wild Blue Yonder
Bluebonnets

Praise for "Out of the Blue"

Loved getting to know Tee and her neighborhood. But wait...don't I already know Tee? The characters are just that friendly. Mary Mead's storytelling follows a perfect arch in this mystery, hitting all the right notes which kept me flipping the pages. I can't wait to visit these characters again. All I can say is Giddyup Cowboy!
— *Barbi*

A wonderful, witty story that ended up being a page turner. No idea who this author is but I hope she makes it big with this series! Bought the second one, and can't wait to start! Kudos Mary Mead!!!
— *Jessica*

Loved it! Couldn't put it down. Didn't see the ending coming, it took me by surprise. I'm ready for the next one!!
— *Melissa*

I don't read a lot of books but heard great things about this one. Was home sick a couple days so I dove in. Read it in 2 days which is fast for me. The characters are realistic, fun, and the plot makes you keep turning pages to find out why these strange things are happening. Great ending to top it off. Highly recommended for any mystery lovers!
— *William*

Praise for "Wild Blue Yonder"

Once I picked up the book I couldn't put it down .... read it in an afternoon. I was right there in the story living it with Tee. This author needs to keep writing ... and quickly.
— *Lea*

Seriously a page turner. I couldn't put it down til I finished it. What's next for Tee and Tim Ms. Mead? Can't wait to find out!
— *Kelly*

I enjoyed this book very much and I can't wait for the NEXT book in the series, "Bluebonnets", to be released so I can find out what happens to all these characters!
— *Cindy*

Bluebonnets

A Monarch Beach Mystery

By Mary E. Mead

Copyright ©2014 Mary E. Mead

This one is for all the guys in the family - Kirk, Jerry, Pete, Hank, Justin, Robert, Luke, Michael, Travis, Ryan, Levi, Dan, David, Liam, Flynn, and Leo.

I am blessed to have them as family, lucky to call them friends.

BLUEBONNETS

A Monarch Beach Mystery

Thank you!

Mary Mead

By Mary Mead

Hi.

My name is Teejay and I'm an idiot.

If this was an IA meeting (Idiots Anonymous) that's how I would introduce myself.

The actual name on my birth certificate is Thomasina Joseffa Bishop. It's just easier to go by Teejay or just Tee.

By nature I am quiet, modest, shy and unassuming. Don't believe it? Just ask me. I'm forty years past birth, five feet nine inches tall and on the slender side since I lost a lot of weight two years ago in a battle with lung cancer. I won. The weight is returning slowly.

The type of cancer I had may return at any time. My doctors assure me if I make it five years beyond my last treatment I can consider myself cured. To that end I have varying tests every six months and so far I'm winning that race.

Most side effects from both cancer and treatment fade away. Some become permanent. The hair that is lost usually regrows. In my case I have a halo – a bright, white circle of hair on the top of my head, crowning the dark blond hair that grew back, replacing the brunette hair I had. It's hair. After being bald for over a year, it stays, even if it's green.

My life was pretty common – married young, two kids, divorced and happy. I didn't much like the cancer, or the treatment. I survived. Now any day that starts off above ground is a good one.

You probably know other women with a similar story.

Mine only tipped off the tracks when Tim came along.

He's one of those side effects I mentioned, one that stayed.

For some reason neither of us can explain Tim can talk to me. Inside my head. Like a telephone call without a telephone. Over long distances. Not even sure how far away he can be and still reach me. Maybe we should check that out one day.

Anyway, during radiation treatment I was told some patients see a flash of blue light; some experience a strong smell of ozone. I'm lucky. I got both – a brilliant flash of bright blue and the stench of ozone.

I can smell lightning half a mile away.

In the case of Tim, I see that same flash of bright blue, smell ozone and get the same effect you get answering your phone. Without the phone. He can talk to me, hear my answers, without a physical instrument of any kind. How? No idea. He just does it.

Tim is gorgeous. Model handsome and then some. He's three inches over six feet, has hair the color of wet sand, smoky blue gray eyes framed by thick dark lashes. Wide shouldered, narrow hipped, sculpted body. Oh, and he's also a very well-known and wealthy celebrity. Did I mention he asked me to marry him? Am I Cinderella or what?

He did, I said yes, and then things got sticky.

Tim is one third of a popular country group called T Three, a fact he kept to himself when he first arrived in town. We have a local band named Bullseye that has done pretty well for itself and tours regularly.

When their travels bring them into our vicinity they throw in a performance for the home folks. The last time they were here, their lead singer, Jerry Mead, recognized Tim, as T. Tom Tanner of T Three and outed him in front of the home town crowd.

Tim in turn invited me up on stage, where he proposed marriage, was accepted, placed a ring on my finger and sang me a song in front of that same home town crowd. I was there, I have the ring, and was so stunned I remember very little of it.

The sticky part was Tim asking his future wife to stand up, me standing up, and some gal none of us had ever seen before standing up at the same time. Then my friends got in the act, and they all stood up, too.

Tim got it straightened out, got the ring on my finger, accepted all the congratulations and got me out of there as quickly as possible.

My first thoughts were who was that woman and why did she stand up. Tim's first thoughts he kept to himself. When I voiced my questions, he promised answers as soon as we got home, and he got fed.

I managed bacon and eggs while he made coffee once we were home.

"And now," I said, pouring a last cup of coffee, "who was that lady?"

Tim sighed, stretched out those long legs and leaned back in his chair.

"Long story, Muse," he began, using his pet name for me. "You sure you're up for it tonight? Pretty late."

"I can manage," I answered.

"Not a pretty story, and it's gonna ramble, take a while."

"I have all night," I said.

He took a deep breath and blew it out.

"You know my dad died when I was fourteen," he began. "He drove trucks with my uncle Merle. They had started their own business when he went over the side. They were just getting started. My brother Matt took over Dad's half, started driving trucks with Uncle Merle. Luke, the middle brother, was in college at the time, and Mama insisted he finish. She used the insurance settlement to pay for school, so she waitressed at the truck stop on the highway to keep us afloat."

He paused to sip coffee.

"Pretty much left me on my own. Tried to keep up with stuff at home, do my homework, all the usual stuff. Then Lurlene came home. Her and her family had lived on the other side of us for ages, just down the dirt road. She was the youngest of three kids, all older than me, so our paths never really crossed beyond a howdy or a wave. She took off when I was ten or eleven, ran off with a farm hand from across town. Big scandal then, different times."

"Still a scandal," I put in. "Even now."

"Well, she was gone for a few years and then she came back. Had two boys, the youngest still in diapers. Her folks took her in of course, her and the boys, although they could ill afford more mouths to feed. She took over the household chores so her momma could work the fields with her daddy."

4

"No social life," he said. "The men around there didn't want to saddle up with a built in family so they pretty much kept their distance. I don't think she ever read a book. She was pretty well strapped into the lonely train by the time she was 22." He grinned at me. "Told you it was a long story."

"I'm still here," I said and he continued.

"You know what's coming. She was a lonely, experienced woman and I was a curious teenager with raging hormones. Should have known better and didn't. I have to admit, I thought I was pretty hot stuff at the time."

"You were fourteen?"

"About there. Didn't even have a driver's license."

"So what happened?"

"She showed up one evening at the house, all dressed up. Uncle Merle was there at the time, back from a trip with Matt. So she sat them all down, said she was pregnant, I was the culprit and she was ready to marry up and settle in. Mama said that wasn't gonna happen. Merle said he'd take her to the doctor for a second opinion. My daddy raised us to be responsible. To my way of thinking I did the deed, I had to take responsibility for it. Next morning I was up and down the road before Mama's feet hit the floor. I proposed, and we headed for town. Had to walk. I didn't have my license. We got to town before the court house opened and were sitting on a bench outside. She was giggling and I was sweating like a mule pulling a plow uphill. About then, Mama and Uncle Merle showed up, along with Lurlene's daddy. They took her straight to the doctor, left me waiting in the truck."

"And?"

Tim sighed and reached for my hand. "I'm sorry, babe. I told you it wasn't a nice story."

"And what happened? Did you marry her?"?

"Oh, hell no. Mama never would have signed for me. It turned out she wasn't pregnant. Couldn't even get pregnant again, some kind of problem when her second was born. Her daddy took her home and Uncle Merle took us all back to our house."

"Was that the end of it?"

"Nope. Just the beginning really. She would walk past the house two or three times a day, every day, until Mama went to the sheriff. He had a talk with Lurlene's daddy and she slacked off. Years went by. I took up guitar, started singing in bars to make a little money. Long story short, I hooked up with my cousin Mark, Merle's boy, and another guy we picked up along the way and formed T Three. We got really lucky. Hit song at the right time. Got an agent, a contract and headed uptown. Thought we were stepping in high cotton. Mama quit the truck stop, Luke finished school and passed the bar, became a full-fledged lawyer and joined a firm in Austin. First time since daddy died things were really looking up."

"Then Lurlene showed up again. Started calling radio stations, television studios, even some magazines. Told people we were married, that the boys were mine, all kinds of stuff she dreamed up. Earned a label as a nut job, and a restraining order from my brother Luke. Then she started showing up where we were performing, followed us all over Texas. Then it was all over the country. She even got into my hotel room one night. Had to have the police get her out."

"Wasn't there anything you could do?"

"Not really. Just call the cops. She went to jail a few times before she finally knocked that off. Things would go along great for a while, and then, there she was again. That woman is just barefoot mean."

"What happened to her?"

Tim sighed again, and squeezed my fingers. "That woman at the Gem? The one who stood up?"

"Her?" I said, and felt a knot in my stomach.

"Yep. That was her."

"How did she know you were here? In Monarch?"

"No idea, babe. None at all. Haven't seen her in years. Thought that was all behind us. Just when you think it's over and forget it, it's right back."

"Do you think she's going to start again?"

"No idea. My biggest concern right now is you."

"Me? Why me? She doesn't know me."

"She does now, Muse. I had to be the big shot, and propose right there in front of God and everybody. Wanted everyone to know you were taken. Showing off for Sheriff John."

"You did a bang up job of that," I smiled at him.

"Yeah, I did. And I put a target right between your shoulder blades."

"What happened to her boys?"

"No idea. Her dad died the next year and her mom sold the place. Don't even know where they moved. Lost track of the family till she showed up after a show a couple of years later. That's all I know. We weren't at the Christmas card stage."

I stood up and stretched. "Not your fault, Tim."

He stood up, too, and carried his cup to the sink. "I could have handled it better," he said, rinsing the cup.

"Hardly. You were a child! A fourteen year old boy is not ready to get married! And certainly not ready to be a father! This one I win, babe. There is no way that was your fault."

He gathered me against his chest and dropped his cheek on top of my head. "Well, maybe this will put an end to it. She heard me propose, too. Now that she knows I'm actually getting married."

He lifted his head and tipped my chin up. "I am, you know."

"You are what?"

"Getting married," he grinned. He took my hand and turned it so the light flashed off the lilac colored stone. "You said yes."

That ended a long day.

We were up so late we slept in the next morning. By the time we got to Kelly's it was closer to lunch time. I was a little surprised to see Sharon in her usual booth. We grabbed cups and slid in across from her.

"Good morning," she fairly sang. "That was quite a show you put on last night. Congratulations, again."

"Thanks," Tim smiled.

"So when's the big event?"

"What event?" I asked, in need of caffeine.

Sharon shook her head. "The wedding, doofus. When's the wedding? Will it be here or back in Texas? You did say you were from Texas, right?" This last she looked over at Tim.

"Yes, ma'am," he agreed. "Born and raised."

"And is everything really bigger in Texas?" She asked with a smile.

8

"Can't testify to everything," Tim smiled back. "Just a whole lot of it."

"I was kidding," she said. "So, seriously, when's the wedding? And here? Or there?"

"Good grief, Sharon," I answered. "We haven't decided yet. You'll be the first to know when anything is settled."

"Okay, I get that. So, who was that woman? Did you know her? I've never seen her before."

Oh boy. Like a bulldog with a pork chop.

I shook my head and looked around for Sally, who was making her way back with the pot of life giving fluid known as coffee.

"Well? Did you know her?"

I clutched my cup and looked at Tim.

He took a deep breath and sighed it out.

"She's a fan," he said. "Been around a while."

Sharon sat back and looked at me and then at Tim. Reaching across the table she lifted my left hand and turned it to admire my ring.

"This is beautiful, Tim. You did very well with this one."

"It was my grandma's," he smiled at her.

"Shouldn't that go to the oldest? I thought you had older brothers."

"Yep, two of them. Luke and Matt."

"Then how did you wind up with Grandma's ring?"

"Asked for it," he grinned. "I loved the story when I was growing up. Decided I wanted it for my wife one day, and when I asked, she pulled it off and handed it to me."

"Oh, a story! Some family history with it. That's always special."

"It's pretty old fashioned. If Tee doesn't like it we can get another."

"I love it," I said, folding my fingers around it. "It stays."

"You going to share the story? Or is it just for family?"

Tim leaned back against the seat. "It's a neat story," he began. "My grandma was named Amethyst. Amethyst Amelia. When grandpa decided to propose he wanted an amethyst ring, although he had never seen one. He couldn't find one in town, so he went into Austin, the big city. He found one in a second hand store there, only he didn't have enough money. He asked the clerk to set it aside for him, said he would be back to get it."

"Did he save up for it?" I was as curious as Sharon.

"Nope. The rodeo was in town. That was the excuse he used to get to town in the first place. He entered the bull riding and won twenty bucks. He took that to a backroom poker game in a bar and won the rest of it."

"That's a nice story," Sharon said.

"Not the end of it," Tim grinned. "He found out after he gave it to her that it wasn't an amethyst. Turned out to be plain glass that had turned color sitting in the window for so long. By the time he found a real one, and bought it, they had two kids and another on the way. She never wore it. That one went to my brother Matt. Grandma wore this one. She wore a silver chain around her neck with a safety pin on it. When she was cooking, she'd clip this ring on the chain with the pin. Always said she didn't want to bite it in a biscuit. She was buried with the chain and the safety pin."

We sat for a minute absorbing the story.

"That's wonderful, Tim," I said, reaching to squeeze his hand.

"Seriously, Muse. It is old fashioned. If you'd rather have something more modern we can get it."

"No way," I snapped. "This one is mine."

He turned his hand over to squeeze mine. "I'm glad you like it."

"Good morning, Tanners! Or soon to be Tanners, whichever is correct," Sally said, joining us. She filled Tim's cup first, then mine. I added cream and inhaled the rich scent, folding my hands around the cup.

"Good morning, sweetheart," Tim greeted her and stood up to give her a hug. Sally's cheeks flushed pink. If she said aw, shucks, I was determined to kick her in the shins.

Tim sat back down, thanking her.

"So when's the wedding?"

Tim laughed and shook his head. "Ladies, y'all are rushing me here. I just got the woman to say yes last night. Give me a little time here to negotiate."

Sally smiled back at him. "I guess you're entitled to some time. You can tell me tomorrow. What can I get you this morning? Or is it time for lunch? You're running a little late."

"What's the special today?" Tim asked.

Kelly's featured the same special during the week – Monday was pot roast, Tuesday was ham, Wednesday was baked mac and cheese, Thursday was chicken and dumplings and Friday was fish. Weekends were chef's choice. Since this was Saturday it was anyone's guess.

"Fried chicken," Sharon replied. "I just ordered the hot ham sandwich. With that chicken gravy, it's the best thing on the menu."

"I agree, in theory. Their chicken is pretty hard to beat, especially when I can take the leftovers home for supper," I added.

Sharon laughed. "I do both. Sandwich for lunch, and the dinner to go. Then I know supper is covered, too. Easy weekend."

"Sounds good to me," Tim agreed. "I'll have the hot ham sandwich."

Sally looked at me, and I nodded, shoving my cup over for a refill before she went to place our orders.

"You awake?" She filled the cup and slid it back. "For a bride to be you're awful slow this morning."

"Ugh," I said.

"You sure you want to marry that?" Sally plopped a hand on her hip. "You may need some time to rethink the situation."

"Go," I said. "Forage for food."

Sally chuckled and headed up front to put in our orders.

"I called the girls this morning," Sharon said, once Sally was gone. "They are thrilled. Melanie especially," she added, referring to her twin daughters. "She said Tim always looked familiar. They both send their love."

"And we appreciate it. You tell 'em both howdy," Tim smiled.

"I'll do that. So, this fan. The gal that stood up last night. Does that happen often?"

Tim laughed. "To be truthful Miss Sharon, I've never asked anyone to marry me before, so I don't know how to answer that question."

"Why all the questions?" My brain finally began to function. "You're certainly full of them today."

"Are you kidding?" Sharon leaned forward. "You knew this stuff. We didn't. Tim is a celebrity. A real one. And he's right here in Monarch! Of course I have questions! Everyone has questions! Think about it, Tee."

I guessed she had a point.

Looking back at Tim, she continued. "If I get too personal, tell me," she said. "There's just so much and it's all so sudden. I get that you guys have talked," she gave us an eye roll with that one, "but from everyone else's point of view, this whole thing is completely bizarre!"

"I don't think bizarre is the right word," I put in. "I'll admit it's a little out of the ordinary, just not in the Twilight Zone range."

Sharon leaned back in the booth, shaking her head.

"Let me put in the right perspective for you," she said. "You have been single for ages. You don't date. You have no social life at all. You almost died from lung cancer, which made you even more reclusive. And I get that, I do. Then it seems like overnight you're out and about. No offense, Tim," she shot him a glance." You and John were all of a sudden pretty darn close."

She held up a hand when I started to speak.

"Hear me out, Tee. You know that's true. You guys were pretty tight there for a few weeks. Then Tim shows up. Out of the blue! Drops out of the sky or something. You've been here most of your life! We know all about you, from your bra size to your SAT scores."

She paused for breath. "The first night, the very first night, he showed up you told me you didn't know him and then promptly took him straight home with you. He stayed the whole weekend! That's bizarre, my dear! Not to mention that from that night, he's here every weekend, he stays with you, and Lord knows he's more protective than a Rottweiler. People talk. I talk!"

Tim squeezed my hand. "She's got a point, babe."

"It's still not bizarre," I argued.

"Hogwash," Sharon replied. "Then he turns out to be famous, and rich, no offense, Tim, but freaking gorgeous and he asks you to marry him? Yeah, Tee, that's bizarre."

"No offense taken," Tim put in with a grin. "Put it like that, I guess it is a little off center."

"Just a little," Sharon smiled back.

I sighed. She did have a point. There were times I didn't believe it and it happened to me. I wonder how Cinderella explained things to the stepmother.

Sally joined us and started distributing steaming plates. Slices of real baked ham, layered over white bread with a mound of mashed potatoes on the side and the whole covered in cream gravy. Healthy, no. Delicious. Oh, yeah. I reached for the pepper.

"Anything else I can get you?"

"More coffee," I answered.

"Iced tea," Sharon and Tim said at the same time.

Sally shuffled back up front.

"Now," Sharon began, fork in hand. "My original question. That woman who stood up last night. Does that happen often? A fan like that intrudes?"

"Not often, no," Tim answered truthfully, picking up his own fork. "It's one of the hazards of the trade. Every band gains a following. And it's a good thing. You need to have fans to be a success. There's going to be a bad apple in every bushel. And it's not just the music business. Movie stars have the same problems. Singers, actors, even politicians. Anyone who's in the public eye."

14

"So she's just an eager fan."

"Yes, ma'am," Tim answered. "You could say that."

Sharon looked from me to Tim and back again. I tried to signal her to drop it and she finally got the message. I knew this was not the end of it but at least it was over for now.

"How do you like your sandwich?" she asked, finally changing the subject.

"Love it," Tim answered when he had swallowed a mouth full. "I love the food here. Almost as good as home," he grinned at me.

"We're taking the fried chicken home," I smiled back. "No home cooking for you tonight."

"Ah, but there will be gravy for breakfast."

"If you're good," I grinned at him.

"Babe, I am always good," he grinned back.

"Good grief," Sharon said. "Pass the pepper."

Conversation dropped off once we started eating, moving on to more general subjects. Tim was always curious, interested in the area and the people. Sally brought drink refills then left to put in the orders to go for fried chicken.

While we waited Sharon brought up the questions again.

"Will you be living here when you're married?"

Tim looked at me.

"Sharon, for the last time. We haven't even talked about it yet. I don't know. We haven't set a date. When we have anything solid, I'll tell you."

"There's just so much to be done! We have to go shopping and get your hair done. Find a place, invitations, flowers, just so many details. You can't leave it all till the last minute."

My turn to hold up a hand. "No."

She blinked at me.

"What do you mean, no?"

"I hate shopping. No shopping. My hair is fine. The rest of it will wait. Relax. Go sell a house."

I have an aversion to shopping. Unlike most women I feel that a good pair of boots and a good pair of sneakers is plenty of shoes. I may have a pair of low heels in the back of the closet somewhere but I couldn't swear to it.

I don't care about clothes, as evidenced by my wardrobe of jeans, sweatshirts and tee shirts. I do wear earrings sometimes and a watch. Otherwise, jewelry is out.

Let me correct the shopping thing a little.

When it comes to books, I can shop all day. I can and have spent hours in a book store just browsing. The yard sales and garage sales I hit every week are mostly in search of books, to replenish the inventory I sell online. Well, I also add a few to the TBR, to be read, pile that resides next to my bed. There are still some titles I can't get on my Kindle and those require hard copies.

The rest of shopping? Not for me.

Sharon braced for an argument. I could read it in her eyes. She looked over at Tim. "Will she have to do interviews? Being your wife, I mean. Will she be in magazines? On TV?"

Tim shook his head. "Don't get me in this, Sharon. That's all up to Muse. She makes her own decisions. I just want her."

"Well, she has to be involved. You're a celebrity!"

I felt a wave of discomfort wash over me, from the ankles up. I am not a celebrity. I have no desire at all to be in a magazine or on television. Just the thought of doing

16

an interview made me a little nauseous. Now we were both looking at Tim.

He reached over and took my hand, his look warm and confident.

"Okay, let's play a little game," he said.

"What kind of game?"

"Trivia game," he smiled. "You're both very smart women."

"This isn't going to end well," I said.

"I'm up for it," Sharon said, leaning forward on her folded arms. "Where do we start?"

Tim shifted in his seat and slid an arm around my shoulders. "You ready, Muse?"

"Sure, why not."

"Okay, ladies. Let's pick a celebrity, one in country music. How about Dolly Parton. You both agree she's a celebrity?"

"Of course," I said, promptly.

"She's a legend," added Sharon.

"All right," Tim smiled. "What's her husband's name?"

Sharon and I looked at each other.

"I didn't know she was married," I admitted.

"Neither did I," Sharon said. "I never thought about it. Is she married?"

Tim chuckled. "She sure is. She has been married to the same guy for about fifty years."

I gaped at him.

"Are you serious?" Sharon sat back. "I think you're messing with us."

"Nope, it's a fact. Her husband doesn't like the limelight, wants nothing to do with show business. He has his own business, nothing to do with music. She does her thing and he does his. Completely separate."

"Wow," said Sharon. "I had no idea."

"Most people don't," Tim said. "She's the celebrity. Not her husband. He's just that, her husband. They've made it work for longer than most average people."

Sharon looked at me and then at Tim. "In other words, Tee doesn't have to do anything."

Tim winked at her. "Exactly. Unless she wants to. It's up to her."

I sat back and sighed, relief warming me. I hadn't even thought about this side of it.

"You still need to get your hair done," Sharon said. "You look like a dandelion."

"Hey, you shave your head. Go bald for a year or so."

"No way," she said quickly. "I know how long you were bald. I know how happy you were to get your hair back. What I'm saying is that you need to get it styled, trimmed, something. Maybe lose the halo."

"Not happening," I said firmly. "I earned the halo. It stays."

"See?" Sharon looked at Tim. "You may want to think about this some more."

Tim pulled me closer to his side.

"No way. She said yes and I have witnesses." Giving me a warm look from under those lashes, he smiled. "She's mine. And she is fine just as she is."

Sharon snorted and tossed her napkin on the table. "You're as bad as she is. You're going to regret it," she said to me. "Once you start showing up in the tabloids, your picture at every checkout stand in the nation, we'll see what you have to say."

18

Sally interrupted us, bringing the white Styrofoam boxes of chicken.

"Thanks, Sally," Tim said, tucking some bills under the salt shaker.

"You are always welcome, Tim," she smiled at him.

That evening Tim built a fire while I finished up in the kitchen, then carried coffee into the living room to join him.

Settled on the couch, we watched the flames catch.

"Talk to me, Muse," he said after a while.

"About what?"

"You've been real quiet all evening. Something on your mind? Second thoughts?"

"About you? Never," I said with a smile. "You're stuck with me now."

He pulled me close. "Nowhere I would rather be. Now, tell me what's bothering you?"

He knew me so well.

With a sigh, I leaned against him and he put his arm around me to snuggle me close.

"The whole celebrity thing. I don't know if I can do it." I found a thread at the hem of my tee shirt and worried it, twisting it one way and then the other.

"Do what, babe? You don't have to do a thing."

"Well, you know what I mean."

"No, I don't know. Tell me."

I thought about it for a minute.

"Tim, I am plain as table salt. For the life of me, I can't figure out why you picked me. I will thank God every day that you did, but I'm never gonna know why. That just does not compute." I sighed, laying my head on his chest.

"I love you so much. I couldn't' stand myself if I held you back."

"What would you keep me from doing?"

"I don't know. I can't put a name to it. Anything."

He sighed, his fingers playing with mine as we watched the fire.

"Okay, let's talk about me. Let me tell you what I want." He lifted his hand and brushed my hair back. "I want you, Muse. I want to be married to you, I want you to be my wife. What we have is permanent and special. I hate that people here think I'm just sleeping with you and I'll be on down the road when the new wears off. It cheapens you, it cheapens me, and it cheapens what we are. I hate that! I want them to see we are real, and permanent. I'm only going to be married once. If you want to stay right here, in this house, in this town, the rest of our lives I am great with that. I will be the happiest man in the world to be on tour and have you to come home to. To know you're here, waiting for me."

"So it would be okay if I stayed here?"

"Absolutely. And if you decide you want to go with me? I would love it. Love having you right at my side, love showing you off. I would be the happiest man in the world if you were right there center front at all of our performances."

"You can't have it both ways," I argued.

Tim laughed and hugged me close. "Yeah, I can, babe. You don't get it. The best thing in the world, for me, is you. I hate being away from you for even a minute. And I love being on the road and knowing you're waiting for me. I can't wait to see you. I don't know what I would do without you. You are my life."

20

"So you would be okay with me staying here."

"Yes, I told you. The most important thing, to me, is having you. The second is having you happy. I promise you, I will dedicate my life to making you happy. Now, you know what I want. How about you? What do you want?"

I thought again, my head on his shoulder. At times like these, I had no doubts. No concerns. He was here. Would I be okay if he was away? For more than a week or two?

"Come on, babe. Share. What are you thinking?"

"I don't want the hoopla."

He laughed out loud. "What hoopla?"

I poked him in the ribs. "You know what I mean. The hoopla. The wedding. The arrangements, the flowers. Who to invite. A dress. All those miserable details. I'm just not a social creature I guess."

"Would you be okay without the hoopla?"

"Are you serious? I would love it! I would love to just wake up tomorrow as Mrs. Tim Tanner. Done deal. Send a few emails to my family, let my kids know, and be done with it."

"You're sure that's what you want?"

I looked at him. "That's what I would like, Tim. It sounds silly to you, doesn't it?"

"Not at all, babe. All I want is you. No hoopla involved in that at all. People forget sometimes that wedding vows are made to God. And each other. Everyone else is just a witness. There's no need for anyone else to even be there."

"I never thought about it," I admitted.

"Just need you and me, babe" he said. "Comes down to this. I want to marry you. You want to marry me. No hoopla."

"Without hoopla, or regret. I don't want you to regret it later on."

"Regret what? Lack of hoopla? Don't want it."

"Okay, then, I guess we agree."

"All I needed to know, Muse," he grinned and kissed the end of my nose. "I was worried you were having second thoughts."

"About you? Never! I'm in it to stay."

"I love hearing you say that," he said, catching my face in his hand and turning me towards him. His mouth came down to renew his claim on me.

Tim liked to get an early start on Sundays when he had to drive back to LA so I fixed his favorite breakfast-sausage, biscuits and gravy – at home. While accustomed to his leaving it seemed to get more difficult every week.

"When are you going to be finished with this project you're working on?" I asked, while we finished our coffee.

"A few more weeks, Muse. The album is finished. Now we have to shoot a couple of videos of the songs, for television. We're launching a line of men's products at the same time, so we have to shoot commercials, photo sessions for stills, that kind of thing. Then we're done."

"What kind of videos?"

"For television. You know. Little mini movie kind of things? Act out the songs?"

"So you're going to be an actor, too?"

He chuckled. "Not much of one. I just sing, maybe dance a little. Depends on the story."

"Who writes the stories?"

"Depends on the song. First the song. Then the story it tells or the story around it. Then it goes into development, story boards and all the details. Then it's hire the actors and find a location."

"There's actors?"

"Sometimes, yeah. Again, depends on the story line. Those are all in production right now. We've shot some of the interiors. Now we need the location."

I thought about it for a minute. "How about here? The beach is pretty scenic. Singer Lake is twenty minutes away and it's pretty up there. The lake, trees, big granite rocks."

He stood up and went to the sink to rinse his cup. "I'll suggest it," he said. "Can't hurt."

"That would be fun," I said. "Maybe they would let me watch."

He hooked a hand around my neck and pulled me close. "I'll see what I can do. Now, walk me out. The longer I wait to leave, the harder it gets."

I followed him out, and watched him load up the truck. With a final kiss, he was off. I watched him out of sight, then went back into the house. Long week ahead.

We talked every day even when he was gone, usually in the evenings, although he could use the mental thing any time he wanted. Mostly we just shared our days and any plans we had upcoming.

Tim knew how much I dreaded the approaching medical tests, my six month check-ups. This time I would not have to go alone. He was committed to being right there with me.

Wednesday night he was late calling, almost nine, which is my usual bedtime.

FLASH

Hey, Muse

Hey, Tim. Busy day?

Yep. Long day. I'm taking Friday off, so we had to cram some extra hours into the past couple of days to stay on schedule. Gonna have to haul it tomorrow too.

You're taking a day off? Is everything okay?

Fine as frog hair, babe. I'll be up Thursday night and we are taking Friday off, so don't make any plans.

I love the idea of an extra day with you. What are we doing?

Trust me?

Of course I do.

Good. It's all planned. The entire day.

Something special?

You'll see. Just don't make any plans. Okay?

That's easy, Tim. I don't do much anyway.

I wanted to give you a heads up. I'm gonna get back to work for a couple of hours. I'll see you tomorrow night.

Can't wait. Love you.

Too.

With that he was gone.

I cleaned house the next day, wanting everything ready for him when he arrived. He didn't give me a time so I got an early start.

I wondered about the surprise he planned and spent half the day in speculation.

Not sure of what time he would arrive I made a big pot of beef stew, hearty with vegetables and meat. While that

24

simmered I put together the dough for fresh bread and set it to rise.

When Tim got home the house was filled with the smell of fresh baked bread, a smell that can't be duplicated.

He came in and dropped his bag, reaching to fold me into his arms.

"Is that bread I smell? Wow, babe. You baked bread?"

"And hello to you, too," I grinned.

He hugged me and went straight to the kitchen. "Man, if I could bottle this smell I'd be rich."

"You are rich," I laughed, filling some thick bowls with stew. "Sit down, it's ready."

He pulled out his chair and leaned to smell the golden brown loaf on the table.

"How was the drive?"

"Long. Boring," he answered, slicing off the heel of the bread.

He spread the bread with a liberal swatch of butter and started eating.

"Oh, man, Muse," he mumbled around a mouth full, "this is heaven. Forget the rest of it."

"Thank you, kind sir, but man does not live by bread alone."

He sliced and buttered another slice and handed it to me before making a third for himself.

"Smells good," he said, sniffing the full bowl I placed in front of him.

"Surprised you can smell anything over that bread," I smiled at him.

"Mmm, wonderful," he said, after swallowing a mouth full of stew. "Nice surprise."

"Speaking of surprises, what are we doing tomorrow?"

"Wouldn't be a surprise if I told you."

"Not even a hint?"

"Nope. Well, I can tell you we're getting an early start. Gonna be a full day."

"All right, fine," I said, digging into my own bowl.

His eyes gleamed, more blue than gray. "Trust me, babe."

"I do, Tim," I said.

With a grin he said, "Remember those words, Muse."

True to his word, Tim had us up, showered, dressed, and loaded in the truck before the sun was up. We made a quick trip through the drive in for coffee and headed for the freeway.

By the time the sun began to peek into the canyons and draws of the foothills we were southbound on the 101.

The scenery morphed into grasslands and pastures as we cleared the foothills. It was still early when we hit the Cuesta grade and dropped into San Luis Obispo.

Lois, Tim's name for his GPS system, interrupted to tell him to take the Marsh Street exit.

"I love San Luis," I said. "One of my favorite places. You picked a good one."

Tim just smiled as Lois directed him right on Broad Street and south about three miles.

"We're going out of town, Tim," I said. "San Luis is back behind us."

"I got this, babe," he answered. "Don't mess with Lois. She knows what she's doing."

"Lois is probably a sixty year old woman."

"Great voice, though," he grinned.

Crossing Tank Farm Road Lois told us our destination would be on the right.

The only thing over there was the airport.

Tim signaled and turned into Aero Way, the curving drive up to the small terminal. From our area, flights to anywhere began here, connecting to either Los Angeles, San Francisco or Phoenix, before continuing to other destinations.

Tim turned again before we made the last curve up to the terminal, hooking a left around the base of the hill and stopping at a guarded gate.

The guard stepped up and asked something I couldn't hear. Tim smiled and showed the guy his ID. The guard stepped back inside his kiosk and raised the gate. Tim nodded to him, replaced his wallet and drove on through, following the road back to some hangars.

On our left a small white plane glistened in the morning sun, looking like something out of Star Wars. Tim pulled in and parked alongside the building.

"Here we go, Muse. Last chance."

I looked into those sparkling eyes, the blue prominent today.

"Okay, last chance for what?"

"Spinsterhood, babe. Step out that door and we are getting married today."

I was out the door and on the ground before he could get his door open, my eyes brimming with tears. His infectious laugh filled the air as he came around and caught me in his arms, swinging me around like a child.

"You best be sure," he said.

"I am positive," I said, hugging him tightly.

He let me go and hooked his little finger through mine, leading the way around the corner of the building.

A trim young man in a tan uniform stepped away from the shadows and came to meet us, extending his hand to Tim.

"Morning, Mr. Tanner," he greeted, shaking Tim's hand.

"Morning, Luis, good to see you again. This is Teejay Bishop. Tee, this is Luis, our pilot."

"Good morning," he said, shaking my hand. "I am so pleased to meet you."

"Likewise," I said, eyeing the little plane behind him.

"Ready to go?" Tim led me toward the plane.

"Yes, sir. Cleared for takeoff in," he glanced at his watch, "six minutes. You are right on time."

As we made our way around the plane, I could see steps leading up.

I am not an experienced flyer. My only other flights was from San Luis to San Francisco and even that propeller driven plane was bigger than this one. Sleek and white, its nose was long and pointy, the stout little wings turned up on the ends.

"Is this safe?" I asked Tim, clasping his hand.

He laughed again, and hugged me to his side. 'Lear Jet, babe. One of the safest planes made. Come on, in you go."

I made my up the narrow steps. A beautiful young woman in a uniform matching Luis' waited at the top of the steps and welcomed me aboard, pointing to our right. "Take any seat, and please make yourself comfortable. We will be leaving shortly. Good morning, Mr. Tanner. It's nice to see you again."

Tim acknowledged her greeting, asked after her father, and guided me to a seat.

"Take the window, babe."

"I don't think I want to look down."

"Afraid of flying?"

"No, I don't think so. I've flown before. It's just this plane is so little."

"More like compact, and it will flat move. Take my word for it. Put on your seatbelt."

The young woman up front pushed a button and the steps rose and closed with a sigh.

"We will be serving as soon as we reach altitude," she said with a smile. "Please keep your seatbelts fastened until the light goes off."

Following her instructions I clicked the belt and looked at Tim.

"Where are we going?"

"Trust me?"

"You know I do. I wouldn't be here otherwise." I could feel bubbles of excitement whirling around inside, like I had swallowed a glass of ginger ale. I was on a private jet, going somewhere with Tim! Wow!

He picked up my hand and kissed the back of it.

"We are going to have breakfast, served by Lillian up there, and by the time we finish, we will be in Las Vegas, where a limo will whisk us away to a Justice of the Peace. There we will be married, without hoopla, just you and me and the Good Lord. You now have about half an hour to change your mind, and I promise you there will be hard feelings if you do."

Looking into those sparkling, dancing eyes I saw my future.

An hour later I cemented it.

We lingered in Vegas long enough for a champagne brunch in a private dining room at one of the luxurious hotels that make the city famous. To be honest I don't remember what we ate.

I spent my time looking between my gorgeous new husband and the antique silver wedding band he had added to my amethyst ring. This one was a narrow band with a delicate pattern of flowers etched into the antiqued silver, a perfect match. Inside one word was inscribed. 'Forever'.

After we ate, the limo delivered us back to McCarran airport where Luis waited beside the sleek little jet.

We were back in San Luis by two o'clock. The drive home took longer than the flight to Las Vegas.

At home, Tim unlocked the front door and scooped me up in his arms.

"Tradition," he grinned and carried me over the threshold. Setting me on my feet inside, he closed the door and bent to greet the cats, who probably didn't even miss us but put on a show of wrapping around our legs like they had been abandoned for days.

Standing again, he gathered me against his chest and smiled down at me.

"Happy, Muse?"

"Ecstatic, Tim. How about you?"

"I am the happiest man to ever walk the face of the earth. You make me complete, babe. This is just the start of a long life together. And when that life is done, I will be put in the ground at your side. This is forever, Thomasina Joseffa Tanner."

"Forever, Timothy Thomas Tanner," I answered, leaning into his kiss.

We stood there, like that, for minutes before he finally stepped back.

"Now what do you want to do," he asked, with his familiar grin.

"About what? Oh, let me guess. You're hungry."

He laughed and hugged me. "That too, Muse. How about the Gem? You up for that tonight? We can grab some pizza."

It was early evening and in all the excitement I hadn't eaten very much in Vegas. I hated to admit I was hungry, too.

"Let me feed the cats, and I'm ready," I said, heading for the kitchen.

"Works for me, babe. I'm gonna grab my new sweatshirt. You want yours?"

"Might as well," I called after him.

For some unknown reason Tim had bought us sweatshirts with Las Vegas emblazoned across the front while we were there. His was electric blue and mine was a deep rose color. After feeding the cats and checking their water, I went upstairs and changed my shirt, too.

Most of the gang was already at the Gem when we walked in and made our way to the back corner table to join them. Tim had grabbed a couple of pitchers of beer on our way back, and put in an order for a couple of pizzas.

He set the beer in the center of the table after he filled a couple of glasses, while we exchanged greetings with everyone. John was even present, sitting next to Sharon. Cora and Archie, Greg and Wanda, his newest lady friend, But Bill, Dave and Jeff filled out the table.

Tim pulled up a couple of chairs and held one for me before taking a seat.

"Nice to see you, Tim," Sharon said. "You came up early?"

"Yes, ma'am. Day off."

"You can take a day off? Huh, never thought about it. I'm surprised."

"Like any job, Sharon. People get sick, need a personal day, whatever."

"You're not sick, though, are you?"

Tim laughed and glanced at me. "No, ma'am, I've never felt better. Wanted a day with my girl."

I felt my cheeks flush and looked over at him. His eyes were dancing, alight with devilment.

"So just a day off?"

"Yep, that about covers it," he chuckled.

Sharon folded her arms and set her jaw. "Why do I feel like you two are laughing at me? What did I miss?"

Tim reached to take my hand. "Just an awesome day, Sharon."

"Okay, now tell me the truth. What did you do that's so special?"

"Actually came up last night," Tim said. "Got up early, drove to San Luis, flew to Vegas, got married, saw a few sights and flew home."

"Well, that does sound like fun. I ---" She blinked. "You did what?"

Tim smiled at her, lifting my hand to show my new ring.

"Oh my Lord!" She shrieked and lurched to her feet, flinging herself at me, hugging me so tightly I was afraid my neck might break. Everyone at the table erupted, all talking at the same time, cheers and congratulations flying.

Over Sharon's shoulder I caught John's look. He wasn't smiling. His clenched jaw throbbed once, twice, before he caught himself and looked away, down at his watch, anywhere but at us. Without a word he turned away and left the table. I lost him in the crowd surrounding us.

Cora had bound around the table to hug us while Archie and Greg pumped Tim's hand. I couldn't hear anything with all of them talking at once. It was long minutes before everyone resumed their seats. My cheeks hurt from smiling so much.

"That's gonna call for a round," Archie said, heading for the bar.

"I'll go with you," Tim said. "I've got a couple of pizzas coming up."

The two guys made their way to the counter, Tim stopping a couple of times to accept more congratulations on the way.

"Wow," Sharon said softly. "Married. Thanks for telling me!" She punched me in the arm.

"I didn't know! It was a complete surprise!"

"You had no idea?"

"Nope. He just said we were going to take a day off."

Her eyes misted over, tears glistening in her lashes. "I am so happy for you, Tee."

My own eyes filled, just looking at her. "Thanks, Sharon."

She squeezed my hand and wiped her eyes with a napkin.

Archie and Tim rejoined the table. Tim put two pizzas boxes in the center of the table while Archie refilled the glasses.

"Here's to the happy couple," he said, lifting his glass of beer. "May you always be as happy as you are today."

Everyone clinked glasses, sipped and cheered before everyone started talking at once.

Cora had commandeered John's chair and leaned around Sharon, asking for details. I tried to answer everyone, losing half the questions in the noise.

Unaware of our own celebration someone pushed the buttons on the juke box and the noise level soared. Tim glanced over at me.

"How about a dance?"

"Love it," I said and stood up to take his hand, grateful to get a few minutes away from the hubbub.

He gathered me in his arms and we swayed along to the slow song, his breath warm in my hair. "Still happy, Muse?"

"Very," I answered softly. "And glad that's over with."

Tim chuckled. "Well, that took care of the hoopla. Went pretty well I thought."

I didn't want to mention John.

"You okay, babe? We had to tell them, you know. If it leaked to the news and they found out that way they would all be hurt."

"I know," I agreed. "And it did go very well. Got it all over with in one fell swoop."

He laughed again. "Almost. Sally is going to be hot when she finds out and we didn't tell her."

I laughed with him, feeling the slight tension John had caused relax and disappear.

From then on it was a night to remember. We danced with each other, everyone else, and even people we didn't know. A full party atmosphere descended, enveloping everyone in the festivities.

I danced with some of the old timers from Kelly's, surprised and impressed with their grace on the dance floor. A couple of young guys that might have been college students whirled me around.

I caught glimpses of Tim dancing with other women, enough distance between them for me to fit. Happily, none of them was Lurlene. I found myself checking all the blonds and was pleased to note her absence.

I even managed a couple of dances with my husband, enjoying the sound of that title. All in all this had to be better than any planned reception.

It was without a doubt one of the happiest nights of my life.

It was late when we finally came back home and I felt it. We had been up so early and so much had happened. The quiet hum of the truck sounded strange after all the noise.

Tim came around and helped me out of the truck.

"Long day, Muse. You must be worn out."

"What about you? You must be tired, too."

He unlocked the front door and held it for me. "We have one more tradition to deal with, babe," he grinned. "I'm not tired at all."

All the excitement and being up so late put us behind Saturday morning. Neither of us really wanted to hike around the yard sales so we had coffee and headed for Kelly's.

We weren't the only ones running on slow. Sharon had barely begun on her coffee when we slid in across the table from her.

"Good morning, Tanners," she greeted us.

We returned the greetings and turned over our cups for service.

"Oh, you're in for it now," Sharon said. "Sally is on the war path."

"Uh-oh," I said, glancing around for her. "What happened?"

"She found out from the old guys about the party at the Gem. Not pleased to be the last to know. You want to be real careful what you order, make sure you can recognize the hot sauce."

As if summoned from a lamp I looked up to see Sally making her way down the aisle with a determined look on her face. I was glad Tim was on the aisle, not me.

"You," she said as soon as she was within range, piercing Tim with a look, "get up from there right now."

Oh, boy. Here we go.

Tim stood up, cautiously, not sure what the dragon waitress had in mind.

Sally never slowed, just marched right into him and threw both arms around his neck, pulling him down to deliver a huge smack right on his mouth.

For a rare change, Tim was the one to blush, right up to the tips of his ears.

"You owed me that," she said, letting him go. "You broke my heart."

"I am so sorry, sweetheart," Tim told her, retaking his seat. "It's John's fault."

She paused for a moment. "John? What's he got to do with anything?"

"He's the law," Tim answered with a grin. "He insisted I could only have one wife. I had to resort to flipping a coin."

"I hope it was two out of three," Sally grinned back.

"Three out of five, Sally. I tried."

Sally laughed and turned to look at me.

"You. Your turn," she said, motioning for me to slide out of the booth. When I did she enveloped me in a bear hug, squeezing my ribs before letting me go. She put both hands on her hefty hips. "I could not be happier if I was dipped in batter and deep fried."

"Thank you, Sally," I said, relieved and sliding back into the booth.

"You take care of him, now," she admonished, shaking a finger in my direction.

"Oh, I am gonna do my best," I said.

"And you're gonna be fine. Both of you. Now, what can I get you this morning?"

"Is it still morning?" Sharon looked at her watch. "Close enough," she added, seeing it was five minutes to twelve.

"What's the special?" Tim asked.

"Roast turkey with corn bread stuffing, mashed and gravy, a side of glazed carrots and garnished with cranberry sauce. Someone must have decided to give thanks a little early this year."

Smiling at her, I nodded. "That's for me."

Tim ordered the same, while Sharon had pancakes and bacon. We sat back and relaxed with coffee.

"Are you okay?" I asked Sharon.

"Sure. Why? Do I look funny?"

"No, you look fine. You just passed on a turkey dinner. With all the trimmings."

"Not that hungry," she smiled. "That was quite a shindig last night. I was so tired I overslept. First time in years."

"We slept in, too," I told her. "Way past my bed time." I was still curious. Like me, she always took the leftovers home for supper, eliminating have to cook. Very odd.

She leaned forward again. "So you're really married?"

"Yes ma'am," Tim answered. "And that reminds me. Did I see a sign in your office about a Notary Public?"

"Sure did," Sharon answered. "That's me. Why? You need something notarized?"

"Yep, whole lot of something. I have about half a ream of paper in my briefcase needs to be signed and then notarized."

"Pre nups?"

"No, Sharon," Tim said firmly. "Everything I have is hers. Has been since we met. These are just the legalities, the formalities, whatever you call them. Lawyers."

"I just asked," she defended. "I didn't mean anything."

Tim relaxed and smiled. "Didn't mean to snap. Don't want to mess up your Saturday. It can wait if you have other things to do."

"We can do it after lunch," she said. "Just next door."

"You sure?" Tim asked. "We can get to it later if you're busy today. Just want it done before I head back."

"Nothing on my plate today," she said. "Unless some rich tourist wanders in and drops his wallet on my desk. Sales have been pretty slow lately."

"We'll bring it by right after lunch then," Tim told her, leaning back as Sally returned with heaping plates and distributed them around the table. "Like to get it done and over with."

"What are we talking about?" Sharon asked, reaching for the pepper.

"Have to get Muse added to everything, make sure she's covered. Bank accounts, insurance, deeds all that stuff."

"For what?" I honestly had no idea what he was talking about.

"Everything, babe. You have to be added to all the investment accounts, everything. You have to sign it all. You can use your own name if you want, you don't have to take mine."

"Of course I'm going to take your name! It's my name now!" I shoved him with my shoulder. "I like being married to you. I want people to know."

"Can I put a sign in the front yard?" He grinned at me.

"Whatever your heart desires," I grinned back at him.

"We'll get to that," he said with a wink and turned his attention to his plate.

The smell was enough to invoke the holidays. Thick, carved slices of white meat turkey were laid over helpings of dressing that would have been a meal by itself. A mound of mashed potatoes, dripping gravy, took up the other third of the plate. The carrots were in a little side dish, along with the cranberry sauce.

Picking up my fork, I leaned over and inhaled all the rich fragrance coming from my plate.

Beside me, Tim looked up at Sally. "Special occasion? This is pretty elaborate."

She patted his shoulder. "No, not really, handsome. Cook just practicing for the holidays. However," she leaned close, "there IS a special occasion at the Gem tonight. Be there at seven." She winked.

"I'll have to see, sweetheart," Tim said. "I just got married you know. Have to check with my wife."

Sally plopped a palm on the table and leaned her weight on it. "Be there," she said. She didn't smile.

"Got it," I said, jumping in. "We'll see you there."

"Good," Sally said, and turned to drift up front.

"What was that all about?" Tim looked confused. "Did I say something wrong?"

"No," I answered. "She's up to something."

"We were at the Gem last night," he said, still looking confused.

I looked over at Sharon, who had remained suspiciously quiet.

She shrugged and poked at her plate, moving a piece of bacon from one side to the other, refusing to look at me.

I shook my head at Tim and dug into the dressing.

He followed suit and let it go.

We finished our lunch, both us so hungry there really wasn't enough to box up.

Sharon finished her coffee and slid out of the booth.

"I'm going right to the office," she said. "Bring those papers over whenever you're ready and we'll get them out of the way."

"Won't be long, Sharon," Tim said, sliding out of the booth. "We're going to go get them right now. Back in fifteen or so."

"See you then," she called back and went on up the aisle.

Tim pulled out some bills and tossed them on the table, picking up the check at the same time. I stood up and led the way up front.

Sally stepped up and met us at the front counter. She rang up our bill, and returned Tim's credit card, along with the slip for him to sign.

"Don't forget, Tee," she said to me. "Seven o'clock."

"Yes, ma'am, I got it," I said and led the way outside.

Back in the truck and headed for home Tim tossed me a glance. "You want to tell me what's going on? Another local initiation?"

"I have to tell you the truth, Tim. I don't know what she's doing. If I had to guess I would say it's some kind of party."

"We had a party last night! Oh, wait. She wasn't there. That's it, isn't it?"

"In all probability. She means well, whatever it is. Did you have something else planned for tonight?"

"Me? No." He reached to put his hand on my thigh and rub it softly. "I have what I wanted. Only other things on my agenda are getting these papers signed and the grass cut."

"I can get the lawn on Monday," I said. "You don't get much time home."

"Nope, sorry, babe. I am the head of the house now. The yards are my job."

"I am perfectly capable of cutting the grass," I argued.

"Never said you weren't," he grinned. "There are some things that fall to the man of the house. You have one, now. Let him do his job." With a wink he turned into our drive. "Believe me, babe, he really wants to do this."

At the house, I hopped out of the truck before he could come around and open my door. "Let me guess," I said. "You will be doing all the outside chores and I get the indoor chores? Like the kitchen?"

Tim laughed and scooped me up and carried me up the steps. Giggling, I took the keys out of his hand and opened the door. "I guess it's a good thing we're older," I chuckled. "Otherwise I'm afraid barefoot and pregnant would be the agenda."

Another side effect I gained from chemo, the onset of early menopause, something Tim and I had discussed before. I wanted him to know, to be sure he understood. I already had my kids. He never would. He decided to love mine and get on with it.

Barefoot and pregnant were never going to be on the agenda.

Tim went up to grab his briefcase while I checked on the cats.

"Left a little something upstairs," he grinned when he came back.

I looked up to see his eyes gleaming, the blue foremost today, over riding the usual slate color.

"And that would be?"

"Just a little sumpin sumpin," he said, gathering me in his arms. He looked into my eyes and I was afraid my heart would stop. So tall, so handsome, so incredibly perfect. I leaned in and pressed my lips against his, savoring the feel of those firm, sculpted lips on mine.

Tim made a little sound in his chest, tightening his hold, returning my kiss with gusto.

After a few minutes he lifted his head and looked at me, his eyes darkening as he met mine. "I love you so much," he whispered, before kissing me again. When he lifted his head again, he caught my face in his hands, turning it up to his.

"You have made me complete, Muse. You are the best thing that ever happened to me. I promise to take care of you, to cherish you, all those vows we made are written on my heart."

His eyes shone with unshed tears as we stood and looked at each other.

"I love you," I whispered back, pressing my lips back to his. With a sigh he bent and scooped me into his arms, holding me tight to his chest. I slipped my arms around his neck as he carried me upstairs.

Although we were running behind we managed to get half a ream of paper into Sharon's office, read through, initialed, signed, stamped and notarized in an hour and a half. Tim still had enough time to get out the lawnmower and take on the lawn when we were back home again.

Since we were going to the Gem, I didn't bother to fix supper. Pizza two nights in a row is okay with me.

While Tim worked in the yard I decided to take my shower and get ready. Getting out clean underwear I noticed a small blue rectangle on top of the dresser. Curious, I picked it up.

A checkbook, filled with pale blue checks.

The imprint in the upper left corner read Teejay Tanner and the address. Flipping the top sheet I goggled. The current balance on the pristine check register read ten thousand dollars.

After my shower I was looking through my closet for something a little dressier than my usual tee shirts and sweatshirts. I was out of luck. I determined right then and there to take Sharon up on the shopping expedition. As much as I disliked the idea she did have a point. As Tim's wife I would be under more scrutiny that normal. Like it or not, I was going to have to go shopping. Thanks to Tim I could afford it.

Tim finished the lawn, put things away and came up for his own shower.

I settled on a blue plaid shirt that at least had to be buttoned instead of just pulled over my head. With clean jeans it was the best I could do.

"Are you sure you don't know what's up?" Tim asked, drying off with a towel, before pulling out his own jeans.

"If I had to hazard a guess, I would say it's some kind of party," I answered, admiring the view. The ridges of muscle of on his chest and abdomen bunched and moved as he reached for a shirt. He pulled a Henley shirt over his head, the blue picking up the blue in his eyes tonight.

"Didn't we party last night?"

I chuckled. "At the Gem? Or at home?"

Tim laughed. "We do seem to party a lot. I love it," he said. He sat to pull on some socks and boots. Looking up at me from under those thick, dark lashes, his eyes gleamed with blue sparks. "As a matter of fact," he began.

"We have to go," I said, back in away from him. "Sally is waiting."

"Oh, yeah," he stood and shook down the legs of his jeans. "Well, let's go then. We haven't left yet and all I can think about is coming back home."

The back corner where our bunch usually congregated was festooned with balloons and crepe paper streamers formed a canopy over the table. A banner on the wall read "Congratulations Tim and Tee" in red letters. The table was laden with beautifully wrapped gifts, the centerpiece an amazing three tiered cake.

The cake alone was magnificent. Pale ivory frosting was a background for cascades of pink and lavender wisteria blossoms all made of frosting that fell from the top to the bottom on bright green vines of sugar.

Two graceful crystal swans were the topper, their curved necks creating a heart as they faced each other.

A separate table to the side was crowned with a beautifully carved turkey and sparkling side dishes surrounding it. A sliced ham nestled close to the turkey platter, with even more side dishes. The rich aromas filled the air. Plates and cutlery trimmed the edges of the table.

Around the table were gathered our friends, who all cheered when we came through the door. Being Saturday night, there were others that cheered too, because they could. That's another joy of small towns. Everybody knows everyone even if it's only by word of mouth.

Tim squeezed my hand and leaned to whisper in my ear as we neared the table. "Hoopla has found us," he said softly.

Sally stood to give us hugs. "Good thing you showed up," she said by way of greeting. "I was afraid I was gonna have to come get you."

Tim gave her a bear hug, actually lifting her off the floor and swinging her around, to the delight of the crowd and the amazement of Sally. Then everyone was talking at once, the jukebox was loaded, and the music tried to drown out the clink of silverware as plates were loaded.

At one point a second turkey was brought out and the carcass of the first removed. I saw Sally and Kathy shuttle side dishes from the kitchen several times and Jennifer, one of the bartenders, kept up a steady pace filling bread baskets. Pitchers of iced tea were plentiful at both tables.

People I only knew by sight milled around with full plates, talking and laughing.

Once the food was finally cleared Jennifer set several stacks of small plates beside the cake.

We opened gifts, oohed and aahed and passed them around, laughed at the gag gifts and smiled at the cards. When all the gifts were opened and admired the cake was cut and distributed to everyone in the bar.

Cora had brought a smaller, pink cake box and set the topper aside for us to take home.

Camera's and phones flashed as we cut cake and passed plates and forks.

Once the cake was done the dancing recommenced and a good time was had by all. I thanked Sally and Sharon numerous times, for the thought and their gifts. Pretty amazing what they had managed to put together in such a short time. A couple of the younger guys I didn't know jumped in to help with clearing up. The music filled the room.

Tim danced with all the women, some twice, and I was whirled around the room once again by an assortment of gentleman ranging in age from Jasper, who is reported to be ninety, to the college guys from last night, who had returned.

One of them introduced himself as Chris and wanted to know if we partied every night.

"Hard to believe, Chris, but it's pretty rare. You caught us just at the right time. Did you get some cake?"

He spun me around and tugged me back. "Oh, yeah. I actually had two pieces. That was the best cake I ever ate."

As I twirled back to him, I nodded at Cora, dancing next to us. "That's the lady who baked it," I said. "She has the bakery here, and everything is delicious."

He caught my waist and swung me another turn. "I'll remember that. I have a real sweet tooth anyway." Another turn and he pulled me back. "Congratulations by the way. I understand you're the new bride."

"Yep, that's me. And thank you."

The song ended and he guided me back to the table where Tim was waiting.

My new friend stepped up and introduced himself to Tim, shaking hands and congratulating him.

"I didn't bring a gift," he said to Tim. "I didn't know about the shindig tonight."

"No need," Tim assured him. "Believe me, it was not expected. Did you get something to eat? Some cake?"

"Oh, yes sir, more than my share. I explained that to your lady here." Chris pulled out his wallet and extracted a card, which he handed over to Tim. "This is for you guys," he said.

Tim took the card and glanced at it. Leaning into him, I read it. 'Trim and Go' was printed across the top of a picture of a lawn mower.

"We have a full service yard maintenance program," Chris explained. "You give me your address and I'll see your yards are done. My gift," he grinned.

"Not necessary, man," Tim repeated. "Really. Just enjoy yourself."

Chris took the card from Tim's hand and reached to tuck it in his pocket. "Please," he said. "I'd feel better about it. Besides, if you like our service, you could be a new customer. Works for both of us. Just call that number and we'll take care of it."

"Fair enough," Tim agreed, and shook Chris' hand again. "Thank you."

"My pleasure," the younger man grinned. "After all, I had your pizza and beer last night and a turkey dinner tonight. Not to mention swinging your pretty new wife around a few times," he added with a smile for me.

"Thanks, Chris," I smiled back. "We really appreciate it."

"Looking forward to seeing y'all again soon," he said and with a small salute, he melted back into the crowd still on the dance floor. A slow song started and Tim caught my hand and pulled me close.

"My turn," he said, wrapping an arm around my waist. "Getting tired of watching you spin around with these other guys." He moved us out onto the dance floor to mingle with other dancers.

"Hey, Hubs, you've been pretty visible yourself with all these ladies."

"Hubs?" He grinned down at me. "I like it."

I tightened my arm around his shoulders, moving closer to the muscled wall of his chest. "So do I," I said, feeling my voice thicken. "So do I."

It was after midnight when we finally got home, taking two trips to get everything indoors. I shoved the top layer of cake Cora had saved for us into the fridge while Tim stacked gifts on the couch and we called it a night.

The combination of excitement, two late nights in a row, plus all the dancing left me worn out. It was almost noon

Sunday morning by the time I rolled over and looked at the clock. I sat up, looking for Tim.

He always wanted an early start on Sunday to avoid most of the traffic on the drive back to LA.

"Tim?"

No answer.

Swinging my legs over the side of the bed, I fumbled around for my slippers and headed for the bathroom.

Once I made my way to the kitchen I found the coffee pot loaded and ready to go. Pushing the button to start the machine I got down a cup and looked around.

In the center of the table was a sheet of paper.

I read: Muse – you were sleeping so sound I didn't want to wake you. Coffee is ready to go, cats fed and I am on my way. See you Friday night. I love you – Tim

Just great, I thought.

He was already gone. I'd missed him.

I went back upstairs and back to bed, leaving the coffee to drip on its own.

The sun was low in the sky by the second time I got up. I felt like myself after a shower. Pulling on some jeans and a sweatshirt I went back to the kitchen.

Pouring out the sludge in the coffee pot I rinsed and reloaded it. While it was dripping I opened the fridge, suddenly ravenous. No wonder.

The first thing I saw was the small, decorated top layer of our wedding cake, carefully nestled in a little box.

I thought about eating it, then decided I should probably share it with Tim.

I didn't want to wait for bacon or sausage to cook. Pulling out some of the plates we had brought home last night, I lifted a lid on a platter of sliced turkey. Yum. Turkey sandwiches.

Once I had eaten I felt a lot better. Checking the time I dialed Tim's phone.

FLASH

Hey, Muse. You awake?

You're on my list, Hubs. Why didn't you wake me?

You were sleeping so sound. You didn't even twitch when I got up. You needed the sleep.

I needed to see my husband. He needed some breakfast before he left.

His rich laughter filled my mind.

I stand corrected, babe. That drive through mistakes a hockey puck for a biscuit. Couldn't even feed that one to the ground squirrels.

Serves you right.

Won't do it again. How do you feel? Pretty hectic couple of days.

I'm fine, Tim. Just overtired. I went back to bed when I found out you were gone and slept till four.

Are you all right? Now?

Heck, yeah, just overdid it. Don't worry. I just missed seeing you. Don't do that again, okay? I need to see you when I can.

You got it, babe. I am fully chastised. Now, should I pick up thank you cards?

Oh, yes! I hadn't thought that far. I'd have to go down to San Luis, or make my own. That would be perfect!

Consider it done. Anything else I can do?

Get this project done, so you can come home. For more than two days.

Top of my list, babe.

All right, I'll let you go.

Don't ever let me go. You promised.

You know what I meant. Have a good night, Hubs.

Had a better one last night, Muse. You get some rest.

If I get any more rest I'll be comatose.

You need it. You have those tests coming up. Get all the rest you can.

I will. You be careful.

Will do. Talk to you tomorrow.

I love you.

Too.

Night, Tim

Night, Muse.

I spent Monday sorting gifts and making a list of people to thank. That took most of the morning. Still feeling a little tired, I made it an early night and was in bed by eight with my Kindle. The cats loved it.

Pretty close to normal by Tuesday I headed for Kelly's after I shipped off a couple of packages of books that had sold.

Sharon had company in her booth.

John Kincaid sat across from her.

When he saw me, he slid out of the booth and stood.

"Don't leave on my account, John," I said when I reached them.

"Morning, Tee. I was on my way. Need to get to work." He gave me a little salute and stepped around me to go up front.

Sliding into his vacated seat I felt his cup. Still warm.

"Did I run him off?"

"I doubt it," she said. "He was headed out anyway. But Bill called in with a problem of some kind."

"What kind of problem?"

"No idea. He didn't say. So, how's married life?"

"I love it," I smiled. "And thank you so much."

"For what?"

"The party, the sheets, everything."

"The sheets, you're welcome. The party was Sally. The cake was Cora."

"Well, thank you. I know you had something to do with it. We really appreciated it."

"Big weekend for you, Tee. Wow. You're married." She sat back, sipping from her coffee. "Now, dish."

"On what?"

"Tim! Did you know he had that much money? All those assets and investments? Lord, girl, you are set for life!"

I had forgotten about all the papers we had signed on Saturday.

"No, never thought about it. He doesn't talk about stuff like that."

"Why would he? Still, I had no idea!"

"He mentioned it a couple of times. It just never really registered."

"It would have registered with me," she said, sitting forward again. "He can afford another house. He wouldn't even have to make payments! He could pay cash!"

Always the business woman.

"Sharon that's all up to him. As I remember he already has a couple of houses. Wasn't that in the papers?"

"Yes, he has three, counting the one his mother lives in. He's just renting the condo in LA."

"I knew that," I said. "Now can we drop it?"

"Drop it? Why! Tee, you're rich! Don't you get it? You can do anything! Go anywhere! Anything you ever dreamed of is right there!"

With a sigh I looked up front, seeing Sally on her way.

"Sharon please don't mention all that. Not to Sally."

"I can't," she smirked. "It's privileged. Besides, she probably has a pretty good idea of what he's worth."

"Morning, Sally," I called, as a warning.

"Morning, Mrs. Tanner. Where's the new hubby? Run him off already?"

"He had to get back," I said. "I'm really looking forward to the end of this project. I hate it when he has to leave."

She filled my cup and warmed up Sharon's.

"So are you moving to Texas? Los Angeles?"

"No idea," I answered. "We haven't even talked about it."

"Happened pretty fast," she smiled.

"Speaking of fast, thank you. You had to scramble to get that party put together."

Sally's plump cheeks pinked up.

"No need to thank me," she said. "Sharon and Cora did most of the work."

"I just want you to know how much we appreciate it. It meant a lot to both of us."

"It's fun to do nice things for nice people," she replied. "Referring to your husband there."

"Oh I know," I smiled. "Thanks anyway."

"All right, enough," Sharon interrupted. "When are you going to decide where to live?"

"I don't know, Sharon! What's the rush? You trying to get rid of me?"

She had the grace to look a little embarrassed.

"It's not that," she said with a sigh.

"She wants to handle your house," Sally put in, pulling her order pad from her apron pocket. "Your aunt's houses. What can I get you?"

"I'll have bacon and eggs and a short stack."

"How can you eat all that?" Sharon asked.

"I'm hungry!"

"Tim is rubbing off on you already," she said. "I'll have the special," she told Sally, referring to the Tuesday special of ham steak.

"You want more coffee?"

"Iced tea," Sharon answered.

"I'll stick with coffee," I said.

Sally made a note on her pad and moved away to turn in our orders.

Sharon fiddled with her napkin. "Tee, I am sorry. Bugging you, I mean. It's a lot of things. I could use a sale right now. And that is at odds with you leaving town, moving to Texas. And you have to admit we've had a long, weird summer. Everything all at once. I'm sorry if you felt I was pressuring you."

"And I'm sorry for being so snappish," I smiled.

"Oh, changing the subject," she said, moving to a different subject, "guess who's working at Tiffany's now?"

Tiffany's referred to our beauty salon, the only one in town if you don't count the barber shop next to the post office, which still has its red, white and blue spinning column out front.

Tiffany is a special lady, to all of us. When I began chemo my hair started to fall out. By the hand full. It was disgusting. One of the first changes in cancer treatment. I opted for the obvious, as do most women with cancer – get it off.

Still struggling with the whole concept of cancer, I went to Tiffany. We've been friends for ages, know each other's families. She took me back to her station and wrapped a cape around my shoulders.

"What are we doing today, Miss Tee?"

I took a deep breath, my throat so tight it hurt to talk.

"Tiff, I have lung cancer. I started chemo and my hair is falling out. I want it off, all of it. And if you cry I will lose it completely."

Without a word, she held up one finger and went through the curtain in the back of the shop. She was gone for almost five minutes. When she came back her eyes were red and a single tear still glistened at the corner of her eye. She picked up the clippers and flipped them on.

"So what are you reading?" she asked.

She earned a special place in my heart that day and she still holds it.

"Who?" I looked at Sharon.

"The blond," she replied, sitting back with a smug look.

My brain spun, trying to find traction.

"Blond?"

She leaned forward and dropped her voice.

"The one from the Gem. The fan. The one who stood up."

My wheels caught. "Lurlene?"

Sharon plopped back in her seat and a smirk. "Yep, that one. I went in to make an appointment for a trim and there she was, working in the back."

"Did you ask Tiffany?"

"Of course I did," she scoffed. "Tiffany said she came in looking for a job. She tested her first, doing someone's hair. Tiff says she's awesome, does great work."

I thought for a minute. It was up to Tim if he wanted their history out there so I kept it to myself, making a mental note to let him know. Looking across the table at Sharon I just shrugged.

"What does that mean?"

"Nothing," I answered. "Good for her? What do you want me to say?"

"Doesn't she have some kind of thing for Tim? Are you jealous already?"

"No need," I smiled at her. "He's taken."

Sharon smiled back, a soft gleam in her eye. "Yeah, he is. He makes that pretty obvious. You are one lucky woman, Tee, you literally have it all. And what a package it comes in."

I was up and moving Friday morning, wanting to have everything done and out of the way. Tim often shows up on Friday night and I didn't want anything to get in the way of my time with him.

I made up our bed with the new pale blue sheets Sharon had given us, tossing the others into the washer. Cleaned the bathroom, vacuumed and dusted before going downstairs and repeating the process.

I didn't slow down until the laundry was folded and put away and all my other implements of destruction had been returned to their place.

Washing my hands at the kitchen sink I tried to think of something that sounded good for lunch. Kelly's Friday special was fish. I liked the fish and often brought it home for supper but today it didn't sound good. I wanted something lighter.

I reached for a towel to dry my hands.

FLASH

Hey, Muse

Hey, Tim! How are you? You still coming home this weekend?

Slow down, babe.

I miss you.

I miss you more. What are you doing?

Is it going to be what are you wearing next?

Now that's a possibility.

Are you still coming home tonight?

Nope. Something came up.

I slumped, resting my arms on the kitchen counter and dropping my head.

You all right, Muse?

Yeah, I'm fine. Disappointed. So what's going on?

Think I have the crew talked into shooting the videos up there. They want some pictures of the area, mostly the beach.

Then you should be able to come home. Take some pictures, even video.

My thoughts exactly, babe.

So you'll be up tomorrow?

Right now I need you to do something for me.

Anything, Hubs. What can I do?

Open the front door. My hands are full.

With a squeal John could have heard I rushed to the front door and threw it open so hard it hit the wall and bounced back to hit me in the rear.

And there he was.

He held his briefcase and overnight bag in one hand and a dozen crimson roses in the other. Their scent was intoxicating, rich and spicy, the old fashioned smell roses seem to have lost.

He stepped in and handed me the flowers, his eyes twinkling.

"You devil," I said, wrapping my free arm around his neck. "I'll get you for that."

He bent to set his bags on the floor before scooping me into his arms and swinging me around. His biceps flexed and I was tight against his chest, feeling those ridges of muscle move under his shirt.

He dropped his head and kissed me thoroughly, taking his time, before he finally let me go and reached around to shut the front door.

"Couldn't resist, babe."

"You're gonna resist," I warned him, going to the kitchen to pull down a vase. "That's not funny. My heart was broken. You're going to do that again and find me laying in the floor."

He moved up behind me, his arms sliding around my waist.

"Laying in the floor could be good," he murmured against the side of my neck.

I nudged him with my elbow and ran water in the vase.

"We'll see about that later. Right now I have to get these roses in some water."

He ran his hands up my sides, kissed my neck, and let me go. Stooping he scratched ears and chins of the feline kids at his feet, rubbing around his legs. I knew how they felt.

Once the cats were dealt with he opened the fridge and got out a beer.

"You want a beer, babe?"

"No, thanks. You can hand me the tea, though."

While I finished with the flowers Tim moved behind me to get a glass, fill it with ice and tea and set it on the table. Taking his seat he watched me bring the flowers to the table and set them in the center. Their heady scent already filled the kitchen.

"Where do you get these?" I asked, fluffing them a little. "It's so rare to find roses that smell."

"Little place in Studio City. Annie found it."

Anne Edwards is his manager, agent and mainstay. According to Tim she can do anything. I was constantly grateful she was happily married. I knew for a fact she put together a wedding flight on a private jet with all the trimmings on short notice.

"Now, tell me," I said, taking my seat across from him. "What's with the videos? Are they really going to shoot them here?"

"I'm hoping," he grinned. "We're entertaining tomorrow."

"What?"

"We're entertaining. A team is coming up to scout around, get some vids, check it all out. I invited them for supper once they're done, gave them our address. Was that all right?"

Typical man, asking after the fact.

"That's fine, Tim, I just don't know what I can put together to feed them. They're used to a lot better than my cooking."

He scooted forward to lean on his folded arms.

"Got it covered, babe."

Of course he did.

"And what are we serving? Does it involve biscuits?"

Tim laughed. "Not this time, Muse. I keep that little bit of trivia to myself. I am not going to share my biscuits and gravy. I asked Annie to call that little Italian place you like. We're meeting there."

"Tahlia's Cuchina? Oh, yum!"

He grinned at me, finishing his beer. "I know you like it. Plus, this way you don't have to cook and I can shove them on their way without being too rude."

"And that's why you're home early?"

"In one, babe."

I watched the flames kindle in his eyes, the blue sparks lighting up the gray, as he reached to take my hand.

"I missed you more this week than ever."

I squeezed his hand, understanding how he felt. There must be more to the ties that bind than just the words. Although we had only been married for a few days, not even a week, it had seemed like forever since he was here.

"I'm glad you're home," I smiled at him. "You have no idea."

He stood up and came around to lift me from my chair and pull me into his arms.

"I have an idea, babe. A very good one."

Saturday Tim had to meet the producer and the music people at the beach by ten for a meeting I declined to attend. We would meet at the restaurant at one.

Shuffling again through my closet unearthed no buried treasure. As much as I hated the whole idea I was going to have to go shopping.

Jeans, tees and sweatshirts were fine for Monarch, pretty much the standard uniform for a beach town anywhere. Any people I was going to be introduced to would in all probability be dressed the same way.

Sharon was right. As Tim's wife, I was going to have to make some concessions. I sure as heck didn't want to embarrass him with my appearance.

Glancing at the clock I knew I couldn't get all the way to San Luis and back by one. Monarch has no clothing stores other than Jade Beach Marine Supply just over the hill, which carries waterproof suits and rubber boots.

I bit my lip and called Sharon.

I explained my dilemma and listened to the silence for several minutes.

"You still there?" I finally asked.

"Yes, I'm thinking. Hang on a second."

After a few more minutes she was back on the line.

"It's warm outside, Tee, so we're in luck. Meet me at Butterfly Gardens. I'm leaving right now."

A gift shop? The tourist trap?

Trusting her, I grabbed my keys and locked up the house.

Beach Street is the short little street that runs behind Main. The far end, beside the beach access ramp, is a little tourist shop, one with post cards, tee shirts and strange creatures made of seashells and rocks.

I had been in it once.

I pulled into the parking lot just as Sharon came in from the other direction and parked next to me.

She was grinning like the proverbial cat when she came around her car.

"Waited till the last minute, didn't you?"

"Not now," I warned her. "Tim didn't give me any notice. I have to meet these people in two hours." Checking my watch, I adjusted my schedule. "Make that an hour and a half."

"Come on," she said, grabbing my hand and tugging me towards the shop. "This is the only shot we have. If your legs were shorter you could borrow something of mine."

"I'll put that on my agenda," I told her as we hurried to the door. "Shorten legs."

Inside was the usual collection found in every souvenir shop in the nation – tee shirts, post cards, cheap jewelry, stuffed animals and small toys. Along the back wall were sweatshirts and windbreakers, all with Monarch Beach blazing along the front or Son of a Beach, a popular one with visitors.

In the back corner was a rack of colorful Hawaiian print dresses. Some were just muumuus, some were wrap around, and some were like a long sarong. Say that three times fast.

Sharon grabbed one of the latter in electric blue and held it against me. Shoving me along she went back up front and looked at the display of plastic and paper leis.

"No," I said. "I will not wear a paper lei."

She cocked an eyebrow at me. "For Tim you would. We just don't need one."

She was looking at the rack of jewelry beside the leis.

There were all kinds of earrings, from studs to long dangling ones, in every color. Sharon picked a couple of carded ones off and we went up front.

"Pay the gal," she said, piling the items on the counter, her eyes still roaming the store.

While the young woman was ringing up the purchases, Sharon called from the back of the store she had one more item. I was rewarded with an eye roll from the clerk, who, in my opinion, should have been happy to have a customer.

Sharon rushed up and added a shirt from the same material as the dress.

"That it?" asked the bored clerk.

"Yes, thank you." I handed over my credit card.

Back at home Sharon gave orders like a drill sergeant.

I was in the long dress and zipped up before I realized it had a slit down the side, from the edge of my underwear down to the floor. When I walked it opened and closed, exposing my entire leg.

"I can't wear this," I said. Sharon was rooting around in my closet so her answer was muffled.

"Yes you can. And you will," she said emerging from the closet with a pair of sandals I forgot I ever owned. "Put these on."

She dumped the little bag of earrings on the bed, pulling them from the cardboard backing. While I fumbled with the straps on my sandals she held them up to my ear, first one and then the other.

"Put these on," she ordered, handing me the long, dangling blue ones. "We can't do anything about that hair, but we can do your eyes."

"I don't have eye makeup," I said. "Except for mascara."

"Well, I do," she said, digging into her purse. "Sit down."

I sat and endured her applications, both grateful she was here, and at the same time resenting the attention. She brushed and poked and did whatever while mumbling under her breath. I was glad I couldn't understand what she was saying.

I stole a glance at my watch. Fifteen minutes till one.

Sharon stepped back and gave me a critical once over. 'Stand up, let's see how that hangs."

Feeling like a five year old, I stood up.

She reached over to tug and pull, then stepped back again.

"Gonna have to do," she said. "Put this on," she said and handed me the shirt.
I pulled it on, grateful for something to cover my shoulders.

"All right," she said finally.

I walked over to the mirror and looked.

My eyes popped with blue, the lids dark and mysterious, upturned at the corners. The long metallic earrings swung below my jawline making my neck look longer. The color of the dress went perfectly with the eyes, accenting them even more.

"Wow," I said. "You do nice work."

"It'll do for now," she said, picking up her purse and stuffing her makeup back in. "You are going to have to do something about that hair."

I looked at my reflection. My hair was just hair. Fine with me. The halo didn't show from this angle, so I just had a cap of ash blond hair. A little hair spray had flattened the sides so they didn't stick straight out.

"Thanks, Sharon," I said, moving to give her a hug. "I owe you big time."

"Get going," she grinned. 'You look fine."

She followed me out and waved as I climbed in the truck.

When I moved my foot to the gas pedal, my whole leg slithered out of the dress. Oh, boy. This was going to be fun.

Tim was waiting for me on the sidewalk in front of Tahlia's. I saw him when I pulled in. By the time I parked, he was there to open the door for me and help me from the truck.

I watched him as I slid out of the truck, to get his reaction.

With his hands on my waist, he stepped back and looked me up and down.

"Lord have mercy," he said finally. "You are sensational, Muse! You really clean up nice."

I blushed, feeling my cheeks warm as I looked down at my feet.

Tim is taller than me any day and today with him in boots and me in flat sandals he was even taller. I had to crane my neck to look up at him.

"Is it okay? Really?"

"Spectacular," he whispered, and brushed his lips across mine. "You're a whole different person." His hands tightened at my waist, pulling me closer.

"Two for the price of one," I grinned at him.

"And I'll take them both," he smiled back. "You look incredible. And if we stand out here much longer everyone in town is going to see your effect on me."

Blushing again, I stepped back.

He reached to hook his little finger through mine and led the way to the front door, the look in his eyes telling me all I needed to know.

Does anyone like to meet new people?

Cancer by its very nature forces its victims to be reclusive. It's a private battle no matter how many family members and friends are there for support. The support is necessary, the battle is private. You lose your hair, your appetite, your weight, your tastes and your body heat. For many, you lose your life.

Not a condition to practice your social skills.

Add to that I have never been an assertive person. Pretty much go with the flow and avoid confrontations or taking a stand.

Meeting these people, some of whom Tim depended on for his livelihood, scared me to put it bluntly. While I was not in danger of using the wrong fork I knew these people were going to be judging me, and indirectly, judging Tim.

I was okay with the locale, giving me an edge, since I knew the chef and counted him among my friends. I knew the food would be impressive to even the most jaded tastes.

Tim stayed close, touching me, holding my hand, pressing his thigh against mine under the table. Everything he could do to keep me aware he was there, that I was not alone.

To be fair, everyone I met was incredibly welcoming and friendly, even explaining some of the more technical discussions they had.

I smiled, nodded, and answered questions when asked. Most of the questions were about the area, few were of a personal nature.

Anne, Tim's agent, manager, whatever title she held, could not have been more welcoming. A beautiful, poised woman in complete control of everything around her. No wonder Tim put so much faith in her.

By the time we arrived she had met Miguel Zambrano, the chef and owner, arranged menus, decorated the table and had everyone seated and comfortable with the drink of their choice.

I was introduced, congratulated, complimented and left alone, except for specific questions about Monarch and San Luis Obispo County. At the same time I was made to feel comfortable and a part of the group. No personal questions came up whether by accident or design.

The meal went off without a hitch, everyone impressed with the cuisine. That one I never doubted, being familiar with Miguel's cooking. By the time the tiramisu and coffee arrived everyone was comfortable.

While they finished dessert Tim walked me out to the truck where I was almost shaking with relief to have it behind me.

Tim hugged me before I climbed into the truck. "Damn, Muse, you were amazing. I am so proud of you I could bust."

"That's probably all that lasagna you ate," I smiled back, yanking the hampering skirt out of the way.

Tim leaned in the truck and ran a hand along my thigh. "Nice legs, babe."

"You have a meeting to attend," I said.

"Uh-huh, I do," he smiled. "And then I have to go home. To my wife." His eyes lit with a promise.

"And your wife has to go see to your supper," I smiled back.

"Forget cooking, we'll grab something from Kelly's"
He lifted his hand to brush his knuckles down my cheek.
"I love you so much," he said softly.
"Too," I said, my heart in my throat.

Behind him Anne stepped out and called him, interrupting us.

"Go," I said, starting the truck. "I'll see you at home."

"Count on it, babe,' he said and backed away.

Glancing in the rear view mirror as I pulled away from the curb, I saw Tim still standing there, watching me leave.

Tim was home by five with exciting news. The powers that be loved our beach, out little town and its environs. They were headed back to LA to prepare for the shoot that would take place on our very own beach.

The best part of that was Tim being home. We were looking at two, maybe three, weeks of working in Monarch. It was difficult to tell who was more excited – me or Tim.

Arrangements had to be made to get ready for the shoot. Crews had to be hired, equipment rented, caterers, all of it beyond me. I did understand that Tim was home, and would be home for a while.

Tim had a few clothes and toiletries at the house although not enough for several weeks. My recent decision to submit to shopping, my least favorite thing in the world, combined with his need for more clothes and necessities determined our need for a shopping trip.

Sunday we relaxed around the house.

Monday we went shopping.

As mentioned, Monarch has nowhere to shop for clothes so a trip to San Luis was scheduled for Monday. I fixed bacon and eggs while Tim dealt with the cats and we were on our way before nine.

San Luis Obispo is a beautiful little town, full of mature trees, friendly people and many little shops of all kinds.

We parked at one end of town and wandered down Higuera, stopping along the way and collecting bags. We stopped for coffee at Broad before going back up Marsh Street on the return trip.

We were laden with bags by the time we got to the Barnes and Noble bookstore.

"How about you wait here and I take this stuff to the truck?"

"Can you carry it all?" I wanted to help and I wanted to go in this store.

Tim dropped a kiss on the top of my head, rearranged the bags, and sent me in the store while he headed on up the street.

I was still browsing by the time he joined me.

"You can't find anything?" He laughed at me. "In a book store?"

He threw an arm around my shoulders and pulled me against his side.

Most of my books for the past couple of years were either collectibles that I resold on line or on my Kindle. I couldn't' remember the last hard cover book I bought. Hard cover books are expensive.

Leaning down to my ear Tim whispered, "I brought the truck. You want a cart?"

With a laugh of my own, I headed upstairs to the mystery section.

"Come on," I called back to him. "You can carry."

Book lovers can relate to my feelings as I looked around at all the bright book spines vying for my attention, the stacks and tables of books all around me. And I could have as many as I wanted.

It was a good thing Tim brought the truck.

We had a late lunch at the Apple Farm on the north end of town, another of my favorite places to eat. The entry is made through their gift shop which features all kinds of merchandise, from aprons to hoof cream.

I had the hot meat loaf sandwich and Tim followed my lead. We finished up sharing a slice of coconut cake and left San Luis so full I doubted I would eat again before Tuesday.

I learned a lot that day. About myself and about Tim.

For one thing I learned shopping can be fun. Tim trying on hats, then finding outfits to go with them had me doubled up with laughter. He kept me laughing all day with his easy humor.

Another thing is his extraordinary taste. I bought things I would never have tried on before, although I did decline Victoria's Secret. Even more, his selections looked good on me, better than the ones I chose. He went to look at guitars while I picked up new underwear.

We spent the most at the western wear shop, where Tim stocked up on his favorite snap front, long sleeve shirts, those he can roll up the sleeves to his elbows. He prefers the small plaid patterns and ginghams to solid colors.

I will be the first to admit that Tim in a small check pale blue gingham shirt is worth walking across the street to see. Actually several streets. I might even enter a 5K run for that sight.

He was recognized only once and happily posed with a couple of girls for pictures. Neither asked for my autograph, or even my name. I was okay with that, even took the picture for them so they could both be in it.

Back at home he did his share of removing tags, washing, folding and putting away, even hanging up his shirts. I learned that laundry can be fun if you're standing alongside someone you love and love to spend time with.

It was late afternoon when we finished up and Tim volunteered to barbecue chicken. While he set up the barbecue I made a salad and peeled potatoes to wrap in foil.

Soon I heard music and looked through the garage to see him sitting on an overturned crate with his guitar, playing along with the radio. He had installed one in the garage, and one in the living room so the house was filled with music when he was home.

I listened for a few minutes, just watching him, before I carried a couple of bottles of beer outside and took a chair by the barbecue.

He quit playing and jumped up when I joined him.

"Keep playing," I said, sitting down. "I love to hear you."

"Just fooling around. You don't mind?"

"You're home, Hubs. You can do anything you want."

He looked up at me through those lush lashes, and grinned. "Not out here I can't."

I chuckled and motioned for him to continue.

He picked up the guitar, listened for a second, then joined in on the current song playing, not missing a beat.

I was perfectly content to sit and watch and listen, the smoke from the barbecue rolling the rich smell of oak burning into the air.

After a while Tim got up to check the coals and set his guitar back in the house.

Joining me he held out his hand, palm up.

"Dance with me, Muse." Hand extended, hips swaying, he moved in front of me.

I took his hand and got up, letting him lead me.

We danced that song and the next and it was fun, just the two of us, out in the fresh air, just being in love.

The next was slow and Tim tugged me into his arms.

I laid my head against his shoulder and closed my eyes, relishing this quiet moment.

"Get a room," John called across the drive way and the moment ended.

"Got one," Tim called back, "this is just a warm up."

With a sigh he let me go and looked up to see John coming over.

"Don't let me interrupt," John said with a grin. "Go right ahead."

"If I throw a stick, will you go chase it?"

"Not tonight," John said. "I'd rather interrupt."

"You want a beer?" I asked before retaking my seat.

"Love it," he said. "Thanks, Tee."

"Tim?"

"Yep, thanks babe," he answered and I went to fetch a couple more bottles of beer.

When I came back the guys were sitting around the barbecue, quite amiably for them. I sat down in the chair next to Tim after distributing beer.

"So what's new, Law Man?"

"Had a visit from your friend," John said, taking a long drink and looking at Tim.

"Which one?" Tim countered.

"Lurlene Martinez," John answered. "Sound familiar?"

Tim nodded and drank beer. "I know her."

John sat forward, resting his elbows on his knees. "Quite a history there."

"That too," Tim said.

John watched for some reaction. When he didn't get one, he continued.

"She came in voluntarily. Wanted to make us aware of her past with you and assure us she is a changed person. Gainfully employed here in town, renting a place in Jade until she can get something here. Spun quite a story."

Tim nodded again. "Okay."

John sat back. "Want to give me your side?"

"Nope."

"Not gonna argue?"

"No need," Tim said and stood up to turn the chicken. "Lawyers have all the records and I can have them send you copies. I have no problem with the woman. Long as she leaves me and mine alone." He glanced at me with that last.

John drank some more beer and looked at Tim, measuring his response.

"She's broken no laws here. Keep that in mind."

Tim carefully set the fork he was holding to the side.

"I just told you, Big John. I have no problem with her. As long as she stays away from me and my wife."

He stressed the last word.

John's jaw twitched once. "All right then. Message delivered. Wanted to keep you up to date."

"Appreciate it," Tim said. "Want some chicken? Supper's ready."

Expecting John to decline and leave I was surprised to see him stand up. "Sounds good," he said. "Can I help with anything?"

"Not necessary," Tim responded, forking chicken onto a platter. "Come on in."

If he was surprised he didn't show it. He pulled the packets of potatoes out of the coals and led the way to the kitchen.

I added another setting to the table and put out the salad and bread.

John slid into a seat and unfolded his napkin. "Smells good," he said.

"Thanks," Tim said, taking his own seat and passing the chicken to John.

I poured tea and took my place, wondering at the change in both of them.

Supper was actually pleasant. The guys talked football and old movies and NASCAR like old friends, even laughing together a couple of times, while I just ate and watched them. Anyone who didn't know them would think they were great buddies.

After supper, John stood up and helped clear the table, even scraping off plates while Tim rinsed and loaded the dishwasher.

I decided I could get used to this.

When John actually moved into the living room and took a seat on the couch, I couldn't stand it any longer.

"So what's up, John?"

"Not a thing, Tee. Wanted to let you guys know about the Martinez woman." He cocked his head and looked at Tim. "You sure you don't want to share your side of it?"

Tim knelt to start the fire in the fireplace, then rolled onto his butt, pulling up his knees and folding his arms across them.

"What is it you want to know, Big John?"

John leaned forward. "What really happened? Her story is that she has been unfairly accused of stalking, that it was you all the time. Following her, harassing her, driving her out of town. She's pretty convincing. Tears and all."

Tim was shaking his head before John even finished speaking.

"I can have my brother send you all the records," he said. "He has the whole legal file."

"I have to tell you, Tanner, I never believed her for a minute. I don't like you, and I am the first to admit it, but I have yet to catch you in anything and heaven knows I've tried. Believe me, I've tried," he grinned. "Her whole story is bogus. I get that. What I don't get is why? Why come in and make a big deal out of it? Are you planning to go after her again? Legally, I mean."

Tim grinned back at John. "No, I told you. I have no problem with the woman as long as she stays away from us. I don't know how she found me up here. I was completely surprised to see her at the Gem the other night. Haven't seen her in over a year. Thought she had finally moved on."

"You're sure there's not more to the story?"

"What is it you want, John? The gory details? What it's like to roll around in the hay with her? Damn, man, I was fourteen years old! You would have done the same thing!"

"Fourteen?" John looked surprised.

"She skip that part?" Tim was on the offensive now. "She skip how she wanted me to marry her? At fifteen?

Take care of her and her boys? How she claimed I got her pregnant when she couldn't have kids?"

John held up his hands in a stop motion. "Hang on, now, Tim. No, none of that was mentioned. Her story is different. That's why I had to ask. I believe you, man, but I still want the facts."

"You want the facts? Here's the facts. I haven't been able to get close to a woman in twenty years. I date one more than once and she gets hurt. Not every time but close enough. I've had girls that got their arms broke, their cars vandalized, all kinds of crap, just because they had dinner with me. So I've stayed away from women. You know what that's like? Is it Lurlene that does it? Not sure. Does she have someone else do it? No idea. Just know it happens. So I stay away from women."

"Hang on, being a little dramatic there. I know your kind. Wannabe playboys hit it rich, think they're the hottest ticket in town," John said. "I really doubt you've stayed away from women."

"You don't know duck squatty," Tim said, rolling to his feet. "You think it's all fun and games? You ever worked in a field till your skin blistered under your shirt? Then played guitar till your calluses bled? For a bunch of drunks who can't even stand up? Who puke on your shoes when telling you how good you are? I doubt it. I've worked in places where the cockroaches shake hands and borrow your toothpaste. I've had more beer spilled on me than you ever drank. You don't know me, John. Far from it."

Tim took a deep breath and blew it out.

"I worked for everything I have. And that includes my wife."

John's jaw clenched. "Let's leave Tee out of it."

"Why? That's the point isn't it? Show her what a bad guy I am? She knows." Throwing a glance my way, his eyes softened. "I told her everything. She knew it all. She married me anyway."

Looking back at John it was Tim's turn. "And you? You get more attention here than I do. How's that working for you, Big John? All these single ladies in a small town fawning over you, bringing you cakes and cookies. How long you think that will last? You still slamming the door before they knock? Running out the back door when they start up the walk?"

Shaking his head Tim came around and sat beside me.

"I know your kind too, bud. You're gonna wind up alone. You're gonna keep pushing them away till no one bothers to knock any more. One day you're gonna be that old guy who yells at the kids to get off his lawn."

"That's not what we're discussing here," John said through clenched teeth. "I'm trying to help. You are not the most popular guy in town, no matter how famous you are. Lot of weird things happened since you started coming to town. People notice."

"Okay," Tim said and shrugged. "You want to help, I get that. Keep Lurlene away from me. Keep her away from my wife. Then there won't be a problem."

"It's a small town, Tim," John said, standing up, too. "You're going to run into her. Tee is most definitely going to run into her while you're off somewhere. I don't want her hurt. That we can agree on."

Tim's head snapped up. "You know," he said. "About the women I dated getting hurt. You did some homework."

John's turn to sigh. He looked at Tim for a long minute. "Some of it, yeah." He held his hands up. "I checked you out pretty thoroughly. Talked to a couple of cops in Austin, another in Nashville."

Tim smiled. "Probably why you suddenly believe me, huh?"

John couldn't help but smile back at him. "Probably had something to do with it."

"Didn't think it was going to be anything I said," Tim said.

"Anyone ever get charged with the assaults? The damages?"

"Nope," Tim shook his head. "Never anyone to catch. Oh, they took reports, several times. Never could prove anything. Lurlene did go to jail a few times. They caught her in my dressing room and my hotel room once. She broke into a couple of places I was staying and got caught by their staff. Nothing that tied her to the assaults or any of the damages."

"Any idea why?"

"Her cheese slid clear off her cracker. I don't know what else I can tell you."

"Never had trouble with other women?"

Tim shook his head. "Not really. There's always fans around, want to get a piece of you. I've had them tear my shirt to get a piece of the sleeve. She's not the only one I've had put out of my hotel room, or the only one arrested for hanging around my house. She's just nuts. She keeps coming back."

"Then try to stay out of her way," John warned. "I can only do so much. She has as much right to be here as you do. If she does anything, and I mean anything, or even threatens to, you call me. Same for you, Tee," he said, looking at me. "Stay away from her. If she does anything you call me. Let me handle it."

I nodded at him. "Will do. I sure don't want any problems."

John turned to Tim again. "Let me handle it. Anything that comes up. I take my job seriously and I am good at it."

"Fair enough," Tim agreed.

John stood up and stretched.

"Thanks for supper, Tee. Sorry we got off on this subject."

"No problem, John. Glad you could join us," I called as Tim showed him to the door. "And thanks for watching out for Tim."

John didn't answer that one, just went on out and Tim locked up behind him.

Tim came back in and dropped on the couch beside me, stretching out his legs, letting his head fall back on the cushions.

I watched him for a few minutes. The sooty thick lashes dark against his cheeks, the perfectly formed lips, and the straight nose. His chest rose and fell with his breathing. I reached over and ran my fingers through his hair.

"He did mean well, you know," I said. I curled my fingers into his hair, lightly scratching his scalp.

"That feels good," he murmured. "I know he meant well," he said, still sitting with his eyes closed. "And it was good of him to let us know what she's up to. He wasn't near the pain in the butt he usually is."

He rolled his head and opened his eyes to look at me.

"Long day, babe. Ready for bed?"

"Oh, yeah," I smiled.

Having Tim home was heaven. The cats trailed him around the house, up and down the stairs while he did a lot of little things. Changed a light bulb, filled the firewood box, even went out and started to organize the garage. He bought a stereo for the garage and replaced my old one with a newer model.

If I had been happy before, now I was ecstatic. I loved hearing him around the house, seeing him outside, the way he sang along with the radio, spontaneously scooping me up for an impromptu dance. The way he tipped his head to listen to a new song. The way he danced around the house.

That man can move, his body like liquid, every muscle tuned to the music.

I asked him where he learned to dance. His response? In a couple of hundred little bars.

Wednesday I was off to the grocery store while he puttered in the garage. Tim had a standing order for meat with Arch, our local butcher, and wanted me to pick it up while I was out.

Tim had brought home the thank you cards and together we had them ready to go. His handwriting is so much nicer than mine that he wrote, I stuffed envelopes. I swung by to mail them on my way to the store.

Tim or Annie, his agent, had picked out three lovely little necklaces with a musical note as a charm, one each for Sharon, Sally and Cora, as a special thank you for all they had done for us. Those he was going to hand out personally.

Pulling into the drive when I got home I found Tim in the middle of the front lawn with the young guy from the Gem, the one who had given us a free lawn cutting.

"I'll get those," Tim called, coming to the back of my truck. He reached in and grabbed a couple of bags of groceries. "You remember Chris," he said, nodding at the younger man.

"Yes, I do," I said, and reached over to shake his hand. "Nice to see you again."

"You too, Mrs. Tanner. Here, let me get the rest of those," he leaned in and picked up the last two bags.

I led the way into the house, through the garage since the door was open.

"Just put them anywhere," I said, indicating the kitchen.

Dave and Cletus are indoor cats, having only been outside once since they came to live here and that was an ugly experience for all of us. Now, if the door to the garage is open for very long, Dave feels the need to explore. He is, after all, a cat.

While the guys carried in the bags and sat them on the table, I watched at the door to be sure a certain yellow feline didn't wander out. When the guys were past me, I shut the door and followed them inside.

"How about some iced tea?" Tim asked Chris.

"Sounds good to me," he said, taking a seat at the table. "I noticed people in California don't drink much tea."

"They drink mostly green tea or herb tea," Tim said. "This is the real stuff. Sweet tea."

"Thank you, Lord," Chris said, accepting the glass Tim held out and drinking half of it. "That's good," he smiled, wiping his mouth with the back of his hand. "Now, that tastes like home."

Tim took the pitcher and refilled his glass then sat down across from him.

"Chris is from the same part of Texas," Tim smiled, drinking his own tea. "We've been swapping yarns about the area."

"Good place to be," Chris agreed. "That reminds me."

He leaned forward and pulled something from his back pocket and slid it across the table to Tim. "I found one of these in my truck, thought you might like it."

Craning my neck I looked to see what it was.

"Hey, man, thanks," Tim smiled. "I'll put it on the truck right now."

It was a decal, an oval with the Texas state flag in the back ground and the foreground a blue field of flowers. In bright letters overlaid it read Texas Forever.

"That's pretty," I said over Tim's shoulder.

"Bluebonnets," he said. "Texas state flower. Up around our part of the country they will fill the fields and hills for miles. Always says home."

I looked again at the sticker. "They're really that color?"

Tim chuckled. "Oh yeah, and that thick. Whole pastures of them. Last a while, die off, and always come back. Texas Forever. Thanks, Chris, really. Nice of you."

"I'll stick it on your bumper on my way out," he said, sliding it out from under Tim's fingers. "Wanted to be sure it was okay."

"Heck yeah," Tim said. "You can take the Texan out of Texas but you can't take the Texas out of a Texan."

The guys laughed together and Tim refilled their glasses with tea.

I finished putting away the groceries while they talked about other things, all Texas related. From what I gathered

Chris was from the same area of Texas where Tim grew up. They talked about places they had been, and did a couple of rounds of remember when and did you ever.

When I grabbed a glass and took a seat beside Tim he filled my glass, too.

"Chris is going to do the lawn," he said when I sat. "First time as his gift. After that I think we're gonna sign up for his service. Gotta support these Texans."

"Up to you," I said with my own grin. "You're the man of the house."

Tim threw me a look, warm and tender, and squeezed my hand.

"Well, I better be on my way," Chris said, standing up. "I'll get that grass down tomorrow. I know you're gonna like the work we do. And I thank you for your business. You have anything you don't like about the service, you call me personal. I'll see to it."

Tim stood up, too. "I'm gonna walk him out, shut down the garage, babe. Be right back."

I retained my seat, told Chris it was good to see him again, and watched them go out through the garage, making sure certain yellow short people didn't go with them.

I got up and started another pitcher of tea. Through the kitchen window I could see Tim, with his hands stuffed in his back pockets, standing at the rear of a white van. After a few minutes he shook hands with Chris and stepped back, watching the van pull away from the curb.

Back in the kitchen, Tim washed his hands at the sink and reached for a towel.

"Nice of him to do the yard for a gift," he said. "Felt like it couldn't hurt to give him a try. You okay with me paying for the next month?"

"It's up to you, Hubs. I don't mind doing it, and you're here a lot more now. On the other hand, he's a nice kid with a new business. No problem to let him do it."

"He's had the business for a while, just new to the area. Him and his brother."

"Seems like a good kid. Hope he does well here. Nice to have a new business."

"Doesn't But Bill have a lawn service?"

"Sure does. Had it for ages. Started working for the previous owners when he was still in high school, then bought it after he graduated."

"Hope they don't cut into his business," Tim said, with a little frown. "Think there's enough work for both of them? I sure don't want to undercut him."

"Sally said But was having trouble a couple of weeks ago. Not sure what happened. He's been pretty grumpy lately from what I hear. I haven't seen him. Depends on how it goes. It might be the perfect time for another lawn service, if he's getting ready to quit."

"Yards here are pretty small," Tim said. "Think Monarch can support two lawn services?"

"Yards are small because the houses are small. Haven't you noticed? You have to get outside the city limits to find the larger homes."

"Is there a reason for that? The small places?"

"Goes way back," I answered. "Folks from the valley wanting to escape the heat in the summer. It's really brutal over there in the summer. So some started coming to the coast for the summer months, building these little weekend places. A lot of them were more like cabins, just two rooms. A place for the family to cool off on weekends during the summer. Then it grew some and whole families started coming over for the summer. When I was a kid half of these places were empty most of the year. You may have noticed how many of the shops in town are two story."

"Yeah, what's that about? False fronts?"

"The owners live above the shops. A lot of them have living quarters up over the business. When we started getting the year round crowd the locals supplemented income by selling out of their homes. Didn't have a real town so they made do by adding another story. Live upstairs, work downstairs."

"Good idea," Tim said. "Help if more businesses were like that."

"Some of them still live over their businesses. Barb's Books is a good example. Barb lives upstairs, over the bookstore. Her only commute is down the stairs."

"Easy to go home for lunch," Tim grinned.

"Is that a hint? You ready for some lunch? I bought the makings for sandwiches," I told him.

"How about Kelly's? We haven't been there for a few days. I want to give the ladies their thank you gifts."

"Sounds good to me," I said, never one to pass up a meal someone else cooked.

He tugged me to my feet and picked his keys off the hook by the back door. We went back out through the garage so he could get the door down and secured.

"You know, babe, if Chris doesn't get the job done, we can always stop the service. I just wanted to give him a chance."

"Yeah, I know. Fellow Texan," I said and noted the Texas decal was already in place in the center of Tim's bumper.

Tim spent most of Thursday on the phone. He had taken over half my desk, already declaring he needed his own. Where we were going to put it didn't come into the equation.

By late afternoon he was full of good news. The video production crew would be arriving over the next few days and shooting was set to begin on Monday. With a tentative schedule of four weeks Tim would be home for almost a month.

We went to Tahlia's Cuchina for supper to celebrate.

Since our dual shopping spree I had clothes to wear. I now spent more time getting dressed, even tried to coordinate colors, a thing I had never bothered with before. I was still in jeans and shirts, but the jeans were skinny jeans and the shirts tended to be Henley's or western styled with snap buttons.

As always, Miguel came to our table to say hello when he saw us, bringing along a plate of bruschetta made with his homemade bread. He visited with us for a few minutes before resuming his chef duties.

The restaurant was busy for a week night which did my heart good. Miguel had worked very hard for a lot of years to have his own place to showcase his recipes. Nice to see someone work for a dream and attain it.

I remembered Tim's story, of working all day and playing music all night, striving for his dream. These guys blessed my life with their success, once again proving that if you want to work for it, the American dream is still available.

Friday morning Tim wanted Kelly's for breakfast so we had a quick cup of coffee and headed to town.

Sharon was in her usual place, fourth booth on the left, working a crossword puzzle when we joined her.

"Hey, Tanners," she said. "Surprised to see you guys out and about. What's going on? How do you like being home, Tim?"

"I love it," Tim answered. "And good morning."

"Morning," she returned. "And you look nice Tee. New shirt?"

"Yep, went shopping," I said and enjoyed watching her spray coffee.

"You did what?" she sputtered, wiping up the table with her napkin. Fortunately she had missed her blouse.

"Went shopping," I smiled. "An entire day of shopping. In San Luis."

"Well, you have certainly made some changes," she said to Tim. "Next thing you know she'll do something about that hair. Work on that, would you?"

Tim chuckled, and reached to run his fingers through my hair.

"All up to her, Sharon. I love her just the way she is."

Being adult, I stuck my tongue out at her.

"I see things are normal at this table," Sally said, joining us with her pad in hand. "Mr. Tim, good to see you."

Tim stood up to give her a hug and she blushed, although he hugged her every time he saw her. I noticed the locket we had given her as a thank you was clasped around her neck.

"What can I get y'all this morning?"

Sharon and I looked at each other, trying not to laugh. Y'all? Really?

Tim ordered two waffles, bacon and eggs while I opted for sausage and pancakes. Sharon had the same and once Sally wandered back up front, she leaned in towards me.

"If she comes in wearing fringe I am going to lose it," she grinned.

"Or parks a horse out in the lot," I giggled.

"She's going to sport a bandana any day now," Sharon laughed, and that set us both off.

Tim looked at us with one eyebrow raised.

I reached over and patted his leg. "It's okay, Hubs. Just your effect on the staff."

"Yeah," Sharon giggled, "gonna be called Kelly's Chuck Wagon soon."

"Over my head," Tim chuckled, "and I think I'm okay with that."

"So I hear we're going to be a movie set," she said when she had wiped her eyes. "When is that going to start?"

"How did you know already? He just found out yesterday."

"Permits," she grinned back. "Fargo Productions called yesterday to get permits. It's all over town already."

"Small town grapevine," Tim said, shaking his head. "Homeland Security could learn from it."

"We don't get a lot to talk about, Tim" Sharon told him. "This is great news. For all of us. Never had a movie shot here. Big doings."

"Not a movie," Tim corrected. "Just a couple of videos and a couple of commercials."

"Isn't that like a movie?"

Tim settled into the seat. "No, not really. We're scheduled for four videos, plus a couple of commercials. They're launching the new product line at the same time as the new CD, so we'll be filming the commercials for those at the same time. Should be about four weeks work. The motor homes should roll in tomorrow or Sunday, be ready to start work on Monday."

"Motor homes?" Sharon's eyes were alight. "They won't be staying at the motel by the freeway?"

"Not every one," Tim answered. "Bringing up trailers and motor homes. They rented one end of the campground, gonna set up a compound there. I guess a few may be at the motel, but the majority are going to be at the beach."

She leaned back in her seat. "What about you? Will you be at the beach?"

"No way," Tim grinned. "I'm gonna be home. With my wife. It's close enough I can walk to the beach although I'll probably take my truck. I already have a place to stay."

"That's a bummer," she said. "I wanted to see inside one of those motor homes."

"I'll see what I can do," Tim told her. "One is assigned to me. I'll make sure you get a tour while it's here."

"You'll have your own? Even if you live here?"

"Sure," Tim said. "Need a place to be on call, change clothes, whatever. I'm not the only one that's involved. There's Mark and Russ, plus the guest stars and the actors. I'll need to be within hailing distance even when I'm not on the actual sets."

Sharon was all ears. "Guest stars? Actors? You guys won't be playing yourselves?"

He chuckled, shaking his head. "We'll be ourselves, Sharon. The videos are like, well, mini movies. Acting out the songs we sing, you know? Those require extra's in the background, that kind of thing. One of our songs is a duet, me and Tammy Scott. Do you know her?"

"Oh yeah," we said together. Tammy was a very well know country singer and country music was big here. "She's going to be here?" Now it was my turn to ask questions.

"Yep, for a couple of days. I don't have the exact schedule yet, that's going to depend on the director and his crew. Plus the weather may come into play. That's always a concern on outdoor shoots."

"A director and a crew," Sharon sighed. "Will they use any local help? Like extras?"

Tim laughed. "I have no idea, Sharon. If they do, you'll be the first to know."

"I better be the first to know everything," Sally said, distributing plates. "Now repeat all that, I didn't catch it all."

"They may need extras for the movie they're shooting," Sharon told her.

Sally's eyes lit up.

Here we go, I thought, and reached under the table to pat Tim's thigh. Glancing at him I saw him shake his head and reach for the pepper. This was going to be an adventure of the first magnitude. I could see it coming.

We hit a couple of yard sales Saturday, since we hadn't been out for a while. Tim had developed a love of yard sales since he'd been coming to town. He bought more than I did these days and of a much wider variety.

I limited myself pretty much to books. He bought caps, jerseys, guitar picks, tee shirts and all manner of unusual items, such as a portable typewriter. Do they even make ribbons for those any more?

When we returned home we found a white van at the curb and Chris in the front yard. Tim used the garage door opener to lift the doors then hopped out to carry the carton of books I had bought inside the garage.

Chris came over to offer his help.

"Got it, but thanks," Tim told him, coming back outside. He dusted his hand on the seat of his jeans and held it out to shake with Chris. "So what's the haps? You been here long?"

"Not too long," Chris replied. "Got the grass cut and edged. The leavings are bagged up in the van. Y'all don't compost do you?"

"No, not yet," Time said. "Good idea, though."

Chris glanced around the yard. "Just gonna grab some clippers and trim up these flower beds. Need some dead heading."

"Speaking of dead heads," Tim said. "Hey, John. How's it going?"

I turned around to see John coming across the drive, a beer bottle in his hand. From that I assumed he was off duty. He didn't wear a uniform so it was hard to tell from his clothes. Jeans and a sweat shirt or tee shirt were his normal attire on and off duty. He told me once he was always on duty so it didn't matter.

John came up and joined us, nodding toward Chris. "New service?"

Chris nodded back, and glanced over his shoulder at the white van. Blue block letters spelled out Trim and Go on the side and again across the double doors at the back. Reaching in his pocket he pulled out a card and handed it to John.

"New in town, not new to the business. We just relocated, move the business wherever we are. I can give you a group rate since you're right next to the Tanners."

"Haven't seen you around town," John said, reading the card before tucking it in his back pocket.

"We've been here for a while," Chris told John. "Me and my brother. It's a mobile business. We can start up quick wherever we are, sort of work as we go."

"Easy to get started? In a new place?"

"Oh, yeah," Chris answered. "We get to a place, first thing we do is find out the licensing requirements. Get a business license, pay the fees, whatever it takes. Never had a problem."

"Sounds good to me," John agreed, taking another long drink from his beer. "Good way to see the country. Where were you last?"

Chris smiled at John, folded his arms and spread his feet apart. Typical guy getting comfortable for a chat.

"Originally from Texas," Chris said. "Pretty close to Mr. Tanner's home territory." He nodded at Tim. "Like I said, we move around. Been in Austin, Fredericksburg and Amarillo in Texas. New Mexico, few months in Arizona and Nevada. Not a lot of lawn work around there, moved on over to Southern California. Working our way up the state now."

"Don't stay in one place too long, huh?"

"Depends on the work," Chris answered. He seemed to be comfortable with the questions, although his eyes had taken on a flat look, maybe from all the questions.

"You need something John?" Tim asked, leaning back against the truck.

"Nah," John answered. "No offense," he said to Chris. "Saw this guy over here and you guys were gone, so kinda watching him. See what he was up to."

"Appreciate it," Tim said. "This is Chris. Chris, this is John Kincaid."

Chris shook hands with John.

"Good to meet you, John," he said. "If you change your mind about the lawn service, give us a call. We are a full service, not just cutting the grass. Plus we take away all the trimmings, do the flower beds, all of it. You keep that card, give me a call if you want to give us a try."

"I'll do that," John said. "Welcome to Monarch Beach. Good to have a new business in town."

"Thank you, sir. I better get to it. I still have another stop to make. Mr. Tanner, good to see you again. Miz Tanner," he nodded at me. "Y'all take care now."

With that he turned and went back to the van. In a couple of minutes he started the engine and gave us a wave as he drove off. I assumed John's questions had sped up his departure.

"Problem?" Tim asked, as soon as the van was gone, looking at John.

"Nope, just checking. He's been over here quite a while. I was watching him before you guys came home. He was looking over the fence, at Miss Ellie's part of the yard, up on the porch. Wandered around the other side. Probably just seeing what needed to be done. Didn't know you had a new service. I was just being nosey."

"Appreciate it, Big John. I'm gonna grab a beer," Tim said, standing away from the truck. "You want another one?"

"I'm good," John answered and Tim went back through the garage to the house.

John turned his attention to me. "You all right, Tee?"

"I'm fine, John. Thanks for keeping an eye on the place."

"My pleasure. You've had more than your share of attention over here lately. Besides, consider it neighborhood watch. Want to know who's out here and why. After all the stuff this summer."

"Thank you," I smiled. "How are you? Things going okay?"

John folded his arms and leaned on the truck, next to where Tim had stood.

"Is that a loaded question?"

"Not to the best of my knowledge. Why? Something wrong?"

John is a big, handsome man, with rust colored hair, big shoulders and a solid body. We've gotten to be pretty good friends the past months. Something was bothering him. I often wished he were more outspoken.

"I'm good," he said finally. "So how do you like the married life?"

Aha. "Love it," I said. "Best thing that ever happened to me. You should try it." I softened that last with a grin.

John grinned back at me, then looked down at his sneakers, shuffling them back and forth on the concrete. "Thought about it a while back," he said, with a small smile.

I didn't want to continue that conversation. "So how's Sharon? You still seeing her?"

He straightened up, walking to the corner to toss his bottle in the recycle tub. "I like Sharon," he said when he was back. "I like her a lot. She's smart and she's funny and she's fun to be with. And it ends right there."

His dark eyes looked straight into mine. Message received. Leave it alone.

Tim chose that moment to wander back out and join us. He moved to my side and looped an arm around my shoulders, pulling me against his side.

"What's with all the questions?" He looked over at John. "You know something I don't know?"

"Not a thing," John said quickly. "Just curious. Like to know what's going on around town, in the neighborhood. You know this guy from before? In Texas?"

"Nope, never saw him before. He showed up at the Gem few weeks ago, when we got married. Gave us a free mow on the grass as a wedding gift. I liked his work, so I agreed to a month. We'll see how he does."

"Seems legit," John admitted.

"And you're gonna go right to work and check on him," Tim added.

"No need," John said. "He appears to be genuine. Just thought you knew him before. Besides, always like to know who's wandering around the neighborhood."

Tim tugged me close again. "Well, come on, babe. I'm hungry. Let's rustle up some supper."

John took the hint and with a small salute he headed back to his house.

Tim led the way into the house and dropped the garage door behind us.

Saturday was a big day.

Tim's manager had called the night before to let him know the crew was on the way. The arrangements were made and production would begin Monday morning with an eight o'clock meeting at the campground.

By the time we joined Sharon the whole diner was abuzz. The half dozen or so old timers that met at the counter applauded when Tim walked through the door, several even turning on their stools to shake his hand as we made our way back to Sharon's booth.

The news had spread faster than the flu.

Contacts from Fargo Productions had been busy.

Kelly's had orders for boxed lunches, cold and hot, for Monday through Friday for at least three weeks. Cora's bakery had also been contacted to provide platters of muffins, donuts and pastries every morning for the same amount of time.

According to Sharon, Archie had standing orders for fresh fruit deliveries over the next three weeks.

Even Sally had the fever.

She launched herself at Tim the minute she saw him.

"Are they going to be needing extras?" Was the first thing out of her mouth, before she even said good morning.

Tim held up his hands and shook his head. "Whoa, hang on. I have no idea what's going on," he told her, loud enough for others to hear. "I won't know anything till after they get here, and get set up." Raising his voice a little he called "Sorry, folks. I have no news."

The conversation around us picked up again.

"Mr. Tim you better be sure I know what's going on," Sally warned, filling his cup first. "Not for myself, you understand, just so I'm in the know. People depend on me."

Still shaking his head, Tim chuckled. "I will let you know sweetheart if I hear anything. The thing is, I don't handle the arrangements. I just do what they tell me."

"Well, you're my inside source, so you let me know if you find out," Sally said, a hand on her meaty hip. "Now what can I get you?"

"What's the special today?"

"Chili and corn bread, side salad."

"Sounds good to me," Tim said, leaning back. "I'll have that and iced tea."

Sally made a note on her pad. "Tee? How about you?"

"Chili is good," I answered. "I'll have that, too."

"Make it three," Sharon added. "Except I want a diet Coke."

Sally chugged up front, stopping to fill coffee cups as she went. I had no doubt she was filling ears along with cups since she was spending a couple of extra minutes every step of the way.

"You're going to be even more popular," Sharon grinned at Tim. "This is the hottest thing to ever happen here."

"Not much I can do," Tim told her. "I'm just one of the cast. Like I said, I do what they tell me."

Sharon leaned closer. "Are you going to get to stay on the set? I saw all those motor homes and trailers going to the beach. Some of them are huge!"

"Me? Heck, no," Tim answered. "I'm going to stay at home." On the last he turned and winked at me. "I'll be home with my wife."

"So how does that work? Will you just drive back and forth as needed?"

"Hope so. If I need to be on site, I can stay down there. They bring in motor homes. They'll be assigned. One of them will be assigned to me. Plus there'll be trucks and trailers with the equipment, all kinds. If they run true to form, they'll set up a compound, out of the way of the public. Some of the crew will stay right there on site, others will stay in motels. I like the motor homes."

"Motor home," sighed Sharon. "I have always wanted to see inside one. I see them going down the freeway or parked over at Jade Beach and I think I'd like that, you know? A home on wheels?"

"They are nice," Tim told her. "Every possible convenience. TV, DVD, microwave, some even have a bath tub. They've come a long way from trailers."

"A bath tub? Oh, my Lord! Can you imagine?" Her green eyes were positively glowing, her whole face alight. "A home on wheels. Drive along, stop where you like, stay as long as you want. All the comforts of home. That's convenient."

"They are that," Tim agreed. "Might be something to think about, Muse."

"Me?"

"Sure," he grinned. "Make a nice honeymoon. See the country."

"I see all the country I want," I smiled, looking into his smoky eyes. "Right here at home."

He leaned over and kissed my nose. "Still have to come up with a honeymoon plan," he told me. "I did the wedding. The honeymoon is all you."

"I don't have a private jet," I grinned back. "You're gonna have to go local."

"Sure you do," he said. "Just call Anne. She made all the arrangements for the wedding. Just tell her what you want and where, she'll take care of it."

"Seriously?" Sharon jumped on it. "Tee! You can go anywhere! Rome, Paris, the Bahamas! Wow, just imagine! Anywhere in the world, right, Tim?"

"Yep, long as we get you a passport," he said. "You can get the application at the post office, or I can have Annie pick one up. Takes a couple of weeks."

"You have a passport?"

Tim grinned at Sharon. "Oh, yeah. Have to have one. We've done some concerts in England, Canada, even Australia."

"Australia really? Which is your favorite?"

"I'd have to say Canada," Tim answered. "Beautiful country, amazing people. The others are great, too, I just loved Canada. My favorite, so far. Lot of places I still want to see."

Looking back at me, Sharon shook her head. "You can see all these places. You can get up tomorrow and go to Canada if you want. Or France."

"Not tomorrow," Tim corrected. "First she needs a passport. Second, I'm working the next few weeks." With a grin at me, he patted my hand. "Hubs has a job, babe."

"I know," I grinned back. "I'm the one packing your lunch."

Tim laughed out loud. "No need, Muse. They feed us on the set. Although, if you bring it down, I wouldn't turn it away."

"I'm counting on that," I said. "I'm as bad as the others. I want to see all I can."

"You'll have a pass," he said. "You get free run of the set."

"Really?"

"Oh, great," Sharon scoffed. "Now we're gonna have to listen to her."

Being an adult I stuck my tongue out at her. "If you're good, I'll take pictures. Let you have a peek."

Tim shook his head. "Have to check on the pictures, babe. May be a closed set. Sometimes we're not allowed to take pictures. We'll find out. They'll cover all that in the first meeting."

"This is really big," Sharon said. "I had no idea so much was involved."

Sally arrived with huge bowls of chili, topped with cheese and onions, the cheese already melting in places. She hurried off and came back with a basket of corn bread wedges, crisp and brown top and bottom, tender yellow inside.

Cathy, the other waitress on duty, followed her with the drinks.

"I will never get around all this," I said, picking up my spoon.

"That's what boxes are for," Sally said. "Although I have to say this is a good batch of chili. You might surprise yourself. Anything else?"

"We're good, sweetheart," Tim answered, scooping up a spoon full of thick, red chili.

Before she left us to eat, Sally patted Tim's shoulder. "You just remember to let me know about the extras. I want to be in that movie."

Conversation dropped off as we all tucked into the chili.

Sally was right. There was no need for boxes, we all scraped our plates. Sharon was picking crumbs of cornbread out of the basket.

"You want some more cornbread?" Sally looked at Sharon, who hastily withdrew her hand.

"No. It's just so good! I love that crunch."

"Butter," Sally said, reaching to take the basket. "Good cornbread needs butter and a cast iron skillet."

"It's the best I've ever had," Sharon agreed. "I wish he would make it more often."

"I'll tell the chef," Sally said.

"Mama makes good cornbread," Tim said, wiping his hands on his napkin. "I grew up on cornbread and beans. At least once a week."

"That sounds good. I'll tell chef that, too. Anything else? Still have some pie left."

"If you have peach, I'll take a slice home," Sharon answered.

"Yes, ma'am. Anyone else?"

Tim looked at me and I shook my head.

"Just the check, sweetheart," he told Sally.

While she went to get Sharon's pie Tim pulled out some bills and stuck them under the pepper shaker, and stood up, extending his hand to help me.

"When will you know about the extras?" Sharon asked.

"No idea, not for sure," Tim answered her, reaching to hook his little finger through mine. "I'll tell Tee as soon as I know and she can let you and Sally know."

"Don't you forget," Sharon warned me. "You know how you can be."

"I'll let you know," I said.

With that as a farewell, we headed up front where Tim paused to pay our tab.

Jasper Riggins, one the old timer's, slid carefully off his stool and came over to Tim, walking with that peculiar bent kneed shuffle so common to the elderly. He held out his hand to Tim.

"Young fella," he said, looking up at Tim, "I want to thank you. Bringing some life back to town. We needed that. Wanted to thank you, personal like."

Shaking the senior's hand, Tim gave him a smile. "You are very welcome, sir. Not sure how much I had to do with it but you are certainly welcome."

Mr. Riggins leaned back and folded his arms before his next question. "Old Connor up there," he nodded to another gentleman, "wants to know if there's room in the movie for him. He don't have the gumption to ask you hisself."

"I don't know, sir," Tim replied. "I just work there. I'll let Sally know if I hear anything. You also might want to watch the local paper. That's always a good source of what' going on."

Jasper snorted. "Not our paper. Gotta thank that inner net for ruining the news. No one reads the paper anymore. Don't even buy it much. Why, I put over fifty years into the printing business and now it's about defunct."

I tugged on Tim's hand. "We need to go, Tim. Have a good day, Mr. Riggins. We'll see you again soon."

The old guy reached to shake my hand, too, before turning back to his stool.

I tugged Tim on out the door.

"That's a trap," I told him when we were outside. "In another minute, Mr. Connor, the one with the red hair, would have come to join him. I've seen them block the entire aisle during football season."

"Ah, another local custom."

"Only when they're excited about something. This is a big deal to this town. Not just the business it's bringing in, but the exposure. They're all hoping for Diane Sawyer."

Tim laughed and opened the door of the truck. "Not likely, babe. I imagine Miss Sawyer has a lot more important things to do than fly out from New York to interview a country group."

Sunday it was on.

Tim's phone started ringing before eight. By the time we sat down to breakfast he had been on the phone eleven times.

He was like a kid on Christmas morning. With each call his eyes lit up, the blue sparks visible clear across the room. Even during breakfast his leg was jumping, tapping out the beat to a silent song.

The crew was on its way. The air seemed alive with all his energy. Dave and Cletus caught his excitement and raced up and down the stairs behind him, weaving around his legs, doing their best to trip him.

In self-defense I sent him to the grocery store while I cleaned up the kitchen and sat down with a cup of coffee.

That gained me almost an hour of calm before the storm really hit.

Tri-tips, a favorite cut of beef on the Central Coast, marinated in the refrigerator beside a huge bag of salad Tim had made as soon as he got home. I had put on a big pot of pinto beans earlier, and they simmered on the back of the stove.

In the driveway, just outside the garage door, the barbecue smoked, sending the amazing scent of burning oak through the kitchen windows.

Tim had just poured off the barbecue sauce when Sharon knocked on the front door.

She came in and accepted a glass of iced tea, taking a seat at the table while Tim and I elbowed each other around the kitchen counters.

"What's the big occasion? Have you heard anything?" She was full of questions.

"Crew's on the way," I told her, slicing two loaves of French bread in half length-wise.

"Are you feeding them?"

"Lord, I hope not," I answered, smearing garlic butter on the cut sides of the bread. "Tim invited Mark and Russ over for supper. They left Santa Maria a couple of hours ago. Should be here soon."

"That's the band, right? The other members of T Three?"

"Yep, that's them. They make up T Three." I finished slathering the butter on the bread and stuck the halves back together, wrapping the whole in foil. Shoving those to the back of the counter, I poured myself a glass of tea and joined her at the table.

"Are you excited? It's really happening, Tee!"

"Believe me, I know. Tim has been running around all morning."

Sharon leaned forward. "This is better than Christmas! I made an appointment yesterday to get my hair done. First thing tomorrow morning. Cora is getting hers done, too."

"For what?"

"Just in case! What if they want to cast some locals? I want to look my best!"

"Sharon, you do know they are just shooting videos, right? The songs from the new album? And a couple of commercials. You know, those annoying little clips that break up the football games?"

"Same thing," she snapped. "It's filming."

"Not really," I said. "I think these are just videos. For television."

She flipped her hand at me in a shooing motion. "Whatever. They're going to be putting images on some kind of film and I want to be in one."

I shook my head.

"Well, I do! I always wanted to be in the movies. This may be my big break. You don't know."

A horn blared and we both started, me slopping tea on the table.

I got up to grab a paper towel and through the window saw a bright red pickup pull up in front of the house. Tim jogged into sight and waved them toward the curb in front of the house, following along as it pulled back into the street and parked in front.

Here we go, I thought, taking a deep breath.

"Who is it?" Sharon was on her feet, too, moving to look out the front window.

"Not sure," I answered, wiping up the tea and rinsing my hands.

We could hear them outside, coming closer. Then it was noise on the porch. I watched Cletus spin and fly up the stairs, the sound of his growl left behind.

Tim led the way through the front door, calling me as he did.

"Hey, Muse, come here," he called, his voice as bright as the sun. "We have company!"

I took another deep breath and moved around Sharon to get into the other room.

"Who's that?" She asked as I slipped around her.

"I don't know!" I hissed back at her and went to join Tim.

The two men in my living room were opposites of each other.

The shorter had clipped, dark hair and the kindest eyes I have ever seen on a human, like warm chocolate. The taller had to be a Tanner. He had the look – dark blond hair worn a little long, tall, rangy build, not as tall as Tim or as well built. Still the family resemblance was evident with the coloring and the height.

I recognized them from the CD covers. The rest of T Three had arrived.

Extending my own hand, I met them with a smile.

"Russ," I said, shaking hands with the shorter guy. "So nice to meet you." Turning to the taller one, "You have to be Mark. Those Tanner looks give you away."

Tim beamed, his smile lighting the room. "Guys this is my wife, Tee."

We fumbled through the introductions, Sharon joined us and we did it some more. Tim moved them all on outside, going through the garage. They were all talking at the same time, laughing, joking, and poking each other, for some reason reminding me of a litter of puppies, tumbling and yapping around each other. They settled outside around the barbecue.

"Wow," Sharon said, her own eyes bright. "What energy! Wish I could bottle that!"

"Grab a beer and join them," I said. "I'm going to just finish up these potatoes."

"Oh, no, you don't! Come on, girl. This is your new family. Get in there," and with a gentle shove, she pushed me ahead of her. "I'm not going without you."

Before I had taken a step, someone knocked at the front door, and I spun around to go that way. Opening it I found a beautiful blond woman on my porch, holding a pink box that smelled heavenly.

"Hi," she said as soon as I opened the door. "I brought dessert. Hope everyone likes cookies. I didn't know how many were here so I went with these. I'm Anne Edwards, T Three's manager. I didn't know if you remembered me."

She stepped in and introduced herself to Sharon while I juggled the box back to the kitchen.

Tim had talked about her so often I felt I knew her. Soft oatmeal colored hair, bright hazel eyes, she looked competent just standing in the kitchen. Her eyes were taking in everything. She wore a long sleeved white blouse under a knitted red vest and tailored slacks, looking both elegant and casual at the same time.

"The guys are outside," I said once I had the box on the table. "Would you like a beer? Or I have iced tea and soda."

"A beer would be good," she answered.

I led the way outside and reached into the cooler to hand her a beer. "Let me get you a glass," I said, realizing Tim didn't put any out.

"Bottle is fine," she smiled, lifting it and taking a long drink. "That is so good," she said. "Thank you. This is a nice place you have." She was scanning the house, the yard and the houses across the drive, taking it all in.

The guys all jumped up when she came out through the garage and were again all talking at the same time. Sharon had followed me and stood there looking lost.

I grabbed two more beers and handed her one. With an elbow I directed her to a couple of chairs.

When we were seated I looked around. Tim had bought more chairs somewhere along the line. Besides the ten set up around the barbecue, a stack of several more rested in the corner of the garage, just inside the door.

A Number Two wash tub filled with beer, soda, and crushed ice sweated next to the folding table that held plates, utensils and napkins, weighted down to keep them from blowing off.

Before Sharon could even ask, two more guys came up the drive and joined the party. One tall and lanky, the other shorter, more solid, with black hair. They seemed to know everyone and more back whacking and noise ensued. Tim brought them over to me and Sharon.

"Muse, this is Ryan," he indicated the taller one, "and this is Kyle. They're our road crew, doing all the setups. We've shared a lot of miles over the years. Guys, this is my wife, Tee, and this is Sharon."

Tim was in his element, his eyes bright and his grin infectious as he wove together his job and his friends.

The new arrivals grabbed soda from the cooler, pulled over a couple of the chairs and sat down, joining right in the conversation that swirled around them. Everyone continued to talk at the same time, punctuated with gusts of laughter, and the occasional thigh slap or arm punch.

Tim put the tri-tips on the barbecue and the air ripened with the scent of beef cooking over oak coals. That smell alone will make people drool. The smoking coals were dotted with foil packets of potatoes.

I drifted back and forth, checking on the rest of the meal.

Sharon showed Anne to the bathroom. When they returned they were chatting like old friends.

By the time the meat was cooked, sliced and set out alongside the salad, potatoes and bread it was like a family gathering. For them, it was. Sharon had joined in completely while I kept a low profile.

I tend towards shy to begin with and I'm not much good in a crowd. An extra five people weren't exactly a crowd but I was still not quite comfortable. I don't entertain much. Never have. I was grateful for Sharon's experience as she took over the hostess duties, making everyone comfortable, checking on food and drink.

By the time everyone was fed, the cookies distributed and the clean-up complete, the sun had set. The shadows of the trees across the street reached across the lawn and touched the driveway.

Ryan and Kyle, the young guys, had left right after supper, as soon as they helped carry leftovers inside and cleared up outside. Anne had excused herself to go back to the motel after a long day, leaving Russ and Mark to sit around the coals and talk.

Sharon and I mostly listened. There were so many 'remember when' tales retold that we felt we had been on a lot of these trips with them.

It was full dark when Tim went back in the house and came out with one of his guitars. Russ stood up immediately and went to his truck, bringing back two guitar cases.

In less than ten minutes, they were jamming, moving from one song to the next without missing a beat. After a bit Tim turned on the radio he had set up in the garage and they played along with that, sometimes singing, sometimes talking over the music, all of it punctuated with laughter.

Sharon had pulled her chair next to mine and sat there, tapping her foot.

"Freaking amazing," she said, leaning close. "Can you believe this? Our own private concert. This is better than the ones you pay for."

I nodded. "They are good."

From out of the dark, Miss Ellie, our elderly renter materialized, carrying a covered dish. She made her way up the drive to where we were sitting.

I jumped up and went to meet her, afraid the music might have bothered her. It was kinda loud even though there were no amps set up.

"Are we disturbing you?" I asked as soon as I reached her.

"Of course not, dear," she answered. "I wondered if I could just join you for a bit. I love the music! Oh, and I brought over some coffee cake." She handed me a foil covered plate.

"Pull up a chair," I said, handing the cake to Sharon.

Greta, Miss Ellie's golden retriever, made her rounds, giving each of the new guys a good sniffing before settling down at Miss Ellie's feet.

Tim introduced her to the guys.

"This is wonderful!" The older woman smiled. "Makes me want to dance."

Tim stood up and set his guitar to the side. "I heard that Miss Ellie," he told her coming to stand in front of her. He held out his hand and swayed invitingly. "Will you do me the honor?"

I swear she blushed as she stood up and placed her hand in his.

Russ and Mark switched to a swing song and by golly, that lady could dance. She kept right up with Tim as he swung her around and twirled her under his arm, her smile bright enough to light up the yard.

Sharon's smile echoed my own as we watched them.

Miss Ellie was light on her feet, her eyes twinkling as she executed a couple of turns. Her laughter followed her moves as she swung around the drive. I found my own smile echoing hers.

Sharon was clapping along, her foot tapping to the music.

When the song ended Tim escorted her to her chair and bent low at the waist.

"Thank you, ma'am," he said.

"My turn," Russ said when they finished their dance. "Get me some music Tanner." He stood and extended his hand to Miss Ellie. "I want some of the action with this nimble lady."

Tim stepped into the garage and turned up the radio. The warm voice of Toby Keith filled the evening air.

"Sharon?" Mark stood in front of her with a little bow and she quickly stood.

"Guess it's you and me, babe," Tim said and gathered me in his arms.

"Having a good time?" he asked as we moved around. "Too much?"

"No, Hubs, it's fine. I really like them. Just different. I'll get used to it."

He hugged me close. "I'm glad," he said softly. "I was afraid my other side would put you off."

"Are you kidding? This is wonderful! Look at Miss Ellie. Can you believe her?"

Tim smiled down at me, his eyes glowing through his lashes. "I can't believe you," he said. "You've really handled the mayhem like a trouper. After this, they'll stay down at the site most of the time. Russ has family a couple hours down the road, so he'll go home for weekends. Mark is home wherever he is."

"Russ has family here?"

"Mm-hmm," Tim murmured. "Somewhere down the road. Arroyo Grande? That sound right?"?

"Yeah, that's the other side of San Luis. Not too far."

"Mark likes to explore, wherever we are. Doubt he'll stay with us. He has a motor home assigned to him so he'll probably stay there and wander."

"It's no problem, Tim," I said. "They're your friends. Your family. This is your home, too. I'm glad they came. I hope they had a good time. And we have a guest room if one of them needs a place to stay."

"Oh, they had a good time," he said. "When they break out the guitars, they're at home."

"Were those the songs from the new CD?"

"Lord, I have no idea," he laughed. "We get together and it's a medley. Pert near every song we've ever heard. We have a lot of them. Been together a long time."

"You sure sound good," I said, nestling into his body.

"Why, thank you, Mrs. Tanner," he smiled back. "You may be prejudiced."

"Nah, I don't think so. How about Miss Ellie?"

"She's good," he grinned down at me. "We'll have to remember to invite her to the Gem some night. She might enjoy it. I was glad she joined in," Tim said. "I was afraid we might have made too much noise."

"I'm pretty sure the noise police would have paid us a visit if we were too loud."

Tim chuckled. "I don't think he's home tonight."

"His loss," I said.

It was close to midnight before Russ and Mark packed up their instruments and called it a night. Russ walked Miss Ellie home while Mark escorted Sharon to her car and they all left.

I helped Tim fold up chairs and carry everything back into the garage. He made sure the coals were dead before he nestled the barbecue up against the side of the house.

"Leave it, Muse," he said, once he was inside. I had put away the leftovers and was rinsing the dishes before loading them in the dishwasher. "I'll finish cleaning up tomorrow. Early morning."

"What time do you have to leave?"

"Not till eight tomorrow. We'll get the schedule at the morning meeting."

"Should I pack you a lunch?"

Tim chuckled and pulled me close, taking the pan from my hand and sticking it into the dishwasher.

"Babe, I can come home for lunch. It's four blocks."

"Well, just in case. If you get busy or something, I can bring you lunch."

"They feed us on the site. I'll keep it in mind, though. Much rather have lunch with you than the crew. Should be

113

a short day tomorrow anyhow. Mostly meetings. I'll be home in time to clean the barbecue. Leave it for me."

"Yes sir," I said, sitting on the bed to pull off my boots. "I can do that."

"Know what else you can do?" Tim bent over me, an arm on each side, his eyes alight.

"Why don't you show me?"

"I can do that."

Monday began the madness.

We were up, dressed, fed and he was out the door by seven, unable to wait another hour, guitar case in hand, eyes alight. With a start that early, my chores were finished before eleven.

I put some chicken to simmer, thinking Tim would want a light lunch, nothing heavy. I needed to check with him on that, not sure if he could sing on a full stomach. At least this way I had options. Chicken pot pie, chicken salad, or even sandwiches.

Tim said he'd be home about noon, so with the chores done and the chicken almost done, I sat down with a cup of coffee and booted up my computer.

No book orders, no invoices, only spam. Someone, somewhere, needs to invent a program that promptly sends all those emails right back to the origin. I live in perpetual hope.

Finding nothing of interest I turned off the computer. Just as I stood up someone knocked on the door.

I opened it to find Sharon standing there with a huge smile.

At least I thought it was Sharon.

She looked different.

Being Sharon, she came on in and headed for the kitchen with a saucy swing to her hips, doing a little dance step before taking a seat at the table.

Following her, I went to get her a cup.

"Your hair," I said, finding what was different about her. "It's amazing! Changes your look completely!" And it did.

Sharon has worn her hair the same for years. It's either a pony tail or a braid, always yanked back away from her face, forcing her face forward.

Now her hair was short, very short, and feathered around her face, the soft curls framing her face and making her eyes look huge. Her normally brown hair sparkled with both red and gold highlights.

"You look spectacular," I told her, setting her coffee in front of her and taking a seat across from her.

"I know," she grinned. "I can't stay away from the mirror."

"I assume Tiffany?"

She sighed. "Yes and no, Tee." She looked up from her new bangs. "Lurlene."

"Lurlene? Tim's stalker lady?"

"Uh-huh. She's working at Tiffany's now. Tiff has a special going right now to help Lurlene build up a customer base. Twenty five bucks. Includes everything – shampoo, cut, style, and color all for one price. Whatever you want. You should try her out."

"No way is that woman getting her hands on my hair," I stated. "I admit, she did a fantastic job on yours. That's the best you've ever looked. Really brings out your eyes."

"Don't hold back, Tee, tell me what you think."

"Oh come on, Sharon, you know what I mean. You look like a movie star."

She giggled and brushed a hand through her hair. "The best part? It goes right back. No hair spray, no stiffness, completely soft, and it's wash and wear. I don't have to learn how to style it. Just wash it and shake it and ready to go."

"You got more than your money's worth this time," I said. "Wait till John sees that."

"You think?"

"If he doesn't make a move, someone else will. Seriously? You look better than you ever have. I wasn't kidding."

"Now you need to get yours done," she grinned. "Just think how good you'd look for Tim."

"Oh, no, not going to happen," I said, shaking my head. "I'm keeping my hair. And my halo."

"I was there, Tee. I know you were bald for a couple of years. You're not bald now! Your new hair is a pretty color! Get rid of the halo, add some highlights and get it styled!"

The second time my hair grew back it came back an oak color with the pure white halo as a crown.

It's mine. I earned it. I'm keeping it. It's hair.

"You are the most stubborn person on the face of the earth. If there's reincarnation you are going to come back as a mule."

I smiled at her. "It's hair."

"And it looks awful! It's all one length, it sticks straight out. You look like a dandelion crossed with a Q-tip!"

"Don't hold back," I echoed her. "Tell me what you really think."

"You know I'm right," she sighed. "We've been through this a hundred times. Now, you're being selfish."

"How do you figure?"

"Tim! Tee, get it through your head, okay? Tim is a celebrity. Even here in Monarch, people know him. They're going to look at you and wonder what the heck he sees in you!"

"That's not true! I am the same. I've lived her most of my life. People know me, too."

"People here, yes. People magazine? No! There are going to be pictures, Tee. And you need to look good! For Tim if not for yourself."

I stared at her, this friend from the crib.

Maybe, just maybe, she was right.

Even the new hairdo could not draw away from her sincerity.

I took a deep breath and blew it out.

"Okay, I'll think about it," I said, finally.

She leaned forward and patted my hands. "Good."

"I didn't agree to anything," I said quickly. "I'll think about it."

"That's a start," she smiled, leaning back in her chair.

The front door opened and the man himself came into the kitchen

"Hey, ladies," Tim greeted, coming around to lean over and give me a kiss. "What's going on? Whoa," he said, stopping to stare at Sharon. "Looking good, Miss Sharon! Nice do. Wasn't sure that was you."

Sharon blushed and batted her lashes at Tim.

"You like it?"

"Love it, girl. You look amazing. What a difference."

I stood up and moved to the stove. "Sorry, babe, I was yakking at Sharon and didn't get your lunch finished. You want chicken salad or a chicken sandwich?"

"Sandwich is fine, Muse," he said, getting out a soda. "Won't be down there much longer. Today is just layout and organization, getting things in order." With a grin he stepped over and looped something over my head.

Looking down my shirt I saw a plastic card about the size of an index card hanging off the cord around my neck. Picking it up I was surprised to see my picture in the center and my name printed right under it. Guest was printed in large letters at the top, and at the bottom were the dates.

"Oh my Lord," squealed Sharon, jumping up to come look. "You have a lanyard! Tee, you have a lanyard!"

"What is this," I asked, looking between them.

"Pass, babe," Tim chuckled. "Gives you access to the site any time you want."

Reaching inside his shirt he pulled out a match with his own picture on it.

"You have to wear it at all times on the site, even if they know you. Security teams may check." He went to the hooks by the laundry door where we hang our truck keys.

"You can put it up here, so you don't forget it when you come down."

I lifted it over my head, handed it back to him and he hung it on the hook.

Dave was immediately entranced with anything that swung and stood up on his back legs to try to swat it.

Tim threw a couple of extra loops around the hook, shortening the swing, and effectively putting it out of Dave's reach.

"Sorry, man," he said, squatting to scratch Dave's ears. "That has to stay right there unless mama is wearing it."

"Did you find out about the extras?" Sharon and her single track mind.

"Sure did," he grinned at her, pulling out the chair next to mine.

"Well?"

I was afraid Sharon was coming over the table after him. Her green eyes shone like lanterns, her fingers curled into her palms.

"You start Thursday," he told her. "Have to be on set by seven, and plan on a full day."

She almost turned over the chair, grabbing it at the last minute, and then launched herself at Tim.

"Really? Oh my gosh! Oh my gosh! I have to go tell Sally! I have to call the girls!"

She spun around to grab her purse.

"Oh, Tim, thank you! Thank you so much!" She scurried back and bent to kiss his cheek. "This is so exciting! I have to go!"

"Hey, Sharon?" Tim called to her before she got out the front door.

She turned to look at him, already turning the knob.

"Tell Sally seven a.m. Thursday morning."

She squealed like a tweener at a Bieber concert. "Oh my gosh! I'll tell her! Thank you, Tim!" And with that she was out the door.

I set Tim's sandwich in front of him and poured him some tea.

"Well, you sure know how to win over the ladies," I said, taking the seat next to him.

He leaned over and kissed me. "Only one lady I care about." He tilted his head and nuzzled my neck, his lips soft as he found my ear.

"Eat," I said, nudging his plate closer. "You have to go back to work."

With a smile, he picked up half his sandwich.

"So both of them are going to be in the video?"

"Mmm," he nodded, swallowing first. "I put Cora and Arch on the list, too, and Greg although I didn't know his last name. Didn't want them to feel I was playing favorites. They can confirm or refuse, whatever they want. It's just a couple of days, so no biggie. They'll make a few bucks."

"I'll call Cora and let her know," I said.

"Thanks, babe. Remember, now. If you come down, you have to wear your lanyard. Keep the boogey man away from you. Insurance regulations for anyone around the set."

"I think I can remember that part," I told him. "You want some cookies?"

Wiping his mouth on his napkin, he wadded it up and tossed it on his plate. "Not today. We're almost done. Should be home in a couple of hours."

"I like this," I grinned at him. "You working here, coming home for lunch."

His eyes warmed as he ran a finger down my cheek. "Me, too, babe. Used to call this my sitcom dream when I was younger. You know, going to work, coming home to the little wife."

We sat and looked at each other for a few minutes, just sitting at the table. Finally I shook myself and stood up to take his plate.

"Git," I said. "The quicker you get to work, the quicker you get home."

120

He stood up and kissed my cheek. "Going, babe, going. Don't forget to call Cora. If they aren't interested I need to let Josh know so he can fill the spots." He pulled his keys off the hook, and went out through the garage.

I heard the whine of the garage door opening and then the thunk as it dropped back in place. Looking out the kitchen window I saw his truck pull out and leave.

Then I got a glass of tea and waited to hear the howl when Sharon told Sally she was going to be in the video, pretty sure the sound would carry. Picking up my phone I called Cora. I wanted to be sitting down when I told her.

Wednesday I saw Tim off to the set before I headed for Kelly's.

The place was hopping, more so than usual.

Grabbing my favorite purple cup from the tray by the door I headed for Sharon in her usual booth.

Sliding in across from her I was struck again by the change in her looks.

Who would have thought that just changing your hair would make such a difference? It wasn't just her hair, it was the look. Maybe the new confidence? Her eyes looked bigger although I know it's impossible to change the size of your eyes without an obvious and expensive surgery.

Confidence can be a huge boost to one's ego. Knowing you look good, not just wondering, can pep you right up.

"Good morning, Tee," she trilled. "How are you?"

"You're sure in a good mood," I said, setting my cup on the table. "What's up?"

"Nothing special," she said. "Just excited. The shoot. Everything." She turned her head to look at two guys standing at the register. Both wore sweat shirts and jeans, the standard dress code for Monarch.

"Those guys are part of the crew. A lot of them are eating here instead of on the set. Sally is ecstatic with all the new people coming in."

Looking up front I saw Ryan and Kyle, the two young men Tim had invited to the house. Seeing me, they waved before collecting a couple of white bags and leaving.

I changed the subject. "Did Cora decide to join you? In the video?"

She sat forward again. "You haven't seen her?"

"Nope, not this week. I was going to swing by the bakery and see what she decided so I could let Tim know. Why? Did something happen to her?"

"She got her hair done," Sharon said, eyes laughing. "She says Archie can't keep his hands out of her hair now!"

More than I wanted to know about the guy that cuts and wraps my meat.

"Yep," Sharon sat back. "She's a new woman. Who thought a new hair style could bring about that big a change. I mean, I was surprised at how much this changed me." She was giving me her calculating look, her eyes wandering over my head. I could almost feel little footsteps across my scalp.

"No," I said. "Don't start."

"Why not, Tee? Cora looks amazing! You have to go see her. You won't believe the difference. She looks like an Italian movie star!"

"Cora?"

"Yes! Her hair is shorter than mine, now, and it's a little pixie cut. Her bangs feather over her forehead. It shines blue! You have to see it."

Cora had always worn her hair in a bun or a coronet of braids pinned to the top of her head. Her idea of dressing up was a pony tail. I couldn't remember the last time I saw her with her hair down.

"I'll have to go see her," I agreed.

The power that is Sally charged the aisle, wrapping both arms around me and squeezing.

"Whoa!" I said, extricating my head from a head lock.

"Thank you!" She grabbed my hand and squeezed it. "Thank you so much! And you tell Tim how happy I am!"

"I'll do that," I said. "Can I get a cup of coffee?"

"Oh, sure, Tee, sorry. I got so excited seeing you. Let me go grab the pot."

"What is wrong with everyone? Have they gone nuts?" I looked around the diner. It was packed, more so than usual, and it seemed everyone was talking.

"Hardly," Sharon said. "It's the filming! Everyone in town is excited. Lord, Tee, this is the biggest thing to happen here!" Leaning forward on folded arms she looked at me intently. "Everyone is making money, Tee. Kelly's is catering the hot meals, Cora is supplying baskets and trays full of muffins, donuts, coffee cakes, and sweet breads every day, Archie is sending fresh fruits daily, everyone! Even the filling station is making extra money! This is big!"

"I didn't think about that," I said. "I guess you're right."

"Of course I'm right! You're probably the only person in the whole town that's not excited about this."

"Not true," I said, holding up my hand. "I'm excited, too. My husband comes home for lunch," I smiled. "That's pretty exciting. Just having him home for more than three days in a row is exciting."

She rolled her eyes.

Sally was back and filling my cup.

"So how do you like it?"

"My coffee? With cream. You know that."

"No, dimwit, the movie! Is it fun? Being down there? Watching it all? I can't wait till tomorrow! I'm getting my hair done this afternoon."

"What's with the hair? Is everyone in town getting their hair done? Talk about crazy! You've all gone nuts!"

Sally straightened to her full height and planted a palm on her hip.

"Excuse me? What is your problem?"

"It's the hair," Sharon put in. "She doesn't want to get her hair done."

"I am NOT getting my hair done," I said, loud enough that three old timers at the counter turned to look our way. "If the entire town decides to cut their hair I will still not cut mine! Do you get it?"

"Someone peed in her Wheaties this morning," Sally said. "What do you want to eat, Sharon?"

Shaking my head I doctored my coffee.

"Pancakes and bacon," Sharon replied. "She's just jealous, don't let it bother you. Are you getting it cut? Or colored?"

"Not sure," Sally answered. "Lurlene is doing everyone else, I think I'll just let her do her thing. If it turns out half as good as yours and Cora's I'm gonna be happy."

"Lurlene?" I sat up and took notice. "Lurlene is doing your hair?"

"She's doing everyone right now, if you'll excuse the expression. Tiffany has an introductory offer going to get Lurlene started. She'll do whatever for one price. Twenty five bucks! Can't beat that price. And it includes everything! Style, cut, shampoo, color, whatever you want."

"She seems to be making a big impression," I said.

"Have you seen Cora?" Sally leaned in close. "She is freaking gorgeous! Who knew? Cut off that mane of hair and darken it and wow, she's a completely different woman. Would you have guessed that?"

"No," I admitted.

"You have to admit that woman knows hair, and she knows what she's doing. The best part is that it is so easy to take care of! This," Sharon indicated her curls, "is strictly wash and wear. I don't have to do a thing but comb it and shake it."

"That works for me," Sally said. "I don't have time to mess with my hair. I'm here from five a.m. to five p.m. and that's seven days a week. I'm using my vacation this week. Might as well get my hair done while I'm off."

"I bet you ten bucks you'll love it," Sharon said.

"No bet," Sally said. "Now, are you eating Miss Mule?" She looked at me.

"Sausage and eggs," I said.

"Thank you," she said, and turned to go put in our orders.

"Are you excited about tomorrow?"

Sharon looked up at me. "Of course, you know I am! To you, it's no big thing. I think you're just happy to have Tim home."

"You're right," I smiled. "I love having him home. And I'm sorry for being snarky."

"I know," she grinned at me. "You still need to get your hair done." She ducked, laying out across the seat like I was going to hit her.

I might have if I was sure no one else would see it.

Thursday morning Tim invited me to the set for lunch.

"The gals are going to be there, Muse. They start work today. You might as well come on down and watch. We can have lunch there."

"Sounds like fun," I said. "What time?"

"About eleven? Eleven-thirty? Remember to wear your lanyard," he reminded me, pulling his own off the hook and slipping it over his head.

"Where do I go?"

"Go to the main gate and they'll direct you back. We have separate parking, too."

"How do I find you?" I wasn't sure I wanted to wander around in a crowd looking for him.

He chuckled, straightening his collar. "Just ask, babe. The actual set is not that big. It's all the trucks and trailers and motor homes that take up the space. We have the whole end of the campground."

"I'll be there," I said. "No point in going to Kelly's when everyone is going to be at the beach."

At the appointed time, I locked up the house and headed for the beach.

Beach Street is just that, a short street that fronts our beach, running only three blocks with a parking lot at each end. A wide wooden board walk connects the two, winding up and down through the dunes that lay between the street and the beach, providing clear walking as well as lovely views of the beach as you make your way up and down the varying heights of the walk. Little built in benches break up the monotony as you go back and forth, inviting you to sit and watch the surf.

The southern lot is the most popular, where most people park and use the ramp or the steps down to the sand. The northern lot is for those staying at the campground or just walking the board walk.

I was surprised to find so little parking available as I cruised past the south lot. At the gate to the campground I was stopped by two security guards in tan uniforms. Showing my lanyard, which I remembered, one of them opened half the gate and motioned me through.

Rolling down the window I asked where the video crew was located.

"Straight down, ma'am," the guard pointed. "You should find parking by that stand of pine trees. The motor homes are to the right and the set to the left."

I thanked him and rolled in the direction he directed.

When our kids were young Sharon and I often brought them down here to 'camp out' even though they were only blocks from home, so I was familiar with the grounds although it had never looked like this. Narrow strips of asphalt curved and bent through the trees, separating sections, so campers weren't stacked like cord wood. Rest rooms were set up in several locations, a couple featuring showers. Most of the time it was quite scenic. Now, totally different.

Great, heavy cables ran in every direction, connecting trailer after trailer, some with steps, some with ramps leading to their doors. Huge trailers snugged against smaller ones, sides open, back flaps extended. Several ropes of triangular bright colored flags swung between some, while others just had a single flag on a whip antenna.

The entire scene looked like a Gypsy camp from an old MGM movie.

I crept down the access road, taking it all in. There was a festive air to the whole place, like I imagined a circus compound would be. Brief threads of music could be heard as a background, along with the dull roar of the ever present surf beyond.

I had to stop to let a small group cross in front of me, all of them dressed as cowboys, with plaid shirts, jeans, boots and kerchiefs around their necks.

Ahead I saw several vehicles parked to the side and pulled my truck off the pavement, parking behind them. Hopping out I locked the truck, made sure my pass was clearly visible and followed along where I had seen the cowboys.

Between the trailers I found a sort of path and I followed it, keeping a wary eye underfoot for errant cables, which were everywhere. Some were as thick as my leg while others were more like garden hoses. The hum and whine of machinery, the cheery conversation of the various guys working, the snippets of music, all of it had a carnival atmosphere.

Stepping out of the last row of trailers I could see a huge green screen set up to the left. It must have been thirty feet across and at least that high. A wooden stage or platform ran along in front of it, raised about five feet above ground level, with steps at either end.

Hay bales were stacked along the back, the top tier six feet or so up from the base. The front of the stage was decorated with instrument stands, several already containing guitars and a maze of cables and boxes.

A group of a dozen or so sat and stood around the hay at the far end, both men and women.

The women I could see were dressed in what we used to call square dance dresses – the ones with full, frilly skirts that swung out in a complete circle when the dancer twirled, with lacy petticoats showing beneath the ruffled hem.

My eye was caught by a lovely brunette with close cropped black hair as shiny as a raven and a bright crimson dress that swung around her as she moved among the group, laughing. The full skirts of her dress whirled and lifted as she moved, giving glimpses of great legs.

I was stunned to realize it was Cora.

Seeing me at the same time she lifted a hand and waved me over.

I made my way around some large crates to meet her.

"Hey, Tee," she called when I was close. "Come on over and meet the gang."

As I joined her I was even more surprised to find that the other striking woman, the one in the emerald green dress, was Sharon. I literally felt my jaw drop.

"You guys look amazing!" I said, joining them. "I can't believe it!"

Cora gave me a hug and Sharon grinned, swishing her skirt back and forth and spinning in a circle, the skirt swinging wide and falling back into place.

"Like it?" Sharon asked, her smile huge. "I want to see how much it costs. I want to keep it."

"I doubt you can keep it," I said, turning to Cora. "And you! Look at you!"

Sharon was right, she looked like a whole different person. Where her hair had always been pulled straight back into a tight bun it not clung to her head in shiny leaves, curling up against her jaw. In the sunlight the stark black gleamed with blue highlights. Like Sharon, her bangs accented her eyes, which glowed like jewels with the makeup.

"I can't get over it," I said again.

"Oh, it's fun, Tee! They even do our makeup. I feel like a star." This from Cora, who is usually the most level headed of our group. "Everyone is so nice, so patient."

"Have you done your bit yet?" I asked.

"Not yet," Sharon said. "We've been in wardrobe and makeup since this morning. Then we had a class on the dance they want us to do. Nothing complicated. I think our first scene is coming up after lunch. Speaking of which, did you come for lunch? They feed us, you know."

She swung an arm at the tables set up in two, long rows. People were eating in groups and singles, every few feet there were condiments and napkin dispensers. There were easily a couple of dozen people chowing down.

Cora laughed. "They feed us with food from Kelly's. They catered it for the time they're here," she said. "It's the same things we get all the time. It's funny to hear these people go on and on about the food when it's our standard

130

fare. There is a food truck," she flipped a hand. "It's here from Jade."

"I don't think they all get that kind of standard food," I offered. "We are pretty spoiled with the quality we get from Kelly's. Probably a nice change for some of these guys."

"And the quantity," Cora added. "I can't believe how many trays of sweet rolls they go through every morning! I had to hire extra hands at the bakery. Julie and I couldn't keep up!"

I felt a couple of strong arms slide around my waist from behind and warm lips touch my neck.

"Hey, Muse, you made it," Tim said. "Come on, let's get something to eat."

He caught my little finger with his and led the way over to the serving tables. Food was being served from one of the big trailers, whose sides opened up. Several guys in white coats were shuttling trays of food to the serving table.

To the right, under one of the pine trees, a food truck's opened windows soared like wings. The smells were rich and full, filling the air with temptation. My mouth watered just from the scent.

I stuck to Tim like a burr, not sure what I was doing.

"Pick one, Muse. The table has meals, the truck over there has sandwiches, burgers, tacos, about anything you could want. What'll it be?"

Sally made a bee line for the food truck. "I smell enchiladas," she said.

The trailer's special for the laden table was chicken and dumplings, a variety of salad plates and an assortment of pies and cakes.

Tim leaned in close. "The trailer is mostly Kelly's, so you know what you're getting there."

Sharon and Cora were lined up behind Sally at the food truck.

"I think the enchiladas. That sounds good. What do I do?"

Tim tugged my little finger and we walked over to join the women.

"Just step up and order," he directed, moving behind me in the line. "Tell them what you want."

"I didn't bring any money," I confessed.

"Don't need it, babe." He reached around to flick my lanyard. "That's your ticket right there."

Plates of food were coming out the window and the gals were stepping up to take them. When it was my turn I ordered the enchilada plate, which included rice and beans and came with a side salad in its own little covered bowl.

Tim ordered the same.

In just a couple of minutes the food was pushed out the window.

"Back to the tables, babe," he said, leading the way.

We went back over to the tables where Sharon, Sally and Cora were already eating. Taking a seat next to Cora, I set my plate down.

Tim set his plate next to mine before taking drink orders.

There were a couple of big plastic tubs of crushed ice at the end of each table. Craning my neck I could see the ends of cans and bottles sticking up.

We told Tim our preferences and he went over and brought them back. We dug into the food like we hadn't eaten in weeks.

I heard several different guys greet Tim as he passed the tables to get the drinks

It was excellent.

Mexican food is a treat in Monarch. I noticed we all went with the enchiladas, everyone's salad sitting abandoned in the center of the table.

"What did those guys call you?" I asked Tim, once he was seated.

He chuckled. "Tom or Thomas? Most of them call me Tom."

"I thought you went by Tim."

"Only to the family. Most everyone else calls me Tom, or Thomas. It's my professional name, babe. T. Tom Tanner, so Thomas or Tom."

"Where did the Tim come from?"

He laughed. "Timothy. My first name, and what the family still calls me. When I got into the music business I thought it sounded awful young, so I started using the T. Thomas. Once we went professional, it was the start of T Three. T. Tom Tanner. That's the three T's." He finished off his soda.

"So it's still okay to call you Tim?"

"Of course. It's my name. Even more appropriate, it's what the family calls me, and no one is more family than you." He leaned over to kiss my cheek. "You about finished?"

Tim again pulled his wrist watch out of his pocket and checked it.

"Did your band break?"

He shook his head and put the watch back in his pocket. "Reflects too much when I'm playing."

I nodded like I understood.

He stood up and picked up his dishes.

"Let's go ladies. Gotta get back to work," he said, picking up my dishes and adding them to his stack. "You going to stay, Muse?"

"I'd like to, if it's okay. Watch this bunch perform."

"Well, come on."

Once again he led the way, back to the huge green screen, pausing only long enough to drop our trash in a can.

When we reached the stage Mark and Russ were there and we all exchanged hugs. Tim found a folding chair and put it behind a rope, to the side of all the cameras and equipment and out of the way of the tall stands of lights, some of them fifteen feet in the air.

With a brief kiss he stepped up to the stage and climbed up the hay bales to take a seat on the highest row. Mark and Russ climbed up to sit on either side of him and another guy came out and handed up guitars.

I took my seat and sat back to watch.

The thing that surprised me the most out of the whole afternoon was the noise. All those people and all that chatter, the music, the amplifiers, the clanking and banging of equipment, the shouting back and forth, all of it. The minute the director blew his whistle it was dead silent. I could hear the surf from the beach and the birds up in the pines.

My friends did themselves proud in the square dance scene.

The dancers performed in front of the band and just below them on the wooden stage. Besides Sharon, Sally, and Cora I saw Archie and Greg from the hardware store swinging around with style and grace. Jasper, Carson, and a couple of the other old timers I didn't know by name sat along the bottom row of bales, complete with cowboy hats and neckerchiefs, a backdrop to the whirling dancers, tapping their feet and clapping. T Three sang and played from the top layer.

They shot it four times from different angles before they took a break.

Tim hopped down and came to squat down by my chair, his eyes bright.

"Well? What do you think? Think it's good?"

"I love it! You knew I would!" I gushed. "And did you see the girls? Wow, who knew they could dance like that?"

"They had a teacher this morning," he confessed. "Just simple moves that look good. They took to it like ducks to water. Be no stopping them now. Look out Gem."

"They do clean up nice," I smiled. "Especially Sharon and Cora. I have to say those new haircuts make a world of difference."

Tim cocked his head and looked at me. "Second thoughts? About your hair?"

I thought about it for a second. "Not yet," I smiled back. "Just admiring my friends."

He leaned close. "If you want to get your hair cut, do it, babe. It will grow back if you don't like it. Or you can buy some wigs. Try out the look. Whatever you want."

"No wigs! I had one when I was sick, and I hated it! It itched and scratched at the same time and that's not easy! No, wigs are out."

He stood up and stretched. "Your choice, Muse. I'm gonna borrow the words of a Randy Travis song. I am in love with you, babe, not your hair. If it all fell out I would love you just the same. Got it?"

I patted his leg. "Yes, Hubs. Thanks. Now go back to work, Thomas. I am going to go home and rustle up some grub for my cowboy."

"You sure? You can stay and we can go to Kelly's for supper after work, save you having to cook."

"Remember your little sitcom dream? About going off to work and the little woman waiting at home?"

"Yes, ma'am."

"I have my own, Tim. The one where I put together a fantastic, home cooked meal from basic ingredients and have it all ready when my husband comes home for supper."

He bent to drop a kiss on the top of my head.

"Got it," he said. "Works for me. Matter of fact, sounds wonderful."

I stood up and brushed off my fanny.

"Can you get out of here okay?"

"Yeah, I think so," I said, giving him a hug. "Don't work too hard."

"Not work, babe," he grinned back at me. "This is pure pleasure. I love it."

"I'll see you at home."

"Yes you will," he said. "Won't be late."

With a little wave I stooped under the rope and started for the front gate.

When I got home the white van of Trim and Go was parked in front and Chris was winding up the hose in the front yard.

"Hey, Mrs. Tanner," he called as I got down from the truck and walked over to the porch.

"Looking good, Chris," I said, admiring the lawn, cut, trimmed and smelling like heaven. "I love this smell," I admitted.

"Me, too," he grinned back. "Fresh cut grass, coffee and orange blossoms."

"I'll go along with all those. You all done?"

"Yes, ma'am, just about."

"Would you like a coke? Some iced tea?"

"You have some sweet tea? Hard to find good sweet tea in California. It's either so bitter you can't swallow it or so sweet it sticks in your throat. No tea flavor at all."

"So I hear from Tim. I keep a pitcher in the fridge, come on in," I said, opening the front door.

"Let me put this hose back and I'll be right there."

I picked up the mail and put it on the bookcase as I went to the kitchen. Getting down two glasses I filled them with ice, poured tea, and set them on the table.

In just minutes Chris tapped at the front door and came on in, coming to the kitchen and taking a seat.

"Can I get you something?" I offered. "A sandwich, cookies?"

"This is fine, ma'am, and thank you. It's warm out there." He took a long drink, emptying half the glass. I got up to refill it.

"You should bring some water," I suggested sitting back down. "Keep you hydrated."

"I normally do. I have a little cooler in the van, but I already drank it all. This was the last stop for today and I wanted to get done."

"I know how that goes," I said, drinking tea.

"Were you down at the beach?" He pointed to the lanyard still swinging from my neck.

"Oh, yeah, for a little while. I have to get supper started so I came on home," I answered, taking off the lanyard and moving over to hang it on the hook with my keys.

"Tim working down there? Is that what's going on? I heard people talking about it, never got the details."

I didn't think I was talking out of class, since the paper had carried the story and the local television news had also done a brief feature.

"Yes, they're shooting a video down there. Actually a couple of them."

"How long does that take?"

"I have no idea, to tell you the truth," I answered. "This is my first time."

"You think more than a week?"

"Not a clue. I imagine it will take a couple of weeks, but don't quote me."

"Oh, that's all right. I'm just nosy. You and Tim known each other a long time?"

Oh boy, how I hate that question.

"A while," I answered. "How about you? You're from the same town?"

"Oh, no, ma'am, just the same area. Tim is north and west of my people, though it's all in the hill country. That's what folks back home call that whole section of the state."

"Pretty country?" My turn for the questions.

"Oh yeah," he grinned. "Prettiest country in Texas to my way of thinking. Especially in the spring when the bluebonnets bloom."

"That's the state flower, right? I think Tim told me that. They're on that bumper sticker you gave him!"

"Yes, ma'am, that's right. There will be whole pastures full of them, look like a bright blue carpet clean over the hills, blue as far as you can see."

"They plant them like that?"

"No, they're wild. Folks back home say that's God's landmark. I've seen acres of them, all blooming at the same time. The next year, they come back, right in the same place."

"Do you know if you can buy seeds?"

"I'm pretty sure you can, though I never tried. They're in the lupine family. Probably check at the nursery or even online. Someone must sell them."

"I'd like to get some for the yard. For Tim."

"I bet he'd like that," Chris grinned, and finished his tea. "You get 'em and I'll plant 'em."

"More tea?"

"No, thank you, ma'am. I need to get going. I sure appreciate it though. Hit the spot." He stood up to carry his glass to the sink. I took it from him and did it.

He had stopped by the hook where my lanyard was hanging.

"This is a good picture of you, ma'am."

"Thank you. My pass, so I can go on the set. The security is pretty tight down there, with all that equipment. And, please, call me Tee."

"Thank you, ma'am. Tee. Now that must be really interesting, seeing all that stuff. I've never known a famous person before. That's why I'm so nosy," he grinned, heading for the front door.

"No problem, Chris," I said, following him.

"I guess I'll see you next week," he said, opening the door.

"You're doing a great job, Chris," I said. "We sure appreciate it."

"Tell your friends," he grinned back at me, going down the steps. "We can use a few more customers."

"I'll do that," I told him, watching as he walked across the yard.

"Say hey to Tim for me," he called back before he climbed in the van and left.

I went back to the kitchen and put potatoes on to bake. I decided on a meat loaf, one of Tim's favorite suppers, and got out some onions.

When supper was in the oven I fired up my computer and went to my favorite shopping place – Amazon. I can shop there all day. Sure enough, several sellers carried bluebonnet seeds. I ordered from two and sat back with a smile. This would be a surprise for Tim next spring.

Friday morning I did all my normal chores and went grocery shopping before Tim came home for lunch. I bought one of the barbecued whole chickens at Arch's store while I was there, intending to slice it up for a chicken salad.

FLASH

Hey, Muse.

Hey, Tim.

What'cha doing?

Putting away groceries, making your lunch.

Will it wait?

Yes, I can put it in the fridge. Why, what's wrong?

Nothing wrong, babe. Just liked having you here yesterday, thought you could come back down here for lunch.

Sounds good to me.

Thanks, Muse. Come on down.

Now?

Why not? We're breaking for lunch. I'll meet you at the gate.

On my way.

Love you.

Too.

I picked my keys back off the hook and headed for the beach.

Tim was waiting when I got to the site.

After a hug he hooked his little finger through mine, leading the way back to the commissary area.

"How's it going today," I asked as we walked.

"Better now," he winked.

I shoved him with my shoulder.

"Well, you asked," he grinned. "Going good, babe. Your lady friends are troupers now. On time and ready to go."

"They are having so much fun," I said. "We are never going to hear the end of this one."

"Hey, come on, it's good for them! Ah, you feeling left out?"

"No way. Although Kelly's is out. No point in going when most everyone I know is down here."

"Long as you're okay with it. Seriously, babe, I can put you in if you want."

"No, thanks, Hubs. You're the celebrity. I'm happy to be the stay at home wife."

"You'd look pretty good on a magazine cover," he grinned, reaching over to fluff my hair. "Come on, let's eat. What are you having today?"

The set up was the same with the big trailer and the food truck in their places. The tables were almost full of hungry people working through plates of food.

I waved to Sharon and my gang, all sitting together at one end of the long row of tables.

"Muse? What do you want?"

I looked up at the board menu. The cheeseburger sounded good and so did the tri-tip sandwich.

"What do you want?" I countered.

"You want me to tell you? Here?" He ran his hand up my back and cupped the back of my neck. His eyes sparkled blue in the sunlight.

"I want the cheeseburger," I said, firmly.

"Tell the lady," he chuckled.

We ordered up and shortly had our food. I was looking for a place two could sit at the tables when he nudged me toward the back of the lot.

"Let's eat in the motor home," he suggested.

"Oh, good," I said. "I'd like that."

We made our way around the eating area and carried our boxes back to the parking compound.

Tim unlocked the door and took my elbow as I stepped up.

"Hang on a second, Muse, let me get some light in here," he said, moving around and opening the curtained windows. Light flooded into the cabin, a slight breeze bringing the sound and scent of the ocean.

I slid onto the bench seat of the dining alcove and opened my box, taking out cutlery and napkins.

Tim squatted at the mini fridge and opened the door.

"What do you want to drink? We have all kinds of soda, beer, and canned tea."

Glancing over I saw the top row of soda, side by side in the door.

I laughed and pointed. "I haven't had an orange soda in years! I'll take that."

He pulled it from the rack along with a Coke and took a seat across from me.

After all the noise on the set, the inside of the motor home was quiet. We could hear the surf breaking on the beach, the rustle of the wind in the pines. The soft sounds were like a cushion for my ears after the noise and bustle of the set.

I listened for a few minutes, just enjoying the sound.

"This is incredible," I said, finally.

Tim chewed and swallowed. "They are nice, babe," he said, looking around the cabin. "I was serious. You might like to take our honeymoon in one. Hotel on wheels."

"Where would we go?"

"Anywhere! Everywhere! Shoot, take a month or so and see the whole country. Or drive up to Canada. I love Canada. Not too big on Mexico, but I do love Canada."

"I better get that passport then, if Canada is in our near future."

"We don't have to go there," he said, reaching for my hand. "We can go anywhere. Heck, we can even just stay down here, on the beach, once the crew leaves."

I thought about it while I finished off the burger. That would be nice, to sleep down here, although I always had the bedroom windows open at home. I slept every night to the sound of the surf coming in the window.

Canada was a thought, too. I had never been out of the U.S.

"Penny?"

"Hmm? Oh, sorry. I was just thinking." I wadded up my napkin and looked for a place to toss it. Tim took it and put everything back in the white boxes our lunch came in.

He stood up and took my hand, tugging me to my feet.

"Come here, I want you to see something."

He pulled me along to the back of the motor home.

I ogled the bathroom as we passed it. Indeed, a bath tub. Who would have thought? Very compact with tub and shower, sink and toilet, yet it was still attractive.

He stepped to the side and motioned with his hand. "Voila."

I went past him and stopped.

There was a queen sized bed in the center of the space with a sliding window for a head board. Each side sported a night stand with its own lamp. Other sliding windows ran along the sides, above built in drawers and shelves. The windows were all curtained with a bright floral print. There were even books arranged on the top shelf, just under the window, and held in place with a little rail.

Turning to look back the way we came, there was another flat screen television, above a shelf of DVD's and CD's.

"Wow," I said softly. "Talk about everything."

Tim bounced onto the bed pulling me down with him.

"Like it? All the comforts of home."

I could have stayed there forever. This was a real mattress, not one of those weird ribbed things that lurk in sofas. This felt like an actual pillow top mattress. There were four pillows, two firm and two fluffy.

The light ocean breeze blew through the whole room from side to side. I could hear it rustle in the pine trees around us, smell their fresh scent. That smell always reminded me of Tim. It was his smell, that clean, biting fresh outdoor smell.

"Well? What do you think?" He leaned above me, propped on an elbow, looking down at me through those luscious lashes.

"Not enough adjectives," I said.

"And the doors lock," he said softly, bending to kiss me.

Later I moved in Tim's arms and poked him.

"You have to go to work," I said. "And I am not about to face anyone. You are on your own this time."

"Mm," he said, turning to face me, running a finger down my jaw. "You think they'll know?"

"Yeah, I think so," I grinned at him. "The only thing more obvious would be a sign."

"How well do you print?"

"Oh, get up!"

His rich laugh filled the motor home.

I felt my face flush, and pushed him with a palm against that muscled chest.

"It's okay, Muse," he said when he stopped laughing. "I'm done for the day. We can shower right here, get dressed and go on home."

I felt my whole body relax. "Now, you tell me." I fell back against the sheets.

"Wouldn't have been as much fun, babe," he said, throwing his legs over the side of the bed. "Stay there, I'll shower first. Not enough room for two of us." He stood up and smiled down at me. "Has to be a short shower anyway. Don't have that much hot water available."

He opened a cupboard at the door way and pulled out a thick, white towel.

The little louvered door to the bathroom opened and shut behind him.

Once we were showered and dressed Tim locked up and tossed our trash bags in a barrel on the way to the parking area. His truck was easy to spot with the Texas sticker dead center on the rear bumper. I noted the bright, blue field of bluebonnets that was the background, looking forward to a bed of them next spring. Talk about a little bit of home.

"The Gem okay for tonight?" he asked, backing out and heading for the front lot where I had left my truck.

"Works for me," I smiled. "I don't have to cook."

He pulled up behind my Explorer.

"You know you don't have to cook for me, Muse. We can eat at Kelly's or have it delivered. For that matter, I am pretty handy with a grill and I can manage in the kitchen. There is no need for you to cook every night."

"I like it," I said. "I told you. I like the idea of cooking supper for my husband. I like having to plan my afternoon around getting supper, plan the groceries around meals, all of it. I didn't cook a lot the last few years. Not worth it for just one person. I have a husband. I want to take care of him. It's my job."

The look he gave me in return could set a fire.

"Come on, babe," he said, opening the door, coming around the truck to open my door. He helped me down and waited until I was belted into my truck.

"I'll follow you home," he said, closing my door.

When we got to the Gem it was packed.

Our usual tables in the back corner were anchored by Sharon, Cora, Arch, Greg and a couple of others. Although

146

it was early for a Friday night, the dance floor was full and a line waited at the bar for service. The noise level was climbing by the minute.

Grabbing a chair by Sharon I had to lean in so she could hear me.

"Who are all these people? Is there another party tonight?"

"The crew," she said. "The guys working at the site." She lifted a hand and waved at a couple of guys coming in. "They wanted to know what we did for fun, and we told them." Her eyes were bright and her smile brighter. "Sally is even going to come down. Isn't it great?" She waved again at yet another pair.

"I suppose," I answered, looking around to see if I knew any of them.

Surprise.

Tim was leaning on the counter talking to Anne, who was decked out in a western shirt, jeans and boots, looking like a regular. Beside them, Archie stood talking to Ryan and Kyle, the young guys that did the T Three setups. Catching my eye, Ryan waved.

I didn't know the names but looking around I saw a lot of familiar faces, just from my trips to the site.

Tim retrieved a couple of pizza boxes and made his way to our table, scooting in next to me.

"Guess who's here," he said, sliding a slice of pizza onto my plate.

From the look on his face, it wasn't someone he cared to see.

"Who isn't?"

"But Bill has a lady friend," he said, taking a slice for himself.

"Bill? Here? Where?"

Tim tipped his head towards the order counter and sure enough, there was But Bill. The unfortunate nickname from high school still stuck. Standing behind him with her hand rammed into his back pocket was Lurlene.

She was dressed to the teeth in tight jeans and a sequined low cut top that displayed her blessings to all. She was smiling and talking to another guy in the line while maintaining her grip on But Bill.

"Do you want to leave?" I asked, leaning close so everyone didn't hear me.

"Nah, no need," he replied. "Long as she doesn't want to share space with me, I'm good."

I watched her for a minute before turning my attention back to Sharon.

"You're looking good, tonight," I told her. "I really love the new hair."

She reached up and flicked her curls that promptly returned to their place.
"Thanks, Tee, I do too. I should have done something like this ages ago. Still stuck in the seventies I guess. I couldn't even find anything to wear!"

I glanced at her dress, a cotton sundress with spaghetti straps.

"You look very nice," I said, accustomed to her usual jeans and blouse.

Before a conversation started, a beefy man in shirt and jeans tapped her shoulder and asked her to dance.

She was up and gone.

Looking around I realized most of our table was on the dance floor.

I finished my pizza, took another slice, and turned my chair a little so I could watch the dancers.

It was like the barn dances from my youth, with all the brightly colored skirts flying and whirling, the boots scuffling along and the guys mostly wearing western cut shirts in bright patterns. The noise level went up another decibel.

I could pick out Sharon, Cora and Sally as they swung by, see Greg and Archie boot scooting right along. The music shifted and the whole dance floor shifted a gear without missing a step.

While I was admiring their moves I saw Lurlene whirl by with But Bill, who looked happier than I had seen him in years.

His face was tilted down to hers as they danced, listening raptly to something she was saying. He truly looked like he was enjoying himself. Lurlene or not, it was nice to see him with someone. He had been alone for so long, since his wife died.

We had gone to supper a few times, as friends. We shared a mutual history but had no spark, just comfortable friends.

Sharon came back and took her seat, patting her face with a napkin.

"Whew, that's a workout." She took a long drink of beer. "I didn't realize how out of shape I am."

"You're looking pretty good out there. Learned some new moves."

She grinned. "It's what we learned yesterday," she confided. "They have a couple that work with the dancers on the set. That was Brad, my dance partner, in the video. We've danced together the last two days."

"Still looked pretty good, whoever it was."

"Thanks, Tee. How about you? You and the man gonna take a turn?"

"Not right now," I said, patting my stomach. "I just inhaled two pieces of pizza."

About then Cora edged up and leaned down to both of us.

"Did you see But?"

"I did," I answered.

"No, why?" Sharon craned her neck to look around. "What happened?"

"Is that amazing or what?"

"What are we talking about?"

"Lurlene," I said, motioning for her to lower her voice.

"The one who did my hair? What about her?"

"She's here with Bill! Keep your voice down, Sharon!"

I felt Tim tighten up on the other side of me and reached under the table to pat his thigh.

"It's all right, Muse," he said softly. "I'm not gonna bite anyone."

Sharon craned her neck, lifting up from her seat and scanning the room. "They're together? Like on a date?"

"For crying out loud, Sharon, I don't know! They are together, yes, and they look pretty cozy. Whether they came together I don't know."

The music fired up again and Sharon and Cora were off, this time with different partners. I watched them spin and weave among the crowd, skirts flying in bright flashes of color, smiling and laughing.

This was their night to shine.

I had mine. Tonight was theirs.

With their new hairdos, the swinging full skirts and the new dance steps they were in the spotlight. Those of us who knew them saw the differences. To the rest, they were just excellent dancers out for a night on the town.

Tim slid an arm around the back of my chair. "Those two are shining tonight," he said. "Sally is, too. I just saw her go by with Greg. She's even wearing earrings!"

Following his look I spotted Sally twirling around the room with Greg and she too was wearing a skirt, this one a definite western design with a wide ruffle at the bottom causing the skirt to flare when she spun around. I was impressed with her legs. Who knew?

Ryan made his way to our table and held out his hand. "How 'bout it, Mrs. Tanner?"

"Please, call me Tee, Ryan, and thank you."

I put my hand in his and followed him into the crowd.

Everyone lined up in a couple of rows for line dancing.

"This okay?" The young man asked.

"I was doing this before you were born," I grinned at him. "Keep up, youngster."

It turned out to be me who had to keep it up. This kid could dance! We were kicking and scooting right along, even slapping boots in time with the music, all I could to do to stay with him.

When the dance ended he escorted me to the table, bent at the waist, thanked me, then he was off for another partner. Seconds later I saw him sweep by with a firm grip on Sally.

I was looking for iced water.

Happily, two large pitchers rested in the center of the table, next to the beer.

Tim laughed at me, and poured a glass, sliding it to me.

"Does this mean you don't want to dance with me?"

"Give me a minute," I said, gulping half the glass. "That boy wore me out."

"He's good," Tim admitted. "He and Kyle both are. Once they get us set up they hit the dance floor wherever we are. I've been watching them for years."

"Years? Are they old enough to be in bars?"

"Oh, yeah, Muse. Just for the last couple of years. Both are legal. Anne is very careful about that."

"I saw her earlier, talking to you."

Tim glanced around the room. "She was here. Don't know where she got to."

"Does she dance, too?"

"Yes, ma'am," he grinned. "It's the music. It's in all of them. Maybe because it's our job, maybe the job is because of the music. You spend years on the road with the music and you learn to dance right quick."

"I thought you just played concerts."

"That's the most of it, lately. Even then, there's always jam sessions or juke boxes. Heaven knows we played enough bars getting started. Those two," he inclined his head towards Ryan and Kyle easing past us, "are also very good musicians. Guitar, piano, drums, you name it."

"Better than hanging around on street corners," I said.

"They're good enough for their own band," Tim said. "One day they'll have one if they want it. Come on, my turn." He held out his hand and I took it, letting him lead me to the dance floor, thankful it was a slow song.

The topics that night were two: the dancers and the hair.

Locals all had to comment on Sharon or Cora's hair. Rightly so. They both looked terrific and completely different. Who knew changing your hair style could be such a change? Sally's looked nice, too.

The dancing was another matter.

The locals could be determined by their foot gear – either boots or sneakers and yes, Priscilla, it is possible to dance in sneakers.

The Gem is mostly a country bar, and tends to country music on the juke box. There is a lot of line dancing and Texas Two Step, although actual real life square dancing is not on the menu. There is also a mix of classic rock on the juke box.

Sharon, Sally, Cora, and the guys, Arch and Greg among them, had these new steps to show off and they did. The locals wanted to show off their new stuff, including the older gentlemen who may have been slower but just as enthusiastic. I recognized some regulars from Kelly's stepping right along with the younger group.

We all enjoyed watching.

Hey, we're a small town, pretty much all the same people from week to week. The dances were new, the execution was new, and it was entertaining, plus we did have some new blood with the crew from the set joining in. The dance floor filled up for every song.

It was a lot of fun.

Those that weren't dancing were admiring the ones that were.

But Bill was indeed escorting Lurlene and they danced a lot. Bill has never been big on dancing although he has shuffled his way through a lot of miles over the years.

Lurlene positively glowed.

She was well built to begin with and she knew how to move it.

By the second hour Bill was just the anchor to her moves. People were backing off and giving up the floor to watch her, some clapping, some cheering, some just tapping their toes and watching.

But Bill watched with the rest of us, his eyes alight for the first time in decades as she shook and shimmied and kicked around the floor, slapping her boots and shaking her shoulders.

When they came to sit at the table we all applauded as they left the floor.

Bill was a regular so they sat with us, as he had done for years. Lurlene simpered and accepted all the compliments on the women's hair, inviting people to 'come on down' and get their done at the reduced rate.

At one point she looked over at me and suggested I come by and see her.

"Thank you, Lurlene, I'll keep that in mind," I said.

"You will love it, Tee," she cooed. "You won't believe the confidence it will give you. We can make that man proud," she winked.

"You've certainly done a wonderful job with Sharon and Cora," I said. "You can be proud of that alone."

"Now, Sugar, listen to me," she said, leaning closer across the table. "I know I could improve on your look. Anyone could."

Ouch.

Trying to change the subject, I complimented her dancing.

"You can really dance, Lurlene. You should be in the video they're shooting."

I said it without thinking, forgetting the situation with Tim and T Three.

154

"I can't, dear," she smirked. "I'm not allowed on the set."

Open mouth, insert boot.

Where do I go from here?

"Well, you certainly can dance. And style hair. I'll be sure to recommend you."

"For the hair? Or the dancing?" She shimmied at me, her shoulders shaking.

"Both," I said, feeling my cheeks flush.

"Why, thank you, Tee," she smiled. "It's always nice to be appreciated. In anything you do. What is it you do? I don't believe I've heard."

I had enough. "I take care of my husband," I snapped back.

Thankfully a guy I had never seen before stepped up and asked her to dance.

She hopped up without even glancing at Bill and headed back to the dance floor.

Things weren't awkward enough, I opened my big mouth yet again. "Bill, would you like to dance? I haven't had a turn with you yet."

"No, thanks, Tee. Think I'll just grab a beer and rest my feet." He got up, turned his back and headed for the counter.

That went well.

Tim stood and tugged me to my feet. "Come on, babe."

I am nowhere near as good as Lurlene but Tim is a wonderful dancer and he leads like a dream, guiding me around and making me look better than I am.

"Sorry," I said when we were moving through the crowd.

"For what, Muse?"

"I sort of threw you under the wheels there."

"No, you didn't. That's just Lurlene. She always manages to put everyone on edge."

"She was right, Tim. I should have remembered she's barred from the set."

"Look at the bright side," he grinned down at me. "At least she knows it. Means it's a safe place to be."

"I still feel bad," I said. "I wasn't trying to embarrass her."

"Embarrass Lurlene? Can't happen, babe. That woman is cast iron barbed wire. I doubt bolt cutters could get through that woman's hide."

"She seems to be attached to Bill. They came together."

He thought about it for a minute, twirling me under his arm and back.

"Maybe," he said, finally. "Her lid's loose but she has a mind like a steel trap. Never sure which way she's gonna snap. Could be sincere, could be one of her nasty little dramas."

Around us the crowd was tightening, pushing us towards the edge of the dance floor.

Tim lifted his head, looked over my shoulder, and promptly took my hand to lead me back to the table. He pulled some bills from his pocket and tossed them in the center of the table.

"Come on, babe, let's head out."

I followed, looking back to see what he had seen that escalated our departure.

Everyone was moving out of the way.

Lurlene and the short guy were dancing again, the one that had so enthralled us earlier.

Only this time, it was different.

156

You could feel it in the air.

What had been a dazzling display sank quickly from bawdy to lewd and was headed for downright obscene when Tim tugged me out the front door. We didn't even say good night to the rest of the gang.

Outside, he led the way to his truck, helped me in, and headed for home.

"Something wrong?"

"Not yet," he answered, his jaw tight. "Just had enough, Muse. It's getting late any way."

This was so unlike Tim.

He didn't speak again till we were back home.

I was filling the coffee pot for the next morning when he came into the kitchen and slipped his arms around me. He dropped his cheek to the top of my head.

"Sorry, Muse," he said softly. "Lost it there for a second."

"You want to talk about it?"

"Not really, babe. Although I guess I should explain." He gave a deep sigh and turned to lean against the kitchen counter, arms folded across his chest.

"I have seen that same scene a hundred times or more."

"Lurlene?"

"Not just her. Women like her. They get to shaking it up on the dance floor, showing off, and they take it too far. That guy she was dancing with thinks he's going to get lucky. But Bill thinks he's going to get lucky and he is going to defend her honor, or watch her walk out the door with the other guy. Either way, no one wins."

"She was fine earlier. Everyone complimented her. She was pretty much the hit of the evening with her dancing.

She came in with But, seemed to be having a good time. We all included her. Why would she do that?"

"Make a spectacle of herself? Who knows? Maybe she can't stand prosperity. She wants to belong so badly that when she's accepted she has no way to handle it. I don't know, babe. I just know that particular scene and I didn't want to see it again."

"Can't blame you for that," I agreed. "You know, if you're not comfortable with the whole bar thing we don't have to go to the Gem."

"It's not the Gem, Muse. I like the Gem. A lot. We can go there, grab something to eat, have a few beers and dance. Hang out with your friends. Just have fun. It's a rare atmosphere for a bar. You don't see a bunch of drunks crying or fighting."

"There have been some incidents," I grinned up at him. "I remember some guy slamming another one into the wall a couple of times not too long ago."

Tim grinned back at me. "He had it coming."

"I'm just saying, the Gem is a bar like any other. If you don't want to go there, we can stay home. Or go over to Jade, or down to San Luis to the movies. We don't have to go there."

"I like going there," he repeated. "I really do. I like your friends, I like the pizza, I like dancing with my girl. I like being treated as Tim Tanner instead of T. Tom Tanner of T Three. They all accept me, the real me, just like I am."

"Then don't let her spoil it for you," I said. "She lives here now, she works here, so she has the right to go there, too. The thing is," I caught his face between my palms and made him look at me. "The thing is, those are your friends, too. Not just mine. You were here first. She'll find out she's not welcome if she keeps up that attitude. That's another side of a small town. We take care of our own."

"Thanks, babe. I guess a lot of it is me, too."

"In what way? You didn't do anything."

"No, before." He sighed. "When you start out in the music business, you are so excited the first time you get a gig. To play in public, you know? Usually it's the neighborhood bar, or one like it. You're excited, you're nervous, and you want to do your very best. Then you get invited back or another guy steps up and says how great you are and gives you another job. You make a hundred bucks or so and you think this is it, I am on my way! That's how it goes, one show after another. Pretty soon you realize that about half of your 'fans' are just talk, a lot of hot air, to puff themselves up, make themselves important or so drunk they could be talking to the wall and say the same things."

We drifted to the living room and sat down on the couch, where Tim continued to talk.

"If you want to make it, you put up with it. Nod, and smile. The women start hitting on you, the guys start wanting to fight you." He chuckled. "Your ego sops it up. You get to the point where you think you're pretty hot stuff. Then it changes. There's some guy waiting in the parking lot to pound you or some gal wanting to jump your bones just so she can say she did. You see the dark side of people."

He sighed again, looking down at his hands. After a minute he picked it up again.

"The thing is you see, well, not the same people, but the same types of people. The guy who wants to fight. The gal who wants to latch on. And there's always someone to tell you how great you are, how talented you are, when half the time they can't find their fanny with both hands and a set of deer antlers. The thing is, those aren't real people. They're like silhouettes, thin as paper."

He shook his head. "I'm wandering all over the place, Muse, I'm sorry."

"I don't mind, Tim. I had no idea. I just thought you're 'discovered' and you're on top."

"It's a lot of hard work. With a lot of fillers, people that just use others. Lurlene is like that. She's playing that poor sucker she danced with, she's playing Bill, and she's gonna play everyone that gets close to her. She's like a puppeteer, pulling strings and watching guys dance."

"Has that happened before?"

"With Lurlene? I never saw her do it. On the other hand, I would bet a shiny new quarter on it. It's why I wanted to get out of there. I didn't want to see it again. I didn't want her to spoil the Gem."

I sat up and turned to face him.

"She can't spoil it, unless you allow it. John has her history. You heard him. If we have a problem we call him. Taken care of. People here will take your side, they won't listen to her tales. Who do you think is going to swing more opinions here? Sally or Lurlene? This is home, babe, in more ways than one."

He looked back at me for another long minute.

"I hope you're right, Muse."

"Count on it," I said.

"I'd still like to wring her neck," he said. "I am so sick to death of that woman."

"Let it go, Hubs. It's over. She's done with you. Try to look on the bright side."

"There's a bright side?"

"Sure. You just have to look for it."

"Is it under a rock? Buried in the back yard?"

"Come on, Tim. Let's be positive. Maybe Lurlene has found her niche. We can share our town."

He thought for a minute. "She did do a heck of a job on Sharon. And on Cora. She seems to have a knack for styling hair. You could be right, babe. I have to admit she did an excellent job on the gals."

I patted his thigh. "There you go. Maybe she makes a name for herself. She has a good start on that already, with the hair thing. She's been with But Bill, they seemed to be a couple, and maybe she'll latch on to him. Hey, this could work out just fine."

"Maybe," he said finally. "I guess that would be okay. Long as I don't have to deal with her."

"Your hair is perfect," I smiled, reaching to run my fingers through it. "No need for you to have to deal with her. Monarch is small, so you might see her at Kelly's, or at the Gem. And we can always leave if she's there."

We sat in the quiet for a bit. I pondered what he had said, people and situations that I had never come across. I was grateful I was spared in our little sheltered town.

I broke the silence. "You know what I can't understand?"

"What's that, babe?"

"How does she afford it?"

"What do you mean?"

"Lurlene. How does she afford it? I couldn't afford to pack it up and move to Texas. I mean, I know hair dressers can find jobs pretty quick, like a mechanic or a waitress. Still takes money to get from one town to the next. Rent, utilities, food and all that stuff. She's single so how does she afford it?"

"Heck if I know. Never thought about it."

"One of those things that make you go hmmm."

With a sigh he stood back up and tugged me to my feet.

"Sorry, babe, I don't normally whine. It's just my turn in the barrel I guess. Let's go to bed."

"You didn't whine. You shared. Thank you."

"For what?"

"Sharing."

"You're something else," he said pulling me close.

"So are you."

"Ready for bed?"

"Oh, yeah."

Sunday I let Tim sleep in while I took my shower and went down to fix breakfast.

I made a pan of biscuits, started frying the sausage, intent on his favorite meal. When the coffee was ready I poured a cup and sipped it while everything cooked. I heard Tim upstairs and got down a second cup.

By the time he came downstairs I was finishing the gravy, the biscuits already on the table, along with his coffee. The eggs stayed warm in a covered bowl.

"Good morning," he said, taking his chair and sipping coffee.

"Good morning," I said, pouring gravy into another bowl.

"I was making a statement," he grinned at me. "Any day that starts with gravy has to be a good one."

I set the gravy next to his plate. "Dig in," I smiled.

162

It was a good start on the day. We ate and talked, about everything but last night. I loved it. It was Sunday, he didn't have to pack up and leave, and we were enjoying a nice, leisurely breakfast.

"So what's up for the rest of the week?" I asked, pouring us each another cup of coffee.

He turned his chair and stretched out his legs.

"More of the same," he answered. "The Kelly's gang has a couple more days."

"Kelly's gang?"

"You know. Sharon, Sally, Cora, Arch and Greg. And that gal he brought Friday night. What's her name?"

"Janet? I think it was Janet. Maybe Joan? She lives over in Jade so I don't know her, just seen her around. She's in the video?"

He nodded and sipped coffee. "Another one of the dancers. Steve, the guy that was dancing with Lurlene the other night, he's in it, too. They have another number to get down. Then we're gonna shoot the commercials while they're here, put them in one of those. Some kind of barn dance scene. I haven't looked at it close. That will finish up with the dancers. Then there's two other songs and done."

"So a couple of weeks left?"

"Sounds about right."

"And then what?"

"Then back to LA for a few days to wind things up there. Do a couple of personal appearances, guest shots on TV, that kind of stuff to kick off the product line, promote the CD."

"Then what?"

He cocked his head and gave me that sultry look from under his lashes. "Then it's time for a honeymoon. Have you thought of anything yet?"

"Nope. On my list. So, just a couple of weeks left?"

"On this project? Yeah, that should do it. What are you fishing for?"

"Then what. What happens when this is finished? Back to Texas?"

He thought it for a minute, sipping coffee.

"Well, wife, we do need to go back there at some point. You have to meet the family. I want you to meet Mama. I want to show you off."

"How much family? I already know Mark."

"Mark's my cousin. Uncle Merle's boy. There's my brothers, Matt and Luke. Mama. Aunt Shirley and Uncle Merle. Odds and ends of cousins. They're going to love you, babe, don't worry about that."

"Just wondering," I said, when what I really wanted to know was where did he want to live. Here? In Texas? Somewhere else? While I wanted to know, I wasn't up to bringing it up for discussion with all the other things on his plate. I decided he had enough to think about for now. It would wait.

Tuesday afternoon I was finishing the laundry when Tim flashed into my head.

FLASH
Hey, Muse
Hey, Hubs, what's going on?
What's for supper?
Supper? You just finished lunch!
Let me rephrase that. What did you plan for supper?

164

Haven't got that far. Did you want something in particular?

If you don't have something planned come down here. We've hit a snag with the generator, gonna be running late. So I thought you could come down here for supper. Maybe stay the night?

In the motor home?

Sure, why not? All the conveniences are here. Put out enough food for the boys, hold them over till you get home tomorrow. They should be fine. What do you think?

You know what? Sounds like fun. I can even bring supper with me.

They'll feed us. I just thought you might like the change. Spend the night here. We can open the windows on the bus and listen to the surf. Or there's all kinds of movies. I'm pretty sure we can find something to do.

Uh-huh.

His warm laugh filled my head.

So it's a go?

Yeah, sounds like fun. What time?

Any time, babe. I'm at the bus now. On call, or I'd come home.

I'll be down in a bit. Need anything from home?

Just you, babe.

On my way.

For a spur of the moment decision it was ideal.

The commissary crew called in a local guy from Jade Beach who put out the full Santa Maria barbecue - tri-tip roasts slowly smoked over oak wood, with spicy chili beans, green salad and garlic bread. It's a favorite meal on the Central Coast, often set up in parking lots for fund raisers during the summer.

We sat with the rest of the crew at the long tables, platters and bowls of food passed around like a huge family dinner. The smells alone would have drawn a crowd.

I estimated forty people but there could have been more.

Once the tables were cleared Tim, Mark and Russ got out guitars and did a few numbers for everyone on the acoustic guitars, since the generator was still being worked on. Battery powered lanterns glowed along the length of the table, giving the whole scene the atmosphere of a camp out, appropriate for the locale.

The guys did a couple of old favorites and invited everyone to sing along, which we all did with gusto, if not with talent.

After that the entire crowd helped buss the tables and pick up the area, finally dispersing with good nights called across the lot. Some headed for town, some for trailers and motor homes.

We were walking back to the parking area, to the motor homes, when a pair of security guards stopped us and checked our passes. They were doing their job, since they all knew Tim by now, and were very nice about it. He talked with them for a few minutes, one even took a selfie with Tim.

At the motor home, Tim fished out a key and opened the door, leaning in to turn on the dimmers before helping me up the step.

The interior glowed with small golden sconces on the wall and the center aisle was outlined on both sides by tiny little white lights set in the floor.

Tim directed me towards the bedroom while he locked up, then followed me.

166

He slid the windows open, then pulled the curtains across them. We could hear the tide coming in, the thump of the waves breaking and the swish of the flattening waves washing against the shore.

"You set?"

"I guess so," I said, looking around. I sat down on the bed and pulled off my sneakers. "This is really nice. You can smell the pines. Smells like you. That fresh pine scent. You might suggest they make one of those products for women. I love that smell!"

Tim turned on the bedside lamp and extinguished all the others. "And I thought it was me you were attracted to. Turns out you just wanted my after shave."

I laughed. "You know better." I pulled off my shirt and tossed it at him.

"Yes, I do. And I'll mention it to Annie."

"This is really nice, Tim." I slid between the cool, smooth sheets.

"Seriously, babe, think about this for a honeymoon."

"You can drive one of these?"

He chuckled and pulled off his boots. "Oh, yeah. I drove a truck when I helped Uncle Merle and Matt. This is just a big bus, easy to drive. Top of the line, too. There's a lot of models smaller. We don't need all the extras, not for just the two of us."

When we got into bed I could sure see the attraction of a home on wheels. This was the high end of the camping life. Easy to get used to. Sure beat the old pop up tent and a sleeping bag on an air mattress that was almost guaranteed to go flat during the night.

We watched a movie, turned off the lights and I slept like a rock. Tim curled around me, the sound of the sea and the smell of the pines surrounded us. All in all we had a great time and it gave me a lot to consider. I could handle days in a motor home, with Tim, seeing the country, sleeping where we stopped.

Tim took a quick shower, kissed me goodbye and went over to the set before I even got out of bed the next morning. I hated to waste their water when I was only four blocks from home, plus I had to feed the cats, so I went back to the house, after I was dressed, grabbing my lanyard and locking up the motor home.

FLASH
Hey Muse.
Hey Hubs, what's up?
Set is down, waiting for a new generator.
You coming home for lunch?
I wish I was. Going to San Luis. May be late getting home. I'll let you know.
What's in San Luis? You going to go get a generator?
Nah, that's up to the tech guys. Anne got us an interview on KJUG. Local radio station. They're doing a live broadcast at some shopping center. We're gonna go plug the CD and the new product line, maybe do a song.
I listen to that station! I'll turn it on. What time?
This afternoon sometime. Maybe two?
I'll listen for you.
We'll be back by supper time. Maybe hit The Gem? That way you won't have to hold supper.
Sounds good to me.
Be careful, Hubs.
Always Muse.
Love you.

168

Too!

Since Tim wouldn't be home for lunch, I fed the boys and realized I was hungry.

It had been a while since I had gone to Kelly's with most of my friends working at the beach. Plus, it was Friday. Fish and chips. Just thinking about it was enough to make up my mind.

I was really surprised to see Sally wielding her coffee pot up front as I went in and more surprised to see Sharon's bright, shiny head in her usual booth.

"What are you doing here?" I said, by way of greeting. "Why aren't you guys working today?"

"This is working," she said, indicating the pile of papers in front of her. "I'm behind on these listings."

"Let me start again. Why aren't you guys at the set?"

"Not shooting today. They're bringing in a new generator. The one that went out was kind of iffy, so they're bringing in a new one. They'll have it up and running by this evening, be ready for Monday. I think we're close to finished. The dancers I mean. Might have to sit around in the background but pretty much over."

"Are you going to miss it? Being on the set, I mean."

She sighed and leaned back in her seat. "You know, I don't think so. Don't get me wrong, I loved it! I owe Tim for giving me the chance. And it was fun!" She sighed again. "Just not me. You know what I mean? I've been independent for so long, my own boss and all that stuff. It was a hoot, and I really did love it, but I'm looking forward to getting back to normal."

"Well, hey, you got a great makeover out of it."

She gave her head a shake, and I watched it all settle right back in place.

"I love this," she admitted. "Best thing I've done in years!" Leaning in closer she added, "You wouldn't believe how many guys hit on me at the set! I could have had supper with a different guy every night!"

"Why didn't you go for it?"

"Are you kidding? Not for me, Tee. I had my thrill just being there. No way would I want that life all the time. Uh-uh, not for me. Who knows where those guys will all be next month?"

I shook my head and grinned at her. "Are we going to have to listen to those one that got away stories for the next five years?"

She laughed. "No, hardly. It was fun. It really was, and I will definitely do something nice for Tim for getting me in. For me, it was one of those things. So glad I did it, so glad it's over."

"I understand," I smiled back. "Tim has told me quite a bit about the life, about being here in town where he gets to be himself as opposed to being T. Tom Tanner the celebrity. Some of the wild things that happen on the road."

"He's welcome to it," she smiled back. "Where is he, by the way? I took back a sweater this morning and Kim said he was gone."

"Replacing the generator slowed things down so Anne got them on the radio. They're doing an interview in SLO. He's planning to be back by tonight. Just a one day thing."

"Everything is okay?"

"Far as I know."

"What station?"

"KJUG. The country station. I guess they're doing a live broadcast down there."

"Oh, yeah! They do that! They have this big blow up jug they put up to mark the location. You know, like one of those moonshine jugs? I saw them once at a shopping center."

"Sounds about right. He said they'd be back for supper."

"What time are they on? Do you know? I'll go back to the office and turn on the radio."

"I think he said about two? Afternoon."

"Just like old times, having you two to wait on," Sally said, sweeping in with her coffee pot. "What's about two? Where's Mr. Tim?"

"He had to make a quick trip to SLO. How do you like being back to work?"

"Love it," she said. "Why wouldn't I? I've been here a long time."

"I know. I'm surprised they managed to do without you."

"It was only for a few days," she countered. "Besides, I came by in the evenings and checked in. Made sure things were okay."

I shook my head. "This place can't run without you, Sally. You know that."

She patted my hand. "Of course it can. It just runs better with me here. Now, why is Tim in SLO?"

"Doing an interview on KJUG," Sharon answered for me. "This afternoon."

"I'll switch on the radio," Sally said. "Hate to miss my man. What can I get you ladies, and I use the term loosely."

"I want the special. It is fish and chips, right?"

"Some things never change, Tee. The menu is one of them. How about you, Sharon?"

"Cobb salad, bleu cheese on the side, please."

"Watching your girlish figure?"

"With those toppings? Be serious. Besides all that dancing, I've lost eleven pounds."

Sally laughed. "Yeah, I hear ya. I lost almost ten. Guess that proves the value of exercise. I have to tell you, I loved it and at the same time I am so glad it's almost over!"

Sharon laughed with her. "See? I feel the same way. Couple more days and we're done."

"I'm still going to get my hair done," Sally added. "You and Cora didn't have to have your hair done every morning. You guys have great hair styles and you don't have to work at it. That's for me. I made an appointment for this afternoon."

"You'll love it," Sharon said. "I don't much like her, but she is a whiz at hair."

"You don't like her?" I spoke up, wondering if this was about the dancing.

"Not especially. Oh, you guys left last Friday. You didn't see her."

"The dancing?"

"If that's what you want to call it."

"Yeah, I saw a little of it. Tim wanted out of there so we left."

"I think everyone did," Sharon said. "I was right behind you guys."

"Did she leave with But?"

"Sure did," Sally put in, "and I'm still having her do my hair. She made a mistake with that dancing, okay? Maybe she didn't think it through. Give her a break. Once, anyway. That may be okay where she's from. I say give her another chance."

"She is great with hair," Sharon put in. "Besides, you don't have to dance with her."

Sally thumped Sharon in the head with her pencil and went up front.

"So you guys are about finished?"

"Yeah," she sighed. "We're mostly background shots for the rest of it. I really am glad, too. I'm not a fan of being anywhere at six in the morning. So," she said, and she had that gleam in her eye. "Have you thought about having your hair done?"

My turn to sigh. "Yeah, I have, Sharon. You look so different and so does Cora. Maybe you're right."

Sharon managed, barely, not to whoop. "Good girl! I bet you can get in this afternoon! Surprise Tim when he gets home! You are going to love it!"

Had she been an oil well she would be a gusher.

"Whoa, hang on, Huckleberry. I said I thought about it. That's as far as I got."

She pulled out her phone. "I'm going to see when she's open."

"Sharon," I began, as she held up a finger.

"Hi, this is Sharon Kelly. I was wondering if you have an opening today?"

I looked up at Heaven.

"Oh, no, not for me! I love my hair! My friend does too, so she wanted to see when you could fit her in."

She sat and nodded, like anyone on the phone could see her.

"Perfect! Thank you so much!"

With that she hung up and smirked at me.

"This afternoon, right after Sally. About three. That still leaves time to listen to Tim. I didn't tell her it was you, so if you must chicken out she won't know who it was."

I opened my mouth to argue with her, then paused.

Why not? Her hair was terrific. Cora's hair was terrific. It was, after all, only hair. It would grow back if I didn't like it. It had grown back before. Twice. I closed my mouth.

"Oh, goody!" She clapped her hands like a two year old.

"You're embarrassing," I told her smug face. "Pathetic."

She leaned forward, her face alight. "I won. You will love it. I will even pay for it."

"I can pay for my own haircut."

Sally picked up on that last.

She set a plate piled high with crispy, golden fries and crunchy brown fish fillets, bracketed by slices of lemon.

"Watch out, that's hot," she warned me, sliding Sharon's salad in front of her. "We know you can pay for your own haircut. The question is IF you will pay for your own haircut."

"Of course I'm going to pay for it," I snapped.

"Well, good for you! About time you did something with that hair."

"With friends like these I don't need enemies," I mumbled, reaching for the pepper.

"Enemies wouldn't care if your head looks like a dandelion," she snickered and went back up front. "I'll get your drinks."

After lunch I still had time before Tim was scheduled to get some paperwork done.

Tim had suggested I quit my little bookkeeping sideline, since I no longer needed the business, giving the job to someone who might benefit from it. I was printing the hard copies of the work I had done this year for my records, having already sent them their copies.

When the printer turned off I boxed them up, labeled the box, and carried it to the garage. Looking around I realized we needed more room.

Tim had yet to bring up all his belongings and we were already out of space to store things. I made a space in the corner, under the shelf Tim had mounted to hold the stereo.

Lifting the carton into place put my eye level with the stereo. Right there, in front of me, was a button that read Record. There was a slot for a CD as well as a little pop out door for a cassette tape.

It took a few minutes to figure out the system, and a few more to find a blank CD, that I inserted into the machine. That finished I tuned in to KJUG, set the timer to record at one thirty so I didn't miss anything and went back in the house, pleased with myself.

I would have a copy for Tim when he got home.

Rinsing my hands at the sink I saw Chris from Trim and Go coming across the lawn to the front door.

I opened the door to catch him with his hand in midair ready to knock.

"Afternoon, Miz Tanner," he said, with a start. "You scared me there. I was just getting ready to knock."

"Afternoon, Chris. What can I do for you?"

"I forgot the clippers and I was wondering if I could just borrow yours? I'm on a pretty close schedule and I hate to drive all the way back to Jade Beach."

"Sure, no problem. I'll get the garage door. You know where they are?"

"Sure do. I'll meet you there." With that he went down the steps and around the corner.

I went through the kitchen to the garage and pushed the button that lifted the garage door.

Chris was there by the time it finished lifting and slid into place.

"Do you need anything else?" I asked.

"No, ma'am that should do it. I'll put them right back when I'm done."

"That will be fine, Chris," I said, going back to the kitchen.

I finished up the rest of the chores with one eye on my watch. I needed to get over to Tiffany's for my hair appointment and Chris was still working in the yard.

I grabbed my keys and went out through the front door, locking it behind me.

I waved my hand to catch Chris's attention when I got to the front yard.

He put the mower in low, pulled the head phones off one ear and looked at me.

"I have to leave for a little bit," I said.

"That's fine, Miz Tanner. I'll put your clippers back as soon as I'm finished up here."

"Just put them up here on the porch," I said. "I don't want to leave the garage open."

"Oh, yeah, I can do that," he said. He looked a little unsure. How hard is it to set the clippers on the step? "If you want, I can put 'em back in the garage and shut the door when I'm through. I promise not to steal the trash cans," he grinned.

It wasn't the trash cans that concerned me.

176

I had orders from Tim to secure the house any time I left. At the same time I was not about to leave the garage door opener over something as silly as the clippers.

"I appreciate it, Chris, but just set them up here on the porch. That will be fine."

For just a split second he looked angry, then he smiled so wide I might have imagined it.

"I'll do that, Miz Tanner. And I won't forget mine next week. Thank you, ma'am."

"No problem," I said. "Have a good day."

"You too, ma'am. See you next week."

With a wave over my shoulder I went over and climbed in my truck, using the remote on the dashboard to lower the garage door. It was about half way down when I turned for the street.

Chris lifted a hand and waved as I turned for town.

I'd be a liar if I said I was confident going to get my hair cut.

I have the security of living most of my life in a small town, where I know most of the people or know of them. Lurlene was outside my comfort zone, even without her history with Tim. To be honest here, so far she had no appeal as a future friend and that had nothing to do with Tim. I didn't care for her. Or her dancing.

Arriving at the salon I was annoyed to find my friend, Tiffany, was absent. Sally was gone, leaving me no allies. Not the best of starts.

Lurlene could not have been more affable.

"Why, Tee, I am so pleased to see you!" she said, as soon as I stepped inside. "I have so looked forward to getting to know you better. This is going to be such fun!

You step right on back here and let's have a look see." She motioned me to a chair in the rear of the room.

I sat down carefully, still not convinced this was a good idea.

Lurlene whipped a black cape around me and snapped it closed in the back.

"Now, let's just see what we have," she began, running her hands through my hair, tipping my head to the left and the right. "Do you have a preference? Any idea what you would like?"

Finding my voice, I said, "I want to keep my halo. It's kind of a trade mark."

I felt her hands go to the crown of my head.

"Are you sure you don't want it blended it? Part of the whole? Or colored to match the rest of your hair?"

"I'm sure. I went through a lot to get it and I'm attached to it," I said.

"Well, of course you're attached to it, sugar, it's your hair! No other restrictions? Would you like me to just make you over? That's what we decided on with Sharon and Cora. They are your friends, right?"

"Yes, ma'am," I answered.

"The lady just ahead of you is another friend?"

"If you mean Sally, yes. We've all known each other for years."

"That's just wonderful. Friends are important in life, make a good foundation, you know? I know we're going to be friends. Good friends. After all, we have so much in common," she winked, and stepped back to give my head another look.

I was beginning to regret this spur of the moment decision, silently vowing to get even with Sharon for getting me into this.

"How about you put yourself in my hands? I promise that man will sit up and take notice! I know him pretty well and I know what he likes. Let's get you shampooed," she said, leading me to the sinks in the back of the room.

"That's fine," I said, taking a seat and settling back. "Just want to keep my halo."

"We'll be sure of that," she smiled and turned on the spray.

I closed my eyes while she shampooed, rinsed and shampooed again. She had great hands and with my eyes closed, she shut up, which was a bonus.

Finished with that, she flipped a towel around my shoulders and led the return to her station. When I was seated she ran the chair up a little then spun it around so I was facing her.

"Here we go," she smiled and picked up a comb and scissors. "I know just what we are going to do."

I was glad I was turned to look at her formidable bosom rather than the mirror. I didn't want to watch. She clipped bunches of hair out of the way and started snipping. Little bits of hair began to rain on my lap. I relaxed a little when none of them were white. She had listened to my request.

The closed eye thing didn't work in the chair.

"Y'all got married so fast," she said, "was there some reason you had to hurry?"

"No particular reason," I answered, being careful to think first.

"A few of the ladies mentioned it was a surprise. I was just curious. I sure don't blame you for grabbing him up when you got the chance. I was afraid maybe your cancer came back. I heard that was a possibility."

"No, nothing like that. It was Tim's idea," I said, on the defensive already.

"Oh he can be impulsive! I know that." Snip snip snip. "Still can't fault you for hurrying him along. A girl has to look out for herself in these times. "

I tried a different tactic.

"How long have you known Bill?"

"Oh, he was so kind when we arrived, so helpful, such a nice gentleman. And so knowledgeable! He just knew all about the area, and the people. "

"And how did you meet?"

She paused for just a minute and I wondered if she realized I was turning it back on her.

"We rented a place in Jade Beach, just over the ridge? He was working in the yard next door and kindly offered to give us a hand."

"Oh, you have other friends here?"

Snip, snip. "Just my boys. They were here and missed their Momma so I came on up here. That little old place they had was too small so we found the place in Jade Beach. We were moving in there, and Bill was working in the yard next door. He stepped in right away, not wanting to see me have to lift heavy things."

"That's nice," I said. "He is a great guy. We go back to high school, known each other for long time. You mentioned your boys? It's always nice to have family around. You must be close."

"Oh, yes, Tee. We're real close, me and my boys. I was so young when they came along most people think they're my brothers! People are always shocked when I say I'm the momma."

I was on a roll now, leading her away from the Tim inquisition.

"How young were you? When you had the boys?"

I glanced up at her face and caught a stubborn light in her eyes.

"Very young," she answered, giving my shoulder a pat. "I'll be right back. I need to get some foil."

She tap tapped to the back and returned with a box of foil strips.

She pulled up a strand of hair and twisted a strip of foil around it. "How did you meet Tim? Were you in Austin?"

"No. I've never been to Texas." I left it at that.

"Then how did you meet? After he came to California?"

"We've known each other for a long time," I said. Not a lie, not really.

She twisted another foil strip around my hair. Trying to answer her questions without giving her any information was becoming a game, taking my mind off my nerves.

I relaxed for the first time since I stepped inside.

She kept on with the foil strips. "Do you know the family? Have you met them?"

"Me? No," I said. "The only one I know is Mark. He's a cousin. Tim told me you were a neighbor, when he was a child." I was proud of that one, stressing the child part.

"We were both very young," she countered. "Our families were close, living next to each other. We sort of grew up together, you know? We were close from the beginning. I may still have some pictures of him, when he was just a pup. I'll have to look. You can come for coffee and we'll go through them."

"Oh, don't bother, Lurlene. I have so many pictures of Tim." Blatant lie.

"No bother," she answered, twisting more hair into foil. "He was such a handsome young man. I have so many stories about him, when we were young. I like to think I taught him a lot," she winked.

"Oh, you play guitar, too?"

Zing, that got her.

"No," she said, her voice cool. "That's not what I meant."

"You sang with him and Mark?" I watched her jaw jump as she clenched her teeth.

"We're gonna let this sit for a little bit," she said, her voice tight. "Can I get you anything? Would you like a Coke? Water?"

"No, thanks, I'm good," I answered, relieved that she was going to let it go.

"Then you sit here for just a bit and relax. I'll be back before you know it."

She tapped back to the rear and I took in a load of air and expelled it, chemicals and all. I concentrated on relaxing. I closed my eyes, took several deep breaths and counted to a hundred.

I lost track of the time.

She was back after a while, taking out the foil, guiding me back to the sinks. Another shampoo, another fluff, then back to the chair and the comb. Risking a glance at my watch, I saw it had been an hour. I hoped the radio show was recording.

Lurlene noticed me checking the time. "I'm sorry, Tee, are you meeting Tim at the beach? I thought Sally told me the set was closed today."

Thanks, Sally, I thought to myself. "Yes, ma'am, it is."

"Now, we decided to drop the ma'am," she said with a pat on my shoulder. "Are you meeting Tim somewhere else? I noticed you checked your watch. I wouldn't want to be the reason you missed him."

"Tim is out of town," I answered, thinking that was pretty vague.

"Oh? Is everything okay? I hope y'all aren't having trouble already. I know how hard it can be to have him around every minute of the day, especially if you're not used to it. He can wear on you."

"We're fine," I snapped a little too fast, her constant poking beginning to annoy me. I am the most laid back, easy going individual you are likely to meet but she was beginning to get under my skin.

"Sugar, I didn't mean a thing! I wanted you to feel comfortable. If you wanted to vent a little bit, I'm willing to listen. Most of the ladies do. In our case, you can't tell me anything about Tim that I don't already know. Believe me, I know all there is to know about that man."

"I appreciate it, Lurlene, and thank you. I have nothing to vent about. Tim and I are perfect, we fit together like pieces in a jigsaw puzzle," I purred. "He is the most amazing man and I am so happy to have him, to be married to him. I don't think we could be closer if we were joined at the hip."
That should hold her.

She was quiet for a minute. "That's wonderful," she said finally. Not so warm and fuzzy now. "I certainly didn't mean to imply anything. It's that I know the Tanner family, very well," she stressed the latter. "They can be trying. Believe me, I know that bunch. I'm just trying to put you at ease, Tee. I want us to be friends."

"That's so nice of you," I answered. "Tim has told me all about his family, and his younger years. We have no secrets from each other."

She busied herself with my hair, taking out the last of the foil strips and tossing them in a tray. Then it was back for another shampoo, then the chair.

The noise of the blow dryer cut off further conversation and in just a few more minutes she stepped back and whipped off the cape.

"There you go," she said, smiling. "All done."

Looking into the mirror my hair looked all right. I don't know what I expected but this wasn't it. It had a nice shape to it, nothing extreme, except my neck felt chilly where she had shaved it.

White stripes radiated from my halo, two on each side, sort of framing my face. To me, it looked like my halo, which I normally couldn't see without a mirror, had somehow melted in a few places and ran forward, making little stripes that pointed to my face.

"Now, sugar, if you don't like it, you come back and we'll try something else," she announced with a smile. "I guarantee my work. I just know our Tim is gonna love it!"

I was so eager to get out of there I hurried up front and paid.

I did not offer a tip.

It was when I got home I found what she had done.

When Tim got home that afternoon he found me at the kitchen table, head down on my folded arms. My cup of tea was cold, my eyes red rimmed from a peach of a fit I threw earlier.

Tim came around and took hold of my shoulders, lifted me up and pulled me into his chest, wrapping his arms around me and holding me close. He rocked me in his arms while I just leaned into him.

"Lurlene?" He finally asked.

I nodded against his chest.

We stood there for more minutes before he finally tipped my chin up and kissed me gently. "We got this," he smiled, wiping away my tears with his thumbs. "Don't worry, Muse. Put on the water for some fresh tea and let me make a call."

"What about supper?" I called after him.

"We'll grab something on the set or hit The Gem," he answered, turning me toward the stove and giving me a little nudge. "Make some tea and let me get on the phone."

I could hear him talking on the phone but not the words. I reheated water and got down another tea bag. By the time the tea was ready, he was back.

"Pour it in a travel mug, Muse. We are out of here."

I shook my head, and got up from the table. "Where are we going? I am NOT going back to that damn woman!" Fresh tears stung my eyes at the thought. My fingers knotted together.

He grinned and turned me toward the door, grabbing my lanyard from the hook and hanging it around my neck.

"Nope. We're done with her."

We climbed into his truck and headed for the beach.

He parked back by the motor home and locked up the truck. Catching my little finger with his, he led me back through the stand of pines toward the set where they had been filming.

We wove through the guys working, through the cables and vans and trailers to a larger trailer parked near the center stage they had built. Tim's manager, Anne, waited for us at the steps.

She came forward and patted my shoulder, then tipped my head down so she could see the damage.

Lurlene had dyed about a three inch, yellow-orange circle, smack in the middle of my bright, white halo. It looked like a large fried egg was flopped on my head, or a particularly large, sick bird had dropped a load and hit the target.

To my horror, she laughed out loud.

"Sorry, Tee. Never seen that one before. Have to hand it to her, that is pretty creative," she smiled, patting my shoulder again. "It's not a problem. Come on in and meet Kim."

With that she led the way up the steps into another salon, this one on wheels. There were three stations inside, sinks, and trays of all sorts of rollers, combs, brushes, and other hair paraphernalia.

"Is this her?" A petite little blond in a full length apron stepped up. She was cute as a pixie, her makeup so light it was invisible yet her eyes were accented with deep color.

"Yes Kim. Meet Teejay. This is Tim's new wife." Annie introduced us. "She needs some work on her hair."

Kim was so little I had to once again tip my head down for her to see the crown.

"Did you do that on purpose?" The little woman giggled. "Sorry, can't resist. Was it a California Condor?" She went off into gales of laughter while my cheeks flamed. Anne's own smile widened.

"Come on, Kim," chided Anne. "Fix it. Make it great."

"Sorry, Mrs. Tanner," Kim said. "Come this way and we'll see what we can do."

Tim patted my shoulder as I went to the back station and took a seat where Kim pointed. "I'm leaving you in capable hands, Muse. I'll be at the bus or somewhere around the set," he called. "Come on back when you're done."

I waved and turned back to Kim.

She spun me around, looking at me from all angles. "Not to worry, Mrs. Tanner. I've won two Emmy's and been nominated for an Oscar. I know what I'm doing. And I am sorry for laughing. It's just so, um, unusual."

She reached out and flipped my hair up.

"It's okay, Kim," I said, sniffing back tears. "If it wasn't my head, I'd laugh, too. Can you really fix it?"

"Oh, heck yeah. This is nothing. We just need to figure out what we want to do. Shoot, I've seen a whole lot worse," she laughed. "Just not recently."

"I just want to lose the egg."

Kim giggled again. "I can see why. You must have pissed someone off real bad to get this."

"Not nearly as much as I plan to in the very near future."

"Atta girl! Let's turn this around on her," she grinned. "We'll make you fabulous."

Two hours later I made my way back through the encampment to the motor home. My step was so light I almost floated. It didn't hurt that three different guys whistled as I went by.

At forty, that's pretty sweet. I sashayed my own butt.

The door to the motor home was unlocked so I stepped up and went inside.

Tim was sitting on the sofa with his guitar and a soft drink. He looked up at me and a slow, sweet smile spread across his face, lighting the blue sparks in his eyes.

"Wow, babe," he said softly, setting the guitar aside. "You look amazing."

He stood up and closed the space between us to gather me gently against his chest.

"Wow. Just wow." His eyes roamed my hair, and my face, and back again.

I felt the same way when Kim had whirled me around to face the mirror.

My hair gleamed. The horrid white stripes and yellow orange yolk were gone. In their place tiny little streaks of champagne, wheat and gold highlighted my hair, spiraling down from my restored halo, making my whole head sparkle as I moved. It was like sunshine on the top of my head, blending down to the softer shades and highlights. Soft feathers of curl framed my face and cupped my ears. It was completely soft, every hair silky, separate and in place without spray or gel. I could shake my head and each hair returned to its proper position, sparkling like sunlight on moving water. I loved it!

Kim had also done my makeup, a thing I have never succeeded in doing. My idea of makeup was mascara and a little lipstick on a really special occasion. She had done the full deal – shaping and plucking my eyebrows, tinting them a darker color. Adding a little blue shadow above and outlining my eyes with a charcoal color, making them look twice as big.

I knew it was good because I couldn't tell I was wearing makeup. Couldn't even feel it on my face it was so light.

Seeing the look on Tim's face made me blush.

"All I can say is wow. You are breathtaking, Muse." The look in his eyes underscored his words.

"Thanks to Kim. And you, Tim. I seem to say thanks a lot lately."

"You're very welcome," he said, tipping my chin up. He raised a hand and touched my hair, then lifted a few strands and let it run through his fingers. "Your hair is as soft as a spider web, and it shines like sunlight."

"Very poetic. You like it?"

"Oh, babe, you have no idea how good you look," he said softly, bringing his other hand up and sifting my hair through his fingers. "Mesmerizing."

"Are you done for the day?"

"Uh-huh." He dropped his head and set his mouth against my neck, nibbling soft kisses. "You even smell terrific."

"Is this going to involve your heart's desire again?" I leaned into him, tipping my head back and locking eyes with him.

"Got it in one, babe."

By the time we locked up the motor home and drove to the house, it was almost dark.

I fed the cats while Tim showered and changed clothes. While I was waiting I remembered the stereo in the garage and went out to check it.

I reloaded the disc and turned it to play.

The recording times I had set were off from the broadcast. When I hit play the first thing I heard was Tim. I would know that voice anywhere. He was talking to someone about the new CD, Blue Monarch, explaining the title and the cover.

I paused to listen. Yep, definitely Tim. I even recognized the deeper tones of Russ as he told an anecdote of his own.

I was still listening when Tim called from the kitchen.

"Out here," I answered.

He stepped into the garage. "What are you doing here?"

I pointed to the stereo. "I taped you."

He grinned at me, shaking his head. "Very nice, Muse."

I pushed the pause button. "I'm very proud of that," I said.

"And I am very proud of you. Come on, let me go show you off."

I flipped off the stereo and followed him back into the house.

I had never looked this good. Ever. Looking your best, or better, puts a bounce in your walk and a sway in your hips, no matter how old you are. I happily strutted my stuff.

"You are hot, Mrs. Tanner," Tim said, holding the door for me.

I giggled like a teenager. "Would it be awful if I said I know?"

"Can't argue with perfection," Tim laughed. "Momma always says he that tooted not his own horn will not be heard. Flaunt it, babe."

We went straight to the counter to order and Jennifer, my favorite bartender didn't even recognize me. She gave me a cursory glance and looked at Tim.

"What'll it be, handsome?"

"We'll start with a pitcher and a couple of specials," Tim answered with a grin.

She pulled a pitcher of beer off the tap and set it up on the counter with a couple of glasses. When I reached for it she gasped.

"Oh my Lord! Tee, is that you?"

I laughed, delighted.

"Of course it's me."

She leaned across the counter to give me a half hug. "You look incredible! I can't believe it! Turn around, let me see the back."

I flipped my head back and forth.

"I have got to go see this hair gal," she squealed. "She is freaking amazing!"

Tim cocked an eyebrow at me.

"She is something," I agreed.

"I can't get over it! Tee, you have never looked this good! I did not recognize you."

Tim took the pitcher and slipped an arm around my waist.

"Come on, Cinderella," he said softly, guiding me back to the corner table. "Please, Lord, let Big John show up tonight," he said, pouring a couple of glasses of beer once we were seated.

"Why? You don't like John."

"Seeing you tonight will send him right up the wall," he grinned. "I do love to kick sand in his shorts."

I laid my head on his shoulder.

"Was I that bad before?"

"Muse, you couldn't look bad if you wanted to. It's the difference. I haven't had my fill of just looking at you and now I have to start all over again."

I smiled up at him. "I'm still me."

"Oh, yeah," he breathed. "And you're mine."

"Oh! Tee?"

I turned to look up at Cora.

"It's me," I smiled. "In the flesh."

"You look amazing! She pulled out the chair next to me and sat, Archie taking the chair on her other side.

Tim reached around us to shake hands with Archie.

Cora just stared at me. "I can't believe it. I thought mine was the best. She is incredible, isn't she? She is changing everyone in town!" She glanced back at Archie. "I wonder if she does guys."

"Oh, no," Archie said quickly, throwing up his hands. "I'm fine with what I have."

I poured two more glasses of beer and slid them over. Not sure how I was going to bring Kim into the equation, I let it go. For now.

Archie leaned in to tell me how nice I looked, Tim went to fetch more pizza.

We were well into that one when Sharon came in and joined us. She was as thrilled as I was, doing everything but climbing on the table to shout and point.

Again, I didn't correct her assumption that Lurlene had done my hair.

They were still talking about it when I caught Tim giving me a quizzical look. He raised an eyebrow and tipped his head to the side.

I smiled back at him waiting for the blue flash in my mind that didn't come. Looking at him again I saw him shrug.

I was the belle of the ball for the first time in my life and I loved it. Every woman should be Cinderella once in her life. I loved the attention, loved the gleam in Tim's eyes when he looked at me, loved his hand caressing my thigh from time to time.

Greg came in with a new gal, this one named Sarah. He introduced her and complimented me yet again. Even Sally put in an appearance, bending to hug me and pat my head, lifting a strand and letting it drop.

"Wonderful," she announced. "Way past due, worth the wait. Now you do Mr. Tim proud. I knew if I did it, you'd get in line. I was beginning to worry I was gonna have to dump something on your head and claim accident." With yet another hug she whispered, "I love it."

More pitchers of beer flowed, more pizza appeared in the middle of the table and the noise level climbed the ladder.

Everyone took turns dancing with everyone else and we were all having a great time. Sharon, Sally and Cora showed off their new moves with some of the guys from the set, who pulled up another table and joined us in the back corner. They were introduced but that went right over my head. I had enough trouble remembering the locals.

Then But Bill showed up.

With Lurlene on his arm.

Let me just say I have never been a confrontational person. To the best of my knowledge I have never been deliberately mean to anyone.

All that was about to change. If I had any dander it was definitely on the rise.

Watching that woman sashay her chubby butt towards our table with that snarky little smirk on her face sincerely ticked me off.

She locked onto Tim the second she saw him, never giving me a glance. She was like a heat seeking missile, straight to the target. Her step quickened even though But had a hand jammed in her back pocket and followed like a caboose.

I felt a mean streak growing up the middle of my back, fed by a rising temper.

It may have been obvious, since under the table I felt Tim's hand tighten on my thigh. Leaning close, he whispered, "We can leave, babe. Any time. Don't let her upset you."

"She's not going to upset me," I assured him. "Quite the contrary. Cinderella is about to bust some bosoms."

Bill had pulled out a chair for Lurlene before taking a seat himself, greeting everyone. He was a long time member of the group and completely at ease. Folks shifted around to make room for them.

Lurlene's focus was Tim, still locked onto him.

I watched her, understanding how Dave felt when he watched the birds out the living room window.

She was barely seated when Cora leaned in to tell her how much she loved my new hair.

"I thought mine was awesome until I saw what you did with Tee. You really outdid yourself this time! I have never seen anything like that! You are a real wizard with hair, Lurlene. You are a welcome addition to our little town."

Sharon chimed in, running over Cora's words. "That is absolutely the most amazing thing I have ever seen in hair! I had to touch it to see if it was real! It's like an illusion or something. I have no idea how you did it."

194

For a brief second Lurlene looked smug, her over lipsticked mouth popping open, turning to smile at me, her eyes finally off Tim.

Then she saw me.

Really saw me.

And my hair.

I smiled at her, my best ten cent smile.

She froze, her mouth half open, her eyes wide open.

"I'm sorry, honey," I drawled sweetly at my victim, reaching across the table to pat her hand. "I didn't tell anyone. I didn't want to embarrass you."

If looks could kill I'd be pushing up a tombstone.

Lurlene's eyes shrank to nasty little slits while her mouth quivered, struggling to smile under the weight of all that lipstick. Words failed her, leaving her gasping like a landed trout.

"Why would she be embarrassed?" Sharon asked. "You have to admit this is the best you have looked in your life! Your hair is almost alive!" Sharon reached over and ruffled my hair, letting it trickle through her fingers. "She has no reason to be ashamed of that. It's liquid sunshine."

"She didn't do it," I said into the silence.

Sharon blinked.

Cora looked from me to Lurlene and back, even Archie looking confused. Under the table Tim's hand tightened on my leg.

"Then who did?"

"Kim, the beautician on the set," I answered. "She's won a couple of Emmys, even been nominated for an Oscar. Tim asked her to do my hair."

Sharon, bless her heart, was all over it.

195

"I made the appointment," she argued. "With Lurlene. You were right after Sally. Sally saw you come in! We were afraid you'd chicken out so she was watching for you!"

Sharon, my best buddy, couldn't let it go. I knew she wouldn't.

"Yes you did. I went to Lurlene," I smiled, my cheeks stretching like the proverbial cat. "She did my hair."

"I thought you said the gal at the site did it. I'm confused," Sharon admitted, reaching for her beer and taking a quick swallow. "Who did your hair?"

"Lurlene did it," I smiled. "The first time. No offense, honey," I jarred down on that word, looking around the silent table. "The thing is, she did a nice job, it was cute, just a little too juvenile for me. As Tim's wife," and I put double stress on that last word, "I have to look more sophisticated so he asked Kim, at the set, to redo it, to give it a professional look."

A pin dropping would have sounded like a cannon firing in the silence.

"It looks very nice," Lurlene mumbled, finally finding words.

She was stuck and she knew it.

"Oh, honey," I laid it on, reaching to pat her hand again. "I want you to know how much I appreciate your effort. It was very clever. If it was just me, I might have left it, for the laughs, you know? It brought out the child in me. As Tim's wife," I stressed the word again, "I have to be more adult. Tim wanted a classier look for his wife." I stressed that last part, and winked. "You know how he can be."

"Well, it's lovely," she said, her ears so red they might erupt. She turned to her escort. "Bill? Sugar, I would love to dance." She was up, tugging on his hand and leading the way to the dance floor.

She was barely out of hearing before Tim started laughing.

"Well done, Muse," he laughed.

"What was that all about?" Sharon asked.

"I'll tell you later," I answered.

"Must have been good," Cora said. "I've never seen you like that! What on earth did she do to you?"

"She put a shot across Tee's bow and her boat got sunk," laughed Tim. "Come on, Tiger, let's dance."

On the dance floor reality set in and I began to feel guilty.

"Let it go, Muse," Tim said. "She asked for it, she got it. Now she knows you have claws she'll back off."

"Was I that mean? I don't know what happened! I just wanted to put her down."

"Well, you did that, babe. And maybe it was time. If nothing else, you put her in her place as far as I'm concerned. Besides, she had to know she wasn't going to get away with that. You could have gone straight to her boss. Cost her the job. She didn't care. The first time they put her in jail for harassing me I wanted to go down and pay her bail. Luke stopped me. She doesn't care. She has no restraints, babe. She will do exactly what she wants to do and the devil take the leftovers."

The next song up was slow and Tim pulled me close, singing the words softly in my ear, his breath warm on my skin. "Forget it, babe. Old dish water now. You said your piece. Maybe now she'll finally back off."

"You know what bothers me the most? It's not even the whole hair thing, or her fixation on you. It's the kids. Her

197

boys. What about them? Those are her children! What kind of life have they had? "

"No idea, Muse. Lost track of them ages ago."

"She said they were here in town. Well, in Jade. That's why she moved up here. To be with her boys."

"Can't help you there," Tim said. "Never had a problem with them. Just her. Never really thought about the boys. They're grown men by now. Maybe they did live here, ask her to come join them. Stranger things have happened. Long as they leave us alone, no problem."

When we rejoined the table Archie spoke before anyone else.

"Okay, folks, we're all gonna agree our ladies have the best hair in the nation," he began, before anyone else spoke, ever the peace maker. "Now, I want the floor for a few minutes." He looked around the table. Lurlene looked like she was going to speak, then changed her mind.

We were all quiet, giving Archie our full attention.

"Thank you," he said. "Hard to get a word in edge wise when these gals get started on fashion or hair," he softened that with a smile he spread around the table like butter on toast. "We all agreed you are all lovely, with the best hair in the state. Now, I have a question for Tim."

"What can I do for you?" Tim leaned forward, eager to get beyond the hair debate.

"It's those motor homes. I'm curious about them."

"The motor homes? Oh, the ones at the camp?"

"Yeah, those. I have always wondered about them. Me and Cora don't get much time off, what with her bakery and my store, hard to get off at the same time. I've thought about one of those things for quite a while. Just get in and go, whenever we can."

"They are nice," Tim said. "The ones at the site are rentals. They have drivers bring them up and drop them off, then come get them when we're through. Used to be big trailers, now everyone uses the motor homes and leaves the trailers for the equipment. The band travels on them during tours."

"I get all that," Archie said. "Here's the thing. This one," he glanced at Cora and gave her a nod. "This one wants a bath tub. Can you believe it? I've suggested going camping and that's her first argument. A bathtub." He shook his head, softening his words when he met her look.

"Motor home is the answer," said Tim, with a grin. "Fully equipped often has a bathtub. The one I have now, the rental, has a tub."

Archie slapped the table with his palm. "There! Thank you!" Turning to Cora, he grinned. "I told you they came with a tub."

"Not all of them," Tim corrected. "There are all kinds of layouts. Different sizes, different amenities, and all different prices. I'm just saying some of them are equipped with tubs."

"What are we talking about in costs?"

"Depends. You can get a smaller rig for two grand, or spend a couple of million on a custom job."

"Millions? For a motor home?"

"Oh, yeah, Arch. Some of those custom jobs go two, two and a half million."

"How custom can they get?"

"Pretty dang custom. You see those slide outs on some, make the rooms bigger, wider, where a section just slides out once it's parked. There are some that go two stories.

The slide outs go up, creating a second story. Stairs and everything."

"Seriously? Man, I can't believe it." Archie was into it now, leaning forward on his elbows, holding the conversation. But and Lurlene got up to dance again while Cora and Sharon went to the girls room.

I felt like the traitor because I was interested in the motor homes, too.

Tim and I had talked about maybe renting one for a honeymoon, driving around the country and stopping where we wanted, then moving on. Although I had no desire for a two story two million dollar custom job.

Arch finally leaned back in his chair, shaking his head. "Man, I had no idea. There's so much to consider. How about driving? Are they hard to drive?"

"I have no problem driving one, although I have my trucker's license. Had to get it to help my uncle with the big rigs. Most of the motor homes don't require a special license. Again, depends on the size. Some of the moderate size ones are just like driving a van. The bigger ones, more like driving a bus. You're just gonna have to see what you want, get an idea of what size and go from there."

"I checked around here already," Archie admitted. "There's a few for sale down in San Luis, but no dealers. Have to go all the way to Santa Barbara for that."

"I've seen a sign driving through there," Tim said. "They have a big motor home and trailer show there, at the fairgrounds. Not sure of the dates but you can find them online. Probably get more information online than I can give you. Like I said, I've stayed in a quite a few, even driven a few and I still have a lot to learn about them."

"Well, I appreciate it, Tim. Thanks. Gives me some ideas."

Lurlene and But had returned and were following the men's talk. I noticed Lurlene stayed out of the conversation, only turning her head towards whoever was speaking, while But sat silently beside her.

"You know, Arch, you can always come down and see the one I have at the site. It's pretty midline. Give you an idea of how they're set up. This one does have a tub," he grinned at Cora.

"Really? Would that be all right?" Archie's face lit up like Christmas morning.

"Sure why not?"

"Oh, man, I'd love that! Tomorrow too soon?"

"Nope, sounds good. No action on the set on weekends. We can meet you there, give you the ten cent tour."

"Why am I meeting you?" Sharon asked as she and Cora rejoined the table.

Archie stood up and waited till Cora was seated.

"Tim says we can go down and see the motor home, you know, tour the inside," he explained, once she was settled again. "We can meet them tomorrow. That sound okay?"

"I'd love it," Cora admitted. "Thanks, Tim! I've always wanted to see the inside of one."

"They are pretty amazing," I put in. "We've stayed down there a couple of nights. Like a fancy hotel. Very comfortable."

That got Sharon into the conversation.

"You guys stay down there? Overnight?"

"A couple of times. All the comforts of home."

"Probably more comforts than I have," Cora laughed.

She lived in a little one bedroom apartment right over the bakery. Many of the older businesses in Monarch had been built with living quarters above the stores. Convenient for the storekeepers at the time they were built, most of the apartments were small, some taking up only half the available space upstairs. Some had storage, like a small warehouse upstairs alongside the apartments. With the canyons running right down to the water's edge, flat land suitable for building was a rarity in the cove that created Monarch Bay. Thus, the early residents built up to make more room.

Cora's bakery was one of those with the living quarters upstairs.

"Sweetheart, I've seen chicken coops bigger than your apartment," chuckled Arch, patting her hand.

Cora ignored him and leaned toward Tim. "Would it really be all right to see the inside of the motor home?"

"Sure, come on down. We can meet at the gate and take you back. You can all come down and see it. How about nine? That suit you?"

"I just invited myself along," Sharon put in. "I wanted to ask before but there was no way I was going to ask to invade your space."

"You could have asked," Tim told her. "Tee has been down there quite a bit. You could have come over with her."

"Didn't want to interrupt," she winked.

"A few times that was smart," he winked back.

"Too much information," Arch said. "We'll meet you there at nine."

"Deal. Front gate at nine." Tim said, standing up and holding out his hand. "Come on, Muse, they're playing our song."

We danced to a couple in a row before heading back to the corner.

"You sure that's okay? Giving a tour of the motor home?" I asked on the way to our seats.

"Sure, why not? No one is working tomorrow, although a lot of the crew will still be on site. As a rule we don't work weekends. Not unless it's a push to get something done."

"That was nice of you, "I grinned at him.

"I'm a nice guy," he returned.

"Yeah, I've noticed that a time or two," I agreed.

But Bill and Lurlene were gone when we got back to the table, their chairs pushed in and their places cleaned up.

Sharon noticed me looking. "They left," she explained. "She turned her ankle dancing and wanted to get it iced since she has to work tomorrow."

"I hope it's not too bad," I said.

"Oh, I'm sure it will be fine," Sharon laughed. "She was limping on her left foot when they came off the dance floor and limping on her right when they left."

"You noticed that, too?" Cora laughed along with Sharon. "I thought I was the only one who saw it. Now they're gone what really happened with your hair?"

I thought about it for a second.

"She made a mistake," I said finally. "I'm sure she won't do it again. You guys look great."

Cora looked a little skeptical while accepting my explanation.

"Well, you look sensational, whoever did it," Sharon said. "Did the gal on the set do your makeup, too?"

I nodded. "You know I'm limited to lipstick and mascara. The best part was Kim taught me to do it. If I can remember. Even gave me samples."

"You will. I'm sure of it. It's a great look."

"She was something else," I admitted. "She wrote out the colors and brands, showed me how to do it. Even gave me swatches of the colors I should wear."

"Hey, we're building a woman," Sharon laughed. "We always had the frame. Now we can fill it in."

"Oh, bite me."

Archie was back with a couple of carafes of coffee and all the fixings, the signal that the evening was winding down. We left shortly after, with reminders to meet at the front gate of the compound at nine the following morning.

We left a little early the next morning, not wanting to leave someone waiting at the gate. Both of us wore our lanyards, just in case.

We showed our passes to the guys on the gate. Tim drove back and parked near the motor home and we walked back up through the compound to the gate to wait for the others.

There were quite a few of the crew on the site, surprising since they weren't working again until Monday. I saw several in cutoff jeans take the path to the beach, carrying boogie boards, while others kicked back around barbecues and hibachis, the smell of wood burning and cooking meat already filtering through the pines.

Tim greeted a few and waved at others as we made our way up front.

While we waited he chatted with the guards on duty at the gate, advising them we were going to take a few people back. They gave it the okay, although they asked Tim to sign them in as visitors and his guests, to keep track of who was on the grounds and to let them know when they left the premises.

Sharon arrived first, with Sally riding shotgun. They parked and joined us at the gate.

"Sally wanted to see inside, too," Sharon said. "I hope it was okay."

"Sure," Tim grinned, stepping over to hug Sally. "You're always welcome, sweetheart." He wrote their names on a couple of sticky labels and handed them over. They in turn stuck them to their shirt fronts.

Arch and Cora arrived about the same time and Tim repeated the process, also writing their names on a clipboard the guard had provided. Once they stuck on badges, Tim handed the clipboard to the guard, who opened the pedestrian gate. When we were through Tim lead the way back to the rear of the compound where the motor homes were parked.

They had all been on the set so it held no interest as we passed through the trailers. Arch waved at a couple of the guys and Sally stopped long enough for a hug from some woman I didn't know.

As we passed the commissary area Tim reached out and snagged a couple of folding chairs and carried them along with us.

When we reached the motor home, Tim set the chairs up beside the door before unlocking it. Once the door was open he leaned in and flipped the light switch before stepping aside and holding the door for the others.

"Have at it," he told them.

The four of them climbed the steps and went inside giggling and laughing.

Tim smiled at me and pointed to the chairs.

"Might as well let them have their fun," he said.

I laughed and sat down. "You're good to them," I said. "Nice of you to let them come see it."

He took the other chair and scooted it close before he sat.

"The first time I was in one of these things I opened every drawer, cubby, and closet checking it all out."

I wasn't going to admit I did it, too.

From inside the giggles continued, along with bits of conversation, ohs and ahs, hard to tell who was saying what. We listened to them for a while, sitting there in the shade of the pine trees.

"Good Lord," Sharon squealed. "There is a tub! Oh, look, Cora, how compact!"

"I want to see," Sally called. "Move over Archie!"

Tim shook his head and smiled at me.

"Kids," I said.

"It is fun," Tim said. "At least, it will give Arch an idea of what's inside one."

"Very nice of you, Mr. Tanner."

"I keep telling you I'm a nice guy," he repeated, leaning close, his eyes darkening.

"Excuse me, Mr. Tanner?" A voice interrupted. One of the guards from the gate walked up, carrying a walkie-talkie in one hand.

Sharon's head popped out of the motor. She hopped down the steps and joined the group, followed closely by Sally.

206

"Something wrong?" Tim asked, meeting the guard.

"Are we in trouble?" Sharon asked at the same time.

Archie and Cora stepped down into our circle.

The guard smiled at all of us, holding up a hand and patting the air.

"No problem, folks. Sorry to interrupt. Mr. Tanner, your other guests are here. You just have to sign them in before we can let them through."

Tim looked at me, raising one eyebrow.

I shrugged and looked at Sharon, who shrugged back at me.

"I'm not expecting anyone else," he told the guard. He glanced at the rest of us.

Sharon and Cora shook their heads.

Sally said, "Not me."

"Sorry for the trouble," Tim told the guard. "This is all of our group."

The guard looked at each of us and blinked.

"Did you get names?" Tim asked.

"No, sir. Excuse me a minute," he stepped back a few paces and turned his back while he keyed the mike on the walkie-talkie. A blast of static responded, peppered with words we couldn't make out.

Returning to us, the guard looked at Tim.

"Bill Williams and Lurlene Martinez?"

Tim's face hardened so fast I thought I heard it.

"NO!" His hands fisted, the left one flying out to strike the side of the motor home. His fist made a dent the size of a salad bowl in the aluminum side of the RV.

Archie, Cora and Sally jumped back while Sharon slid behind me. The guard took three steps back and raised his clipboard like a shield.

Tim's eyes were wild, almost black, the blue gone completely.

In the few short months Tim and I had been together I had only seen him angry one time. In that instance he had picked up a grown man and tossed him against a wall, holding him there without the least effort.

I reached to touch him, putting my hand on his shoulder. Like touching granite. His biceps bulged like boulders.

"No," he said again. Then he roared it. "NO!"

The guard took another step back.

"They are not with us," I said to the guard, keeping my hand on Tim's arm.

Tim swore, something very rare, and slammed his fist against the motor home again. The others backed up again, everyone getting clear of him.

"Tim, come on," I said, reaching up to stroke his arm. "It's okay, babe."

He shook his head, flipping his hair back away from his face.

"She is not coming back here," he said through clenched teeth. "No way in hell."

"She's not coming here, Tim. It's okay." I tried to soothe him, rubbing my hand up and down his arm. "Relax. It's all right."

I looked over at the guard and smiled at him while I rubbed Tim's arm.

"I'm sorry," I said to him. "This is a misunderstanding. Those people are not with us. We're finished anyway."

The guard pointed at the dent in the RV's siding. "He's gonna have to pay for that," he said, and pulled a pen out of his pocket to make a note on his clipboard. "Those are private property. I saw him hit it, dent it. He's going to have to pay."

"Not a problem," I said. "Just give me a price and I'll write you a check."

Beneath my palm I felt Tim's muscles begin to relax.

I drew in a deep breath.

Looking around at my friends I could see their concern, their eyes wide with alarm.

Archie wasn't sure if he should run for help, run for cover or just run, the whites of his eyes showing all the way around.

"Everything is good," I assured them, trying to make my stiff lips form a smile.

The guard raised his walkie-talkie. "I am going to assume you don't know these people. Is that correct?"

"It's a misunderstanding," I answered. "They are not with us, not part of our group. We're finished here, anyway. I can go talk to them if need be."

Lifting the walkie-talkie to his mouth, the guard keyed the mike. "Dan that's a negative. Those people are not with the party."

He kept a cautious distance as he backed away from Tim. "You will need to sign out at the gate, Mr. Tanner. Also sign a damage form for the motor home. I have to report that."

"We'll do that," I assured him. "We'll be right there."

The guard turned and left, looking back over his shoulder a couple of times. Probably to see if Tim was going to put another dent in the RV.

"Are you okay?" I asked Tim, my main concern.

"Fine, Muse," he said, and shook himself like a wet dog. With a sheepish grin he looked around at the others.

"Sorry, folks. Lost it there for a minute. I apologize for that outburst."

"No need," Arch said, stepping back up and tentatively patting Tim's back. "No need at all, man. I want to thank you again for having us down."

The guard was out of sight.

"Sorry, Arch," Tim said again.

"No need," Arch repeated. "Come on, I think we're done," he said, taking Cora's arm in one hand and Sharon's in the other.

"Hang on," Sally called, stopping them. "Head over to Kelly's. All of you. Brunch is on me. I'll meet you there."

"That's okay, Sally," Tim said. "I'm not hungry."

"Hey, wait a minute!" Sally slapped her hands on her hips and faced him. "I don't give out invitations often and when I do I expect them to be accepted. We'll all go to Kelly's," she looked into Tim's face. "Brunch is on me. I won't take no for an answer."

"Thanks, Sally," Tim said, and leaned to give her a hug. "Guess we'll meet you there."

"Let's go," I said, following along behind the others. I reached to link my little finger with Tim's and tugged him along, watching him carefully. Even with that slight connection I could feel him trembling, more like humming, a low vibration through his body.

He glanced over once at the damaged motor home before following me, quickly catching up to walk beside me, our hands linked.

"Sorry, babe," he murmured.

"You have nothing to be sorry for," I said, shaking our joined hands. "Stop it."

The others were silent all the way back to the front gate.

210

I was relieved to see Bill and Lurlene were not waiting there. Evidently the guard had relayed the message. The relief shivered down my back in a wave.

At the gate the others pulled off their little paper badges and handed them to the guard, thanking Tim again. Sally repeated her invitation to brunch, more of an order, and the look in her eye was scary enough I knew we were all going to Kelly's.

They moved off while Tim signed some kind of paperwork on the clipboard. The guards talked softly among themselves, pulled out some more paperwork from the little kiosk and had Tim sign that in several places.

They shook hands all around and let us go after tearing off a copy and giving it to Tim.

With a sheepish grin, Tim took my hand, leading me back to the compound where we had parked.

After a few minutes I glanced up at him.

"You okay?"

He nodded and kept moving. "I don't lose it often, Muse. I'm sorry." He took a deep breath and blew it out. "That woman gets to me. She just tears me apart! I swear I want to wring her neck and throw her off a bridge! Be done with it! She's driving me right out of my mind."

He kept on for a couple of minutes and I let him rant, glad he was talking, getting it out of his system. Was I afraid of him? Not in the least. I knew I would always be safe with him.

For Lurlene? I began to have some doubts.

What on earth possessed her to think she was included? I couldn't even remember if she was at the table when we were talking about it. The history she had with Tim she had to know she was not included. How many times had she been arrested for trying?

We reached the truck and Tim opened my door and helped me up, pulling the seat belt snug and clicking it closed. He cupped my face with one hand and I leaned into it.

"I am so sorry, babe. That was way out of line," his eyes were so soft, the regret shining from them. "That's gonna be a two steps back with your friends."

"It's done, Hubs. Come on, let's go eat."

He gave me my favorite three cornered grin and stepped back to shut the truck door.

"I could eat," he admitted and I knew he was all right.

By Tuesday the shooting was complete and everything was being packed up for the return to LA. I spent most of Tuesday cleaning the RV, although Tim insisted it was not necessary. Mostly I swept up sand we had tracked in and checked to be sure we had removed all our belongings. The big motor home had become a home away from home over the past few weeks, accumulating errant socks and tee shirts.

No more had been said about the incident Saturday.

Tim talked to the transportation captain, gave him the insurance information as well as our home address, and the assurance he would pay for the damages to the RV.

Wednesday we were back to the old routine – up early for Tim's departure, his briefcase and overnight bag sitting by the front door.

We had his favorite breakfast of eggs, sausage, biscuits and gravy before he had to leave for the drive back to LA.

The positive side being it was Wednesday, they didn't work weekends, and he would be home Friday night. Even the overnight seemed a long time to be separated after having him home for so many weeks.

Once breakfast was finished and the table cleared, he kissed me and carried his stuff to the truck. He came back in to kneel and tell the boys goodbye, distributing chin scratches and belly rubs. They had no idea he was leaving, they just wanted their share of his time. I felt the same way.

I stood up to follow him out and he stopped me.

"Sit down, Muse, have some more coffee. The fog's in, it's cold and wet out there. Stay in here where it's warm." He hugged me, holding me tight to his chest and picked up his belongings. From the front door he called, "See you Friday, babe. Love you!"

"Too!" I called back and heard the door close behind him.

Dave and Cletus sat for a minute watching the door in case he was coming back, then set to cleaning their assorted body parts.

I heard the engine kick over on the truck and stood up fast to see him drive off. As soon as my face appeared in the window he waved, knowing me too well. He blew a kiss, backed out and was gone.

How could someone become so important in so short a time? I had been alone for years, more than ten, and got along just fine. Even when I was going through the whole cancer treatment with all the chemo and radiation five days a week. Now I hated to have him gone, hated the idea of sleeping alone and waking up alone.

With a sigh, I got up and started the dishes.

I had avoided Kelly's all week, not wanting to discuss Tim's outburst, knowing that both Sharon and Sally were curious.

Sharon knew Tim had a history with Lurlene but not all the details. As far as I was concerned it was up to Tim to share the story or not, as he chose.

The fog had been thick last night, the overcast still with us and the day was pretty dreary matching my mood perfectly.

Friday I wanted to do something special for Tim's supper so I got out the ingredients and started some bread dough. That's such a warm and welcoming smell when fresh bread comes out of the oven.

While the dough was rising I started a pot of beef stew, braising the meat and setting it to simmer with onions and carrots.

In short order the house smelled delicious, dispelling the damp from the weather.

As a general rule the hotter the inland valleys got, the more fog came in to Monarch Bay, keeping us cool throughout the summer months.

Tim didn't get out of LA as early as he hoped so I turned off the stew when it was ready. It would be quick and easy to reheat when he was home.

Two beautiful, crusty golden loaves of bread came out of the oven and cooled on the counter, the whole house now smelling of fresh baked bread and rich beef stew. I was anxious for Tim to get home.

FLASH
Hey Muse.
Hey Hubs. You on the way?

Nope, I'm here. Just getting off the freeway. Need anything from the store?

Just you, Tim. Supper is ready.

On my way, babe. Ten minutes.

Be careful. Fog's been in most of the day.

Will do. Clear up here.

See you soon.

Love you, babe.

Too.

With him only minutes from home, I turned the stove to simmer under the stew, so it would be warm, and set the table, getting out the thick earthenware bowls that belonged to my aunt.

I set a loaf of fresh bread in a basket so Tim could slice it when we ate.

Standing back, I admired my efforts. With the bright colored bowls, the smells of stew and bread from the kitchen, Tim should be impressed.

I was pretty proud of how nice it looked.

Having the time, I went in and turned on the lamps in the living room, and lit the fire I had laid earlier. There, everything was perfect. I stepped back and admired it.

Ten minutes went by, and I was still admiring it.

Twenty minutes went by, and I turned the fire off under the stew, the cast iron holding heat for quite a while.

At thirty minutes I was picking up my phone.

FLASH

Hey Muse.

Where are you? Everything okay? I was getting worried.

Little accident, babe. I'm fine! Don't worry, okay? Need you to come get me.

What happened? Are you sure you're okay? Where are you?

I'm fine, babe. Bumped my head. That's it. Just need a ride.

Where are you?

Top of the grade, just this side of the freeway. The exit ramp.

On my way.

Thanks, babe.

Be right there.

I grabbed my keys and was half way out the door when my cell phone rang.

I yanked it out of my pocket, locking the door behind me, and heading for the truck.

"On my way," I said.

"Hello?"

"John?"

"Yeah, it's me. Hate to bother you, Tee, when you're headed out but you need to come pick up Tim."

"That's where I'm headed," I told him, climbing into the truck. "Is he okay?"

"Slow down, Tee. He's fine. They're bringing him up now."

"Up from where? I just talked to him! What happened?"

My truck roared to life as I turned the key, backed up, turned and made for the freeway, the big engine singing as I gave it the gas.

"Up from the creek. He went off the road coming into town. He's fine, but the truck is pretty messed up. He asked me to call since his cell phone is somewhere down there in the truck."

216

It is illegal in California to drive while talking on your cell.

"On my way," I said, and clicked off, tossing the phone in the console.

The off ramp for Monarch is a sharp circle to the right that circles back over the freeway. Then it's a series of tight turns and a sharp curving grade that brings the road down through a canyon to sea level, or close to it.

By the time I was half way up the grade I could see the glow of red and blue emergency lights through the trees at the top, the bright yellow caution lights flashing a slower message.

At the top of the grade I slowed down to a crawl. A couple of officers in fluorescent vests were directing traffic, using the heavy flashlights and lanterns. The lookie-loos were blocking the road as they crept along.

Traffic backed up along the entire bend in the road. As I made my way past the squad cars lining the other side I kept glancing over to the shoulder.

The whole scene was nightmarish, like a science fiction movie of an alien landing, with all the colored lights flashing, the men yelling to each other, the crackle of walkie-talkies, and the rumble of idling engines. The air was filled with exhaust fumes.

I finally caught a glimpse of a tall figure in a cowboy hat. He was leaning against a squad car, arms folded, long legs stretched out in front of him, while rescue teams in reflective suits and fluorescent vests worked around him.

A tow truck flashed yellow lights that reflected off Tim.

I didn't realize I was holding my breath until I let it go in a tremendous sigh. Tears stung my eyes and blurred my vision as I crept past the scene.

I had to pull past the curve to find a place to turn around, then ease back into the line of traffic going the other way, looking for a place to pull off the road. I finally got over and parked behind a squad car.

Getting out of the truck I was stopped immediately by an officer waving a flashlight, sweeping the beam across my eyes.

"Sorry, ma'am, no stopping here. Please get back in your vehicle."

The voice was familiar and as the light dropped out of my face I recognized Officer Chuck.

"It's Tee," I said. "I came to get Tim."

He flashed the light briefly back in my face.

"Oh, sorry, Tee. He's over there with John. Watch your step. There's not much room on the shoulder."

He shone his light on the edge of the road as I joined him, leading the way down the hill to where the men were working in tight groups.

Trees and brush crowded the shoulder, which was just a narrow, dirt, edge, pebbled with small rocks and gravel. We wove our way through the men in vests and helmets, stepping over cables and around sawhorses.

As soon as I was close enough I ran to Tim, wrapping my arms around his waist and hugging him tightly.

"Hey, Muse," he smiled, wrapping one arm around me. With the other he was holding some kind of pack against his face. "I didn't see you coming."

I burst into tears. Relief roared through my system, buckling my knees for a minute. Tim held me against him, dropping his cheek to the top of my head.

"I'm okay, babe," he said softly. "I'm fine."

"I hate to break this up, but I need you to sign this statement," John interrupted. "I want to get back to work."

Straightening up I stepped back a little from Tim, retaining my grip on the hand that wasn't holding the pack to his face.

"Be just a few minutes," he said, squeezing the hand in mine. "Get off the road before you get hit." He turned me toward the shoulder of the road and guided me to the narrow edge.

"You sure got here quick," John greeted me, a little frown between his eyes.

I didn't say anything, just looked at Tim.

With a shrug, he turned to Tim. "Not much I can do," he told him. "No license plate number, no witnesses, no description of the vehicle. You didn't see anything at all?"

"I told you," Tim sighed. "It was a white truck or van, something big enough to shove my truck over. I felt it hit the back, saw a flash of white as it went past. By then I was fighting the truck down the slope."

John made some notes on his eternal clipboard. "You didn't see him behind you?"

"For the last time, John, I didn't see a thing! Headlights, yes. They were set up high so it was a truck or van of some kind. I glanced in the mirror when it hit me, then I was over the side. I had my hands full."

"All right. Do you think his vehicle suffered any damage?"

"No idea. He clipped my left rear and spun me to the right. I was over the edge and riding it down before I really knew what happened. Sure glad it didn't roll."

John looked down the side of the canyon, where portable spotlights centered on the back end of a silver pickup. The heavy cable from the tow truck snaked down the side and connected somewhere underneath. Broken branches and snapped trees pointed to the truck from both sides, marking the trail it blasted through the undergrowth.

Men thrashed around beside the truck, calling to each other and yelling orders, punctuated by the static of the hand held radios and the rustle of the brush snapping back and forth around them.

The tow truck let loose a squeal, whined and groaned and someone shouted, then the back end of Tim's pickup quivered and broke through the brush, a taut cable popped tight as it pulled the truck up the steep embankment.

The various bright lights glittered off the bumper as it was towed up onto the asphalt, the bright blue of the Texas sticker centered on the chrome.

The tow truck driver managed to get the truck turned, so it sat parallel to the road, tipped a little to the side on the shoulder. Two tires were flat, throwing it off balance.

More men worked around it, freeing and winding cables.

Tim walked over to look at the front end, tugging me along with his little finger looped through mine. The grill on the truck was crushed in, the hood popped up and bent and the windshield was cracked. A billowy white air bag drooped from the dashboard and across the front seat.

John was taking pictures, making his way around the truck, getting it from all angles. Other guys in fluorescent vests were winding cables. The air crackled with walkie-talkies and static, voices called out and lights flashed here and there.

I wandered to the edge and looked down into the rugged ravine, still lighted in places as they began to bring the lights up. Broken branches snagged them and had to be manually cleared.

I could hear the faint gurgle of the creek somewhere at the darkened bottom.

I shivered and went to look for Tim.

I found him looking over the truck, shaking his head. He tried to open the driver's side door. It was jammed shut. He made his way around to the other side and got the passenger door open by applying some muscle. Reaching inside he pulled his bag from behind the seat.

He turned to John.

"Am I done here? Tee's cold. I want to get her home."

"Yeah, go ahead," John called back. "I know where to find you if I need you."

Tim climbed back up to the road and led the way, weaving between rescue vehicles and men still working. The shoulder was crowded with personnel and flashing caution lights as we made our way back to where my truck was parked.

Traffic was still creeping along. People trying to see what happened were guided by men with flashlights. Out of habit, I went around to the driver's side and climbed in, waiting for Tim to get in the passenger seat and buckled up.

When he opened the door, the interior light came on and for the first time I saw his face.

The entire left side of his face, from forehead to jaw, was bright red, already beginning to purple with bruise, the cheek swollen, the eye beginning to blacken.

I caught my breath and reached to touch his face gently.

"Tim, you're hurt!"

He shook his head, leaning away from my hand. "Just the air bag, babe. Good thing I had one. It's not as bad as it looks."

"You're sure you're okay?" I started the truck and edged back into traffic, signaling I was coming over.

"Yep, fine as frog hair, Muse. Sorry I scared you." He reached across and patted my thigh. "Guess I was just eager to get home to my bride."

"I'm happy to see you. I missed you. I would have preferred you just drive up, you know, skip the drama." I patted his leg in return. "Could have been worse."

"Missed you, too," he said, looking out the side window.

"What happened?"

"Just got off the freeway and was headed home. I felt a thud, the truck lurched and spun to the side, and over I went. Fought the wheel till I hit that tree and the airbag deployed. That's what caused this," he waved a hand at his face. "Whew, I have a headache I'll tell you."

"No one stopped? The guy that hit you didn't stop?"

"A nice couple from Jade saw me go over and stopped. They called 911. I didn't get their names. I'd like to thank them."

He pressed the ice bag back to his cheek.

"I wonder why the guy who hit you didn't stop."

"No idea, babe. Scared? Didn't see it? No way to know for sure. Just lucky it didn't roll. That could have been really ugly. This isn't the first time that's happened to me. Guess I'm just unlucky that way."

"What do you mean? It's happened to you before? Being run off the road?"

"Couple of times," he answered, shifting the cold pack to his jaw. "Maybe I'm not as good a driver as I think I am. Don't worry, babe, that was years ago."

"Being run off the road is NOT common, Tim! When did it happen before?"

He turned and looked out the window. "Austin, few years ago. Twice in a year."

He turned to grin at me. "I got rid of that truck. Thought maybe it was cursed. You've heard of those lemons, right? How some vehicles just seem to attract problems?"

"Heard of it, yes," I agreed. "Had one? Never."

He was quiet the rest of the way home, his head back against the head rest.

The first thing he said when I opened the door was "What is that smell?"

"Depends," I answered, closing the door behind him. "Is it a good smell or a bad smell?"

"Smells delicious," he said, following his nose to the kitchen.

I flipped the stove on again, to warm the stew, again, and poured him a glass of tea.

"Sit down. Supper's ready, just needs to be warmed up."

He picked up the knife and sliced the heel off the loaf of bread, shoving it in his mouth without even butter and chewing. He closed his eyes and made a sound that I could not interpret.

I filled his bowl first and set it on the table. He was already reaching for the bread.

"Man does not live by bread alone," I warned him. "Try the stew."

"This man can live on this bread," he chuckled. "Did you get this at Cora's?"

"No, I did not get the bread at Cora's. I made the bread."

"You made the bread?"

"What is with you? That air bag hit your ears? Yes, I made the bread. Measured, sifted, kneaded and baked."

"I knew there was a reason I married you," he grinned, picking up his spoon.

"Uh-huh," I smiled back. "Eat. Then I'll get you some more ice."

After that it was mostly Tim making satisfied little noises as he ate. Most of the loaf disappeared along with two bowls of stew.

When he finally finished eating, I ordered him to the couch while I made another ice pack for his face. The bruising was darker now, from his hairline to his jaw, the left side of his face was crimson, even the white of his eye was pink. On a good note, the swelling seemed less, his face not quite so distorted.

I took him the ice, turned on the TV and went back to the kitchen.

When the kitchen was clean and the dishes done, I went in to join him.

He was sound asleep, both cats nestled against him.

I picked up the fallen ice bag and covered him with an afghan before picking up my Kindle and settling into my chair.

The next morning the swelling was almost gone, the crimson had faded some, although he had an amazing shiner, his blue eye shining out of a black and purple circle. He showered and came downstairs, still talking on his phone.

"Here ya go, Muse," he said, handing me his phone. "Get a shot of this for me."

I obliged, taking a picture of his blackened eye and forehead. I handed back the phone, breaking eggs in a bowl for his breakfast.

He made a call, then came in and took a chair at the table.

"How much do you like having me home?" He asked when he was seated with a cup of coffee at hand.

"I love it, and you know it. Why?"

"Not going to be able to do any guest shots or promos with this face. Anne says take the week off."

"That's heartbreaking," I told him, setting the scrambled eggs on the table. "However will I manage?"

He filled his plate, giving me a weird lop-sided grin.

"How does it feel?"

"Only hurts when I laugh," he grinned, then winced. "Literally."

Tim laid around the rest of the day, watching old movies, playing his guitar. The cats loved it, getting up only long enough to eat and going right back to snuggle with him when he stretched out on the couch.

His only complaint was the headache, the eye not seeming to bother him.

I monitored the time he used the ice pack, not wanting him to get frostbite.

We had leftover stew for supper and he was back to watching TV while I cleaned up the kitchen when someone knocked on the front door.

"Got it," he called. I heard him open the door.

"Call the plumber, babe, sewer backed up."

With an eye roll he could hear I called out "Come on in, John."

"In," he called back. "Wish I had done that to your face," he told Tim on his way to the kitchen.

"Not in this lifetime," Tim said. "You take me on, you better pack a lunch."

"Uh-huh," John said and came into the kitchen. "On you it looks good."

"You hungry? I have some beef stew here, and homemade bread."

"I could gag it down," he answered, taking a seat at the table, pulling off his cap and hooking it over the chair. "Thanks, Tee."

Tim came in and took his usual seat while I filled a bowl with stew and nuked it to warm it up. I set it in front of John, with a couple of slices of bread.

"Beer or tea?"

"Tea would hit the spot," he managed around a mouthful of bread. "This is great, Tee. Did you make this?"

"Did you have a purpose here or did you just come to eat?" Tim folded his arms across his chest and watched John.

"Can you see out of that thing on your face?"

"Perfectly," Tim answered. "Looking at you, wish I couldn't."

"Gentlemen," I said, taking my own seat at the table.

"Where?" They said at the same time and then both laughed.

Tim behaved while John polished off a couple of bowls of stew and two glasses of tea, only making small talk until John finished eating.

226

When John leaned back and patted his stomach, I got up and set his dishes in the sink.

"Excellent, Tee, and thanks. Didn't get to lunch today. That hit the spot. I always was a fan of your cooking. By the way, your hair looks terrific."

"Now that you've fed your face is there a purpose for this visit? Other than just irritating the crap out of me?" Tim asked.

"That's always a pleasure," John smiled. "Gives me a reason to live. However," he added, pulling a folded paper out of his shirt pocket, "I brought you a copy of the accident report for your insurance company."

Tim unfolded the paper, glanced over it, refolded it and stuck it in his own pocket.

"Thanks, John Q, appreciate it. I'll fax it down tomorrow."

"You remember anything else about the wreck?"

"Nope, just those headlights, flash of white. You get anything more?"

"No, not yet. Those folks that stopped and called it in came down and gave us a statement. They were looking at you, running off the road. He said it was a van, she said it was a pickup truck, so there you have it."

"So no help at all."

"That's about it," John said. "Your phone, registration, all the stuff in your glove box is at the station. You can pick it up any time. Tow truck guys bagged it and brought it to the station. Screen on your phone is broken."

"I'll get down and pick it up. Thanks."

"Oh, I live to serve," John grinned.

I sat down and joined the guys. "Otherwise how are things, John?"

Looking at me, John smiled. "Hear you had a run in with Ms. Martinez."

"You heard about that? From who?"

He shook his head. '"Just word around town. By the way, your hair really does look great. Glitters like rain on water."

"Thanks, John," I said.

"She's married," Tim said.

"Yeah, but I won't hold that against her," John shot back.

"You best not hold anything against her if you expect to keep breathing."

"Careful there, sport. Officer of the law. Terrorist threat. You can go to jail."

"Wouldn't count on it," Tim smiled. "They'd have to find the body first."

"Knock it off, both of you," I said. "Thank you, John."

"To get back to what I was saying before I was so rudely interrupted," John said, turning to me. "What happened with Martinez?"

"Just a little misunderstanding," I said.

John cocked his head to the side and gave me a long look.

"I looked in Friday night at the Gem, had a beer. You were all at the back table together. No bloodstains. Thoughts things were good. Then I hear there was some kind of showdown with you and the Martinez woman. Now, what really happened? And before you ask, I already checked. She drives a blue Honda sedan."

I said. "More tea?"

John slid his glass across to me and I refilled it.

He looked at Tim and lifted one eyebrow, a trick I never mastered. "You want to tell me what happened?"

"She messed up Tee's hair," Tim answered. "Deliberately. Gal with the production company fixed it. Lurlene got a lot of compliments on how nice Tee looked before Tee told them the truth. Kind of irked her. End of story."

"Do you think she had anything to do with Tim's accident?" I interrupted. "Why did you check her car?"

"Just doing my job, Tee," John smiled at me. "So you're sure it was a van? Not a car?"

Tim thought for a second. "Doubt it. Pretty sure from the get go it was a van or a pickup."

"All right, then. Let me ask you a couple more questions. Have you had any other problems with her? Besides the hair I mean. She been bugging you? Following you around?"

"She's showed up at the Gem the last couple of times we've been there. She's been with But Bill, so she's sat at the same table."

John nodded. "Uh-huh, heard that. Got an ear full on her dancing, too."

"We left," I said promptly. "When she started the dancing thing, I mean."

"Also noted," John said, draining his glass. "No other problems with her? Problems with her family?"

A little line formed between Tim's eyebrows.

"What family?"

"Sons. Two of them. Not giving you any problems?"

Tim shook his head. "Don't know 'em. Don't care to. Nothing to do with me."

John smiled at Tim, looking smug. I wondered what he was up to now.

"No? You have one of them working for you. Other one used to."

Tim's head snapped up. "What are you talking about? I don't know her kids. Haven't seen them in twenty years or more."

The smile on John's face widened. He leaned back in his chair and folded his arms, all the while watching Tim.

"Yeah, you have. At least one them," John told him.

"Spit it out," Tim snapped.

John chuckled and leaned forward, watching Tim. "Chris Martin ring any bells?"

"I don't know any - - -" Tim's voice trailed off and he blinked. "Chris? The lawn kid?"

"Gold star, Tex," John smirked. "Birth name Cisco Luis Martinez. AKA Chris Martinez AKA Chris Martin. So far no attempt to defraud so he can use any name he wants. Business license for the yard service reads Ray and Chris Martin. Assume Ray is the other son."

Tim sat back, a stunned look on his face.

"You said one of them worked for Tim? Before this?" I asked as I got up to start a pot of coffee. This was going to be a while.

"According to the Texas Department of Safety, Ray worked as an electrician in Austin for the T Three Texas Tour about two years ago. That sound familiar?" he asked, looking at Tim.

Tim blinked a couple of times and shook his head. "I can't believe it. Damn kids have been right under my nose all this time." Looking up at John, his brow furrowed. "Ray Martin doesn't ring a bell but if he worked with the set up crew or the production crew, they'll have a record of it."

John gave Tim another smile. By the glint in his eye, he was enjoying this. "Why, yes, yes they do. Already checked. And I have already checked out their van, which is white."

Tim sighed. "Anything? Was it him?"

I filled cups and passed them before taking a seat at the table.

John leaned forward to pour cream in his coffee. "No marks on their van. None I can connect to the accident. It has the normal scratches and scrapes you'd expect from a yard service vehicle. Your truck being white, too, doesn't help. Half the vehicles in Monarch are white. If we had a paint chip, anything to compare, might be able to eliminate some of them. Right now, nada."

Tim cradled his coffee cup in his hands and looked over at me. "That really irks me," he said. "I was nice to that kid! Hired their service!"

I patted his hand. "I know you liked him, Hubs. You even let him put that sticker on your truck."

"What sticker?" John asked, looking at Tim.

"Texas bumper sticker," Tim answered. "He had an extra one, gave it to me."

"Where is it?"

"Where do you think it is, John? It's a bumper sticker. It's on the bumper. Back bumper." He gave a curt little grin. "Wanted him to know I appreciated the gesture."

"What's it look like?"

"Oh, you know. It's a bumper sticker. Oval, about eight inches," Tim held his hands in front of him. "Picture of bluebonnets, blue flowers for the uneducated. Texas state flower. Texas spelled out around the top in red letters."

John gave Tim a measuring look. "On your back bumper," he grinned.

"That's what I said," Tim snapped back.

"Good way to mark your truck," John smiled. "Tell it apart from the other white Ford trucks."

Tim looked at John, groaned, and drank coffee. "Serves me right for being nice to the kid."

"You don't know it was him," I said, defending Chris. "That doesn't mean he did it. Why would he? We've been good to him!"

Tim looked at me from under those thick lashes. "His momma," he said. "Might have a whole lot to do with the price of beans. Most boys look up to their mommas."

"My thoughts exactly," John said, standing up and pushing in his chair. He smiled at me." Your hair looks beautiful, no matter who did it, Tee. Like sunlight on water."

"How poetic,' Tim grumbled, getting up to walk John to the door.

I smiled at John. "Thanks, John. You want to take some of this bread home?"

"No, he doesn't," Tim said.

John laughed out loud.

"I guess not, Tee. Thanks. Supper was delicious. I'll stop by during the week, when the infestation is over."

"Then it won't be this week," Tim responded. "I'm home."

"Oh, well, can't win 'em all. You'll leave sooner or later."

"Not without my wife I won't," Tim snapped.

232

John shook his head and opened the front door and struck a pose, one hand aloft, the other on his heart. "Tomorrow is another day."

He opened the front door, then turned to Tim. "You're welcome."

"For what?" Tim got up and joined him at the door.

"The information," John said. "Told you I was good at my job. Now don't go starting anything with them. I'm watching them. And you. Got it?"

"I got it," Tim said, his handsome face drawn into a grimace, like he had an upset stomach. "Thanks, John," he added reluctantly.

"Welcome, Tex. By the way? That shiner is a good look on you. You get tired of playing cowboy, you might try being a pirate."

With a grin he swung his right hand from his knee to over his left shoulder, mimicking the sweep of a cape. "Alas, dear friend," he intoned in a deep voice before he left, "I must be away."

I could hear him laughing all the way across the lawn.

"He is seriously disturbed," Tim grumbled, locking the door.

"I think he's been practicing," I laughed, happily surprised by John's response to Tim's barbs. "You have to admit he won this round, finding out about the boys. Do you think the boys did it? Caused the accident? Ran you off the road?"

Tim ambled back over to retake his seat, stretching those long legs out to the side. He closed his eyes and let his head rest on the back of the chair.

"I like to think I'm a pretty good judge of character and I just got blind-sided," he said. "Evidently a couple of times. Guess I'm not as good as I thought I was."

"Do you think they knew who you are? I mean, as far as their mother is concerned."

"Oh, yeah, I'd bet on it," he answered. "Not a real common name, not like Smith or Jones. Then there's the group, T Three. If they were working for the crew they would know which one I am. Far as I know we're the only trio with that handle. I can't believe that damn woman would make a career out of following me around and her kids wouldn't know it, so yeah, I think they know who I am. Especially Chris, Muse. He's been in the house, the garage. My guitars are in the garage. There's T Three CD's around here."

I cleared the table, rinsed the cups and loaded the coffee pot for the next morning. Tim sat at the table, legs stretched out, arms folded, that little line between his eyes. I left him alone.

I was upset about Chris, too. We had both been taken in by him. I remembered the times I had taken him a cold drink while he worked, the times he had free run of the garage and the house. Maybe I wasn't a very good judge of character either.

Drying my hands on a towel, I looked over to Tim, till sitting there, staring into space.

"Tim?"

He shook his head, and looked over at me. "What 'cha need, babe?"

"Do you think we should change the locks again?"

"Why?"

"Chris. He's been in the house, the garage, all over the yards."

He thought about it for a minute. "Guess it wouldn't hurt," he said finally. "I'll do it tomorrow."

"I'm sorry, Tim."

He looked up at me. "Sorry? For what?"

"I know you liked him."

He stood up, pushed in his chair and stretched, both arms over his head. "Still do," he said. "Not sure how to handle this."

"What? He can't keep coming here!"

"Why not, Muse? He hasn't done anything. Not that we know of anyway."

"He lied!"

Tim nodded and reached to hook a hand around my neck, pulling me close.

"Not technically. I never asked for references. Never asked anything. Not a good start on being a husband."

"What on earth are you talking about now?"

"You, babe. I'm head of the household now. My job to provide for you, take care of you, see to your needs. I should have checked on him myself before I let him in the house."

"That's too protective," I said. "I liked him, too."

"Past tense?"

I thought about it. Chris had not done anything to us, not that we knew of anyway. He had omitted his relationship to Lurlene, and he had to know there were issues with her and the Tanners, especially Tim.

At the same time, he might have needed the work, or perhaps he was putting distance between him and his mother. I decided to use caution.

One thing Tim was right about for sure.

Chris had done nothing to us.

Nothing we knew.

Tim's headache lasted through the weekend so we were pretty quiet. By Monday his head felt better and the swelling was gone although the left side of his face was still discolored. The deep purple shiner withdrew into a shadow of its former self.

Tim spent the time lazing around the house and doing chores – changing the locks on the doors, adding shelves in the garage – when he wasn't working on songs and practicing with the acoustic guitar. He used his laptop to Skype with Anne and some other people throughout the week.

I always peeked when I heard him talking to someone, not wanting to wander in and interrupt some meeting by popping up in the background. Dave, on the other hand, considered the laptop an invitation to join the fun, sitting in Tim's lap and swatting the moving faces on the screen.

Everything was pretty much back to normal by Friday.

Anne, Tim's agent, had scheduled an appointment with an eye specialist in San Luis for Friday, at the request of the insurance company. It was an early appointment so we were on the road by seven Friday morning.

Tim loved San Luis. Once the doctor gave him a clean bill of health he wanted to roam around town for a while. The while included lunch, shopping, and an early supper before we finally headed home.

It was dark by the time I made the exit for Monarch Beach, swinging around and back over the freeway, near where Tim had his accident. As we passed the scene I saw two yellow sawhorses flashing with caution lights connected by yellow caution tape. The break in the brush was visible where Tim had gone over.

We were both tired from the long day so we skipped the Gem and settled for a movie after we unloaded the truck and fed the cats.

After breakfast Saturday I cleaned up and brought down a load of laundry.

Tim was standing at the sink, looking out the window.

"You okay?"

"Hmm? Oh, yeah," he smiled. "Just thinking. Guess I better get that grass cut today. Looking a little shaggy."

I shoved the load of sheets into the washer and came back to the kitchen, putting on water for tea.

Shoving Tim with my hip I told him to sit down.

"Now, what's wrong?" I asked when we each had a cup of tea.

"Nothing, babe, really. Noticed the lawn was getting out of hand."

"You're still upset about Chris? I know you liked him."

"Yeah, I did. Who knows? He may still be back." He stirred his tea, his eyes seeing something else.

"You do realize he could have been the problem?"

He looked up at me. "In what way?"

"We were just talking about her boys. At least I was. Wondering about them. Maybe it's been them all along. She might be completely innocent."

"Muse, no offense, but I had to have her put out of my hotel room. Twice. I can tell the difference between her and a teenage boy. Especially naked."

Oops, I forgot those incidents. "Still, some of the other accidents could have been the boys. Being run off the road, the other times, in Texas. Your house being burned down. That could have been them."

He thought for a minute or so. "So, you think the whole family is after me? That's a little farfetched, babe."

"Not really," I argued, leaning forward. "Think about it, Tim. What if those boys have been raised to hate you, to see you as the enemy? I wondered about a woman who would blatantly stalk a man, let alone one with two kids at home? That takes a special kind of crazy. Lurlene might qualify."

I could see the little line form between his brows, which meant he was thinking.

I pressed my advantage. "You have to admit, Chris had every chance in the world to tell you who his mother was. He didn't. He never mentioned that he lived that close to you, or that he knew who you were. He hunted us up, remember? At the party at the Gem? He came right up to you, gave you a card for free yard service as a wedding gift. He knew who you were, Tim."

"Why? That's my stumbling block, babe. Why? Why would he do anything to us? I never did anything to him. Lord knows you were good to him."

"He hasn't done anything," I corrected. "Not that we know of. Just the sin of omission, not telling you who he was. And that's a big thing! His mother has gone to jail! Because of you! Think about it. Where was he while she was in jail? Where was his brother? You said she was never married. So where did the boys stay?"

"You think two teenage boys, on their own, planned all those accidents? Trying to hurt me? For what I did to their mother? I didn't do anything to their mother. She brought it all on herself."

238

"Exactly my point," I said, slapping the top of the table. "You don't know what she told them! They only have their mother's viewpoint! I doubt she bothered to tell them she was the stalker, or that she was sneaking into your room. They may not even know she was following you! They only know what she told them, Tim. And they're not teenagers any longer. They're grown men, and have been for a while."

"You could be right, I guess," he admitted. "Pretty sad way to grow up. Chris still seemed like a good kid, you know? He knew his stuff when it came to yards and plants and he did a good job."

"Well, if the part he told us about moving the business all over the country was true, he's had a lot of experience. I'd like to know how long they were here, in Jade, before she showed up."

"You think she sent them here? How would she know where I am?"

"You think it's a coincidence? After twenty years of that woman hounding you? She knew you were here."

He thought about that, I could see him turning it over in his head.

"There's another thing," I said. "John said they worked for you, in Texas. On the tour. They must have hidden that from you."

Tim shook his head. "Not really, Muse. I don't know everyone on the tour, or the crew that sets up. I don't even know all the guys on this last shoot! There's technicians, electricians, lighting guys, sound guys, drivers – way too many for me to know personally. It's possible they worked the tour, I don't doubt what John said. Doesn't mean I knew them."

"I'll bet they knew you! You were the star! Wasn't one of your 'accidents' being electrocuted? Can't you see that is not a coincidence? They have been after you! With or without their mother, those boys have been watching you for quite a while." I sat back, confident I had solved at least part of the events from his past.

Tim stood up and stretched, picked up his cup and took it to the sink.

"All possible, babe. I admit that." Bending, he dropped a kiss on my nose. "Lawn still needs to be cut."

I sighed and sat back in my chair. "Will you do something for me?"

"Anything, Muse. Name it."

"Be careful. Please? It's one thing to have some dingy woman on your case. Two grown men and a dingy woman could be very dangerous. What if they're as fixated as she is? Just watch yourself, okay?"

"Intend to, babe. Already figured that part out. I'm gonna get out the mower."

"Be careful," I called to his back.

He turned around and grinned at me. "I can't mow the lawn in body armor, babe. Or carry a shotgun and the edger at the same time. I'll be fine. You can watch from the porch if you're worried."

"Smart ass," I said, softening it with a smile.

"And I can sing," he said with a wink and went out through the door to the garage.

Monday Tim headed back to LA for, hopefully, his last trip. The production company wanted one more photo shoot for the promotions tour. The apartment where Tim, Mark and Russ had stayed during the months in LA had to be cleaned out, which also meant Tim would be hauling more things home.

We were running out of room at the house.

Housing in Monarch began with small houses, many of them rustic cabins, where the people of the San Joaquin Valley escaped the brutal summers. For them even the brief respite of a weekend in the cool canyons and beaches was worth the drive.

Later it was the retirees from that same area that built along the shores of Monarch Bay. Jade Beach, to our north, had long been a community of fishermen and their families. As the retirees moved in they chose the smaller, quieter Monarch Beach to build their homes, most of those small one bedroom places.

My aunt's property, the three houses on an oversized lot had originally belonged to a retired fisherman from Jade. He built the largest of the three, the one I occupied, for himself and his wife. The two facing houses were for his son and his family, and the smallest one, the one occupied by Miss Ellie, was for his mother.

My house, and the mirror image across the drive that John lived in, were quite large for the time they were built. Both had two stories with two bedrooms and a bath upstairs, a luxury at the time.

Still, the rooms were small, large enough for a double bed, dresser and night stand. Even a queen size bed would be a tight fit.

For me and two cats it was perfect. For me and Tim and two cats it was getting a little snug, and he still had things to add. Just from LA. What about Texas? I had no idea what he had back there in the other houses he owned.

Might be time to look for storage space.

Beach Storage nestled on a couple of acres between Monarch and Jade. That might be a good idea for our extra stuff, things like Christmas decorations, and Tim's extra recording equipment. Something to think about when he got home.

I wrote myself a note, knowing how wonky my memory can be, and headed to Kelly's, rewarding myself with pot roast and veggies, the Monday special.

When I got to the diner Sharon was in her usual booth and I joined her.

"Where's Tim?" The first thing she said to me. "Are the videos out yet?" The second thing.

"LA and no idea. He'll let us know the release date."

"Why is he back in LA? I thought he was done?"

Sally came down the aisle with the coffee pot and filled Sharon's cup.

"Back up, and start over," she said. "I don't want to miss anything."

"Nothing to miss, Sally," I told her. "Tim went back to LA for a couple of days. Some kind of photo shoot, then he has to help clean out the apartment they stayed in. Should be home in a few days."

"When does the promo tour start? For the CD and the men's products. Mark said that was coming up right after they finished shooting the videos."

I had no idea Sally was that close to Mark although I wasn't surprised. That woman knows everyone in town, their parentage and their history. She is the encyclopedia of Monarch Beach.

"Next week I think," I answered. "I want the special and iced tea, please."

242

"Got it, and you? Are you eating or just taking up oxygen?"

"Same," Sharon told her, finishing her coffee and shoving the cup away.

Sally went to place the orders.

"You know anything about storage?" I asked Sharon, once Sally had brought our tea.

"Like what? Closets? Organizers?"

"No, the kind you rent. Those little room things."

"Oh, okay. Yes, I know about storage facilities. The one here, Beach Storage, is down by the beach, obviously. The manager is an ex-marine or something military. They have an excellent reputation since she took it over. Before that, it was pretty much a den of thieves."

"So it's safe? Now?"

"Everything I've heard lately has been positive. Why? What are you going to store?"

"We're outgrowing the house," I replied. "Tim has a lot of stuff and he's bringing up more. And that's not counting the stuff he still has in Texas. Since the storage place is close, thought we might rent a place there, you know? Move the Christmas decorations, extra recording stuff and all the things we don't use often over there. It would still be close enough to get to quick if we need it."

"You know what would be better?"

"What?"

"Buy another place," she grinned. "I have a lot of them for sale."

Stepped in that one, I thought.

"You know that's up to Tim," I said.

"He can afford it! He could buy all of them!"

"You have to take that up with him."

"Why? You're married. You have as much say as he does. You really think he would tell you no? Seriously?"

"No, I don't think so. I also don't think he would like for me to make decisions without him. He's kinda proud of being head of the household."

Sally came up, delivering plates of pot roast, potatoes and veggies.

"I think he makes a good one," she put in, sliding the plates into position. "Wouldn't mind having him take over my household. Shoot, he could sit around the house and hold me all he wanted." She laughed at her own joke.

"You know he has a single brother, right?"

"Yes, I did know that," Sally answered. "I'm looking forward to his visit."

"He's coming to visit?" Sharon was interested.

"I have no clue," I said, raising my hands in defeat. "I'm sure at some time he'll be up. I mean, he is family."

"When he does, I'm looking forward to it," Sally said, turning for the front. "I want me a Tanner."

"So do I," Sharon chuckled.

"You do know you're talking about my husband, right? With me sitting right here?"

"I do," Sally called back over her shoulder.

"Of course," Sharon said. "Did you think we were talking about Brad Pitt?"

Shaking my head, I took a long drink of iced tea.

With a sigh Sharon leaned on her elbows and lowered her voice.

"Honey, it's not your husband we want. It's what you have in your husband."

"That makes no sense at all," I said, taking a bite of mashed potatoes and gravy.

She sighed and leaned back. "It's not Tim," she explained, "although he is hot, I'll tell you that. It's the way he looks at you that we want. We'd probably be happy with Rip Van Winkle if he looked at us like Tim looks at you. The way he watches you, touches you every chance he gets, the complete closeness you two have even right now, with him in LA. You are so secure in each other. I don't completely buy that talk inside your head thing, whatever it is. What I do see is his attention to you, always on you."

She pulled her plate over and sprinkled it with pepper. "I can't explain it, Tee. I guess it's jealousy. We want what you have, not who you have."

"I get it," I said, "and thank you."

How do you respond to that? Everyone wants that kind of relationship, don't they? I knew exactly how lucky I was to have it and I valued it. Discussing it? I don't think so.

With the leftovers of my pot roast boxed up and in a bag on the passenger seat I decided to go check out the storage facility myself, before I suggested it to Tim.

It's only a few minutes from anywhere in Monarch to anywhere else in Monarch so I was at the storage facility in just minutes.

The tan buildings with dark brown trim spread in orderly rows behind an automatic gate that looked secure enough to keep out a dinosaur.

The office was bright and clean, fresh with lots of green plants. The walls were hung with seascapes and waterfront paintings. Classical music played softly in the background. The woman behind the counter put aside a Kindle and stood to extend her hand.

She was tall and slender, with short cropped blond hair and beautiful pale blue eyes, like Paul Newman. She appeared to be mid-thirties. Her grip was strong without being painful.

"Hello, can I help you?"

"I hope so," I said, shaking her hand. "I wanted to get some information about storage."

She picked up a bright green brochure from a stack on the counter and handed it to me.

"This is our price list, which will give you an idea of the expense. I can also guarantee that you'll have more to store than you think you do. I also suggest you rent a size larger than you think you need. All rents are due on the first and we have a late fee if not paid by the tenth of the month. If you do not pay your rent as agreed, we will sell your belongings. I think that covers it." She pointed to the brochure in my hand. "On the back you will find some tips for storing your belongings that might be of help. Is there anything else?"

"I think that covers it," I said. "Thank you."

"You are very welcome," she smiled. "If you are interested, I can put you on a waiting list. Our vacancies are usually around the first of the month."

"I'll have to talk to my husband first," I said. "I will let you know, though, and thanks again."

"Any time," she said and sat back down, picking up the Kindle. "We're open seven days a week. The hours are on the brochure. My name is Rayme West, I'm the manager here. I hope to see you again soon."

I went back to the truck and headed for home.

When Tim called that night I told him about my idea with the storage.

"Good idea, Muse! I know I've been taking up a lot of room already."

"That's fine, Tim, I don't mind. It's just that we're running out of space. Even with shelves you put in the garage it's getting pretty tight around here. This lady says we have to go on a waiting list if we decide we want to rent a unit."

"No problem there. Have her put us on the list now."

"What size? They come in all sizes."

"Medium? You know what, I'll go over and talk to her when I get home. Maybe she can show us one, give us an idea."

"Okay. I'll put the brochure on the desk. How's it going there?"

"Good. We have a studio shoot tomorrow, then cleaning out the apartment. That shouldn't be more than a day, day and a half. Have to pick up a new truck. Tired of riding with Mark."

Tim's truck had been declared a total loss by the insurance company. Between driving mine at home, and riding with Mark to LA he was ready for his own again.

"So you'll be home by the weekend?"

"Oh, yeah, should be, babe. Saturday at the latest, good Lord willing and the creek don't rise."

I laughed, loving his voice in my ear. "You can swim any creek that comes along," I told him. "I have faith in you."

"I can get to you if the whole Pacific Ocean drops in," he said softly.

I had a quick flash of Sharon's words this afternoon. "I know, Hubs," I said. "I know."

Tuesday evening I ate a light supper, cleaned the kitchen and curled up on the couch with the new Louise Penny mystery. She is a favorite author and I had looked forward to it all day.

Naturally, the minute I got comfortable, someone knocked on the door.

I got up and opened it to find John.

"Come on in," I said, gesturing to the living room. "Would you like some tea? A beer?"

He sat in an armchair and stretched out his legs, much like Tim does when he's home.

"I would love a cup of tea if it's not too much trouble. The fog is in early and it's damp."

"Just be a minute," I said, and went to the kitchen, turning the stove on under the kettle and getting down the teapot and cups.

"What's going on?" I asked, leaning against the door frame while the water boiled.

"Long day," he sighed. "One of those that just never seems to end."

"I've had my share of those," I said, remembering the long tedious hours of chemo.

"Where's Tim?"

"He's in LA," I answered. "Winding up things down there."

"When did he leave?"

"Monday morning. Why?"

It was not like John to be concerned about Tim's whereabouts.

Before he could answer the kettle whistled and I went to get the tea. Placing the teapot and cups on a tray I carried it to the living room and set it on the coffee table.

"Have you seen the Martinez woman?" John leaned forward and accepted his tea. He smelled it and took a sip. "I love tea," he said with a sigh. "I don't know why I don't drink more of it."

"I drink a lot of it," I smiled. "Hot and cold. Too much caffeine to drink coffee all the time." I sat back with my cup. "No, I haven't seen Lurlene. Why? Is she up to something again?"

He sighed again.

"She's missing."

That got my attention right quick.

"Missing? Says who?"

"She never showed up for work on Monday, never got home Monday night. Bill came in with Ray this afternoon and filed a report."

"Ray? The son?"

"Uh-huh, the older one. Bill has been seeing her. He's close to the boys, too. Bill said he took her to San Luis Sunday for a movie and supper. He took her home about nine Sunday night, stayed for a bit, then left. Last anyone saw her."

"What about her sons? Don't they live together?"

"Yeah. In the same house. Ray was out till late, and the other one, Chris, went to bed early. Had to work Monday. He heard her come in, didn't get up."

"Tim was home Sunday night," I said firmly. "He was here, with me, all night. We went to bed early because he had to be up early to leave for LA. Mark picked him up here."

"Whoa, Tee, slow down. I didn't accuse him of anything."

"Not yet," I snapped. "Who else have you talked too? You just assume Tim did something."

"No, that's not true. I'm just doing my job. Tim has a history with that woman. I wanted to know if she has been bothering him, or you. That's all I asked."

He leaned forward and refilled his cup.

"No, and no," I told him, setting my cup on the table. "To the best of my knowledge we haven't had any contact with her, not since the last time we were at the Gem together. That was several weeks ago."

"She hasn't been here around the house? At the Gem?"

"I haven't seen her, John. Not since that night at the Gem when we had our little run in."

"The hair thing?"

"Yes. That was it."

"You didn't do anything about that? Call the beauty shop? File a complaint?"

"No, why would I? Tim had the lady at the compound fix it, and she did a lot better job than Lurlene ever could."

"I agree," he smiled. "It's really lovely, and as a rule, I don't notice women's hair. It shimmers, like water."

"Thank you," I smiled. "I had my say with her, John, and it's done. I don't carry a grudge and why would I? Like you said, my hair came out on the plus side."

He stretched over and set his cup on the table. "It looks great," he said again. "So, no other problems with her? She hasn't been following Tim? Harassing him? No hanging around the neighborhood?"

"No, not at all. Not that I know of."

"Okay, then. I have to ask, Tee. The son, Ray, insists she was seeing Tim."

"Really? I thought she was seeing Bill. The last couple of times I saw her she was with him."

John shook his head. "That is one wacko family," he said. "Just between us. That's not the official stance. According to Ray, she has been seeing Bill and that made Tim jealous. She was worried about his jealousy getting out of hand. Again, according to him. She told him she was beginning to be afraid of Tim. Said Tim was following her."

"That's horse hockey! There is no way he was following her! When he's home we do everything together! When would he have time to follow her? No way. Didn't happen."

"Didn't say it did, Tee. Cool off. I've read the file on her, a couple of times. I don't believe Tim had anything to do with her. Much as I hate to admit it, you two are pretty solid. Can't see him with anyone else. The thing is the son has filed a missing persons report. Bill signed it, too. They both listed Tim as a person of interest. Right now, we need to find her."

"Did you call Tim? Ask him?"

John looked me in the eye. "No. I didn't. Before you snap at me, I didn't because I don't think he has seen her, or had anything to do with her. As part of my job, I have to ask. You notice I didn't make an official request. I stopped by on my way home. As a friend. Not as a cop."

"Thanks, John," I said with a smile. "I'm glad to hear it."

"Don't get me wrong, Tee," he returned with a smile. "Doesn't mean I like him."

I laughed. "Oh, you might surprise yourself, John."

"Not gonna go that far. Not yet. Still, the guy is likable. And honest. I've checked him ten ways from Sunday. He's clean. Respected. On the other hand, Martinez has a file three inches thick that goes way back, through four different states. She's on record, and none of it positive."

"What about the guy she was dancing with? Have you talked with him?"

"The guy from the Gem? Not yet. He was part of that production crew. Haven't found him yet. Still checking with agents and people in the industry, those that were hired for that shoot."

"Ask Sharon or Sally. They might know his name. They got to know quite a few of the people on the set."

"On my list," he smiled, standing up and stretching. "Thanks for the tea."

"You are always welcome. You're one of the few who enjoys hot tea," I said, standing up and following him to the door. "I'm always happy to see you."

"Thanks again, Tee," he said, his dark eyes warm. "You might ask Tim if he's seen Lurlene. She disappeared around the same time Tim went south. Maybe she just took off, following him again. Tell him to keep his eyes open, just in case she's on his trail."

"Will do," I said. "I hope that's not the case. That woman is bizarre."

"She is that," he agreed. "We'll find her. In the meantime, you be careful. Keep the house locked up."

"Always do," I smiled. "Tim's instructions."

With a little salute he left, waiting till he heard the lock click before I heard him go down the steps and head home.

I leaned against the door for a second before picking up the tray and carrying it back to the kitchen.

I admit I wondered if she had followed Tim to LA. If she was even now trying to get into his room. Wouldn't be the first time. I would not be surprised to find she was there, in LA, or somewhere in southern California, although it did seem she would tell her sons if she was leaving town.

Plus, her job. She had been working for Tiffany for about a month, not long enough for vacation. She surely would have called in sick if she was just taking a day off.

Turning off the lights I let the cats lead the way upstairs. Time to call Tim.

Talking to Tim always made me feel better, even if it was only for a few minutes.

I told him about John's visit, which set him off.

"Why doesn't he just call me? He has my number."

"He just stopped in on his way home," I answered. "I'm only telling you, so you'll know what's going on. In case he does call. He told me he didn't think you were involved."

"Does he really think I would even talk to that woman?"

"No, I don't think so. It's part of his job, Tim. He has to ask questions. He said the older boy had filed a missing person report. Think about it. If you were missing she would be the first one I would suspect. You can't blame him for asking. And he came here, instead of calling me to the station. He also said you should watch for her down there, in case she just followed you. She may be down there where you are."

"He can call me, or he can wait till I get home." I could almost hear his jaw set over the phone. "He can stay out of the house when I'm gone."

"Which brings me to the next question. When are you coming home?"

"Friday for sure, maybe Thursday. The apartment is going to take at least a day, even with all three of us working on it. Then I have to get a truck. I don't like having to ask Mark or Russ for a ride every time I want a snack. Did you call the storage place today?"

"No, I will. I just don't know what size we want."

He thought for a minute. "Something big," he said. "I'm gonna have some of Mark's stuff, too."

Oh goody. "Define big."

Tim chuckled. "About the size of the garage. We can always go smaller once we get stuff sorted."

"Or fill it up," I smiled, even though he couldn't see me. "That too, babe."

We talked a little longer, about his day, and hung up.

I gathered my Kindle and got into bed, wondering how much stuff of Mark's we were going to have. And how long we were going to have it. Maybe Monarch Beach was the future compound for the Tanner clan.

I called the storage place and put our name on the waiting list the first thing Thursday morning, knowing that my memory can take a dump without warning.

Tim would be home tonight or tomorrow and I wanted everything ready when he arrived. The laundry was done, the house was clean. He had done the lawn before he left.

Chris had still not made an appearance, nor had we heard from him. I assumed our days of full yard service were finished.

Evidently it was up to me to plant the bluebonnet seeds that resided in a drawer in the kitchen. One more thing on my To Do list.

Tim was home late Thursday, with a new truck, a white Ford 150 pickup exactly like the previous one. The back was fully loaded, tarped and tied down. I cringed at where all this was going to go.

We were up so late Thursday night we slept in Friday morning. I had stocked the kitchen while he was gone, so I made a full breakfast of Tim's favorites – sausage and gravy, biscuits and scrambled eggs.

While we ate he sorted mail that had come in over the last couple of days.

"We have to go over to the boat yard in Jade. You know where it is?"

"Yep, sure do. Just the other side of the storage facility. Down by the pier. What's at the boat yard? Are we buying a boat?"

"No, babe. That's where they towed the truck, the wrecked one. I have to go claim any personal belongings and sign off on it. It's salvage now."

"As long as we're out, we can go by the storage place and you can take a look."

He stood up and pushed in his chair. "Deal," he said. "I'll get my boots."

The boat yard in Jade Beach has been there forever. At one time, before the sanctions on fishing, the harbor had been an active, busy fishing port, with lots of commercial fishing boats anchored in the safe bay.

Marine materials and repairs were a big business in those days, the boat yard the center of a bustling trade. Now, it was home to several charter boats and sports fishing boats, the fleet of fishing vessels having moved north to the shores of Washington state and Alaska.

Tim went in to the office and returned a short time later with a rotund little man in overalls, sporting a captain's cap aboard a full head of white hair.

Tim gestured and I hopped out and joined them.

We followed the gentleman's directions to the back wall, where we found Tim's truck backed into a parking space, the rear gate up against a block wall fence.

The nose of the truck was shoved in, dented into a curve where it had met the tree going over the side and sliding down the hill. The windshield was cracked behind the sprung and bent hood. Inside the cab the air bags dangled limply from the dashboard.

Tim went around and popped open the passenger door so he could empty the glove compartment into a couple of tote bags we had brought with us.

The ban on plastic bags in our county meant everyone owned at least half a dozen cloth carriers.

He loaded up the bags, felt around under the seat, tilted it forward and checked behind it. A pair of flip flops and two pairs of rolled up socks went into the tote.

"I think that's it, babe. You see anything else?"

"Nope. Why the socks?"

"Beach," he grinned. "Didn't want sand in my shoes."

He shut the door and went around to the rear of the pickup, leaning over the side to look in the bed. Dead leaves and small branches littered the floor. A couple of Pepsi cans were crushed up in the corner. Must be a gift from the towing guys. Tim never drinks Pepsi.

Tim edged between the truck and the wall and pulled out his phone, taking several pictures of the bumper sticker right in the center of the bumper.

"Do you really think that marked your truck?"

"Have to admit it makes sense, "he grinned at me. "Don't have to admit John was right. The insurance company wanted a picture of it. Now which way to the storage place?"

At the storage office we were told a large unit would be ready on Saturday by twelve so Tim filled out the contract, paid for three months plus the deposit and a lock.

Back at home, it seemed silly to unload his truck only to load it back up the next day to take to storage. Tim checked the tie downs and backed the truck up close to the garage door.

After breakfast Saturday Tim began to bring things down from the guest room closet, things he had stored there while he was in residence. The entry was full by the time he left to go unload his truck at the storage facility.

He spent Saturday afternoon and early evening moving things to storage. He made several trips, emptying a lot of the upstairs closet, and most of the garage, keeping just his guitars at home.

Tim and guitars were like me and books – he never met one he didn't like. He had spent one evening explaining the difference to me, in tone, feel, and resonance. I didn't get it. I did, however, understand the compulsion of just one more. Witness my full bookshelves.

We were fortunate the marine layer had kept the day cool while he was loading and moving and unloading. I put on a pot of soup to simmer all day, not sure when he would be finished and made two loaves of bread.

It was dark by the time he finished up his last load. We ate, cleaned up, and put on a movie he had bought in LA. We were in bed by eleven.

Sunday morning we lingered over coffee, having put away a huge breakfast, the only kind Tim likes.

We had been talking about the three weeks he was going to be gone with the promo tour, hitting fifteen cities in three weeks, when John called my cell phone and invited us to the station.

"What the hell does he want?" Tim groused. "He lives across the drive for crying out loud. He can't just walk over here?"

"He's at the station, Hubs," I soothed.

"So? Is he going to move there? Is he locked in a cell?"

Picking my keys from the hook I walked around him to the front.

"Are you through?"

He shook his head. "I am having a talk with that guy."

I sighed. "Tim, it has be official for him to call us down to the station."

He got up and followed me out to my truck, still grumbling under his breath. I was pretty glad I couldn't understand his words.

The police station in Monarch was the Union Hall in the forties. The lobby is small, more of a vestibule, with a counter to the left as you go through the double doors. Straight ahead is a regular door, with a small glass pane in the top center.

The officer on duty must push a release button for that door to open, and that gives you access to the larger duty room. Through that door another counter is to the left and behind that are the desks, filing cabinets, desks with lamps and computers. To the right is a row of old fashioned, wooden, folding chairs, the kind with the slatted backs. That passes for a waiting room.

Further down the aisle is a short corridor that leads to the interrogation rooms and a couple of small offices, one of which is John's. I've been there before, can you tell?

We stepped up to the front counter and I gave the guy on duty our names. I told him Detective Kincaid was expecting us. He looked down at a paper we couldn't see, and directed us to take a seat in the waiting area where Detective Kincaid would come get us when he was ready.

He pushed the buzzer releasing the door, and in we went.

And all hell broke loose.

When the buzzer sounded, Tim opened the door and stood to the side so I could precede him. I went through, automatically turning to the left, to the second counter.

Tim followed right behind.

We were both looking to the left, expecting another officer at this counter.

Behind us a guy waiting in one of the wooden chairs exploded up, turning the air blue with his cussing.

Without warning he reached behind him, caught the chair and hurled it – right into the back of Tim's head.

Tim went to his knees, barely catching himself before his face hit the floor.

I didn't think.

I looked down, saw Tim on his knees, blood beginning to run down the side of his neck and drip onto the floor. I grabbed the chair by the slatted back and slung it right straight back at the guy who threw it.

The chair caught him right in the face, the crack of his nose breaking audible, blood gushing from his nose onto his shirt, the floor and the chair.

He howled like a wounded moose.

Other cops were there, from everywhere.

One bent to Tim, another grabbed my arms and turned me towards the counter, pressing me against it while pulling my arms behind me.

Tim threw off the guy helping him up and grabbed the one holding me and pitched him back down the aisle.

Two more grabbed Tim, bending him down and trying to cuff his hands behind him, while he tried to fight them off. I kicked at one of them, adding my own yelling to the mix, and the guy behind me shoved me hard, smearing the blood from his bloodied hands all over my shirt.

I bounced off the counter with a stapler in my hand and went for the bloody guy who was kicking at Tim although not connecting.

A shrill whistle split the air, causing all of us to freeze in position.

John was there, giving orders and shouting at the officers.

He caught my arm with one hand and pulled me back to his side, getting me clear of the action that was now frozen.

He threw me a quick glance. "Stay Tee! Right there!"

"I am not a dog, and I will not be yelled at like one."

I charged around him, trying to get to Tim, who was down on his knees, attempting to get up from the floor.

"Tee! Now! Get back! Don't make me cuff you."

His hand around my bicep tightened. He tugged me back again.

I took a deep breath and blew it out.

"Tim is hurt," I told him. "Get him some help."

Another officer bent over Tim, helping him to his feet again.

Two rivulets of blood ran down Tim's neck, from underneath his hair to the collar of his sweat shirt, which was soaking it up in splotches.

"Enough!" John roared.

Things settled a little as two officers dealt with the bloody nose guy, whose face was swathed in paper towels held in place by one of the cops. The other poured water from a bottle and swabbed at the guy's chin and neck.

Tim was upright, with the help of a third officer.

John still held me by the arm. He turned to look at me. "Are you all right?"

"I'm fine, dammit! Tim's hurt! Call an ambulance!"

Two firemen had joined us from the Fire Department next door. One of them was swabbing at Tim's neck while the other checked his head.

"All right," John said, finally letting me go. "Get these guys to emergency. In separate cars! I'll be right behind you."

The two firemen took Tim out through the front. I heard the door buzzer and saw him led out.

FLASH
Are you okay?
Fine. You're hurt. Go with them.
I'm all right Muse.
You're bleeding, babe. I'll meet you at emergency.
You're sure you're okay?
I'm fine. Go! I'll be right there.
See you there, babe.

Yes, you will.

"Come on," John said, taking my arm again. "Let's get you out of here."

I watched two officers, one on each side, escort the guy with the bloody nose, his face still packed with paper towels, the whole front of his shirt stained dark with blood.

The firemen were cleaning the floor with more paper towels and red rags.

John guided me out the front door. On the sidewalk he turned me around and looked me over, tilting my head left and right.

"You sure you're okay?"

"I'm fine, John! Let's go. I want to see Tim!"

"Slow down, Tee! We're going, all right? My truck is back here."

He led me around the corner, through the chain link gate, to where his truck was parked. He beeped it open before we reached it and helped me in.

On our way he glanced over at me. "With a chair? Dang, girl! You nailed that guy!"

"He deserved it! Did you see him hit Tim! Without warning! He just hit him for no reason!"

"Easy, girl." He checked traffic and turned toward the emergency center. "That was Ray Martin."

I paused in my rant. Ray Martin?

"Lurlene's son?

"That's him."

"Did you find her?"

"No, not yet."

"So what's his problem? He slammed that chair at Tim! For no reason!"

262

"We'll talk later, Tee."

"About what? What did you call us down there for? You set him up!"

"No I didn't! You best slow down or we're going right back to the station."

I took a deep breath and blew it out. In my lap my hands were shaking. I clenched them together until they stopped.

John pulled up at the emergency center and I was out the door by the time the truck quit rolling. He called something to me but all I wanted right now was Tim. I was through the doors, leaving him to follow.

I passed the lobby and went straight back to emergency, being well acquainted with it by now.

I found Tim easily by following his voice. He could be heard for a block.

I pushed back the curtain and stepped into his cubicle, going straight to his side. The nurse shot me a look and recognized me from previous trips. She went back to cleaning Tim's wound.

"He's going to need some stitches," she told me. "It's not that bad, just a laceration. He'll have a headache for a few days. The doctor will be right in."

Tim's hand reached for me and squeezed.

"You're sure you're all right?"

"I'm fine, Tim," I replied, squeezing his hand in return.

"Please hold your head still," cautioned the nurse.

I took up a position at the end of the examining table where he sat, keeping his hand in mine.

"He all right?" was the first thing John asked when he joined us.

"He'll need a few stitches," the nurse replied. "I'm going to have to shave a little of this hair. The doctor may want a CAT scan to check for concussion. That's why he's the doctor," she smiled. "We'll wait to see what he says." She stepped out, pulling the curtain back.

"You set me up," Tim accused John, his eyes going cold.

"I didn't do squat," John told him, pulling a stool around and seating me at the foot of the table, so I could still hold onto Tim.

"That was Ray," I told Tim, sitting down. "The guy that hit you."

"Who the heck is Ray? I don't know Ray! Oh." I saw it sink in. "Lurlene's son?"

"The one and only," John put in. "That's why I called you guys down, so you could see what he looks like. I had questions, too, just thought it would be a good idea for you to know what he looks like. He was there to see if we found his mom."

"Did you find her?" I asked.

"No," John said, looking over at Tim. "We found her car."

The nurse chose that time to step back inside, rattling the curtain as a warning of her presence. With a pair of scissors she clipped some of Tim's hair, catching it as it fell and tossing it in the waste basket. He flinched a couple of times but was otherwise silent while she worked on him.

When she finished she stepped back and assured us once again the doctor would be right with us before she slid outside the curtain.

As soon as she flipped the curtain back, Tim looked at John. "You found the car? Her car?"

"Yeah," John nodded. "You're sure you haven't seen her? Maybe took a minute to talk to her?"

Tim sighed. "I gotta tell you, Sherriff John, sometimes you irk the snot out of me. No. I have not seen her. Or talked to her. Or even smelled her. What's going on? Can you just tell us without all the cops and robbers stuff? If I was guilty of an overdue book fine you'd be all over it. I'm innocent, bud, like it or not."

John grinned at Tim. "You're right about that, Cowboy. This is something different altogether."

"Are you ever gonna tell us what happened?"

John pulled his cell phone out of his pocket, thumbed it a couple of times and held it up for Tim to see. "This is her car," he said. "We found it off the road, into some bushes, on the road to the lake. Looks like it was run off the road. The driver's door is locked and the window is busted out. Someone went in after her."

"And the first thing you do is assume it was me," Tim shook his head. "Why? Why would I go after her? I don't want her!"

"Easy, Tex, I'm doing my job. I did not accuse you of anything."

"Please turn off your cell phone," said Nursie, coming back around the curtain. "Cell phones must be turned off while inside the building." She shot me a look at the same time. I let go of Tim long enough to raise my empty hands.

The woman that followed her was obviously said doctor. She had that no nonsense air about her as she stepped up to pull on gloves and probe Tim's head.

"Ow," he howled. "That hurts."

Using both hands, she separated his hair, peering at his scalp. She prodded his head a few times, eliciting one more yelp before she stepped back and snapped off the gloves.

"Your x-rays are clear, show no internal bleeding. I think you'll be fine. You may have a headache for a few days. I'll send a few pain pills with you if it gets too bad, otherwise ibuprofen. If your vision blurs, or the headache lasts more than two days, come back and we'll check it again." Turning to the nurse she said, "Sutures", and snapped on another pair of gloves.

The nurse held out a tray with scissors, needles and thread and I looked away. I held John's warm brown gaze while the women worked on Tim. He seemed to understand how I felt about needles, giving me a small smile and a thumbs up when they were finished.

"That does it, Mr. Tanner," said the doctor, snapping off the second set of gloves. "I would suggest you take better care of your skull. This is the second time this month you've been in here with head injuries. It's not a rock, Mr. Tanner. It will crack if you continue to pound on it."

"For the record, doc, I didn't hit myself in the head. Or run into a wall on purpose. Thank you, ma'am. I will try to follow your advice." He looked over at John. "For the official record, I will shoot the next jackass that hits me in the head."

"Can't say that in my presence, Tim. Terrorist threat. I'll have to take you in," John said with a grin.

"Oh, okay, let me define that for you," Tim said slowly, enunciating each word. "I will shoot the next yahoo that hits me in the head."

"So noted," John smiled at him. "Next shooting, I know who to pick up."

The nurse managed a bandage on the back of Tim's head, then wound some gauze to hold it in place. "Keep it clean," she told him, stepping back. "Wear a shower cap for a few days to keep it dry. If you have any problems return to the ER. Doctor has given you these pills which should help with the pain. The instructions are on the envelope. There's a few papers for you to sign and you're free to go."

Tim scooted off the table and took a couple of shaky steps. I got in under his arm and helped him till he got his balance. John followed us to the front desk where Tim signed papers in half a dozen places. He thanked the lady at the desk then headed for the doors.

"Slow down, Cowboy," John called from behind us. "You're with me."

Tim stopped and looked down at me. I nodded. He sighed.

"My head hurts too bad to roll my eyes," he told me, and I knew he was all right.

"Stay here, I'll get my truck," John said at the door, jogging around to the right.

"Are you sure you're okay?" Tim's first question when John was out of sight. He reached to cup a hand around the back of my neck and tug me close. I resisted laying my head on his chest with all the blood on it, vowing to throw it away as soon as we got home.

"I'm fine, Hubs. How about you? You really okay?"

"Getting sick and tired of these headaches," he admitted, "but yeah, I'm okay."

We stood together, his arm around my shoulders, and waited for John.

When we reached home John helped Tim into the house while I went straight to the kitchen to put on some coffee, being pretty sure the last thing Tim needed would be a beer.

Tim settled at the table, mumbled a thanks to John and watched John take a seat across from him.

"Now, what's this about the car?"

John pulled out his cell again, thumbed it, and handed it over to Tim. I leaned in over his shoulder to see the screen.

The picture was a shot of the driver's side window of a blue car, the color showing in the metal around the window frame. The glass was shattered, only a few beads visible in the lower corners.

Through the window bits of glass glittered like diamonds, covering the driver's seat, even some on the passenger's seat and sprinkled on the floorboards.

John thumbed the screen again, and a second photo showed the base of the car door, the same blue color, the same empty window.

On the ground beneath the door frame was a glove, what looked like a typical leather work glove. The glove was partly under the car so not really clear, the curled fingers almost beckoning.

The next shot John thumbed up was the rear of the car, showing the license plate number and the way the car was pulled to the side of the road, not quite off the pavement, the nose angled in towards the brush.

"Where is this?" Tim asked, having looked at all the pictures.

"Loomis Drive," John answered. "The road to the lake."

"When did you find it?" I asked.

"Early this morning. Fishermen called it in around five. Anything else you see?"

I shook my head.

"What is it you want to know?" Tim asked.

I got up and filled three mugs with coffee and put them on the table with the cream pitcher.

John's turn to sigh. "That glove look familiar?"

"Looks pretty common," Tim said. "I have some like that, use them when I work in the yard."

"Where do you keep them?" John's voice had an edge as he watched Tim.

"I'll get them," I said, jumping up and going through to the garage.

Tim kept the garage much neater than I ever did. He had put up shelves and pegboard, mounted the tools to the wall where they were easy to find. The lower shelf held a couple of wire baskets where he tossed his gloves.

I flipped on the lights as I went in and walked straight to his work area. There was one glove on the wire basket. Only one.

I looked under the shelf, around the floor, even checked the other shelves.

One glove.

In a hurry, I checked all the shelves on both sides of the garage, even looked into the trash barrel.

One glove.

I picked it up and took it inside, closing the door behind me.

Both men looked at me as I came back into the kitchen. I held Tim's eyes, shaking my head slightly.

He sighed again, and leaned his head on one hand.

John looked up at me, his eyes asking the question.

I handed him the glove, the one glove.

He turned it in his hands before looking up at me. "The other one?"

"It's not there," I said, looking at Tim. "I checked all over the garage."

"I didn't do it," Tim said, still holding my eyes with his.

"I know," I said, taking my seat.

John's shoulders drooped as he drank some coffee.

"When's the last time you saw them?" John asked.

"Lord, I don't know," Tim answered, closing his eyes.

"John, can this wait? Look at him, he's worn out! He can't think with that lump on his head! Can't it wait till tomorrow?"

"Speaking of lumps on a head," John said, looking up at me. "You broke his nose and knocked out a couple of teeth. He was in the ER right down the hall from Tim."

I felt no remorse. "He deserved it!"

John laughed out loud. "I'm not gonna argue with that, Tee, but you really laid him out. He's threatening to sue."

"Let him sue! I have witnesses, police witnesses that saw the whole thing!"

"What are we talking about now?" asked Tim. "What witnesses?"

"Your dainty little wife busted Ray Martin's nose all over his face, not to mention he lost a couple of teeth and had a couple of stitches put in his bottom lip. He was two cubicles down from you at the ER."

"You did that?" Tim asked, looking at me with wondering eyes. "I heard it, didn't see what happened."

"She nailed him right in the face with the chair," John said, grinning. "Believe me, man, he got worse than he dealt out. She was taking him on with only a stapler when I got to her."

Tim's eyes lit up as he looked back at me. "Good job, babe. Proud of you." He held up his palm for a high five. I slapped his hand with mine, feeling my face blush.

"Let him sue, Muse," Tim chuckled. "Luke can take care of it. Be worth it to hear him testify a hundred and twenty pound woman took him out in a fight."

"Come by the office," John laughed with him. "It's all on tape. Video system picked it up. Chuck already texted me about the tape. One more item for the Teejay file."

"Oh, I want a copy of that," Tim laughed along with him.

John shook his head and stood up, taking his cup to the sink.

"You want some more coffee, John?"

"No, thanks, Tee. I'm ready for this day to be over. Tanner, get some rest. You will have to come into the station and give a statement. In case you're interested, the tape clearly shows Ray hitting you with that chair, first. He won't have a leg to stand on in court."

"Did she take out his legs, too?" Tim laughed.

John joined in and I let them have their laugh, glad they were laughing together, even if it was at my expense.

"I'll see you guys tomorrow," John said, heading for the front door. "I have to caution you, don't leave town, yada, yada, yada. You know the routine. We'll get back out there tomorrow, check the scene. Her car's been towed in already. It's at the storage yard. We do have to talk about this, and you'll have to sign a statement about the assault. It can wait a day or so."

"Thanks, John," I said, following him to the door. "For everything."

He paused and gave me a long look from those warm, chocolate eyes. "Be careful, Tee."

"I will, John. He didn't do it," I said.

"Never thought he did," John said, softly. "If I thought he had anything to do with it he'd be in jail. Lock up behind me."

"I'll be careful," I assured him.

He gave me a smile, and opened the door, his eyes still on mine.

The minute he swung back the door a series of pops, like firecrackers, went off and John flew past me, hitting the floor hard. I dropped to my knees beside him.

"John! Are you okay?"

"Get out of the door, Muse!" Tim was beside me, shoving me out of the doorway.

He hit the wall switch above us, turning off the lights and carrying me to the floor. The house was plunged into darkness, the only light coming from the kitchen behind us and a glow from the open door. He was covering me with his body, crushing me against the floor.

FLASH

Are you okay? Are you hit?

I'm okay, Tim. What happened? Is he hurt?

Not sure, babe. Ease over, next to the wall. I have to check him.

Be careful! What happened?

That was gunfire. I think he's hit, gotta check. Stay low. Can you get the lights in the kitchen?

Yes, on my way.

Stay low, babe.

With that he nudged me on my way.

272

I kept as low as I could, using my elbows to pull myself across the floor, bumping into a chair before I could reach the light switch. I lifted up enough to flip off the lights before dropping back to all fours. I crawled back to the entry, staying close to the wall.

In the dim light coming in the still open door I saw Tim scoot across the floor, heard John groan. In the dark it was hard to tell what was going on as I made my way back to the open front door, staying to the side, against the wall as Tim had instructed.

I could hear Tim talking softly to John. I scooted over enough to help him half slide, half roll John back in the house. He groaned when we moved him, so I knew he was alive.

When his legs were clear of the door, Tim kicked it shut, cutting off most of the light.

"Stay down, Muse. I'm gonna check the back."

"How bad is he?"

"Not sure, babe. He's alive. Can't tell till I can see him. Stay here. Let me check the back door. I'll grab a flashlight."

I heard him go past me towards the kitchen. My eyes were adjusting to the dim light coming in the front windows. John was just a form on the floor. I got to his side and felt around for his hand. When I found it, I grabbed it with both of mine and squeezed, wanting him to know he wasn't alone.

He gave me a little squeeze back and sighed.

"Are you okay?" I whispered.

He grunted and let go of my hand. "Does being pissed off count?" His voice was tight but strong.

I giggled, I hope from stress. "Works for me," I whispered back.

A bright beam of light hit John right in the eyes and he flinched away squeezing them shut.

"It's me, Muse," Tim said softly, putting his fingers over the lens of the flashlight, creating a weird reddish glow. He was bent at the waist, sliding along the wall behind me. He eased around me and knelt by John.

"Where you hit?" he asked, just as softly.

"Chest," John answered with barely a whisper. "Not too bad. Think it grazed me."

"You be okay while I check outside?"

"Yeah, my body broke my fall. Wait a second." I heard John shuffle around on the floor. "Here, take my gun. Don't shoot anyone unless you have to."

"Thanks, man. Try not to move. I'll be back."

Tim shone the dimmed red glow at the floor, which helped me track him back to the kitchen. Dave was right behind him, enjoying the new game. I hissed at him, trying to catch him but he was out of reach.

I heard the click of the back door and held my breath. Another soft click meant it was closed again. I hoped.

"Tee?" I heard John's quiet call.

Scooting on my butt, I managed to get beside John.

"Right here, John," I said, keeping my voice low. I reached out to pat his shoulder.

"You okay? Did you get hit?"

"No, I'm fine. Looks like you made someone mad," I said.

"Or someone is mad at Tim," he countered. "Hard to tell against the light."

I leaned in and took his hand.

274

"No offense," I whispered back, "I hope it was someone after you."

I heard his chuckle. "See how you are? Fickle woman."

I smiled in the dark and patted his shoulder again. "I told you I meant no offense."

"None taken, Tee." I felt him lift his shoulder, trying to turn to his side. He groaned.

"Wait, John. Tim will be back. He'll help you."

"I got it," he said tightly. "Give me a boost, huh? Help me sit up."

I moved around where I could use both hands to help lift him to a sitting position. Shifting my hands to support him I hit a slick, wet spot along his ribs. He groaned at the same time.

"Sorry," I said. I could feel something sticky on my hands.

"I'm good," he hissed.

Before I could answer we heard footsteps on the porch. John froze, his muscles going tight under my hands.

Something tapped against the door.

FLASH

Open the door, Muse.

I got to my feet and rushed to the door, unlocking it and throwing it open. Tim came through and caught me in his arms, crushing me against his chest. With one arm he reached for the door and shut it behind us.

"All clear," he said in a normal voice. "As far as I can tell."

He reached back and flipped the lights on before moving to kneel beside John.

I saw the blood smears all over the entry floor. Without thinking about it I went to the kitchen and grabbed some paper towels and a bottle of water. I ran water from the sink over a wad of the towels and wrung them out.

"Muse, call 911, get an ambulance," Tim said. "Leave that for now. Crime scene."

"No," John said. "No ambulance."

I joined the guys and handed Tim the roll of paper towels and the water.

He was trying to pull John's bloodied sweatshirt up so he could check his wound. In places it was stuck to his skin, causing him to grunt and cuss.

I opened a drawer in my desk and handed Tim some shears.

He quickly cut open the front of the shirt and peeled it back.

The left side of his chest clearly showed the wound, a small scarlet hole, a little smaller than a dime, just under the nipple. From there a deep purple line stretched around his ribs toward his back. His entire chest was smeared with blood, already turning brown.

"Easy," Tim said, tilting John to the side. "Muse, swab his ribs here," he indicated an almost circular patch on John's back.

Leaning around Tim, I poured some water on a wad of towels and carefully swabbed the area, trying not to do more harm.

As the blood rinsed away a small bump, about the size of a pencil eraser stuck out, right in the center of the discolored skin on his back.

"Careful, babe. I think that's the bullet. We've got to get him to the ER."

All during the examination John alternated cussing and grunting, his jaw clenched until the muscles stood out in relief. He struggled to get to his feet.

"Hold on, John," Tim said, getting to his feet. He bent and helped John stand. "Let's get you to the truck."

"It's okay," John argued, his voice thick. "Just help me home."

"No can do, man," Tim said, keeping a grip on John's arm. "The bullet is still there, under the skin. Make sure you don't lean back when we get you in the truck."

"I don't want to go to emergency!" John gritted his teeth with the effort.

"No choice, Big John," Tim grinned at him, helping him to the door. "Evidence. I would think as a cop you would know that."

John uttered a nasty word between his teeth.

"Grab your keys, babe," Tim grinned at me. "And put this gun somewhere out of sight. He can pick it up later."

He handed me the pistol John had given him.

I took it with two fingers and carried it to the kitchen, surprised at its weight. Where do you hide a gun? I opened the door to the microwave and put the gun inside before grabbing my keys from the hook on the wall.

I drove us back to the ER while Tim kept an arm around John, tipping him forward, to keep him from leaning back into the bullet.

"Don't snuggle," Tim warned him.

"You're loving this, aren't you," John said between his teeth.

"Sorry, big guy, I prefer my wife," Tim replied.

Of course, we got the same nurse that had just dealt with Tim's head. She had to wonder what the heck kind of people we were.

On the positive side the ER had all of John's medical info on file from his previous stay there when he was poisoned.

He was taken straight back while Tim and I took seats in the little waiting area.

On the negative side, the tiny coffee shop was closed.

After an hour or so a guy who looked like he wasn't old enough for a driver's license came out and told us they had removed the bullet and were stitching up John. He would be ready to leave shortly. The bullet had been recovered and given to John.

It was another hour before we collected John and headed home.

There were two squad cars at the house, one local and one CHP. An official pickup truck with the Sherriff's insignia on the door blocked the drive.

The front porch was decorated with yellow tape. A portable spot light lit up the whole yard, showing men moving around between the street and the porch.

Tim used the garage door opener to get us back into the house through the garage. John wanted to go home right away. Tim talked him into a cup of tea first, and helped him inside.

Once inside I put on the water while the guys opened the front door and talked to the officers there. I saw Officer Chuck long enough to wave, before turning to the kitchen.

We hadn't eaten so while the water heated I set a pan of bacon in the oven and got out the eggs, grating some cheese to make a semi omelet. I set the table while everything cooked.

By the time the guys came back in and took seats, I was dishing up fortified scrambled eggs, bacon and toast.

How anyone could get shot and eat was beyond me.

I had a piece of bacon and a slice of toast. Tim and John polished off every morsel on the table.

"Thanks, Tee," John said, leaning back in his chair, careful of his bandaged back. "That hit the spot."

"More tea?"

"No, thanks, I'm about ready to fall down. That anesthetic wore off and I hurt like hell. I just want to get down, get off my feet for a while."

Tim stood up to help him if necessary. "I have some of those pain pills they gave me for my head if you want one."

"They gave me some," John said, patting his pocket. "I just want to get to bed."

"You need help?"

"No, thanks. You had your chance. You're not getting in my bed."

Tim walked him out through the garage. Although the police had cleared out while we ate, Tim said the front porch was strung with yellow caution tape.

He walked John to his steps and waited until John's lights came on before I heard the garage door drop and he came back in the kitchen.

"More tea?"

"No, Muse, I'm whipped. My head hurts. We have got to quit these late nights," he smiled, stretching. "Leave this, I'll help clean it up tomorrow."

"Go on to bed," I said. "I'll toss these in the dish washer. Won't take a few minutes."

"All right, babe," he said, yawning widely. "Good job, tonight. Guess I'll keep you another day or two." His smile warmed me all the way to my toes.

"You're just afraid I'll hit you with a chair," I grinned at him, clearing the table.

"That was what I meant by good job," he grinned back.

Cletus' growl woke me the next morning, a sure sign someone was outside. I eased out of bed and grabbed my robe, leaving Tim to sleep. There were dark circles under his eyes, almost as dark as the bruises had been.

Looking out the window I saw a squad car at the curb. A van with the county seal on the side was parked across the street, its red lights blinking off and on.

Officer Chuck, arms folded across his chest, was talking to John in the middle of my lawn. They were both looking at my porch.

I dressed quickly and went down to make coffee.

Knowing the guys would be hungry and probably tired of bacon and eggs, I got out the trusty box of Bisquik and whipped up a dough that I pressed into the biggest pan I had. Dotting it with butter I shook brown sugar and cinnamon over the whole thing and shoved it in the oven.

While it baked I fried up some sausage patties and set them to drain.

There was a light tap at the front door. I hurried to open it before it woke Tim, and admitted John.

"Morning," he said. "Tex still sleeping?"

"Yeah, how do you feel?"

"Sore," he said. "Smelled the coffee."

"Sit down," I said, getting out another cup. "What about Officer Chuck?"

"He's on duty," he groaned as he took a seat, reaching around to lift his arm. "What is that smell?" He sniffed the air.

"Coffee cake," I answered, sliding his coffee across the table. "What are you doing out so early? Shouldn't you be resting?"

"Rather know who took those shots, and why. Not to mention at who. Tee, this is serious. Someone is trying to kill old Tex. I thought so before and now I'm pretty sure of it. That guy's had too many close calls. He's gonna run out of lives pretty soon."

I took the coffee cake out of the oven and set it to cool while I scrambled some eggs.

"Did you find anything?"

"Dug three more bullets out of the woodwork. That's it so far. No footprints across the street, nothing that can be identified. The gravel there, the dead leaves and all the other stuff, doesn't take prints. Could have been someone over there, in the trees, could have been from a car. Did you hear anything?"

"Just those pops. Like firecrackers. Then you hit the floor."

"How many did you hear?"

I thought for a minute. "Four or five, John. I'm not sure. It happened so fast. Really, when you hit the floor that was all I saw, or heard. I was trying to see what happened to you."

"Morning, Muse," said another voice and Tim wandered in to take a seat at the table. "Morning, John Law. How's the chest?"

"Sore. How's the head?"

"Sore. Thanks, babe," he said, when I slid him a plate of sausage and eggs. "To what do we owe the honor?"

"Have to talk to you," John said. "Like it or not, there are steps I have to follow. A woman is missing. Search parties are looking for her as we speak, been out there since dawn. Someone shot at this house. Someone is after you seriously trying to take you out."

"I've been right here, sound asleep," Tim interrupted.

"Okay, I still have to do my job. I have all kinds of paperwork to fill out. I have a woman missing. I have been shot. Your house has been shot up. By the way, your porch is gonna need some repairs. They're trying to get it cleared out now. So, let's get started. Where were you Saturday?"

"Right here. You could have looked out your window and seen me."

"I wasn't home, I was working. You were here all day?"

"Sort of. In and out. I moved a lot of our belongings to a storage facility. Over in Jade. Beach Storage."

"I know it. Were you with him?" John asked, looking at me.

"Nope. I was home. I packed up stuff while he moved it. You know, brought it downstairs, taped up boxes, that kind of stuff."

"In other words, you have no alibi for Saturday."

"When did she go missing?" Tim scooted his plate to the side and pulled his coffee cup closer. "Thanks, babe that was delicious. You found the car Saturday night?"

"Early Sunday. Couple of guys going fishing found it. They saw it on the side of the road, window busted out, and stopped to see if someone needed help. They looked around a little bit, then called it in. Chuck was the first on the scene. A couple of deputies met him, beat the bushes for a while, and found nothing. No sign of her. Volunteers searched all day out there. Sherriff's posse going in today to continue the search. They have horses. Some of that terrain's too tough for ATV's, going in on horseback."

"I'm telling you I had nothing to do with it," Tim stated flatly. "The gal at the storage place can vouch for me being there. They have video surveillance on the property. Has to show me there."

"I believe you, Tanner. That's not enough to clear you. You had the opportunity. Lord knows you had reason. Add to that you don't have a solid alibi. Then there's the glove. You admit you have gloves like that. One of yours is missing. On the surface it looks bad."

"All right, I get that," Tim nodded. "You called me in for questioning before you knew I didn't have an alibi. Why?"

John's turn to sigh. "I called Ray when we found the car. He insisted you did something to his mother. Bill Williams was with him, claimed you had been harassing her, trying to get her to leave town."

"Whoa, back up. Bill who?"

"But Bill," John said. "His name is Bill Williams. He says Lurlene complained to him about you, that you were trying to get her to leave town. He said she told him she was afraid of you."

"Hearsay."

"Cool off, Tim. They haven't accused you, not really. Your name is the only one they can suggest. According to them, and I am only repeating what they told me, Lurlene said you had accosted her. Her story is that you wanted her out of town. Before you start, let me finish. She has told them, both of them, on several occasions that you have asked her to leave town, and that you don't want her seeing Bill. She has told them a variation of this on several occasions. They are concerned."

"Sounds like they are," Tim argued. "I'm telling you, I have not spoken to that woman. She came into the Gem when we were there. She sat at the same table. I did not speak to her. You can ask all of them – Sharon, Greg, Cora, Archie, all of them. We did not exchange a single word."

"Good enough. That's some corroboration. Now what about your gloves? You explain that?"

"I can," I said, interrupting. "Chris."

"Right," Tim grinned at me. "Good girl! Chris has been in and out of the garage for weeks. He could have taken one."

"The other brother?"

"Yeah, he's the guy who's been doing the lawn. You even checked on him once, for prowling around over here."

John pulled a small notebook out of his shirt pocket and made some notes with the stub of pencil stuck in the fold.

"Is that all?" Tim got up and carried his dishes to the sink.

"For now," John said. "I may have more questions later."

"I have to leave Wednesday," Tim said, retaking his seat. "Promo tour. Three weeks. There's people depending on me, John. I can't keep ducking out on them. We've had to reschedule twice already."

"I don't see a problem," John said. "You've notified me. Give me a copy of the itinerary so I know where you are at all times, and for heaven's sake, stay with the program! I'll put it in the file. Tee going with you?"

"No, she's gonna stay home," Tim answered.

"That settles it for me," John smiled, standing up. "You won't leave her."

"Not in this lifetime," Tim said.

"I may need to talk to you again. I'm gonna give you a pass on this tour thing. Keep your phone on, just in case. And seriously? Stay with the program. Don't even go for a soda without someone else along."

"I will, Big John, count on it."

"You need to remember I'm on your side, Tex. Right now, I'm the best friend you have. If I thought there was even a sliver of a chance you were involved I would lock you down. There's one other thing. Like it or not, until it's proved otherwise, those shots were meant for you. Your house. In the dark, against the light, we're pretty close in size. That's attempted murder. Don't go wandering off by yourself."

"Running Tim off the road could be attempted murder, too," I put in. "He could have been killed! Those shots weren't the first time he's been in danger."

"I agree with you there, Tee. That's another reason I think those shots were meant for him. This tour thing may be the best idea all the way around. Gets you out of town. Gives me some time to look around without having to worry about your hide."

"Watch out for Tee," Tim said. "While I'm gone."

"Intended to," John said. "That's the only place you're vulnerable. The best way to hurt you is to hurt her. You think about that?"

"Every minute of the day," Tim admitted. "That's why we're still living here. I hate to tell you this but I like the

285

idea of you being across the drive when I'm gone. In a legal sense only."

John nodded. "Got it. Now, I still need you to come in and make a formal statement, just to have one on record. I'm not the only one looking for Lurlene. Sherriff's office and CHP are on it, too. I need that statement."

"Am I gonna get gob-smacked in the head again?"

John chuckled and shook his head. "Not that I'm aware of, and believe me, I am sorry about that. Although at the same time, I think we could sell that video of Tee going after Ray."

"I still want a copy of that tape," Tim grinned back.

"Be careful, Tex. This is one ugly mess. I still don't like you. On the other hand, I don't want anything to happen to you. Not unless I do it."

"Understood," Tim nodded. "Thanks for keeping an eye on my wife."

"I'll talk to you later." Turning to me he tossed a small salute. "Thanks for breakfast, Tee. Delicious as always."

"You're welcome," I smiled back at him.

Tim got up and followed John to the front door. I saw them actually shake hands although I couldn't hear what they said. Strange behavior for those two. I refused to admit to either of them that I was worried.

More than that, for the first time, I was afraid.

Not for me.

For Tim. I prayed the third time was not going to be the charm.

I agreed with John. I was glad he was going to be out of town for a while.

Tim left on Wednesday.

286

Thursday's local paper had a small report on the missing woman, just a couple of inches on page three, about her car being found.

The scream sheets, those ridiculous pulp papers at the checkout stands, were another story.

One of them featured pictures of Lurlene's car, with a close up inset of the glove on the ground beneath the broken window. The headline read 'Tables turned on stalker'. Another actually used Tim's name in connection with her history, although it did not say he lived here in Monarch. Her residence was given as Jade Beach, which most people would not connect with Monarch.

Tim called that night and told me about the papers, warning me to be careful about reporters calling or showing up. He apologized several times, no matter how many times I told him it wasn't his fault. I wanted to see what the papers reported yet I didn't want to buy one.

The official search was called off, the posse loaded up their horses and returned to their origins. On the weekend there were some volunteers who took up the hunt, including a troop of Boy Scouts from Morro Bay.

I talked to Tim several times a day, whenever he had the chance.

The tour was going well, they were having a good time and for the first time, he was homesick.

He missed me, the cats, the beach and its sounds and smells.

Anne had handled reporters asking about Lurlene's disappearance and any connection to Tim. The pulp papers moved on to Brad and Angie and the latest ranting's of Charlie Sheen.

I kept busy with little things. Mostly just puttering. I got the bluebonnet seeds planted along the driveway and in the front flowerbeds. Cleaned drawers and cupboards. Now that some of our belongings were in storage we had more room.

John stopped by several times, usually in the early evening for tea. We had supper a couple of times, sharing a pizza and a couple of beers.

There was no news on the missing woman.

Days passed.

Weeks passed.

Lurlene was still missing.

But Bill and the Martin boys called John every day wanting a progress report.

Bill, on his own, had contacted the FBI, causing more paperwork for John. An agent came up from Santa Barbara, reviewed the facts, looked at a few pictures, toured the site and went back south. Sadly, her history was against her.

I watched Tim and T Three on several different shows, taping a few for him. Most of the stations gave them a copy of their appearances so there was no need to tape them all.

I found it strange to see him on the TV screen.

It was him. It was his voice. And at the same time it wasn't Tim. There was something unreal about seeing him sing, laugh and talk with interviewers, hard to accept this was my husband, the same guy that slept curled around me when he was home. The one who loved gravy and home.

When he was due home I went into a cleaning frenzy although nothing was dirty. I even washed all the curtains in the kitchen and dining room and rehung them. Once that was all done I got out the mower and started on the lawn.

The bluebonnet seedlings were up and growing like weeds, beautiful compact, bluish green little plants that would reseed themselves over the years.

The grass cut and raked I started on the edging, being careful to keep the grass out of the flower beds where the seedlings thrived. Several already sported tiny buds.

I was edging the area along the street when a white van pulled to the curb and parked.

I froze, edger in hand.

But Bill got out and came around the front of the van.

I turned the edger off and called out a greeting, relieved it was him and not Chris. I wasn't sure how I felt about Chris. I did know I was glad I didn't have to face him without Tim.

"Doing a nice job there," Bill called as he met me at the curb. "Old Tex let you down?"

I blinked at him.

We had known each other since high school. He even asked me to Prom, although I declined. After his wife died we had supper together a few times, as friends. Never in all that time had I known him to be rude or offensive.

"I like yard work," I replied. "I've been doing it since I moved here."

"I know that. I've tried to do it for you a couple of times. Guess my lawn service wasn't good enough for you. What is it? The accent? Something about that redneck drawl?"

"I don't know what you're talking about."

"Oh, sure you do, Tee. It's about me. And you. I've never been good enough for you. Even in school. You don't see me. I'm just good ol' But Bill."

I blinked at him, not sure where this was going.

"You think I don't know about that? The But thing? Shoot, always have. It's a habit. I don't mind. I tried to stop it but it's a habit. It don't bother me. It bothers you. You, your friends, all think you're so hip and cool. Know what? You're not."

He stepped up on the curb, moving closer to me. "I found a woman. A real woman. Three times the woman you like to think you are. Did that bother you? Old But Bill having a woman? Did you and Sharon and Sally sit up there in your diner and pass judgment? Let me tell you something, missy, that's a booth in a worn out diner, not a throne. No one cares what you think. Any of you."

I took a step back, unsettled by the look in his eyes. They looked empty, dead, no one home.

"I don't know what you're talking about and right now, I don't care. I think you've said enough." With that I turned away and fired up the edger.

He took another step and grabbed my arm. I dropped the edger and spun away from him, yanking my arm free, stumbling a little and losing my balance. I lurched sideways to regain it, not wanting to turn my back on him again.

"You're covering for him, I know you are! He's done something with her! Is she still alive?" He reached for my arm again. "I deserve to know!"

Before I could respond a horn honked.

I looked at the drive and saw John pulling in, stopping just off the street. He climbed out of the truck and headed toward us, sunglasses covering his eyes.

"Hey guys, how's it going?"

"Good," I called quickly. "You ready for lunch? I'm almost done here."

John, bless his heart, picked up right away. "I'm a little early. Take your time."

"That's okay, this will wait," I said, picking up the edger and starting for the porch. "See ya later, Bill," I tossed over my shoulder, not looking at him.

"Any news?" Bill ignored me, turning his full attention on John.

"Told you, Bill, you'll be the first to know if I find anything."

"Won't be voting for you next election," Bill said. He turned away from us, walked around the van and climbed in. Without another word he drove off.

"I sure am glad to see you," I said, with a deep sigh. My knees felt shaky, unsteady.

"What's going on? Things looked a little tense when I pulled in."

"Come on in, John. I'll make some coffee." I leaned the edger against the wall and went up the steps into the house, John following along.

He took a seat at the table while I started the coffee, my shaking hands spilling the grounds all over the counter.

"You all right? You need some help there?"

"No, I have it," I said, pushing the button to start the coffee. "Just weird."

"In what way? What was going on out there?"

"Him," I said. "I've known him for years, John! Decades! We went to high school together. I've never seen him like that. He was almost in a trance or something, rambling on."

"About what?"

"I don't know! I think Lurlene. Does that make sense?"

"How do I know? I didn't hear him. What did he say?"

"It was jumbled," I admitted. "Something about him never being good enough for me or my friends. Then he said something about me not wanting him to have a woman." I shook my head, getting down some cups and filling them.

"He's been stuck in my craw since she disappeared, him and the son both. They're calling every day, some days more than once." John poured some cream in his coffee and gave it a stir. "He's taking it pretty hard."

"Has there been any news?"

"Nothing," he said, sipping coffee. "They keep insisting Tim did something to her."

"They think he killed her? Why? This has been going on for over twenty years! Why would he decide to kill her now? Makes no sense at all."

"I agree, Tee. The thing is, we don't know what she told them. To be fair, I'd take your word over hers any day of the week. They feel the same way, at least Bill does. She'd lie and he'd swear to it."

I put some cookies on a plate and slid it over to him before taking a seat.

"I don't get it," I admitted. "Whatever she told him, Bill knows me. He's known me a whole lot longer than he's known her! Why would he take her word over mine? You'd think he would have come and talked to me."

"Maybe that's why he was here. To talk to you."

"Then he sure as heck went about it all wrong," I complained.

"Come on, Tee," John grinned. "You can be a little testy when it comes to Tim. Maybe you misunderstood."

"Oh, now it's my fault?"

"No, not what I said," he answered, holding up a hand. "What exactly did he say?"

I took a deep breath and blew it out. "I'm not even sure," I said. "Something about him never being good enough for me."

"You have a history with him? From the old days?"

"No! I mean he asked me to Prom in high school and I didn't accept. After his wife died we went out a few times, nothing special, you know? Just friends. I was single, so was he. Then I got sick. Nothing since then."

"How about Tim? He have a problem with him?"

"Not that I know of. Tim's always polite to him. They only see each other at the Gem, and that's rare."

"No disagreements? Arguments?"

"No," I said. "Wait. We did have one problem. Well, not really a problem. I guess you'd call it an incident? We took some of the gang down to tour the RV, before the production crew left. Archie was curious about the inside, and they all wanted to see it. Tim took them down to see the inside – Archie and Cora, Sharon, and Sally. The guard came back to tell Tim the rest of the party was there and it was Bill and Lurlene. They weren't invited. Tim told the guard no, and they were turned away. We never did see them. They were gone when we left."

"That could do it I suppose," John said, taking a cookie. "Maybe it embarrassed him, in front of her. Guess that could set wrong."

"I guess," I said. "Still, she had to know she would never be included in anything Tim did! With their history? No way!"

"Yeah, she should know. Bill may not know that. He only has her version of things."

"That's just my point! Even if he believed her story, why would she want to go where Tim is? Doesn't make sense! If she's so afraid of him, why would she want to go where he is?"

John nodded. "Good point, Tee. I may ask him about that."

I shook my head. "It doesn't make sense, John, any of it. Why is she even here? If she's so concerned about Tim, why move up here?"

"All things I've thought about," John smiled. "According to Ray he and Chris moved up here, liked it, and asked their mom to move up here with them. Then, according to their story, Tim found a way to move here, too. To stay close to her."

"You know that's a lie. Tim moved up here to be with me. For crying out loud, you think he would go to all this trouble, marry me? Just to be close to her? Hogwash."

"Agreed. I told you, I've read the reports. All of them. Several times. Bill hasn't. We're back to him being told a different story. Hard to fault the guy. He seems to care about her. He's gonna take her side."

"Okay, still, why go after me? Why was he here? I mean, come on. I have nothing to do with her! No wonder Tim wanted to get away from her. That woman is poison!"

"Who knows what's going on with him," John sighed. "I just want to find her, get this mess cleaned up."

"Do you think she's still here?"

"Again, Tee, who knows? From the evidence at her car, when it was found, it appears she was run off the road and someone smashed in the window and took her out. There's

294

no blood. So she was alive when she was taken. From there? No idea. The searchers have been up every canyon around there, all around the lake. Nothing."

"Have they given up on the search completely?"

"Officially, yes. The volunteers are still at it, on the weekends. Bill has put up a reward. That's gonna be public Friday. He put up $25,000 for information. That might bring someone out of the woodwork. Otherwise it's church groups and scouts. Bill and the sons are still actively looking last I heard."

"I hope they find her," I said. "It's a scary situation. What if it has nothing to do with Tim? What if another woman disappears? Have you thought of that?"

"It's a theory," he admitted. "We're working on several scenarios. She could have followed Tim, be off somewhere after him. She could have left with someone else she met here. Someone could have taken her. All active right now. Just have to keep after it. I am good at my job, Tee. We'll find out what happened to her."

"I hope you do," I said. "It's a little scary to have her just disappear."

"When's Tim coming home?"

"This weekend, I hope. I haven't talked to him today. Last night he was in Cincinnati, next stop New York. That's the last stop. Then he'll be home."

John stood up and put his cup in the sink. "How about supper tonight? I can pick up a pizza and some beer after work. You've fed me often enough."

"Sounds good," I said. "I could use the company. I'll look forward to it."

"Around six? That okay?"

"Great. See you then."

"It's a date," he said. "Thanks for the coffee."

Tim was home!

Better than Christmas! I didn't know how much I missed him until he was back home, sleeping upstairs.

With all the flights, drives, shows, hurry up and waits over the past three weeks, not to mention the time difference, he was worn out.

He got in late Friday night, loaded with gifts, dirty clothes, and a box full of CD's and DVD's, copies of the videos as well as the new CD. The cover on both was the Monarch Butterfly, wings spread, against a background of tree bark. In this case the traditional pattern of black on orange was changed to black on blue.

He dumped his things at the front door and scooped me into his arms while the cats wound around his feet.

He was home.

Biscuits were ready for the oven, sausage cooked, ready for gravy as soon as I heard him move around upstairs.

By the time he showered and came downstairs, the table was set and breakfast ready to serve.

He came around long enough to give me a hug and a long kiss before taking his seat.

I poured his coffee and sat down across from him, content to just look at him. He looked tired, something rare for Tim. I think he had lost weight over the weeks.

"I missed everything, Muse," he said, filling his plate. "I missed you so much it hurt. I missed the cats chasing my toes, I missed the sound of the ocean, the smell of the sea. All of it. Right up there in the top was this - biscuits and gravy. Your gravy. You make the world's best cream gravy. I tried it everywhere we ate breakfast and none of them was as good as this." He scooped a huge fork full of biscuit and gravy into his mouth and closed his eyes while he chewed. "Heaven."

"You are so prejudiced," I chuckled.

"No, babe, true fact. Best gravy ever." He opened his eyes, winked at me, and loaded up another mouthful.

"So things went well? The trip was a success?"

"Hard to tell," he said, swallowing. "We'll know in a few weeks. Have to see how the sales go. Especially the new products line. The CD took off right away, a lot of them were pre-ordered. The men's products are a crap shoot. Have to wait and see."

"I know that one is going to be a hit. That smell is amazing, so fresh and clean. I'm telling you I would follow that scent anywhere!"

"Maybe I better lodge a complaint," he grinned. "Don't want you following some guy home when I'm not here."

"You wear it, Hubs. It's you that makes it so great."

Tim laughed and split another biscuit. "In that case I'll bathe in it."

"Seriously, that line is going to go over with the ladies. I think you should look into a woman's line, too. Something that fresh and clean smelling? Instant hit."

"I suggested it to the company," he said. "Told them my wife thought of it."

"Your wife thought of you," I told him.

"Too," he smiled, his eyes the rare, deep blue.

After he finished eating and the table was cleared I poured him an extra cup of coffee and rejoined him at the table.

"I have presents," he said after he added cream to his cup. "There's a DVD of the videos, all five of them, and a

CD of the new album for each of the cast. The DVD's are limited edition, not for sale. Thought your friends might like them."

"How about 'the gang'? They're your friends, too."

He smiled at me. "I guess maybe they are."

"They are, Tim. You've put down a few roots, Hubs, like it or not."

"I like it," he smiled. "And for you, babe, tee shirts. One from every city we hit. Thought you could start a collection. I'll get them later. Right now, I am just glad to be home."

"Good. Now, what do you want to do today?"

"How about San Luis? You up for that?"

"Always. Are you sure you want to go? You've been traveling nonstop."

"I need some guitar strings. Didn't want to take an extra day in LA just for that. I wanted to get home."

When it came to anything beyond groceries Monarch was not the place to shop. For other things, you made the trip south to San Luis.

"Ready when you are," I told him, taking my cup to the sink.

San Luis is a beautiful little town with the mission planted at one end. It's vibrant and alive, compact and lovely, with all kinds of little shops and places to eat. Tim's favorite music store was just a block from Barnes and Noble so we could both browse.

We spent an afternoon wandering, looking and eating, even took in a movie.

The sun was going down when we left the theater, laden with bags and packages. At the truck we unloaded and locked up before deciding on where to eat supper.

298

"How about the Apple Farm?" I suggested. "You'll love the desserts."

"Do they have anything besides dessert?"

"Oh, yeah, Hubs, they have excellent food. The thing is, they also have excellent desserts and I know you."

I gave directions to the other end of town, to the Apple Farm, which is a restaurant and inn, not a farm. The entrance is through their gift shop and past their bakery. I had to shove Tim through that part.

After we ate nothing would do Tim but a return to the bakery where he added another bag and a pink box to the load in the truck.

I held the box while Tim unlocked the truck.

He stood there, with an odd look on his face.

"Tim? Here, babe, stick this in there."

He still stood, looking over my shoulder, back toward the restaurant.

"What?"

"That woman," he said. "The one that just went in the gift shop."

"Where?" I shifted the box and turned to look back.

Tim was still looking where we had just left. "She's gone," he said. "Woman in a green top and black pants."

I didn't see a woman in green. There were two guys that looked like college kids and a family of five between us and the entrance.

"What about her?" I hitched the box around again.

Tim shook his head and took the box, slipping it behind the seat before helping me into the cab. "Probably just me," he said, closing the door.

When he was belted in and aimed for the freeway he glanced at me and chuckled. "I must be tired," he grinned.

"I could have sworn that was Lurlene back there. Except she was thinner and had dark hair. Something about the face, the way she walked. I must be losing it, babe."

Talk about throwing a wet blanket over the fire.

The last thing I wanted to talk about was the missing Lurlene. Even the dog teams the county brought in found no trace of her. She had simply disappeared.

Had someone busted the window out of that car and dragged her out? Was there a chance, even a slim one that another woman was going to be taken?

Lurlene was haunting us all, even in her total absence.

Sunday morning Tim was off right after breakfast, heading for the hardware store.

The front door and its frame looked pretty ragged. The bullets did enough damage, splintering wood in the framing as well as the door. The forensics guys digging out the bullets made small holes bigger ones and all of the holes were circled with yellow paint, splintered and shredded wood.

While I cleaned the kitchen Tim made his list and went to get supplies.

Tim loves working around the house. Fortunately, he's also very good at it. For me? Hearing him around the house is one of my greatest pleasures, whether he's tinkering with the barbecue, loading the fireplace, playing with the cats, or like today, working on the house.

I love hearing him whistle or sing as he works, so completely focused on what he's doing he has no clue he's also singing or whistling.

He had rattled, hammered, scraped and whistled for an hour or so when I heard him talking.

I talk to myself. A lot. He never does.

I opened the front door and found John Kincaid on my front porch. No blood was shed so I assumed things were all right.

"Hey, John, didn't know you were here," I greeted him. "Can I get you some coffee? Tea?"

"Hey, Tee. Love some iced tea."

"Tim?"

He straightened up and stretched his back. "Yeah, Muse, I can take a break. Tea sounds good."

I stepped out to see what he was doing.

The front door was now bare, no framing at all while the porch was littered with pieces of raw wood molding. The door itself sported a couple of sanded holes where the bullets hit.

Sand paper, saw, level, hammer, nails and more littered the porch beside cut pieces of molding.

"What do you think?" Tim asked.

"Looks good," I told him, wondering who in the world we could call to clean up this mess. "I'll get the tea. You want it out here?"

"Naw, I'm gonna take a break."

"Probably should get that wood filler in," John said, leaning close to the damaged door. "These holes are pretty deep. What did you use to clean them? A harpoon?"

"I know what I'm doing," Tim said, following me in the house. "Are you coming in or going home? Lord knows you never work."

I led both of them to the kitchen and got down glasses while Tim washed up at the sink and John took a seat.

"Oh, I do work, Tex. Never doubt that. Nero Wolfe never left the house and look how many cases he solved."

"You are putting on weight," Tim said. "You may get to his size. Doubt you'll equal his mental capacities. Better stick with putting on weight."

John grinned at him and patted his belly. "Your wife's cooking. Can't beat it."

"I see you put away enough of it," Tim growled and took a seat across from John.

I set their glasses on the table and poured one for myself.

"Speaking of cases," I said. "Is there anything new on Lurlene?"

John shook his head. "Nope. Not a thing."

"Tim thought he saw her in San Luis," I said.

John sat up. "When? Where? Why the hell didn't you report it?"

"Slow down, Sheriff John," Tim said, holding up his hand. "I just saw a gal that reminded me of her. Something about the way she walked. If I thought it was really her I would have hogtied her and brought her back."

John was eager for details now. "Where did you see her?"

"In San Luis. The Apple Farm restaurant. Well, the parking lot anyway. This gal was thinner and had dark hair."

"She works with hair. Changing her hair color would be no big deal."

"I could change the color of my hair in an hour," I put in. "Over the counter hair dye is everywhere. Archie carries it."

Tim nodded. "I guess she could have lost weight, dyed her hair." With a shrug he sat back. "Could also have been a complete stranger. We may never know what happened to her. I, for one, don't give a fig."

"You should," John warned him. "You're still the primary suspect. There's an awful lot of people think you had something to do with her disappearing."

"Me? What did I do? I haven't seen her!"

"You just said you did," John corrected. "Did you see her or not?"

"I said I saw some woman who reminded me of her. I've been looking at blonds since she disappeared. This gal had dark hair."

"Does your wife know you check out blondes?"

"You'd be out of your depth in a puddle."

John chuckled and drank tea.

"Like it or not, there is a chance she dyed her hair and lost some weight. Maybe she just moved on down the road." I brought the pitcher of tea to the table for refills.

"Why?" John asked. "What would be the purpose?"

"To get at Tim, "I said, taking my seat. "Maybe this whole thing is a set up."

"She'd bust out her car window, crawl through broken glass, give up her job, move, and dye her hair and all this to get at Tim? That's a little far-fetched, Tee."

"Not for her," I argued. "She's done weird stuff before. She's got some allies now, with her boys and Bill."

"I suppose you think she shot at Tim, too?"

"Would not surprise me," I said. "She's a loon."

Tim had been quiet for a few minutes. Now, he looked up at John.

"Do you still have those pictures on your phone? The ones of her car?"

"Sent them to email, at the station, for enlargements. Why?"

"There is something about that window bugging me. Can't put my finger on it," Tim said. "I saw them in the gossip sheets. Wanted another look see."

"I can go get them if you really think it matters," John offered.

Tim thought for a minute, that little line forming between his eyebrows. "You mind?"

"Oh heck no," John said, standing up. "I live to serve your every whim. That's why the squad car says To Protect and Serve. Protect the populace and serve the celebrity." He pulled his keys out of his pocket. "Be right back."

"Since you're going out anyway," Tim called to his back. "Leave your sarcasm at the door."

"Can't," John called back. "It's one of those services I offer for free."

"He's something else," Tim said once the door was closed.

"Heard that," came John's voice from the front lawn.

"Do you really want to see those pictures or are you just yanking John's chain?"

Tim looked up at me from under those thick, dark lashes, the blue highlights in his eyes sparkling. "Would I do that, Muse?"

"Every chance you get," I laughed. "Are you hungry? You want a sandwich?"

"I want something," he chuckled, waggling his eyebrows. "I just don't want to be interrupted by that clown. A sandwich would be good, babe. Might as well count on a second for the lawman. Lord knows he never eats at home."

I got up and went to the fridge, getting out the cold cuts and fixings for sandwiches. By the time John got back there was a platter of meats, cheese, sliced tomatoes and lettuce on the table beside a stack of bread.

Tim was slathering mustard on a piece of bread when John came back.

"Am I interrupting lunch?" He asked, pulling out his chair and sitting. He laid a large manila envelope to the side of his plate. "Or just in time?"

"Eat," Tim said. He put together a sandwich and took a huge bite before he reached for the envelope John had put on the table.

While John and I made sandwiches Tim pulled out a stack of color enlargements and thumbed through them, setting a few aside. When he had them sorted the way he wanted he slid one stack back into the envelope.

He finished his sandwich, looking at the photos he had set aside. He shuffled through them several times. When he was done he sat back with a grin.

"Solve the case, Tex?"

Tim grinned at him, arms folded across his chest. "She wasn't taken."

John wiped his mouth and sat back, assuming the same position, arms folded across his chest. "You know that how?"

Tim turned a photo and slid it across to John.

"Look at that one. That's what was bugging me."

I craned my neck to see the picture.

It was the photo looking through the shattered car window. The blue window frame formed an outline for the picture. Inside the car the shards of glass glittered like diamonds, sprayed across the driver's seat, some of them all the way to the passenger seat. The floorboard was darker but a few pieces glittered there as well.

I sat back after I had looked it over, seeing nothing unusual.

"So?" John said.

"Look at it," Tim smirked, one eyebrow lifting.

"I am looking at it, Sherlock," John snapped. "What is it you think you see?"

Tim leaned forward on his elbows. "The glass. Look at the glass."

John sighed and leaned over the picture. "What am I seeing?"

Tim shook his head and reached over to tap the photo. "The glass. In the seat."

"What about it?"

"It's in the seat," Tim said with a sigh. "In the seat, Sherriff John."

"I don't get it," John said, leaning back.

"If someone smashed in the window to get to her, the glass would be in her lap. Or it would hit her back and fall to the floor if she turned away. Look at it, man. No one was sitting there when that window broke. The glass is too even, the spread too even."

John sat forward and pulled the picture closer. I leaned in for a better look. Tim grinned.

After a couple of long minutes John leaned back and looked over at Tim.

"I think you're right," he said.

"I know I'm right," Tim grinned.

John shook his head, pulling a few more of the photos over to his side of the table. The kitchen was so quiet we could hear the clock ticking.

"So you could have seen her," John said finally. "She could have set this up."

"Not sure about that," Tim told him. "The only thing I see is that she wasn't sitting in that seat when the window was smashed. No one was. That seat was empty when that window broke."

"So you think she smashed it?" I asked. "That she left it like that and took off? Where would she go? She'd be on foot."

"No idea," Tim said. "Maybe she was gone when someone else found the car and smashed the window. Maybe someone smashed the window after she got out. I'm just saying she was not in the driver's seat when that window broke."

"She could have had help," John said, gathering the pictures together and shoving them into the envelope. "One of the boys, or some guy, followed her and helped her set it up, then drove her somewhere else."

"Why?" I asked. "All this to set Tim up? For what?"

Tim sighed again. "That woman has no hamster in her wheel, babe."

"I don't see what the gain is," I continued. "Everyone knows you didn't do it."

"Not everyone," John said. "Tim is the leading candidate. You're second, Tee."

"Me? Why on earth would I do something to her?"

"Tim," John answered.

"Muse wouldn't hurt a fly," Tim put in. "Let alone go after some poor deranged soul."

"Tell that to Ray Martin," John laughed. "She put a pretty good whipping on that boy."

"That was different," I said. "I was defending myself! I didn't start it!"

'No, but you sure as hell ended it," John chuckled. "Never even needed to use your stapler."

I blushed, my neck a thermometer as the red climbed to my cheeks.

"It's all right, babe," Tim soothed. "I was proud of you. Even if I didn't see it."

"On video," John reminded him. "Drop by any time."

Of all the things I didn't need was these two bonding. I much preferred them sniping at each other.

"All right, all right," I said, getting up and clearing the table. "That door is not going to fix itself. You need to get back to your project. You can pick on me any time."

"Wouldn't dream of it," John grinned.

"Uh – huh," I smiled back. "I'm gonna remember this the next time I bake bread."

"You need any help with that door?" John asked. "I'm off today."

"Yeah, if you have the time," Tim said, standing up. "I could use some help with that molding."

"Show me what to do," John said, pushing in his chair. "I'm hell with a hammer."

Together they moved outside, to the front porch.

While I cleared up and loaded the dishwasher I could hear their voices back and forth although I couldn't make out the words.

Then they started laughing.

Together.

Scary.

In the meantime he and John switched to beer, sawed, hammered, nailed and laughed the afternoon away. By the time they came in to wash up Aunt Johnnie had a newly repaired and repainted front door. They even repainted the window casements so it would all match.

I was still admiring their handiwork when Sharon drove up. I waved and waited for her on the porch.

"What's up?" She called, coming up the walk. "Haven't seen you in a while. Everything okay?"

"Great," I answered. "How're things with you?"

She came up the steps and gave me a hug. "Good here. Hadn't heard from you, wanted to make sure everything was all right."

I opened the door and let her precede me.

When she saw John, she stopped so quickly I ran into her.

"Hey, Sharon," the lanky lawman said, wiping his hands with paper towels. "How you doing?"

"I'm good, John, how about you?"

"Fine," he answered and leaned back against the counter, watching her.

She looked over at Tim. "Hi, Tim. Good to have you back."

"Sharon," he greeted her. "Anyone up for a beer?"

"I'll have another," John answered. "I'm off today."

I raised a hand. Tim opened the fridge and started passing bottles of beer.

"Oh, why not," Sharon said and accepted one.

"Let's sit outside," I said. "Admire the guy's handiwork."

With that we all trooped back to the front porch. Sharon and I sat in the rockers while Tim sat on the top step and John sat up on the rail. The sun was behind the trees now so the porch was dappled with late afternoon light.

"Have to admit you guys did a good job," Sharon told them, after carefully inspecting their work. "I'll know who to call for repairs from now on."

"Once in a while work," Tim laughed. "I have a job, thanks."

"Me, too," John said, toasting Tim with his beer.

"Speaking of your job," Sharon said, turning to face John. "Any news?"

"No, sorry. Nothing new," John answered, with a quick glance at Tim.

Sharon sighed and turned back to me. "Are you worried?"

"Me? Why?"

"There may be a maniac out there! For crying out loud, Tee! That woman has been missing for over a month. Not a sign of her!" She fanned herself with her hand. "I get so nervous when I have to go check on a house by myself."

"Don't go by yourself," John put in. "Take someone along if you're uneasy."

"That's going to look like I'm scared," Sharon returned.

"You are. Better safe than sorry," John said. "If it bothers you, Sharon, take someone along for the ride."

I saw her eyes narrow and the tick in her jaw before she took a swallow of beer.

"You going to give me a police escort?"

John laughed. "Hardly. Not enough man power." He glanced at me. "Take Tee along. Give her a stapler and you're safe as church."

Tim laughed along with John, although he reached over and patted my knee.

"I don't get it," Sharon groused.

310

"Inside joke," I told her. "Seriously, though. Are you really concerned about being alone?"

She sighed and leaned back in her chair. "Never was before," she admitted. "Lately, though, I hate having to go check on the country houses. Or meet a stranger to show a house outside of town. Just a little creepy."

"We have a pretty safe town," John told her.

"Oh, yeah, right," she countered. "The vet got killed, Tee almost drowned, Tim was thrown down a well and run off the road. Not to mention we have a woman run off the road and abducted. Pretty safe, all right."

I watched them, back and forth, like a tennis match. Glancing at Tim I saw he was doing the same thing.

"So what's for supper, Muse?" He asked when the silence became a little uncomfortable.

"What would you like?"

"We have those steaks need to be cooked. How about I throw them on the grill. Maybe a salad and some bread?"

"Sounds good," I said, standing up. "Would you like to join us, Sharon? John?"

"Sure, "John said, standing alongside me. "Can I help?"

"Come on," Tim said, standing up and leading the way inside. "You can help me get the grill going." He stepped inside with John right behind him.

Sharon looked over at me. "Those two are pretty chummy. When did that happen?"

"Today," I answered. "I think. Who knows with those two? So what's with you and John? You seemed kinda testy there."

She thought about not answering me. I could see it on her face. Then she sighed. "I invited him to supper and he refused."

"Why? Did he say?"

"Said he was busy with a case."

"Very possible, Sharon. Cut the guy a break."

"I have, Tee. More than once."

"Then quit trying," I said, leading the way into the house. "Come on, help me with supper."

After we got the salad in the fridge and the bread ready to go on the grill we joined the guys outside.

They had set up the chairs and filled the cooler while we were inside. John handed us each a beer before taking his seat again. I noticed he sat on the other side of me, rather than next to Sharon.

The smell of the burning oak drifted across the yard, into the trees across the street. The late afternoon sun turned the smoke from the barbecue into a golden cloud that hovered above us.

I closed my eyes and let my head rest on the back of the chair, the drone of the guys talking football soothed me, almost as good as the sound of the surf.

"Are you really that worried about going out of town?" I asked from my relaxed position.

"Yeah, I am. Sometimes. I don't know, Tee, it's weird. I think I spend more time looking in the rear view mirror than ever before. If I'm at a house that's off the road, up in the canyon somewhere, I listen for a car. Or footsteps. I get so tense! It's silly, I guess, but you never know! So many strange things have happened this year, unusual things. Sitting here, in the sun, in your driveway, with two grown men within touching distance, I'm fine. Not a care in the world. Out Prince Road, or Travis Canyon, up one of those barely paved roads, I'd make coffee nervous."

"I can go with you," Tim offered. "When I'm home anyway."

"I can go, too," John jumped in. "For that matter, I have to cruise out that way about once a week or so. Let me know when you want to go and I can give you a ride. Or follow you."

Sharon looked up at the guys. "Thanks, guys. I appreciate that. I may take you up on it." She gave a little giggle, her cheeks pinking. "I know it's silly. I'd just feel better if I wasn't alone out there."

"No problem," John said. "I wish you'd told me earlier. I'd be happy to help. Any time. With anything."

Her eyes teared up when he said that. Or maybe the smoke from the barbecue blew into her eyes.

We ate and cleaned up, Tim built a fire in the fireplace and we talked long into the night. Tim told stories from his travels and John countered with tales of some of his cases and the people he'd dealt with before moving to Monarch. Sharon shared some of the stranger requests people had when looking for a home.

My life was so mundane I had nothing to share.

It was after midnight when John stood up, stretched and carried cups into the kitchen. Tim promptly helped while Sharon gathered her purse and sweater.

"I'll walk you out," John told her. "Thanks for supper, Tex."

"Thanks for your help," Tim answered.

The four of us made those small comments people make when ready to leave.

John reached around Sharon and opened the door for her.

Sharon's smile widened, squared, and became a scream, one that ripped through the open door and echoed through the house.

Tim grabbed me, yanking me up against him, his head swiveling left and right.

John slammed the door and pulled Sharon to his side, hitting the switch to kill the lights at the same time.

"What?" Tim whispered, still clutching me against his body with both arms.

John's voice was just as soft. "Tee, take Sharon upstairs." He turned her and gave her a nudge. "Go with her, please."

The only light now was the weak glow of the porch light coming through the side windows.

Tim moved me around and sent me to the stairs with Sharon before moving up next to John.

From the shadowed stairs we heard the murmurs of the guys talking, unable to make out their words. Sharon gripped my hand as we sat on the steps.

Leaning in close I copied John and whispered.

"What happened?"

Her cold fingers tightened on my mine.

"An animal," she whispered back, her voice thick with fear, trembling in the dark.

"What kind of animal?"

"I think it was a dog. Not sure." Her voice shook. "It had no head."

I felt my own body go cold. I gripped her hand even harder. "Are you sure?"

"Good Lord, Tee, why would I make that up!"

I flashed back to early spring, when she had stumbled on the heads of dogs nailed to posts on one of her properties.

314

No one had ever been charged.

I pulled Sharon over for a hug and we huddled there.

Below us, the guys had gone to the kitchen and out through the back door.

We waited.

FLASH

Hey, Muse, it's okay. We're coming back in.

What is it?

Animal carcass, babe. Across the front door. Don't look.

Had no intention of looking. Are you guys okay?

Fine. We're at the back door, coming in.

Okay, Hubs.

"It's okay, Sharon, they're coming back."

I let go of her shoulders and stood up, heading back downstairs."

"How do you know? What if it's someone else?"

"I know," I told her. "Tim told me," I said, tapping my head.

We heard the guys coming in from the kitchen as I flipped the lights back on, not even considering the animal on the other side of the door.

Tim came straight to me and hugged me, tipping my chin up to look into my eyes.

"You all right, babe?"

"Okay, Tim. You?"

Whether it was Tim's reaction, or his own, John went around to tug Sharon into his arms and hug her. I heard him ask the same question of her.

"We have to call this in," John said, over Sharon's shoulder.

"Got it," Tim told him, pulling his cell phone from his pocket.

John let Sharon go and stepped over to the front door.

"Back up, ladies," he ordered. "You don't want to see this."

"I'll make coffee," I said, catching Sharon's arm and tugging her along. The Monarch panacea – coffee and lots of it.

We went through five pots of coffee, two coffee cakes and three packages of cookies before the crowd began to thin out.

Officer Chuck and two of his buddies were there, taking pictures, measuring, stringing more yellow tape across my front porch.

California Highway Patrol was there and two deputies from the Sherriff's Department. The county had sent the forensics van back.

It was getting to be like old home week seeing the same faces and vehicles. At least this time none of us was wounded, although Sharon was pretty green around the gills for most of an hour.

"You want to stay at my place tonight?" Sharon asked when the teams began to drift away. The sky to the east was a pale gray, beginning to relieve some of the shadows in my yard.

I yawned widely, almost unhinging my jaw. "No, thanks, Sharon. It's almost daylight now."

She moved over to peek out the window.

"Looks like Tim and John are coming back in," she said, just as the front door opened and the two men came into the house. Their faces were grim, their eyes tight as they came to the kitchen.

"You guys up for some breakfast?" I offered. "I can fix some bacon and eggs or sausage and biscuits."

"I am hungry, Muse," Tim said, coming over to hold me against him. "You've done enough. How about we let Sally take over? They should be open pretty soon. How about you two? You want to go to Kelly's?"

"I could use some food," John admitted. "I am about coffee'd out. Sharon?"

She nodded. "Yeah, I think we all need to refuel. Been one long night."

"Let me grab a sweatshirt," I said. "We can take my truck."

We filed into Kelly's a much quieter group, taking our seats in the fourth booth back. Sally was right behind us with a steaming pot of coffee which smelled delicious even though we had been sucking it up for hours.

It was early, the old timers at the counter made up the majority of the patrons. They nodded as we trouped past them, a few mumbling greetings.

I wondered if the news was already out.

Sally put an end to my wondering.

Filling cups around the table, she looked at each of us, then shook her head.

"Rough night," she said, setting the pot down and pulling out her pad. "Just a little more madness I guess. We heard first thing this morning. What can I get you folks? On the house."

Tim raised one hand, the one I wasn't clinging to. "I'm starved, sweetheart. I'll take one of everything. Whatever is hot on the grill. And I'll pay. You can't keep giving away food."

"How about you, John?"

"I'll have what he's having," he answered, stirring cream into his coffee.

Sharon ordered pancakes and I went with the Spanish omelet.

"I'm sure sorry that happened to you, Tee," the waitress said, before starting back up front to put in our orders. "That's sick and disgusting. I hope they hang that guy when they catch him."

"We don't hang criminals any more," John told her. "Wish we did at times."

"Then we should start again," Sally snapped. "Might slow down some of this craziness if we had a corpse hanging off the bridge again."

She trundled her way up front.

Tim turned to me. "Again?"

I let go of his hand and pulled my coffee closer. "Long time ago. Cattle thief."

"They hanged him?"

"Uh-huh. From the old bridge over the creek."

"Doesn't look high enough."

"That's the new bridge. Rebuilt in the forties. The old one was higher. Wooden arch. There's pictures of it at the City Hall, in the halls."

"She might have something there," Sharon added to the conversation. "Who does things like that? That's beyond sick."

"Did they find anything?" I asked. "Did they tell you anything?"

John shook his head. "Not really. The county guy said the dog had been dead for a while. Wasn't a fresh kill."

"Do we have to talk about it?" I shivered. "I'm over it. Enough."

318

Tim looped an arm around my shoulders and snugged me tight against him. "Sorry, Muse, that's going to be the story for a few days. It's already public knowledge."

I closed my eyes and breathed in his scent, the fresh pine smell, even after this long, long night. A vague scent of oak smoke still clung to his shirt, along with the pine.

"It's the same guy isn't it," Sharon stated, not a question. "He's back."

"Probably never left," John said. "Just backed off, or moved his operation after you found his old one. That kind of sickness won't go away, honey. It's bone deep." He reached over to pull her against his side, mimicking Tim. "Somewhere out there is a madman. We just have to hope he limits his activities to animals. That's bad enough."

"I'm gonna ask," Sharon said. "Do you think he got Lurlene? Do you think he's telling us that?"

"Whoa, slow down, Sharon," John said, retrieving his arm. "We don't know anything yet. This guy was pulling this stuff before she ever came to town. That site you found was way last spring."

"Still, what if she caught him? What if she saw him killing dogs? Caught him in the act? What if he took her out?"

Her green eyes were glazing over, fear sparking like tears.

"Shhh," John comforted. "Let it go, Sharon. Let it go. We'll find him. We'll catch him."

She leaned back and looked at him. "You don't get it! That guy put that animal on her porch while we were sitting there! We were right there! All night! He came up onto that porch, with a dead animal, while we were laughing or eating or something." Tears filled her eyes, threatening her mascara. "We were right there. I was parked in front."

"She has a point," Tim agreed. "We never heard a thing."

I spoke up. "Had to have been earlier. Cletus would have growled. He's the best watch dog I've ever seen. He would have told us someone was on the porch. It must have been while we were outside, in the driveway, and didn't hear him."

"Lord, that's worse!" Sharon cried. "He was wandering around on the grass with a dead animal, right there! What if we'd seen him? What if one of us had looked that way, or gone around to the front?"

"Safety in numbers," John comforted. "He took a hell of a chance with us sitting that close. He had to have parked down the street and walked over. We would have heard a car door."

"I don't care how he got there," Sharon snapped. "We were right there! Think about it! What if he'd had a gun? This town is not safe, John, no matter what you say. Something ugly is here. It's been here."

In one of the few tender moments I have ever seen from John he reached a hand behind her head to cup her head and pull her down on his shoulder.

"It's all right to be scared," he told her softly. "We'll get the guy, Sharon. I promise. In the meantime, stay with me if you're worried. I have a guest room."

Tim was still, watching the couple across the booth. Under the table his hand squeezed my thigh.

"Thanks, John," Sharon said, just as softly. She lifted her head and gave him a long look before she looked over at us. "I'm sorry, guys. I lost it."

"No problem, Sharon. You don't have to apologize to us. We were there," Tim told her.

Sally interrupted the moment bringing plates of food. When the table was loaded she returned with fresh coffee for everyone.

"Is there anything new?" She asked, leaning a hip against the side of the booth.

John shook his head, chewing on a piece of toast. When he disposed of it, he tilted his head to look up at Sally. "You've been here forever. Has this kind of thing happened before?"

"Why don't you all eat first, then we can talk," she answered. "For the record though, I don't recall anything like this. You have to remember this was originally a fishing town. Well, a town next to a fishing town. Jade was quite the center when California had open waters. The houses here were offshoots of the families there. Then the retirees from the valley started moving over to get out of that heat. That's why so many houses are small here. Originally built for one or two people.

Once the fishing went north, the seniors pretty much had the place to themselves. With the ocean and the lake they could supplement their income eating fish. Mild climate, grow a lot of their own food. A good place to live. This other stuff is new."

"Every town has its crazies," Tim put in. "Shoot, back home they celebrate eccentricity. You wouldn't believe some of the things I heard growing up. Anyone like that?"

Sally's mouth curved up in a wide smile. "Well, to tell you the honest truth, Mr. Tim, the only really odd person I've noticed is the one you married. I've seen her sit here for half an hour like she's in a trance, just staring into space or at the table top, or whatever. Just freeze and sit there."

"Present company excluded," Tim laughed. "Anyone else?"

Sally thought for a minute or two. "I can't think of anyone else. You know the oldsters," she dropped her voice to a rough whisper. "The morning regulars? Some of them are a little strange but who isn't at that age? You know old Dan talks to himself. Has since his wife passed. He still talks to her. Even asks her to pass the salt and such. Then there's Phil. He rarely talks at all, writes down his order before he comes in and hands it over. They're odd, yes. I put it down to age. I'd trust every one of them with my life. Crazy? Maybe. Torture an animal? No way."

Someone up front called her and she turned and left us.

We busied ourselves with food for a while, until everyone was shoving their plates away and pulling coffee cups closer. Sally had brought refills a couple of times without any more comments.

When she came to clear the table Tim handed her his credit card. "Take care of yourself, sweetheart," he said as he signed the slip she brought back. "Can't lose my favorite waitress."

"You think something else is gonna happen?"

He patted her hand and tucked his card back in his wallet. "No idea, Sweet Sally. Just want you to be extra careful. Those videos with you gals in them getting a lot of play on television. Don't want some handsome country man to come in here and sweep you off your feet."

She giggled, a thing she saves up for Tim, and went back up front.

John leaned back and looked at Tim. "You think there's a chance someone in the film crew is involved?"

"With the dogs? No. That was going on before they even considered coming up here."

"Okay, I'll go along with that. How about Martinez? You think she went off with some guy from the shoot?"

Tim shook his head. "No clue, John. With that woman anything is possible. I've seen her do crazy things for years and years. The only thing I'm certain of with that woman is you cannot figure her out. I wouldn't put anything past her."

"How about animals?" John asked.

Tim looked between John and Sharon and back again. "I don't think so. Gut feeling. Would I gamble on it? No. Again, I don't think she was up here when that was going on. Do we have an idea when she moved up here?"

"According to Ray she just moved up here a couple of months ago. He says he and the younger one came up here last fall on a camping trip, liked it and moved up. Mama came to visit, liked it, and moved up to join them. He says they had no idea Tim lived here. Claims Tim came up after they did."

Tim snorted. "Hogwash. She's been following me for twenty years. You can't possibly believe that story."

"You wouldn't think so," John agreed. "That's his story. The younger one agrees. The first time I talked to her that was her story, too. She said Tim used Tee to get in with the locals."

"Just a minute," Tim started.

John held up a hand. "I didn't say I believed her. No one did. Maybe her boys although after this long, they have to know what she's doing." John leaned forward on folded arms. "Those guys are men now, not little boys. They have to know something's wrong with their mother. I've checked on them. They're clean. Get great references from everywhere they've worked. Your own crew gave them high marks the year they worked for your outfit," he said, looking at Tim. "Nothing in their records anywhere."

"They still have to know she's nuts," Tim argued.

"It's a perspective thing, Tex. Those boys grew up with her. She's their history. The only story they know is hers. To them, she's perfectly normal. It's you that's out of line. To them, you're the dangerous one."

"That can't be right," I said. "Why would Chris hunt us up? Offer his services? He had to know who Tim was and he still worked for us. Came in and ate with us, had coffee, like anyone else would. He knew who Tim was. You'll never convince me otherwise."

John shrugged, and slid out of the booth.

"Not gonna argue, Tee," he said. "Right now, I've been up all night, I'm stuffed and I'm tired. I am going to go home and take a nap. Glad it's Sunday."

We all stood up and headed for the front. Tim stopped to talk to a couple of the old timers, some of his biggest fans. We waited on the sidewalk for him. The sun was up and bright, no fog or overcast this morning, a beautiful day. We could hear the tide coming in, feel the vibrations in the ground of the waves breaking on the shore.

At home John walked Sharon to her car before joining Tim at the bottom of the porch steps. Yellow caution tape still fluttered between the uprights on the porch, effectively sealing it off.

I didn't want to see it, so I went around to the garage and waited for Tim there, leaning against the garage door, enjoying the warmth of the sun.

In a few minutes I heard John call his good byes and opened my eyes to see him crossing the drive.

He waved and I waved back, straightening up.

Tim joined me and we went in through the garage.

Like John, I was tired. We had been up all night, eaten a large meal and my own eyes felt heavy. Without a word we locked up and went upstairs for a nap.

It was late afternoon before we woke up.

I had that groggy feeling of not enough sleep, my eyes felt like sandpaper when I blinked. I moved around in slow motion.

With that huge breakfast we weren't really hungry so Tim made a couple of grilled cheese sandwiches and called it supper.

We were watching the news when Cletus growled and ran for the stairs. Tim was up and at the front door almost as fast as the cat.

I sat up from my place on the couch when I heard him talking.

He was standing there, talking to John, when I joined them. "What's up?"

"It's all right, Muse. John was taking down the tape. I'm gonna clean up the front porch, get this tape out of here, hose it down."

"I'll make a pot of tea," I said.

I left them to it and went to the kitchen. While the water boiled I could hear them outside and with recent events, I found comfort in those voices.

I pulled down the trusty box of Bisquik and put together some scones using frozen blueberries.

The men came in and washed up, Tim smelling the scones.

John came in and took his usual seat.

I poured the tea while the guys helped themselves to scones and butter.

"These are really good," John said, around a mouthful. "Are these from Cora's?"

"No," Tim answered. "Can't you smell them? She made them. From scratch."

John shook his head and grinned at Tim. "Of course she did. I was smelling her cooking long before you showed up. I just like to rattle your chain, keep you on alert."

"Speaking of alert," Tim said, taking a third scone. "Did any of those county guys say anything about the dog? About this happening before?"

John swallowed and sipped tea. "One of the Highway Patrol guys remembered something like this a few years ago. Before I came up here. Happened south of here, in one of those undeveloped areas along the coast. Maybe ten miles from here?"

"Same thing? The dogs?"

"He said similar. They found some carcasses. No heads."

"Do you have to talk about it now?" I felt squeamish just hearing about it.

"Sorry, babe," Tim said quickly. "One last thing. Can you check with him again? Find out when that was?"

"Sure. You think it's important?"

"Could be," Tim said. "I remember when something like this happened in Houston. Can't recall the details. Just know they were gruesome. Sorry, Muse."

"I know, Hubs. There's no way around it. Do you think the animal thing is really connected with Lurlene?"

Tim sat back, turned his chair and stretched out his legs. "Comes back to the same thing," he said. "She wasn't up here when Sharon found those other dogs."

"That we know of," John put in. "The only timeline I have is the one she and her sons gave me."

"Still, if her disappearance was linked to the dogs, we would have lost someone before," Tim argued. "I just can't see her being taken. She's a wily one. To me, it makes more sense that she either took off with some guy, or tried to follow me on the tour. She's done that before. Maybe she's stuck in Nashville or Memphis."

"I tend to agree," John said. "I don't know the woman like you do but it seems more likely to me that she took off on her own. The whole thing with the car window smells like a set up."

"What does it accomplish?" I asked, pouring the last of the lukewarm tea. "She doesn't gain anything. No one here is going to believe Tim did anything to her."

"Not quite true," John said. "Some people have been looking at Tim. There's a faction here that blames him for everything, from the dogs to her." He held up his hands, palms out. "I know, I know, Tee. Settle down. I'm just saying, some folks think Tim showed up about the time all the trouble started – the dogs, the pranks all summer."

"That was the college kids," I snapped. "You caught them. With Tim's help I might add. Sharon may be scared but I'm not. Until I find out different, I think she's taken off with some guy. Did you ever find that guy she was dancing with?"

"Not yet. He took another gig, up in Wyoming. Sherriff is still trying to locate him." He stood and carried his cup and plate to the sink. "Thanks for feeding me again," he said.

"Thanks for helping with the porch," Tim countered.

"No problem, Tex. You gonna be around this week?"

"Far as I know, should be home for several weeks. Fall tour is about six weeks out."

"Good," John said, walking to the front door. "I'm gonna talk to the CHP again, about what happened down south. See if anyone remembers anything else."

"Let me know," Tim said, following him to the door.

Tuesday Tim was cutting the lawn when he noticed the bluebonnets in the flower beds. I saw him from the front window stop, squat and reach for the little plants. Carrying my coffee I went out to the porch.

"Something wrong?" I asked, leaning over the railing.

His eyes were alight with blue sparkles when he looked up at me.

"You do this?"

"Do what?"

He straightened up and came up the steps to join me on the porch.

"That is awesome, Muse. Now my territory is really marked."

"What are you talking about?" I tried to feign innocence.

"The bluebonnets. Texas State flower, babe. Growing right there in the yard."

"Hmm, imagine that," I said, trying to sound surprised.

He caught me around the waist and pulled me close. "How did you pull that one off?"

"Amazon," I grinned at him, setting my cup on the railing. "I was hoping they would bloom before you saw them."

He cradled me against his chest and dropped his cheek on top of my head. "Nice, babe. That is very special. I'd know those leaves anywhere." Lifting his head, he tipped my chin up so I was looking into his eyes. "Very special, Muse. Much like you," he said, kissing me.

"Get a room!" John yelled, pulling into the drive and stopping.

"I swear that guy is physic," Tim said.

"You mean psychic," I chuckled.

"No, I mean physic," Tim told me, turning to look at John, who was coming across the grass. "Hey, John Law, what's going on?"

John came right up the steps to join us.

"Scouts found a jacket Sunday," he said. "Way the heck up behind the lake. Boys identified it as belonging to the Martinez woman."

"Is it hers? Do you think they may have found her?"

"Don't know yet, Tee. It was way up the mountain. Can't get up there with the ATV's, too rough for the choppers. Need volunteers for a new search up there." He grinned up at Tim. "Can you ride a horse, Tex?"

"Can a duck swim?" Tim grinned back. "You need me?"

"Need every man we can get. You qualify," John said. "Grab your hat and let's go."

Tim was moving before John finished talking.

"Are you serious?" I asked, picking up my coffee.

"Sure am," John smiled. "Sherriff's posse is the only mounted group in the county and they're strictly volunteer. They have the horse power. Short on man power." He winked at me. "I volunteered Tim."

"You're going, too, right?"

"Wouldn't miss it," John laughed. "You might want to fix him a thermos, grab some bottled water."

"I'm good to go," Tim said, coming back. He had pulled a sweatshirt over his tee. He had switched out his sneakers for his boots, and his straw cowboy hat sat firmly on his head. His eyes sparkled with blue highlights.

He bent to kiss me quickly. "I'll be back, Muse. I love you."

"Too," I told him as he opened the front door. "Be careful! Both of you."

"I'm always careful," Tim called back.

"I'll watch him, Tee, keep him out of trouble," John said.

Like little boys heading for camp, they were across the lawn, jogging to John's truck. They loaded up, backed, and with a wave were off.

I took my cup back in the house and refilled it, hoping that maybe, just maybe the mystery of the missing woman was about to be solved.

Tim flashed my mind when they reached the lake, letting me know they were heading up the canyon. John had reported some difficulty with cell service when they got above the lake, into the recesses of the canyon itself.

When they reached the base camp, he flashed again to say there was no cell service at all, not even one bar. We were fortunate he didn't need his cell.

The excitement in his voice was catching. I could feel his energy as he talked.

He told me about all the horses, how crisp the air was, how much he wanted me with him.

Cora was up there with sandwiches and donuts since Archie was helping, too.

I wished him good hunting, told him I loved him and let him go, knowing he was having a good time even if it was on a grisly quest.

I was glad Archie was with him since Archie had grown up here, too, while John was a recent addition, only moving here a couple of years ago.

I gave a brief thought, very brief, to going up and joining in.

Horses are not my thing. I would wind up serving coffee and waiting for the men to return. Nah, not for me.

By nine they still weren't home so I warmed up some soup and called it supper, fed the cats, and curled up on the sofa with my Kindle, settled in for a long night if necessary.

It was after ten when Cletus bolted upright and growled.

He had been curled behind my knees where I rested on the sofa and now he was up and all ears. Dave popped up beside him, both of them eyeing the front door.

He never growled at Tim.

Pushing myself upright, I swung my legs to the floor and got up.

Cletus growled again, a long, vibrating sound, much louder than a purr. He looked at me, then dropped to the floor and took off for the stairs, belly low to the floor. Dave ran with him.

I went to the front window and peeked outside.

Someone was on the front porch.

I was reaching for my phone when someone knocked.

I put on the chain and opened the door a crack to find But Bill standing there, clearly lit by the porch light I had flipped on at dark.

"Hey, Bill, what can I do for you? It's kind of late."

He stepped closer.

"Tim wants his jacket," he said. "I came down to get some more supplies and he asked me to grab his coat."

"Oh, sure, hang on a sec," I said, shutting the door so I could release the chain.

I swung the door open and motioned him in. "Come on in. I'll grab his coat. Be just a second."

I left him standing at the door while I hurried upstairs and grabbed Tim's coat from the guest room closet. Heavy rust colored suede with a sheepskin lining, he had never needed it in Monarch.

I went back downstairs, looking for Bill.

The front door was shut.

At the foot of the stairs I looked over to see him in the kitchen.

"Here's his jacket," I called, holding it up.

"Would it be too much to ask for coffee? I could sure use some."

"Of course," I said, wondering why he didn't just hit the drive through. I had already filled the coffee pot for tomorrow so it was just a matter of pushing the button and getting down the mugs.

"It will just be a couple of minutes, Bill. Have a seat."

He took a seat at the table while I got out the milk and sugar, setting them on the table. I opened a package of cookies and put several on a plate that I set in front of him.

When the coffee finished dripping I filled the cups and took a seat.

For the first time tonight I noticed Bill's eyes.

The normally warm, caramel colored eyes were dark and sunken, set back in dark circles. There was a strange, almost red, glint in the corners.

"Are you okay, Bill? You look awfully tired."

"Oh, fine, fine." His eyes roamed the kitchen, left and right and back again, turning his chair a little and repeating the action. I began to wish I had just left him on the front porch and shoved the jacket through the chained door.

For that matter, why didn't Tim tell me Bill was coming? The first finger of concern tickled my back.

"You know, you've never had me over for coffee," he said, taking a sip and adding sugar. "I hear John and Sharon, Cora, all of them talk about having coffee here and this is my first time. After what? Thirty years?"

Surprised, I occupied myself with a long sip of my own.

"Nothing special here," I said. "I can't imagine anyone talking about it."

"No, I guess you wouldn't. You're the center. Always the center."

No answer for that one.

"So how's it going up there? Have they found anything new?"

Those haunted eyes locked on mine. "Up the canyon? Where your precious pretty boy is? No, nothing new. They have Lulu's jacket. With the blood on it. They've sent that to the lab or some such. He's gonna be up there a while. If they start to break up my boy will put something else in their path. Draw them off."

What on earth was he talking about? He had lost me minutes ago.

"Bill, I'm sorry. It is late and I'm tired. Tim will be home soon."

"No, he won't," he said. "My boy will take care of that."

"What boy are you talking about?" Bill had no children that I knew of. And who was Lulu? Did he mean Lurlene?

"My boy! My son!" He shouted, slamming his hand on the table so hard the coffee sloshed out of my cup. I reached for a napkin to wipe up the spill.

"Hey, sorry, Bill, take it easy. I didn't know you had a son."

"Of course I have sons. Two of them. When Lulu came into my life, I took them all in. My family. My boys."

"Lulu? Do I know her? I don't think I've met her."

"Stop it, Tee! Just stop it!" The hand slammed the table again. "OF course you know her! She did your hair. Did her best for you. And what did you do? Had it redone! Embarrassed her in public, pointing it out. You should be ashamed of yourself."

"Lurlene? You mean Lurlene?"

He shook his head and calmly took a sip of coffee. Reaching, he took a cookie and bit off a corner, eyes roaming the kitchen.

"My woman," he said softly. "My life. He took her from me."

"Who took her, Bill? Do you know who took her?"

"That phony cowboy! He's tried for years! Now he's got her. And he's going to pay! Now it's his turn. His turn." He took another bite of cookie, a few crumbs sticking to his bottom lip.

I felt fear tightening my chest. My fingers went cold, even pressed tightly to the cup.

"It's late, Bill," I said again. "Can I fix you a cup to go? They must miss you at the search."

"What? Oh, the search. I haven't been up there. My boy is up there. He has it all under control."

"I thought you were helping," I said, easing my feet under the chair. I stood up slowly, reached for the coffee pot. "Can I fix you a cup to go? You should probably help your son."

He shook his head again, violently, side to side. "No! Too late, Tee. Too late. He's got to pay. Pay for what he did to my family! He took her. Do you know how that hurts? No, of course not. You get everything you want. Everyone loves Tee Bishop. Tee never gets hurt."

I kept still, hoping his mind would wander again and take him out of here. Hoping Tim would flash into my mind.

Bill took a deep sigh and carefully placed both hands on the table, looking down at them, arranging them exactly in front of him.

"You were supposed to be mine," he said, looking up at me. "Did you know that? I paid the forfeit. Made the sacrifice but you never knew. Never noticed. I did it all," he murmured. "And what did you do? WHAT DID YOU DO?" He shouted the last, so loud the cabinet doors rattled.

Fear choked me, closed my airway. I was having trouble drawing breath.

Bill raised his head and looked me in the eye.

"I made the sacrifice, Tee. You were supposed to be mine. You screwed it up. Again. I wasn't good enough. I paid the price, damn it! I paid! I got the house ready for you, and everything! And what did you do? You brought in this pretty boy, this completely strange man! Where did he come from? Just out of the blue, there he is! And you marry him! You married him! Had a big party at the Gem, celebrated it. What is wrong with you? I paid the price. You were mine. Mine," he repeated and I could see those sunken eyes fill with tears.

"Bill I am so sorry," I said softly. "I don't understand. I have no idea what you're talking about."

"You don't want to know!"

"I do," I said. "I really do. Can you explain it to me? Maybe I could make you a sandwich and you could tell me about it."

He took a deep breath and let it go. "Too late, Tee. Too late."

I had to keep him talking, had to hope Tim and John would be back soon.

"Never too late, Bill," I said. "Tell me about the sacrifice. Help me understand. Remember when you helped me with algebra? You made it clear. I would never have passed that class without your help."

"You remember that? Thought you forgot all about it."

"Of course I remember! I would have been lost without your help. You were so patient. Help me now, Bill. Explain it to me, just like algebra."

"The sacrifice," he said slowly. "The dogs. Good dogs. Anubis. The Egyptian deity. I had to give him dogs, good dogs, not mutts. Really good dogs. I had to give him the dogs and he would give me you. You were my reward. And he was going to do it! He told me! And you took up with some complete stranger, right off the street!" He sobbed, a deep, throbbing sound from his chest. "You were under the spell. Anubis' spell. Before I could get to you he showed up! He stepped in, between us!"

Tears squirted from his eyes, running down his cheeks, dripping from his chin. His fingers squeezed the cup so hard his knuckles were white.

"Anubis?" I asked while praying for Tim to come home. He saved me before.

In my mind I called for him, constantly calling his name.

Bill shook his head yet again. "I made the deal with him," he explained. "Three dogs for you. Took a while to find three good dogs. I made the sacrifice. Then Tim showed up. Took you away. So I made another sacrifice. Anubis sent me Lulu." He sighed deeply, the corners of his mouth turning up as he said her name. "She wasn't you but she was good. So good. A good woman. A good mother. She came to me and gave me a family, sons."

He rambled on for minutes about Lurlene and how good she was, saliva gathering in the corners of his mouth.

I let him ramble, trying to formulate a plan of my own. How long could he talk?

He was between me and the back door and the door to the garage. There was nowhere to go, no way to get around him. Even the kitchen knives were behind me, tucked neatly in their drawer.

Where the heck was Tim?

"I loved you, Tee. So much. I settled for Lulu, I admit it. But she made it worthwhile. We were happy. She brought the boys, made me complete. I'm a good father. Good to my boys. Paid the bail for Ray, got him a good lawyer. He's a good son. Taking care of your man right now."

"My man? You mean Tim? Ray is with Tim?"

"Oh yeah," he said and for the first time relaxed a tiny bit, leaning back a little. His fingers eased up on the cup, color flooding back as the relaxed. "He put the jacket up there, Ray did. He's got her blouse in his pack. If they try to give up and come home, he'll plant that one. Has blood on it, so they'll hang in there, keep on looking."

"Ray is planting the evidence?"

"Of course, Tee. Why on earth would Lulu be up that canyon? You all think you're so smart but you're not. Had to get your watch dog across the drive there out of the way. Had to get that fake cowboy out of here. Ray took care of it. That's my boy. Told him what I needed and he did it."

"Okay, then. Lurlene or Lulu was never up there? Do you know where she is? Is she all right?"

"What do you care? You hated her. You were so jealous of her talent, her looks." The tears came back, escaping down his cheeks. He angrily flicked them away. "She found the dogs."

"You lost me, Bill. Lurlene found the dogs?"

He nodded and swiped at another tear. "Yeah, she found the heads. I had 'em in the freezer till I could get them staked up. She didn't understand. Scared her. But she'll be back," he assured me. "Yeah, Anubis will send her back. Right now, she's just a little skittish. We're getting married, you know? She wants a big wedding but I'd be happy with a judge. Still her choice. What she wants."

"Oh that will be nice," I said. "We could give her a bridal shower. Sharon and Sally would love to help."

"STOP! Don't do that! You and your bunch will not do anything for her. But I will! I'll give her everything." His voice dropped again. "Everything I saved up for you. Your loss." His eyes cleared a little and went back to roaming the kitchen, across the cabinets, to the window and back again.

"Come on, Bill, you know better than that. Remember your first wedding? We had a big shower for Joyce."

Another look came into his eyes, a softer gleam.

"I do remember that," he said. "That was supposed to be you, too. Only she got pregnant."

"She was a good woman," I said calmly.

"So is Lulu," he said. "So is she. But he took her. He took her away from me. Selfish bastard! Wants all the women! I'll get even, Tee. I am going to take you from him. It's time he lost."

Still standing by the coffee pot, I eased my weight to the side, and slide over a few inches.

"I tried to kill him, you know. Ray tried a couple of times. Damn man has more lives than a cat. Can't kill him. Can't even hurt him bad. Till now," he said and the soft look left his eyes. "Until you."

"I don't follow, Bill. Can you explain it to me?"

"Sure, Tee. It's easy. Can't kill Mr. Big Shot. Can't even hurt him much. Till now."

"Now?"

"You, Tee. I can't get at him but I can hurt him. Hurt him bad."

He leaned back to reach under the table, to his pocket.

He pulled out a gun. A very small, black gun that he pointed right at me.

"He took you from me but I am going to take you away from him. Permanently."

FLASH

Hey, Muse, you still awake?

Tim! Help! Tim it's Bill!

What? Talk to me, Muse!

But Bill is here, with a gun. Oh, Tim he killed the dogs. He told me. He's lost his mind, babe.

On my way.

You can't get here in time, Tim. I love you. You are the best thing that ever happened to me. I want you to know that.

Hang on, babe. I am on the way.

I love you, Tim.

You hang on! Fall down! Strip! Do whatever you have to do. Don't you dare give up! Talk to him.

"What is wrong with you? Do you get it, Tee? Is it sinking in? Don't faint on me, now. Pay attention! You are going to die! You will be the best revenge on him! See how he likes it, right? Let him live with himself, knowing he's the reason you died. Do you see the justice? Do you?"

Talk to him, Muse. Keep him talking. Say anything, just keep him talking.

Listen, Tim. Listen! Bill killed the dogs. Some kind of sacrifice. Ray tried to kill you. It was Bill and Ray together. Tell John.

I'll tell John! Talk to Bill. Keep talking to him.

"What is wrong with you? You think I won't pull this trigger? Look at me!"

"Bill, please. Can we talk about this? Why do you want to hurt Tim? He's done nothing to you. Not really."

"What?!" He slammed the table with his free hand, the sound echoing through the house. "I told you what he did! He took my woman. Twice! Twice, Tee. He took my family. Why? He doesn't need them. He doesn't even want them."

That strange red glint was back in his eye.

My knees began to quiver, to get that shaky feeling, that feeling that they are going to bend the wrong way.

"Bill," I kept my voice low and soft, my throat closing up on tears. "We've known each other a long time. We go back a long way. Do you remember the class reunion? That first one?"

His eyes focused again, looking back at me. "The one at the lake? The five year one?"

"Yes," I said, forcing my lips to smile. "The one where Sally fell in the lake? You had to swim out and get her. Remember? Joyce was so proud of you."

For a minute, maybe two, he looked normal, looked like But Bill. Then his eyes glinted, sparked, and the tears began to flow again.

"No, Tee. You have to die. Funny, isn't it? I wanted you for so long but you wouldn't have me. Now, now it's different. Now you want me but I don't want you. You hear me? I don't want you! No more! I can get Lulu back. She'll come back. And you know what? You know what? We will watch that bastard you married suffer. Me and Lulu, together. We will watch him dry up and wither away."

"Do you know where she is, Bill?"

For just a brief second, he lowered the gun, the small black hole in the barrel dropped an inch or two before snapping back up.

"Who?"

"Lurlene. Lulu. Do you know where she is? Is she waiting for you?"

I struggled to think, to come up with anything to keep him talking. At the same time, I prayed for God to protect Tim. Not easy to talk and pray at the same time.

"Of course she's waiting for me," Bill scoffed. "She's my woman. We're getting married. You're not the only one who can get married. We're getting married and my boys are coming to work in my business. Changing the name to Williams and Sons Yard Care."

"I am so glad Lurlene is okay," I said, sincerely. "People have been worried about her, you know. They are out there now. Looking for her."

He laughed. The last thing I expected.

"They won't find her," he chuckled. "She's smart. She's wily, like a cat. She ran when she got scared. The dogs scared her. She's gonna come back, though."

"She's in San Luis," I said. "We saw her."

"Lulu? You saw Lulu?" He hunched forward, the gun still pointed at me.

"Uh-huh. She's there. We saw her at the Apple Farm."

His eyes cleared again. "Really? She liked that place. We ate there a couple of times. I'll go down and get her."

"You should probably hurry, Bill. It's late. Very late. She's going to wonder where you are."

"What? She knows where I am." That weird glazed look came back in his eyes and I felt my own tear up.

"Bill, please. Do you want me to beg? Do you want me to cry?"

"Oh, no, Tee. I'm sorry. I really am. But nothing worked out the way it was supposed to."

He lifted the gun, carefully aimed it at my head, squinting one eye.

He was maybe five feet away.

He couldn't miss.

"Bill, please. Don't do this."

"You have to die," he repeated. "He has to suffer."

Tim I love you, I screamed in my head.

I saw Bill's finger tighten on the trigger, the knuckle turning white.

I squeezed my eyes closed.

Lord, forgive me.

BANG!

Made in the USA
San Bernardino, CA
25 August 2014